Fallen Star

by

Allison Morse

Fallen Star

Cover Art by *Tina Lynn Stout*

The Wild Rose Press, Inc.
PO Box 708
Adams Basin, NY 14410-0708
Visit us at www.thewildrosepress.com

Publishing History
First Vintage Edition, 2016
Print ISBN 978-1-5092-0872-2
Digital ISBN 978-1-5092-0873-9

Published in the United States of America

Praise for Allison Morse

FALLEN STAR

"Readers who love a strong, independent heroine will automatically fall in love with this story. Twists, suspense, and intrigue will keep readers turning the pages…"

~Manhattan Book Review

THE SWEETHEART DEAL

"Morse successfully weaves a lively romance together with a tale of complex corporate skullduggery that often feels like a gripping thriller."

~Kirkus Review

~*~

"A fast, fun read with a sweet but intense romance."

~San Francisco Book Review

~*~

"*THE SWEETHEART DEAL* is a romantic and intelligent novel that will have readers clamoring for more…"

~Pacific Book Review

~*~

"*THE SWEETHEART DEAL* is a happily unpredictable novel about one clever woman, her by no means supportive family, and a romance she is determined to deny."

~Long & Short Review

Kate struggled to absorb all the visual input.
The flickering light from the screen pounded against her skull and gave her a throbbing headache. She couldn't shake the feeling something wasn't quite right in the footage.

She concentrated on the minutiae, cataloging every detail, particularly what occurred when the camera continued to run after a take was done.

There was part of a child's polka dot skirt slipped into the frame after a take.

That must have been her mother.

Burly techs walked at the outer edge of the frame, over thick cables winding across the floor like snakes.

Details, details. All were there, in perfect focus, with deep focus.

"Oh, my God." Kate clamped her hands over her mouth.

It's not what's there, she realized. *It's what's not there.*

Dedication

For the many friends and fellow writers who have
been generous with their time and insights
as I struggled to bring this book to life.
~*~
In particular, I wish to thank brilliant Molly Sackler,
who supported this project from the very beginning.
~*~
To Hollywood!

"But soft, behold! Lo, where it comes again!
I'll cross it, though it blast me. Stay, illusion!
If thou hast any sound or use of voice,
Speak to me!"

~Shakespeare, Hamlet.

Prologue

Hollywood, California 1964

In a gold sequined gown and holding a lit cigarette, Gloria Reardon loomed out of the huge movie poster. The picture was old, but with its splashes of yellow and red, it popped like neon against the nicotine-stained wall of the dingy office. And Gloria, breathtaking Gloria, eclipsed the puny room, smiling as if she knew it couldn't possibly contain her dazzling self.

"You look like her," the photographer said, as he glanced up from his 35 mm camera set on a black tripod.

"I do?" Kate tried not to let her words run faster than her thoughts—a major impossibility. "I mean, I've been told I do. I have the same red hair and green eyes, but..." She sighed and looked down at her navy and white jumper and the knee socks her mom insisted she still wear to school. Was it really possible that one day, her thirteen-year-old body could be as beautiful as her infamous grandmother's?

"Unclasp your arms, and roll back one shoulder," he said. "No. Slower."

She tried, but her movements were jerky while her hands fidgeted. Something in the scratchiness of the man's voice made her uncomfortable.

The office hadn't been what she'd expected either.

The entry room had cigarette burns in the carpet, and the musty smell made her nose itch. But a bunch of tripods holding lights, scrims, and umbrellas made up for everything. This, she knew, made film magical.

She tried rolling her shoulder again, but this time, she pretended to be her grandmother. Not that Kate had ever been lucky enough to meet Gloria. Her movie star grandmother had died eons ago. But Kate had thumbed through family albums filled with pictures of her and had seen her movies on TV late at night. With these artifacts, she had studied the sly sparkle in the actress's eyes and had practiced the careless bravado as Gloria tilted her head just so, and rolled her shoulders with feline ease. And, now, as Kate conjured up these images, she realized that she was doing it, too. She was being Gloria.

Click, click, click.

"Yeah, that's it," the photographer said.

Despite knowing how silly it was, she smiled at the poster as if seeking her grandmother's praise. "It's like she's immortal. I mean, it's been over twenty years since she was murdered—" Kate sucked in her lower lip and stared at the ground. "You know died." She looked up. "Still, there are magazine articles, posters, and books constantly being published about her, and—"

"You talk a lot."

She grimaced. "I'm nervous."

"Don't be."

"I know. I investigated you." Kate stood tall.

The man looked up from the camera and stared at her with an odd stillness as if maybe he was the one posing.

She shook the thought away. She *had* checked him

out.

"I went to the library and found an article about you in an old Hollywood Reporter."

The man exhaled and spun the silver and black camera off the tripod.

"It wasn't easy to find either. I had to search through stacks and stacks of old issues, but I did." She stepped forward. "And, there you were. Your picture and everything, and it said you were a director."

He smiled and placed the camera in a protective cover. "Determined."

"Dogged." She stuck out her chin. "That's what I'm called."

With the camera now slung around his neck, he squatted and tilted it up at her. "So tell me, dogged Kate, how much do you want to be an actress?"

"More than anything." Her hands waved in the air as she twirled, and he, with the camera, shuffled around her. "To be in a movie means everything. To be transported…to be somewhere else…to be someone else. It's wonderful."

She spun again, and he followed.

God, it felt like dancing.

He stilled, and so did she.

"Is it so hard being just Kate Bloom?"

She looked away and hoped he could not see her gulp down the pain.

Click.

The click of the camera reminded her of the sound of the lock on her mother's bedroom door when she would seal herself in with her bottle and fear, while Kate, sitting alone in the living room, turned up the volume on the TV so she wouldn't hear her mom crying.

"Kate." The man's voice was gentle.

She blinked and wiped the moisture from her eyes.

He stood and placed a hand on her shoulder. "Are you all right?"

"Please put me in one of your films." She looked up at him and thought she'd crumble if he said no.

He let go of her shoulder. "Truth is…I don't think you're ready. I'm sorry." He walked around the room and switched off the lights for the photo shoot.

"But—"

"Your features are like your grandmother's, but she was more than that. Gloria Reardon was a screen goddess…a siren. Your pictures are stiff. Come back in a couple of years." With the camera in his right hand, he headed toward the small hallway that led to what Kate assumed was where he developed the film.

"Wait. I can be less stiff. Please, I can be like Gloria."

He turned and looked at her.

She snatched up the canvas beach bag she'd brought and pulled out the glittery gold gown. "I found the dress in the poster…like you asked. We have a ton of her stuff locked in the garage. I'm not supposed to go through those boxes, but I did, and I found the gown. I can be her if you want. I pretend to be her all the time. Let me try."

His eyes widened at the sight of the dress, but still, he shook his head. "I think you're too much of a little girl to pull off a dress like that."

"I can do it." She dashed to the bathroom before he had the chance to say no.

In the small bathroom, there was a full-length

mirror and a makeup box. She looked through all the different choices of powders and creams and settled on a light peach blush and a soft pink lipstick.

She stepped into the dress and did up the side zipper.

Staring at herself, she blinked again and again.

The color on Kate's cheeks accentuated the startling red of her hair, which fell in sinuous waves onto her bare shoulders. The bodice of gold scalloped over her new breasts like seashells. The dress, which was tight at the waist, fell loose from her hips to the floor in a long cascade of shimmering folds of metallic fabric.

For the first time since she'd begun sneaking into the garage to play with Gloria's things, the glittering dress almost fit her perfectly. With a sense of wonder at her own grown-up image, her hand skimmed down the curve of her waist, and her toes danced inside the pinpoint shoes. She was a woman.

She swung open the door from the bathroom into the office hallway.

The photographer was there, waiting.

She hopped back a step.

"Nice." His voice was gruff. He moved in closer and brushed a stray lock from her face. "I was wrong; you are old enough."

She stepped away from him and into the hallway. His touch made her skin crawl.

"Come on. I've got another setup in the back, and it will make that dress come alive."

She turned and saw the door at the end of the hallway was open.

Her throat went dry. "I...changed my mind. I need

to go, please."

His thick hands clamped onto her shoulders. "I'm going to make you a star. Like Gloria. It's what you want, right? *More than anything.*" He spun her around like she weighed nothing and shoved her into the room. A room with a bed.

"No!" She tried to run around him.

He caught her.

She screamed and kicked, anything to break free, but his hold remained tight and his outstretched arms kept his body safe from her attack.

He knocked her hard, and she fell on the bed. His entire body crushed down on her.

She screamed again.

"Quiet!" He shook her.

Her head bounced against the mattress, blurring her vision. She fought to escape, banging and wriggling against his mass.

"That's nice, baby." His breath, which was wet against her cheek, reeked of cigarettes and stale coffee. "The more you move, the more I like it."

She froze.

How had she been so stupid? She was stupid. Stupid.

"No. Please, no." Quick, convulsive gasping breaths were followed by tears streaming down her cheeks.

The man groaned as his sticky tongue lapped up her tears.

Vomit burned at the back of her throat.

His hands were everywhere...on her breasts...pinching her crotch.

She prayed to disappear. Her eyes sought sanctuary

away from the sight of him. Movie posters lined these walls, too. But these had little color or thought to their designs and had triple Xs in block letters, with grainy photos of women with large breasts popping out of their bras or with their mouths wide open, and on each poster the man's name was inscribed as the director.

The room spun and the din of a hurricane roared in her ears until it was replaced by the wrenching and eerie tones of a woman sobbing.

They must be her own cries. But it didn't sound like her. It was too old, too world weary and filled with a chasm of grief.

Grace had come, and she detached from what was happening. It was as if she had stepped out of her body and was viewing the scene from afar.

She watched the man rub against someone else's body. Someone who wore gold dresses, someone whose figure was so voluptuous it was a siren's call—someone not her.

Kate deep down knew it was a lie. But what could she do? He was so much stronger. Better to disappear.

The man yanked up the gold dress, and the sewn beads scraped her thighs.

Damn it!

She felt that. And, she felt him: his hands, the stink of his odor.

Hot anger erupted inside her, dissolving the icy fear.

The man stood, freeing her from his girth, but his legs pressed onto her own like a vise. Seemingly sure of her passivity, he didn't even rush as he unzipped his pants and pulled them off.

He leered at her. "You do look like Gloria. Just like

her."

"I'm not her!" Kate bucked to her right, and due to surprise, this time she was able to roll away from the pressure of his legs. She grappled at the side table for anything she could use against him.

He bent toward her and tried turning her back to him.

But she found her weapon and slammed his head hard with the camera.

She scrambled off the bed.

He lunged at her.

She turned and kicked him in the groin.

He crumpled to the floor. "Bitch!"

She ran out of the office.

Chapter One

Nine Years later

Kate Bloom tugged at her denim jacket appliqued with a Sisterhood Is Power fist. She'd made it through the funeral arrangements. Just. Now standing in her mother's small house, she knew she should be figuring out what to do with all this stuff, but instead all she could think about was the hollow look in her mom's eyes before she'd succumbed to cancer.

Pushing her fists deep into her pockets, Kate felt embraced by the sound of a woman weeping. The haunting voice was unbearably sad and strangely comforting.

The buzz of the doorbell quieted the lament.

She wiped away a tear that ran down her cheek.

Depersonalization. That's what the psychology text books called the phenomenon. That feeling of being disconnected, disassociated from your own body, your feelings, your own voice.

After that horrible day she'd been attacked by that so-called director, she'd gone to the library and researched the topic. The book said it was not at all uncommon to experience depersonalization during a traumatic event, or once triggered, during times of immense pressure…

She glanced around her mother's house as she

walked to the front door.

Or, extreme sadness.

She opened the door. There, in the merciless California light, stood her great-aunt Lillian, looking…old.

When had that happened?

Lillian Baker, the once commanding stage actress, had begun to wilt. Her lips were pale, particularly in comparison to her helmet of dyed-red hair. All her life Kate had heard stories about how Lillian had arrived in Los Angeles with her younger sister Gloria, ready to take it by storm. While Gloria became a star, Lillian had been relegated to studio character roles and now, TV bit parts. Kate couldn't help think when she looked at Lillian that this disappointment was etched in her deeper than the lines on her skin.

"Darling, don't hunch." Lillian strode by Kate and into the house. She then spun on her heels and struck a pose as grand as anything Bette Davis could muster. "Or is standing upright a sign of conforming to the oppression of movie images?"

"They *are* oppressive," Kate said. "At least, old movies are. They perpetuate destructive stereotypes of women. I'm going to change that."

Lillian lifted one imperious brow.

Costumed for a day of rummaging, her aunt had swapped her customary colorful caftan for a starched button-down shirt, a brown vest, and brown breeches. The ensemble cried out for a riding crop. But then again, her aunt's sharp tongue made the crop redundant.

"I am," Kate said. "The short documentary I made during my first year of grad school threw a grenade at the L.A. porn industry."

"Hardly a grenade. No one has seen your film, and only one man was arrested."

"Yeah, but it was the right one."

Lillian cocked her head, and her voice softened. "The right one?"

A memory, like nausea, wafted through Kate. She smelled the tar and ash of the man's cigarette breath and felt his sweaty hands everywhere on her body as he tried to rape her.

"It's nothing." She averted her glance and turned away from her aunt's perceptive examination.

On the mantel above the colonial fireplace with its faux pillars, her mother's antique clock ticked. A dusty hand-painted porcelain base lamp shaped like a pug sat on an end table.

"Well," Lillian finally said, "what are you going to do with the house and your mother's things?"

"I don't know." Kate shrugged. "Once the semester is over, I'll figure it out."

"Poor Audrey." Lillian glanced around the modest three-bedroom, one-bath home as if she were surveying a prison yard. "After a childhood of luxury, she ends up here."

"Not that again," Kate shot back, happy to have anger provide a respite from the suffocating gloom. "Of all the terrible things that happened to her, this is the least of…"

She halted in mid-rant and gazed about the familiar living room.

The truth was, for her mom, this house had been a prison. Too afraid to venture out much, she had tried to keep the terrifying world away with her dark drapes and state-of-the-art central air. And, even inside the home, everything was kept sealed or wrapped in plastic or locked away behind cabinet doors. Including her mom's prized collection of animal and doll figurines that was never to be played with—only admired through glistening cabinet windows as untouchable as the characters on a movie screen.

Her mom must have felt that locked behind the window of a china cabinet, her dreams could be safe.

Staring at the collection, Kate's eyes misted.

She turned and grabbed a box of extra-large garbage bags from the coffee table and handed it to Lillian. "Go ahead. I've already unlocked the garage. Gloria's things are in the back. I'll meet you there."

"Thank you for letting me go through my sister's belongings." Lillian shook her head. "Why your mother was so cruel and wouldn't allow me access to these things earlier, I'll never know."

Their gazes locked.

Lillian shrugged. "Well, I suppose I do."

Kate didn't want to get into that old argument again.

****

Thirty minutes later, covered in dust, Kate and Lillian were in the jam-packed garage tackling Gloria's boxes.

When Kate had returned home from the BS photo shoot nine years ago, she'd sealed up tight Gloria's dress along with all her other things—the way her mother had always wanted it. Kate hadn't looked at any of Gloria's belongings again...until today.

The aroma of wet carpet and mold wafted out of the boxes. And just touching the thirty-plus-year-old gowns and tarnished costume jewelry made her queasy.

After depositing a load of Gloria's things in her car, Lillian strode back to the garage. Halting, she pointed to a large wooden crate at the front of the garage. "What's that?"

Kate walked over and stared at the rectangle of splintering wood. "I don't know."

Lillian shrugged and returned to the back wall where Gloria's dusty boxes were lined up.

A UPS packing slip was still neatly folded and attached to the splintering wood crate.

Kate figured that it must have arrived when her mom was sick, and that her caretaker had forgotten to mention it.

She peeled the slip off the crate. It was addressed to her mom, Audrey Reardon Bloom, from a Charles Needham of a Culver City address. She called over to her great-aunt. "Who's Charles Needham?"

Lillian halted from stuffing several of Gloria's smaller mementos into a plastic bag and looked up. "I don't know. Why? Is that who sent the crate?"

Kate nodded.

Underneath the packing slip was an envelope. She tore it open and read the letter. It was from a law firm stating that a bequest was inside. Attached to the letter was a note written in a shaky scrawl: *Audrey, I'm sorry I wasn't brave enough to give this to you when I was alive. I wish I could have saved her instead of her legacy. Keep it safe. Chuck.*

Give her what?

She tugged at the crate's top. It was ridiculously heavy and had been nailed shut.

She walked to the toolbox and found a hammer.

A choked cry came from the back of the garage.

Kate looked up to see her aunt holding a white oblong box and trembling.

It was *the* white oblong box—the one that the police had, for a time, believed contained the object used to bludgeon her grandmother to death.

She cringed. She'd forgotten to warn Lillian that this elegant and empty box, along with many of Gloria's other personal effects found in her dressing room the day she died, had been returned to the family a year after Winston Nash's conviction had been overturned on a technicality and the case had been closed.

Kate hurried to Lillian's side. "I'm sorry. I should have told you we had this stuff."

Her aunt tossed the oblong box aside. "It doesn't matter." She turned and went back to culling through Gloria's belongings with renewed vigor. She pulled the yellowing pages of the police incident report. "Have you read it?"

"Sure. Like Mom said, everything pointed to Winston."

Lillian thumbed through the document. "I still don't believe he did it."

Kate simmered with an old anger. "Come on! There was a ton of evidence all pointing to him and only him. Just because he was a man and rich, he got off. It's disgusting."

At least some justice had been done. Winston Nash, the golden boy of radio, stage, and screen, had never worked again. Instead, he had become a joke: an obese alcoholic, relegated to being a professional guest of the minor nobility and the superrich until his death ten years ago.

"You sound like your mother." Lillian shook her head. "I just wish you and she could have understood that my defending Winston didn't mean I was disloyal to Gloria."

"It did. And then you abandoned Mom."

"It was Audrey who wanted nothing to do with me. What could I do?"

"You were the adult. You should have..." Kate's voice caught. "You should have loved her."

And me.

Luckily, she hadn't said that.

"You're right. I should have." Unblinking, Lillian walked by Kate as she headed to the car, the police report in one hand and a garment bag in the other.

Kate returned to the UPS crate at the front of the garage and slammed the hammer against it. The wood framing fell to pieces.

Staring down, she saw a sealed cardboard box. She ripped off the tape and flipped the lid open. Light bounced off a container with a shiny handle on top.

An odd sensation of heat rippled across her skin, and with it, a premonition of what it might be began to solidify into something more than fantasy. Trying to remain calm, she told herself that it couldn't possibly be what she hoped it was. It had been lost...destroyed...right?

Her heart pounded as she used both hands to lift the metal container. She undid the latches. Inside were two round 35 mm motion picture canisters.

"Lillian!" she shouted.

As she pried off the top of the first canister, she was assaulted by the pungent smell of vinegar. The film appeared brittle. She was afraid to touch it in case it turned to dust in her hands. But she had to know. With the tips of her fingers and holding her breath, she unwound a small piece of film and looked at it. There, captured in the frame, was Gloria—the costume, the set behind her...there was no mistaking it. These reels were from *Emperor Smythe*. It was the infamous missing footage from the day Gloria was murdered on that film set.

"Lillian! Quick, Lillian!" Kate returned the footage to the canister and closed it up.

Her great-aunt hurried back. "What? What is it?" Her eyes widened as she gazed at the canisters.

"I can't believe it. Can you believe it? I can't believe it!"

"Is that what I think it is?" Lillian asked.

"The footage. *The* missing footage." A heady sense of excitement filled Kate.

"That's not possible. The studio destroyed it. Let me see."

Kate stood in front of the shiny canisters, blocking her aunt from coming too close. "No, it's too delicate."

"This is monumental." Lillian clasped her hands together. "Winston's vision shall be restored. The critics will no longer doubt. He shall be hailed as the greatest director of all time and this film, his masterpiece."

"That's not why it's important!" Kate grabbed her aunt's shoulders. "Don't you get it? Mom said the camera was rolling the day Gloria died and that it caught their fight."

"So?" Lillian shrugged and stepped away from Kate. "Everyone knows about the fight on the set. There were plenty of witnesses and news reports."

"And all with different versions of what was said. It's different to *see* it. You know it is. We've got to call the police or press or something. It's past time we crushed the cottage industry of speculation and exploitation of Gloria's death."

The garage was too full to pace in, and Kate felt her words burst out with the force of an exploding water main. "You know the books: *Why the Mob Killed Gloria*, or *Screen Goddess or Secret Spy,* or *Aliens Abducted Gloria*. The world needs to know the simple truth: she was murdered by her brutal boyfriend, the famous director. End of story."

"Wait, darling. Calm down." Lillian shook her head. "If you run off without thinking, the studio will swoop in and take the footage, and then it will never be seen."

"I won't let them."

"Is that so?" Lillian said, the words dripping with sarcasm. "By yourself, you're going to fight Golden State Pictures for the rights to screen the film?"

Kate looked down at the two canisters. She'd seen the film's curled edges and sharp smell and knew those were signs it had vinegar syndrome and was too fragile to be shown now...maybe ever.

She also knew Lillian was right about the studio. J.B. Sutton's money still controlled it, and everyone knew the portrait of the megalomaniacal industrialist Emperor Smythe was supposed to be him. That's why he bought Golden State Pictures in the first place, to destroy the film before it could be released.

Kate rubbed her eyes as if trying to force them to see a way to beat the powerful J.B. Sutton. *God, to be so close to the truth and yet...*

17

"I have an idea," Lillian said. "I know someone trustworthy who can help us with that footage...to store it and hopefully restore it."

Kate dropped her hands and looked at her aunt.

Lillian wore a wicked grin. "And I have another idea."

"A good one?"

"A pip." Lillian winked.

Kate couldn't help but smile. Sometimes, she really loved her aunt. "What is it?"

"I need time before I tell you."

"No." And in other moments, her aunt was...well...Lillian!

"Darling, a lot of pieces need to be put together, and delicate negotiations must be done first to even know if my scheme has a chance. Give me time to think it through...unless *you* have an idea?" Lillian's right brow lifted with dramatic condescension.

Kate didn't have a plan—not yet. "How much time do you need?"

"A week."

"Okay." Kate bent down and carefully placed the two canisters back into the cardboard box. "But just for a week. If there's no plan by then, I'm making it public."

Chapter Two

Five days later, Kate sat on her threadbare vintage loveseat in the shabby Silver Lake apartment she shared with her best friend, Natalie. Wedged between downtown L.A. and the stately homes of Los Feliz, Silver Lake was in transition—at least, that was what her landlord claimed when he'd upped their rent the previous month without bothering to fix the leaky pipes.

She rubbed her eyes from another night of too little sleep and put down the feminist essay, "Sex in Cinema: An Inquiry into the Mythos of the Hollywood Bombshell."

How could she think about theory when she had just made one of the great film discoveries of all time? And then, like a fool, handed it over to Lillian, just like that.

Great aunt she may be, but a particularly absent one for most of her life.

Still, Lillian had a plan to protect it, and Kate didn't.

She jumped to her feet. Her aunt had asked for a week. It didn't sound like such a long time. But then she'd promptly left town.

Trying to not completely obsess, Kate paced the room and focused on her hand-me-down furniture, the old studio's Fresnel light next to a Queen Anne chair, and then Natalie's painting. It was a large canvas of a woman in a drawing room on top of which a collage of products, like tampons and eyeliner, were piled along with cut out pieces of a woman's body parts.

Disturbing. Yes. But it was important!

Natalie swung open the front door and breezed through the living room toward her bedroom. Her peasant skirt with paint splatter from art class billowed as she moved.

"I'm sorry I'm late."

Kate looked at the clock. "Oh, shit! We are."

The Herbert Collier Prize for best grad short film was going to be announced in an hour.

"I can't believe you're not ready. The contest is all you've talked about this entire semester." Natalie looked at her quizzically. "What's going on with you? You've been weird lately."

Kate stared at the ceiling. "Nothing."

"Give me a break. First the nightmares—"

"There're just dreams. I don't even remember them."

That was a lie.

She turned from her friend's penetrating gaze and ran to her bedroom, her socks sliding on the wood floor as she yelled back to Natalie, "We're going to be late, and I've got to get dressed."

Peering in her closet, Kate grabbed her bulky jean jacket and stuffed an errant lock of hair under her baseball cap and thought back to last night.

She did remember part of the dream. It was of her, sitting in bed, trembling and feeling so scared, so alone.

And then she wasn't alone. In the darkness, someone...something moved toward her: a presence, unseen, but revealed in substance by the sensation of moist heat twisting around her like smoke spiraling up a narrow chimney.

Kate shuddered at the memory.

She reminded herself that when she woke up—really woke up—her room was empty and her nose tickled from the dry California air.

It was a dream. That's all. It had just felt real.

Still, she couldn't help but notice her nightmares began the day after she'd found the film.

****

The theater at Melnitz Hall was packed. Five of the best short films made by UCLA graduate students would be screened tonight, and hers was one of them. Whoever won would meet representatives from three film studios and receive a summer internship at the American Film Institute. Her classmates wished her luck, but Kate was so nervous, she could do no more than smile and mumble a reply. She scanned the audience. Most were the usual suspects—film students and professors. In the back sat the invited studio representatives, most wearing apache scarves and suede jackets, trying to appear young.

What would they do if they knew she possessed the missing *Emperor Smythe* footage? The thought of their haughty demeanors devolving into a frenzy of questions calmed her nerves.

But it didn't last. As soon as the lights went down and the first flickers of her black-and-white short appeared on screen, Kate's nerves really took over. She leapt to her feet and waded through the row of people, banging several knees along the way, and then she fled up the theater aisle.

In the dim light, she didn't see the man standing in the back until she crashed into him. His hands clasped her shoulders and kept her from falling.

Why hadn't she seen him? The guy was as big as a football player. She looked up.

"Nice to meet you, Kate," he said with a jester's smile, engaging and hinting of mischief.

She froze. How did he know her name? Before she could question him, he walked down the theater aisle and disappeared in the darkness.

Who the hell was he?

Her mind raced through the possibilities. He didn't look like a student. He seemed older, but not by much. He was not handsome. His face was too wide and his wavy hair too feminine. But there was nothing womanly about his square jaw.

Thinking about how intensely he looked at her through John Lennon glasses made her shiver.

Creepy. That's what he was.

After the five finalists' shorts were shown, everyone was ushered to the Faculty Center for the reception and announcement of the prize. When she walked into the Center, Kate saw Natalie's black curls bouncing up and down and her hands expressive as she spoke with fellow art students.

Kate wandered toward the food where a group of starving undergrads huddled around three large platters which looked as if a bomb had gone off in the middle of them. Limp pieces of celery and carrots were strewn haphazardly along the perimeters while all that remained in the center was a smudge of onion dip.

She was too nervous to eat anyway.

She sat on a brown woven couch directly across

from the podium where the winner would be announced, and dreamed how incredible it would be if she were named the winner. Unlike the studios, AFI wasn't a cesspool of corporate greed; the Institute was a place where filmmaking came first and film restoration was at the forefront.

Natalie came over and handed her a plastic cup filled with cheap Chablis. "Yours was the best. You're going to win."

"I hope so." Kate sipped the wine and cringed. It tasted like rubbing alcohol with notes of bark and orange punch. Then she spotted the mysterious man's wavy hair. In the light, it was amber brown. He was talking to her professor not more than ten feet away.

Kate tilted her head toward them. "Who's he?" she whispered to Natalie.

Natalie scrunched her face and looked perplexed. "Professor Phillips? I always said he was cute."

"No, not him. The guy next to him."

Natalie shrugged. "Not as pretty, if you ask me."

"I'm not asking you." Was Natalie always this aggravating?

"He is kind of hunky." Her friend's gaze darted about, apparently to get a better look. "Kind of like a praetorian guard in a Cecil B. DeMille movie."

"You think?" Kate had a flash of him barelegged in Roman armor, and her mouth just hung open.

Natalie laughed. "You're gaping."

"Am not." She jutted out her chin. "It's just that he knew my name, and I've never seen him before. Wouldn't you call that strange?"

"Yeah." Natalie grabbed her arm and tried to lift her from the couch. "So let's find out who he is."

On cue, the memory of that day nine years ago invaded her. The vibrating pain when the man knocked her onto the bed and the terror when his mass crushed down on her.

Kate pulled back as the familiar panic set in. "No."

Her long-time friend, and the only person Kate had told about what had happened that day, collapsed back on to the couch next to her and gave her a gentle nudge. "Oh, Kate."

Peering down at her clenched hands and her body covered by oversized clothes, she saw what Natalie must see when looking at her: the pretense of a fighter but really still the victim—like her mom, like Gloria.

She glanced back at the big guy with a jester's grin and thought one day she'd get over what happened to her when she was thirteen.

She tensed and tugged at her jacket.

Just not tonight.

The ear-piercing shriek of electronic feedback filled the room and returned her attention to the podium.

Dean Garrido, a rotund man with a big smile stood too close to the mic and gestured for the crowd to quiet down. "I'm delighted all of you could be here for the third annual Herbert Collier Prize for Best Short by a graduate student. Let me begin by thanking my fellow judges. Please give a hand to our own Professor Phillips." Her favorite film teacher walked up to the podium and stood next to the dean.

When the applause died down, Dean Garrido continued, "I'm sorry to say the head of AFI's internship program had to cancel. But I'm pleased he sent in his place a young man who sat where all of you did just three years ago when he was named the first winner of this prize. After his internship, he went on to sell several scripts to Skyline Studios."

"Schlock Studios is more apt," Kate muttered.

"Be good," Natalie said.

"And last week he finished directing an episode of *The Partridge Family*," Dean Garrido said.

Kate rolled her eyes.

Natalie stifled a giggle. "You're such a snob."

"Now," said the dean. "Let's have a hand for fellow Bruin, Dylan Nichols."

Kate's jaw dropped when Mr. Mysterious strode to the podium and gave a big, theatrical wave to the crowd.

****

She didn't win. Worse than that: she didn't even come in second, but a paltry third place.

She congratulated the winner and then rushed outside, afraid she was going to do something stupid like cry. She'd really wanted that internship.

Just up the brightly-lit Charles E. Young Drive between Schoenberg Hall and Franz Hall was the inverted fountain, one of her favorite spots on campus. The area was deserted and a bit spooky, so she turned back to the friendly lights of the Faculty Center.

A classmate talking to some friends outside the center waved to her. She waved back. Then she got the uncomfortable feeling that someone was behind her, watching her.

She spun around and saw a dark shape slip out of sight somewhere near Franz Hall.

"Hello!" she called out into the night.

There was no answer—just the rustling of bushes

in the distance. The odd thing was, Kate didn't feel scared. She knew she was in sight of the stragglers outside the Faculty Center; but that wasn't why she didn't feel afraid. Even though she hadn't seen enough to say if the figure she glimpsed was a man or a woman, she'd have sworn it was someone familiar…someone who didn't intend to harm her.

Still, she ran back to the reception. There was no need to test her hunch.

****

Back inside the Faculty Center, Kate threw away the remains of her second piece of slightly stale chocolate cake and tried to fix a face to the presence she'd felt hovering outside.

The thought was interrupted by the booming baritone of Dylan Nichols saying something about *her* film. She turned and saw him in the corner of the crowded room talking to Professor Phillips. She had to know what he was saying.

When she was only steps away, Professor Phillips said to Dylan, "I think Kate's one of my best students. That montage sequence in her film is terrific. The images cut so quickly, you lose sense of the object reality and are subsumed into the internal frenzy of an observer. I was surprised you didn't think she was ready for the internship."

"She's talented and I liked the way she used deep focus to…"

For some annoying reason he'd stopped. She inched closer.

Dylan laughed. He had a nice rumbly laugh, but then he said, "But her work is the same old deconstruction bullshit you'll find at every college."

Her hands clenched.

"Forget about connecting or communicating something to others," he continued.

Her shoulders were now so tight she swore they brushed her ears.

"Her work is just oh-so-intellectual and clever in that self-important, juvenile way."

Kate leapt forward. "Juvenile? What *I* do is juvenile? True, my film is no *Partridge Family*."

Dylan gave her a wicked grin. She tried to ignore how his smile alone made her legs wobble.

"Ha!" With one of his big paws, he gave her a hearty thump on the back that almost toppled her. "I knew you were there. That's what you get for spying."

She wanted to say something brilliant and biting. Instead, she stood there like an idiot.

He leaned toward her. He smelled of musk and the zing of minty fresh soap. "Hey," he said gazing into her eyes. "I didn't mean what I said about your film."

"Really?" She found herself inching closer to him.

He took a step back and grinned. "At least not *all* of it."

She reeled as if she'd just been drenched with a bucket of ice water.

Professor Phillips stepped between them. "Kate, your work is excellent. Don't let him get to you."

"I certainly won't."

Professor Phillips excused himself and looked at Kate as if he expected her to follow him, but she'd be damned if she would go while Dylan still had that smirk on his face.

After Professor Phillips left, she narrowed in on Dylan. "How did you know my name?"

"Er…easy." He looked about the crowded room and then nodded in the direction of her professor. "Phillips told me you looked just like Gloria Reardon. I'm a big fan of her films."

"I do not look like her."

He tilted his thick-lensed frameless glasses down. "Yes, you do."

Fine. Maybe she did. God knows, she'd been told often enough that she was the very picture of Gloria. But if personality counted for anything—and it should—she was nothing like her grandmother. In fact, nine years ago she'd promised herself she'd never be like Gloria. Ever.

Dylan gave a playful tug at her baseball cap. "Even though you try to hide the resemblance."

Kate shook him off. "It's always about looks, isn't it?"

"Hell, yes. We're working in a visual medium."

She stood tall. "Visual, fine. But that's no excuse for objectifying women as merely the embodiment of male fantasies and not real people at all."

"Uh-oh! Do I hear the righteous ranting of a Gloria Steinem acolyte?" His smile was cheeky.

Damn him.

A petite blonde in a clingy black nylon pantsuit, with a plunging V-neck and exaggerated bell bottoms appeared and rubbed against Dylan's side like a cat.

Double damn him.

"It's a lot better than pretending to be Hugh Hefner. Talk about last decade."

"Maybe," he said with a sly smile. "But as I recall, Steinem was a Playboy bunny." He gave her a wink, and then he and the blonde walked away arm-in-arm.

What a jerk! Her hands clenched, and she wanted to punch something. Which she knew was an overreaction. Still, he was such a...

Natalie came up to her.

"Chauvinist!" Kate declared.

"What?" her friend asked.

"He winked at me in front of his date. Talk about gross."

"What do you expect? He's a Hollywood director," Natalie said emphatically, as though the term *director* explained all self-aggrandizing behavior.

And, of course, it did.

Natalie continued, "When it comes to colossal egos these days, male directors are even worse than actors."

"How true." Kate laughed. "Well, I'm glad I never have to see him again."

Chapter Three

Kate unlocked the outer security gate to Lillian's West Hollywood apartment complex. She had finally been summoned to hear her aunt's plan.

At first glance, the Spanish-style courtyard of the complex appeared like an oasis. She imagined the 1930's architecture with its peppermint bushes and lemon trees had once sparkled with the promise of easy living. Now the pink cement was chipped, and weeds choked the plants.

She knocked at her aunt's door.

The door swung open, and there stood a smiling Dylan Nichols.

Kate fell back a step.

"Hello, hello," he said, as if he was satirizing a greeting instead of making one.

Gaining her bearings, she planted her feet and demanded, "What are you doing here?"

"Me? I'm a friend of Lillian's."

"What's going on? Don't tell me your judging my film was a coincidence."

"Hell, no! I was there to check you out."

She crossed her arms.

"Not like that." He laughed. "Hey, you didn't expect me to give up a couple of paying gigs this summer without finding out who I'd be working with, did you? That's why I knew who you were the moment

I saw you. Lil's the one who told me you looked like your grandmother."

"What do you mean work together?" She charged past the brute. "Lillian!"

Her aunt stood by her faux marble mantel in the living room. She was wearing a purple and yellow caftan and several strands of colorful beads, as if she were part of a harem in some old Valentino picture. Kate knew her well enough not to be fooled by her overdone costume. Lillian's mind was quick, and her temperament terrier-like when challenged.

It ran in the family.

"Darling, ladies don't yell, particularly to their aging aunts who happen to be in the next room."

"Sorry. But what's *he* doing here?"

"He's a friend."

Kate leaned close to her aunt and whispered, "I thought we weren't going to tell anybody about…you know…"

Dylan's voice sounded behind her. "You mean about the *Emperor Smythe* footage?"

She stared at her aunt in disbelief.

"Now, dear, I told you I had a friend who could help us. I've worked with him before. He's a filmmaker."

Kate flung her hands up in exasperation. "*I'm* a filmmaker. He makes pulp movies and TV shows."

Unperturbed, Dylan said, "And what have you done besides making a couple of shorts?"

"It's not what I've done." Kate stood tall. "It's what I plan to do."

Both Lillian and Dylan gave her a blank stare. "I'm going to be part of what's happening now, to be part of the independent cinema scene and not merely a vehicle to perpetuate sexist fantasies."

"Ha!" Dylan said so loudly that she actually jumped. "If you really want to make changes, you have to be *in* the business."

"Sell out." She scoffed. "I'll never do that."

The bastard laughed and looked at her like she was a child even though he was, at most, just a couple of years older than her.

She turned to Lillian. "What can he do that I can't?"

"Darling, Dylan spent over a year working at AFI's film restoration program."

He lifted his ridiculously wide chin. "I can restore that film. This footage may be some of the most important ever discovered. If it's not handled correctly, it may be ruined."

"His skill is highly recommended," Lillian said. "He's also ambitious enough to agree to work on the restoration as long as necessary."

"It'll be an honor to preserve it," he said.

Kate shook her head. "And doing so will make you famous in film circles. I'm sure that has nothing to do with your motives."

Dylan feigned innocence and then broke into a brilliant smile. "No, nothing at all."

Kate turned to her aunt. "Does that mean the film is ours?"

"Not without a fight," Lillian said. "What I've learned is that your possessory claim to the footage is tenuous. Even Winston's estate, with his unusual retention of rights to the script and to the final edit of the film, probably won't stand up against Golden State

Pictures' claim and their hordes of lawyers."

Kate deflated. "Sutton's going to take it from us?"

Lillian smiled mischievously. "I said *probably*. One thing just might give us a chance against them. I was thinking, how better to beat a school of sharks than by using another one?"

"Who?"

"Somebody who loved Gloria and has turned out to be the biggest shark of all—Jarvis Benjamin…Gloria's former agent and now the head of Infinity Studios."

Dylan shook his head. "Lil, I'm still not sure that's a good idea."

Kate dismissed Dylan with a look. "I think it's a wonderful idea. Mom mentioned him. She liked Jarvis."

"Yes, the only one in Gloria's set that Audrey did like," Lillian said.

"But Golden State Pictures produced *Emperor Smythe*," Dylan said. "That's who you should be dealing with. Adding someone like Jarvis to the mix, particularly if he's half as fierce a competitor as he's rumored to be, might—"

Lillian raised a perfectly penciled eyebrow. "Precisely the point. He is indeed fierce."

"I love it." Kate clapped her hands. "Lillian, I think you're the shark."

"But Dylan's correct about one thing," her aunt said. "Trying to use Jarvis's studio to fight Sutton's studio is diving into treacherous waters."

Kate grinned at her aunt. "You can't wait, can you?"

"Don't worry, my darling. If things get tough, I'll even get out the tiara Count Markov presented to me. Men are so easily impressed by a good wardrobe."

Lillian took Kate's face in her hands. "Something you should remember."

"Nice try. But I'm not changing my *wardrobe*— not even for Jarvis Benjamin."

****

Kate had never felt as uncomfortable as she did sitting on the black leather couch in the reception area outside Jarvis Benjamin's office.

Their appointment had been scheduled for two-o'clock, but it was now close to six.

Lillian and Dylan sat nearby. He was reading the old swashbuckler novel *Scaramouche* while her aunt dozed.

Kate squirmed. The entire set-up made her feel like she'd been plunged back into the Middle-Ages and was waiting in the great hall to petition the king.

Here, caste levels were well defined. All the secretaries were women, and all wore plain, sensible dresses with regulation two-inch heels. The men, young executives, wore tailored black or navy blue suits. Each one entered and exited Jarvis's office with a bowed head and fear etched on his face. Occasionally, she saw a man she pegged as someone from a different class. These men were overly tanned and donned casual but expensive suede jackets. Kate surmised that they were knights-errant—the ones who went out among the people to scour the land for talent. The longer she waited, the clearer it became that she, Lillian, and Dylan were peasants.

Finally, a thin woman in her late fifties appeared and shook Lillian's delicate hand so hard that Kate thought she might break it. The woman wore a beige jacket and matching skirt with a tan, wide-collared shirt. The only thing that wasn't drab about her ensemble was the glint of silver that pulled her ash-brown, perfectly angled pageboy neatly behind her ear.

"Miss Lillian Baker, I don't know if you remember me. I'm Beatrice Talbott." She had a clipped, east coast prep school accent. "I'm Vice President of Development here at Infinity Studios, and I work directly with Mr. Benjamin on all projects."

Not a secretary, thought Kate. *Very cool.*

Beatrice continued to rattle on as if by rote. She didn't look at Lillian's face but just over her shoulder, as if her mind was already on the next task of the day. "Please accept Mr. Benjamin's apologies. He wanted to meet with you in person, for old times' sake, but he's much too busy today, so he asked me to handle your matter personally."

Lillian rose. "That is very kind of you. But, our proposal is sensitive and for Jarvis's ears alone."

"Miss Baker, I assure you, I have Mr. Benjamin's total confidence. Anything you tell me will remain between me and him."

Lillian sat. "Nonetheless, we will wait to speak with Jarvis. However long it takes."

"Suit yourself. But it won't be today. He's much too busy." Beatrice twisted the silver object in her hair with her thumb and forefinger.

That's when Kate realized it wasn't a barrette but a pen she had nestled behind her ear.

Beatrice turned and pointed to one of the three secretaries, whose steel and wood laminated desks were lined up like sentries in front of Jarvis's office. "Check with Janice, there, and see if she can fit you in to his schedule on another day."

After Beatrice left, Dylan leapt to his feet. "That's BS!"

Lillian shot him a look that would halt a charging bull.

Ignoring the warning, Kate huffed and rushed the barricades anyway.

"Stop!" Lillian commanded.

Kate ignored her aunt and the screams from others for security, as she darted past the three secretaries and swung open Jarvis's office door. "We're here to offer you the deal of the century, and you don't even bother to see us?"

Jarvis, a scrunched man with a slightly lopsided face and faint blue eyes, shot her barely a glance. "Deal of the century? Sounds like a load of crap."

She sucked in her lower lip.

The room exuded power with its panoramic view of both Hollywood and the San Fernando Valley. Two of the walls were glass, but their brown tint darkened the interior. Crammed between the oversized pieces of furniture were two long glass cases that housed a collection of antique pipes and silver matchboxes, all adding to the opulent but oppressive feel of the office. When she first looked at the man himself, he appeared small behind his vast desk, and with his asymmetrical jowls, some might laugh and think could this really be the man who caused such trepidation throughout the Hollywood kingdom?

But she knew it would be a mistake to be taken in by his inelegant features.

The real force in the office was all Jarvis Benjamin.

"Get out of my office, whoever you are, otherwise

my security's going to throw you out on your ass."

"Happy to do it, Boss," a man said behind her and his thick hand clasped down tight on her shoulder.

Lillian, Dylan, and an assortment of secretaries had crowded into the room.

"Oh dear," Lillian said a bit winded and shaky. "Jarvis, I'm so sorry—"

"Lillian Baker." Jarvis's expression softened as he rose and gestured to an empty chair. "Please take a seat. It's good to see you again." He shot Kate a look less kind. "Let me guess, anyone so ballsy and rude must be Gloria's granddaughter."

Ballsy. Rude. Not the normal type of gushing and idealized language she was used to hearing to describe her grandmother.

Kate liked those strong descriptors. So much so, she decided to give him a pass on his male-centric terminology. She also concluded that where Jarvis had, at first, appeared squat, on closer inspection, he could be best characterized as solid. His muscular forearms and intimidating gaze made him look like a seasoned street fighter, even if his slightly baggy black suit and power tie were luxurious. He was also a lot younger than she'd expected. She'd bet he was in his early fifties, which meant he had been younger than her when he first became Gloria's agent.

He turned to his staff. "It's okay. I'll handle them." He thumbed through a pile of files on his desk, pulled one out, and read from it. "Kate, right? And you're Dylan." He looked up at them. "See? I was expecting you, until an emergency came up." He gestured for them to sit in the chairs next to Lillian on the other side of his desk. "But I'm a sucker for a gutsy broad, so I'll give you ten minutes."

Jarvis sat Sphinx-like as he listened to Lillian weave her tale. When she revealed the discovery of the missing footage from *Emperor Smythe*, even the famously omniscient Jarvis Benjamin's jaw dropped.

For her finale, Lillian pushed a letter across his mahogany desk. Kate knew it to be from an attorney for Nash's estate. "If you will use the power of your studio to back Kate's and the Nash estate's claim, they will both support Infinity Studio's control of the footage."

Jarvis tapped his fingers on his desk with the steady pace of a metronome. "No."

Kate glanced at Dylan, who looked like he was going to bolt from his seat and declare the whole day a waste.

"Kate's claim to the footage is weak," Jarvis said. "And even recognizing that Nash had a sweet deal of a contract where he retained certain rights, I'm sure my lawyers will tell me the film is Golden State's product. I'd end up with nothing but legal fees and—"

"We knew you'd want more," Kate interjected.

Lillian glanced at her with a tight smile before she returned her attention to Jarvis and her performance. "Yes. So I went to Santa Barbara and spoke to the Nash estate's attorney personally. The estate has agreed to give you an option to buy Winston's original script at a reduced cost. Think of it. Infinity Studios will have the sole right to remake the film."

"No one's ever gotten them to agree to sell it at any price." Jarvis's eyes narrowed. "Can you really deliver that?"

Lillian smiled. "Yes. Unlike you, or anyone else in Hollywood for that matter, the Nash estate trusts me.

But there are conditions."

She cocked her head like a coquette, a part Hollywood never let her play, before continuing. "In return for the right to remake *Emperor Smythe*, you will use your resources to champion Kate's and the Nash estate's claim of the found footage against Sutton's studio claim. We know you may not win. We just ask that you try."

Jarvis ran his index finger across his polished desktop. "And?"

Lillian turned all business and rattled off the terms like a law partner instructing an associate. "The estate gets one percent of gross profit on the remake, and if we prevail on the right to distribute the original, one percent profit on that, with the condition the Nash estate gets to approve the final cut. Kate here, a talented filmmaker in her own right, only asks to work with the editors, get in the union, and gain the experience." Her performance complete, Lillian leaned back as if expecting him to come to her.

Jarvis shrugged. "Golden State Pictures would probably accept those terms just to have you go away and not challenge their claim. Why do you need me?"

Kate stood. "The footage needs to be seen. Sutton may agree to our terms, but if he gets it, he'll bury it. Everyone knows Smythe is based on him, and the missing footage was the most damning part of the film. In fact, until finding the footage, I'd assumed, like everyone else, he'd been the one to destroy it."

Jarvis stared at her. And she realized the blue of his eyes was not faint at all, but more like the color at the center of a flame.

She gulped before continuing. "What we want is a

guarantee that the film will be preserved and shown, no matter what happens."

"I'm surprised preserving Winston's film is so important to you…considering…"

"I don't give a damn about Winston! It's that my mom—"

"Audrey."

"Yes." Kate smiled. He had remembered her. "She claimed the camera was left rolling the day Gloria was killed and recorded Winston threatening her on the set. I want the world to see him terrorizing Gloria and know without a doubt that Winston killed her."

"Ah. Revenge." Jarvis leaned back in his leather chair. "Who do you think you are—the goddess Nemesis?"

"No. Justice." Kate took a step toward his gargantuan desk.

He stared at her for a while, his face unreadable. She glanced at her aunt, who appeared to be holding her breath. Finally, he laughed, the sound all the more warm because of the sense it was rarely used. "Good answer."

Kate rolled her shoulders back in triumph. After all, she had just made the most powerful man in Hollywood laugh.

Dylan interjected, "Of course this is assuming we can save the footage. It's in bad shape. I'm not sure it is even salvageable."

"But you want to try," Jarvis said.

Dylan nodded.

Jarvis pulled a one-page document in his file and glanced it over. "I've looked into your background. You apprenticed at AFI under Ken Bresnick. He gave you a glowing recommendation. I also had a reader take a look at some of your scripts, and he said you're not without talent. My question for you is, why? What do you get out of all this?"

"For one," Dylan replied, "*the* Jarvis Benjamin notices that I'm not without talent, and maybe you'll give me a shot at adapting Nash's script for the remake."

Jarvis's expression remained flat.

Dylan cleared his throat. "And to be able to bring back to life the famous lost reels of what may be the greatest film ever made would be amazing."

"*If* I agree to your conditions, then you all must agree to mine, number one being that I control everything: strategy, marketing, restoration. Everything."

They nodded. How could they not? During the course of the meeting, Kate had watched Jarvis's expression flit from impatient, to cold, to seductive, to calculating.

Jarvis turned to Lillian. "I'll talk to my lawyers. I smell a sizable profit with the remake, benefiting from all the publicity about the discovery of the old footage and the inevitable rehashing of the scandal. The public loves that stuff."

"But—" Kate began.

"Don't worry," he said. "I'm still going to try to win the rights to the original footage. If those reels you found show the world how Winston bullied Gloria, then I'm all for that, too."

"Did you love her?" she asked.

Dylan coughed.

Lillian looked horrified.

"Of course." Jarvis's eyes softened. "We all did."

"But you were different from the others. That's what my mom said. You weren't trying to claw a piece off Gloria like everyone else. You were her friend."

"I hope she thought that." Jarvis gave an awkward laugh, looking as if the years had melted away and he was a kid again. His expression was short-lived.

His mouth tightened and his eyes narrowed as he returned to the subject of business. "My first order is we keep this quiet until my lawyers are prepared to take on Golden State Pictures. Is that understood?"

Kate opened her mouth to protest.

Jarvis silenced her with a steely look. "Only until the footage is fully restored and ready to be shown, I promise. I want to make sure no one—not even Sutton—can stop us from getting the film in that condition. The preservation process should start right away, but not in a public facility."

He turned to Dylan. "Because you already know of this discovery, I'm going to trust you with the restoration."

"Great!" Dylan said.

"I get to assist," Kate said.

"Fine," Jarvis said. "Okay, Dylan?"

"Yeah, sure."

"Good. Write me a list of what you need, and I'll set up my guest house as your lab." Jarvis stood and motioned them toward the door.

Kate held her ground. "I'm not going to just hand over the film to you. My claim is possession. Where that film goes, I go."

Dylan stood next to Kate. "The process includes some volatile chemicals. The restoration shouldn't be done in anyone's house."

Although a good four inches shorter than Dylan, Jarvis stepped in front of him as if he were nothing more than set decoration. "My Bel Air home has a cottage far enough away from the main residence and should work fine as a lab."

"I don't know," Kate said.

"Tell you what," Jarvis said. "If you insist the film not leave your possession, why don't you and Lillian be my guests and stay at the house until the restoration is completed?"

Her aunt's eyes brightened at the suggestion, but Kate wasn't so sure.

Jarvis turned to Dylan. "I assume you don't need to camp out at my house, too."

"No, sir," Dylan said.

"Good. It's settled."

"Oh, we couldn't possibly." Lillian's smiling face didn't match her shaking head. "That would be too much of an imposition."

"I usually stay at my beach house. I'm hardly ever there, and the place is large. I'll have it arranged." Jarvis held his office door open as they filed past him into the reception area.

The three of them walked out of the building in silence. Once they were safely in the parking lot, Dylan whooped. "Goddamn! Am I crazy, or did that bastard just say yes?"

"Don't call him a bastard," Kate said. "He's on our side. And I thought he was fascinating."

"Huh? Don't be fooled by that fatherly twinkle in his eyes when he looked at you."

"He had no such thing," she said.

"You're right...the look he gave you wasn't *fatherly*," Dylan said pointedly.

"He's just a savvy businessman."

"You're both correct," Lillian said. "A man doesn't climb out of a rough upbringing and beat all the silver-spooned lads to be the top man in Hollywood without knowing how to be ruthless." Lillian stabbed an index finger at Dylan's chest. "And you behave, because we just got ruthless to work for us."

Kate hugged her great-aunt. "You did. You were incredible!"

"Oh, it was nothing. I'm just an actress who believes in preparation."

"Except," Kate said, "I'm not sure about living in his house. I think being there would be weird living with some old guy I don't know. I mean, running into him in the kitchen wearing shorts and eating toast."

Lillian sniffed. "I doubt Jarvis owns shorts."

Chapter Four

A long private road covered with a thick canopy of green wound up a hill until the lane widened into a circular driveway. At the top was a six-car garage larger than her mother's home in Claremont. Kate parked her 1968 VW bug behind her aunt's Lincoln and gazed at the house.

A faux-Roman villa with its textured white stucco walls and brightly tiled roof of reds, gold, and green may have looked beautiful in an open field in Tuscany. But here in the hills above urban L.A., it was garish. Still, Kate delighted in the eclectic touches that rebelled against the estate's mostly traditional style. The front yard centerpiece, a large garden fountain, wasn't a marble replica of something found in Italy. Instead it was a mid-century modern sculpture, all steel and angles. In that vein, the landscape design imposed structure onto nature. Bougainvillea were shaped like office towers along the perimeter of a geometric grass plane framed by cement and stone. Yet, in defiance to such order, untamed English roses spread, climbed, and insinuated themselves throughout the austere landscape, and up against strong masculine lines of the villa.

Kate wondered if these touches came from a professional designer. She preferred to think they were from The Great Jarvis Benjamin himself.

The great? Right. She chuckled.

Why did she always think of him with that title? At first she had used the moniker in jest. Now she thought it fit him. In his office, he'd filled the room with power, like a gunslinger, steady and watchful, with the potential to strike only a hair trigger away.

Slamming her car door shut, she concluded the grounds were, in fact, perfectly Californian. The verdant terraced garden juxtaposed against the golden brown hillside gave it the appearance of a movie set, not a real place at all.

She dragged her two fading suitcases from the backseat and placed them on the pristine sandstone driveway. She then went to the front of the car and lifted the stiff latch on the forward trunk to retrieve the two carefully wrapped film canisters.

An Asian man with a sharp chin and a determined expression glided down the two front steps and along the stone pathway toward her car. He announced he was Kiyoshi and snatched up her suitcases.

"Wait, please don't bother," Kate yelled after him.

Ignoring her, he hurried into the main house, leaving the arched front door open.

She shrugged and lifted out the steel film reel carrying case. After closing the trunk, she headed toward the house with the case in hand. When she was half-way to the door, she flinched at the sound of crackling and popping overhead. Startled, she looked up. The canopy of eucalyptus branches shading the stairs shook violently. She blinked, and a blast of scalding heat shot across her cheek making her gasp. Her grip on the cool film case tightened as a humid wind lapped at her skin. In just a few seconds, the noise, heat, and commotion of the trees ended.

Whoa. What was that?

Must have been the summer wind. She took a deep breath, lifted the heavy case against her chest, and jogged toward the house, trying to ignore the nagging fact that the day up until now had been still and everything else in the garden, even the open front door, hadn't moved an inch.

Once inside, she saw no sign of Kiyoshi. Instead, an angular woman with the fierce eyes and broad cheeks of an ancient warrior greeted her. She smelled of ammonia and freshly squeezed lemons.

"I'm Jimena. I'll show you to your room. Your aunt is already settled."

Kate smiled awkwardly. "Right." She followed Jimena up a magnificent mahogany staircase and down a cream-colored hallway to a guest room.

It was lovely, a suite more than a room—all soft colors, gauzy curtains, and a pillowed window seat.

She placed the film carrying case in a shaded corner of the room and peered out the window at the backyard with its garden patio butting up against the house. Groomed terraced steps weaved down the hillside to a second patio, where a glistening swimming pool was perched beside a drop-off to the canyon below. At the edge of this patio was the top of a wood handrail that seemingly led off the cliff. From what Dylan told her, that must be the staircase to the cottage where the film would be properly stored and where she'd be working each day on the film restoration.

She gulped. From this vantage, the trail looked like a step-off into an abyss.

Jimena opened one of her suitcases and began to unpack her things.

"No, please," Kate said. "I can do it."

"If that's what you prefer." Jimena slammed the suitcase shut.

"I didn't mean…"

"Miss Bloom, you don't insult me by letting me do my job. It's the opposite."

"Oh, right. Sure, go ahead then." Watching someone handle her things was just plain weird.

Sucking in her lower lip, she thought about how much her mom had hated anyone touching her stuff. Guilt rushed through Kate. It had been wrong to have rented her mom's house furnished. But with so much going on in the last month, with the semester ending and the restoration beginning, it was the easy thing to do. Besides, the past was already much too present.

Kate looked about the room and then noticed it had three closets. She almost laughed. Three! One was in the main sleeping area, and two more were in a dressing area, which had a built-in vanity and walls of mirrors. This then led to a large, sunny bathroom.

"The bathroom connects to your aunt's room. Mr. Benjamin thought you'd be more comfortable located near her."

"I would. Yes." Kate turned. "Is Jarvis here? I'd like to thank him."

"He's here only for the night, but he doesn't wish to be disturbed." Jimena removed Kate's denim jacket from her suitcase and looked at her loved, and somewhat tattered, garb with distaste. The housekeeper held the jacket by her fingertips and took it to the dressing room. Kate beat her to the dressing alcove and opened the closet door. Hanging there several long gowns, one a gold lamé dress. She stiffened. It was *the* gold lamé dress—Gloria's.

Eyes wide, Jimena smiled. "Ah, look at that." She pulled out the gown. Its beads shimmered in the light. "Your aunt said she had put some things in your closet. The dress is so beautiful." The maid held the garment up to Kate. "It was designed for you, no?"

Kate's throat constricted. Just the sight of it made her want to jump in the shower and scrub away the memory of the man.

"Miss, are you all right?" Jimena asked.

"Yes." Kate shook herself and grabbed the dress. She charged through the bathroom and burst through Lillian's bedroom door. "What is *this* doing in my room?"

Lillian turned from arranging her cosmetics on the dressing table. "What do you think? It's to wear."

"No way." She pushed the garment into her aunt's hands.

Lillian sighed and draped the gown on her arm. "I realize Gloria's designer gown does not compare to the charm of your blue jeans and hiking boots."

"Lillian, we've been through this before."

"Tish-tosh." Her aunt flicked her hand in the air. "It occurred to me that there may be an occasion to dress formally here. A girl should always be prepared."

"I'm a woman, not a *girl*. That term is derogatory."

Lillian rolled her eyes.

"It is. It infantilizes us. Besides, I'd look ridiculous in the dress. It's no longer the 1940s, you know."

"Quality is forever." Lillian turned Kate toward the mirror and held the dress in front of her. "Letting the world see how special you are is letting the world see *who* you are."

Kate stared at the gown draped against her body and knew intellectually she shouldn't blame the dress, or her naïve stupidity for causing the assault to her so many years ago.

But, she only knew it intellectually.

She turned from the mirror and tugged at her baggy T-shirt. "Makeup and fancy costumes are masks, a way to hide the real person."

Lillian gazed pointedly at the excess fabric of Kate's work shirt. "Oh really? More than oversized clothes and hiking boots are?"

"Maybe."

Lillian handed the dress to Kate then crossed to a small scalloped desk with long spooled legs. "Come, see what else I brought." She unlatched a wood box with an inlaid enamel border. Inside were rings, bracelets, clip-on earrings, some ridiculously-gaudy, others, Kate noted, not so ridiculous.

"Most are costume jewelry, although some quite lovely." Lillian retrieved a shiny green necklace. "Glass, not jade, I'm afraid. Gloria wore this in *Madame X*—terrible film, but wonderful wardrobe."

Kate waved away the bauble. "You keep it."

"I'll keep them for you." Lillian wrapped the piece up and smiled. "I loved the old days. Including the studio system you're always trying to tear down. They managed to repackage dull everyday life as an opulent world filled with glamour and wit."

Kate inched toward the box and let her fingers explore its treasures.

"One couldn't keep it up, of course," her aunt continued. "But there were moments when it felt real. Like at an opening or grand party." Lillian had a glazed, far off look as she hummed an overly romantic tune.

The melody plucked inside Kate like a forgotten memory. A lullaby sung on a starlit night. It reminded her of a time long ago, when she was little and endlessly alone, reading a book or thumbing through an old photo album, and she'd imagine Gloria by her side, warm, almost tangible, wrapping around her like a hug, and for a while, she'd felt loved.

Kate picked up a swan pin and watched it twinkle in the light. The brooch's only spot of color was a red eye. Small clear sparkles outlined the simple elegant lines of the bird.

Lillian's gaze fixed on the brooch. Then she leaned back and clapped. "Well done. You just may have a bit of me in you after all. That one is *not* costume. White gold, a ruby eye, and tiny diamond studs."

"Oh?" Kate's voice leapt to a soprano register.

"Don't worry, my darling. It's not worth that much money. The diamonds and ruby aren't much larger than specks. It's just well-made and well chosen. Enjoy. That's what it's for."

Lillian closed the jewelry box. "Jimena said dinner is at seven, and I wouldn't dare be late."

"See you down there." When Kate got back to her room, she realized one hand still clutched the jeweled swan and the other the gold dress. She sighed. Round one went to Lillian.

****

Several hours later, Kate was back in her bedroom. Dinner had been delicious: homemade lasagna and crisp green salad. She'd been glad Jarvis had not joined them. She was too tired for small talk.

Kate slipped on her favorite extra-large, extra-soft,

white T-shirt and stretched out in the bed. She hoped the over-the-top plush bedding of Jarvis's guest room would finally provide her much needed rest.

It wasn't working.

Each creak or thump of the unfamiliar house made her tense and clutch at the sheets as if any moment her door would swing open and she'd be...

Get a grip!

She turned to her other side, then turned again, shifting her pillow to under her head. A fitful sleep finally came and with it a dream filled with misty tears of her own, of her mother's, and someone else's, too.

The drapes looking over the backyard began to sway as if alive. Kate got out of bed and went to close the windows. The curtains lashed around her. Then she saw the windows were shut, yet the curtains continued to billow and sway. Her heart raced as she watched shadows flitting around the patio garden below and darting across the dark lawn down to the edge of a cliff and dropping into a black chasm.

"*Run.*" A woman's voice echoed up from the abyss. Kate jumped back from the windows.

"*Leave,*" the voice said, closer this time. Moist heat like the breath of an animal swirled around her.

The presence was here.

She dashed back to the bed and pulled the covers tightly around her.

Everything in the room shook until the window exploded, shards of glass spraying everywhere.

Her skin felt on fire, it pricked and stung with searing pain. She sat up and threw off the blanket. The room spun. A metallic smell filled her nose. The heat turned sticky. She looked down and saw her body dripping with blood.

She screamed.

The door to her bedroom swung open.

"Good God," Jarvis said. "What's the matter? Are you all right?"

She writhed in the bed and had no ability to form words.

Jarvis ran to her and held her shaking body. "Tell me what happened. What's wrong?"

Taking in a deep breath, she extracted herself from his embrace.

She gazed about the room and blinked. There was no blood, and the pretty room was bathed in the soft pink of dawn. The curtains hung still, and the windows were unbroken.

"I'm so sorry. It must've been a nightmare."

Jarvis rose. "Is that all? I heard you cry out. It was…chilling. Like you were dying." His gaze became diffused, haunted, as if he were watching something terrible that only he could see. Then he came back to himself and said, "A nightmare? Do you have those often?"

"Oh, no… Yes, I do. I'm so sorry I disturbed you." Kate jumped out of bed, forgetting she was wearing only a T-shirt and panties.

Jarvis swept an admiring glance over her bare legs. She jumped back into the bed and pulled the sheet up.

He cleared his throat. "I better be going. I have an early meeting, and you need to get dressed."

Chapter Five

After a month of sitting in the overly air-conditioned cottage, with its thick smell of acetone and the other pungent chemicals used in the restoration, doing nothing but peering into a magnifying glass, inspecting one film frame at a time to find scratches, the glamour of the project was waning.

Still, she couldn't fault the location, nestled on a hidden expanse below the pool. Even if the stairs leading to the cottage were treacherous, the little house was inviting with its arched doorway, white stucco plaster, and tile roof that matched the style of the main residence.

Jarvis had certainly spared no expense. Against the back wall, there was a state of the art flatbed editor, looking like any long horizontal table, except that fastened to it were multiple spools to run the film and sound separately. Off to one side of the cottage was a splicer on a small desk. Against another wall sat a couch, next to which was the very impressive temperature controlled safe. In the center of the room was another table with two hand-cranked vertical spools that threaded film through a secured back-lit flat area, where each frame could be inspected and cleaned.

The click of Dylan's switching off the flatbed brought her out of her musings. "Quitting time." He handed her a rag and carried the filmstrips back to the safe.

Kate groaned. Quitting time meant cleaning time. So did starting time, leaving for lunchtime, and also whenever Dylan said it was time.

The man was more dust phobic than Howard Hughes. But Dylan had explained, in his most dictatorial manner, that dust was a death sentence for the fragile film. So clean they did—constantly.

Her hands burned. The skin on them peeled off like the thin membrane of an onion as she exchanged form-fitting surgical gloves for bright pink household ones.

Once they were finished with the cleaning, Dylan held the door open for her, and for once she was too tired to object to the sexist gesture.

She trudged up the steep stone stairway careful to keep away from the rickety handrail. She was looking forward to what had become her after-work ritual—a twilight swim. Since moving into the mansion, she'd go to the pool house and choose from an assortment of bathing costumes. She called them "costumes" because they weren't like the simple sports swimsuits she normally wore. No, these had a structure to them that squeezed her torso into that of Esther Williams. She could almost imagine Fernando Lamas diving into the pool with her.

After swimming her laps, she'd always leave the pool to find a pitcher of ice water and a bowl of fruit had magically appeared on a poolside table.

It was getting to be quite an elegant lifestyle.

Today, when she had reached the top of the stairs, she was surprised to see Jarvis, Beatrice Talbot, and her aunt lounging on the pool patio. Well, only Lillian lounged. Jarvis and Beatrice sat upright on the green cushioned couch in black business attire.

She hadn't seen Jarvis since the first night of her stay. He nodded to her then resumed his conversation with Beatrice. Kate felt an irrational resentment toward his intrusion—and even more so for the stony Beatrice, who had been by several times to bark orders and to complain the restoration was taking too long.

After trailing her up the stairs, Dylan now scooted by Kate and made a beeline for the cheese and crackers on the mosaic coffee table in front of the couch.

Beatrice scribbled in a small leather notebook. The woman always had it handy. Other than her burgundy notebook and flashy silver pen, Beatrice's tastes ran monochromatic.

Kate had done a little research. She learned that Beatrice was the first woman to reach the heights of VP in the studio's male-dominated structure. She had begun her career as a secretary at some tony New York talent agency. Then, over thirty years ago, she met Jarvis. She must have seen something special in him, because she went to work in his fledgling agency soon thereafter.

After reading Beatrice's short bio, Kate had bubbled with questions about how she'd managed to break the glass ceiling during the chauvinistic 1950s. But every time she tried to talk to Beatrice, she'd gotten the brush-off. Kate didn't know whether Beatrice's obvious antipathy was aimed specifically toward her or to life in general, but she decided to keep her distance from the woman.

Dylan sat next to Lillian, chomping on what looked like a water cracker piled with brie. "Great news," he said. "We've finished the first reel."

"About time." Beatrice's gaze narrowed in on Kate, and then she shot toward her like a missile.

The angular woman lifted Kate's jacket by the lapel and ran her finger across the swan pin that was fastened to it.

"I haven't seen that in a long time," Beatrice said.

Kate blinked down at the bauble. In the sunlight, the swan's ruby eye twinkled back at her.

When did she begin wearing Gloria's brooch?

Beatrice turned from Kate as abruptly as she'd approached. "Jarvis, isn't that the trinket you gave Gloria? To celebrate the signing of her studio contract, I think?"

Kate's mouth went dry as she was conscious of everyone staring at her and the glittering pin.

"Sure did," Jarvis replied. He smiled at Kate. "It suits you."

"Was that Gloria's?" Dylan approached with reverence. "Cool!"

She squirmed away from him. "There's some of her stuff in my garage, not a lot. Most of what's left of her is what's preserved on film."

Beatrice clicked her tongue. "And a beauty she was, too. Wise of you to trade on your grandmother's fame."

Kate shook her head. "That's not—"

"Of course, you are. It's a tough business, no shame." Beatrice surveyed her like she was something to be purchased. "You're right, Jarvis. She's a mess. I suppose hair and makeup could fix her up. The face, except for her nose, isn't bad and probably her body, too, but who can tell under those ridiculous clothes." She turned to Jarvis. "But if you're also right, and she has half the presence Gloria had on screen, she'd be an asset."

Not waiting for an answer, Beatrice plucked her pen from behind her ear and scribbled something in her notebook. "I'll have Mike set up a screen test."

"Wonderful!" Lillian clapped her hands.

"Screen test? No way!" Kate cried. "I don't want to act."

Dylan snorted.

Kate glared at him.

Beatrice tucked her notebook into her big black purse. "Of course you do. Everyone wants to be a star."

"Not me."

Jarvis put down his glass and stood. "I know you asked for the opportunity to work with an editor, or someone on the technical side, but no one notices them." He put his arm around Kate and gave her a squeeze. "I promised I'd help you get into the business. But you'll have to do the rest."

"I'm *not* an actress."

"Whoever I call an actress is one," Jarvis said. "Don't be so modest. Lillian told me you've taken acting classes at UCLA, and she said you're not bad."

"Yeah, well, not bad isn't good. I only signed up for those classes to be a better director."

"Women can't direct," Jarvis said.

"That's not true." Kate stuck out her chin. "What about Agnes Varga and Lena Wertmuller?"

"Foreigners."

Kate brightened. "Yes. And that's where the innovation is."

"But not the money," Jarvis said.

"You're worse than Dylan."

"Undoubtedly." Jarvis chuckled. "Okay, you want to direct. I won't stop you. But no one will give a million-dollar budget to a kid with no experience."

"All I'm asking for is a chance to get some technical experience. Kick me out if I can't perform."

"I will." The sharpness of his gaze left no doubt about his sincerity. "You should take the acting opportunity."

"Why do you want me to test? There are a million other girls who'd jump at the chance, who've worked hard for it."

"Hell, I know why," Dylan said. "You want to see if she can play Gloria's part in the *Emperor Smythe* remake. That's the reason, isn't it?"

Kate shook her head. "Absolutely not."

"The publicity would be dynamite." Beatrice's lips narrowed into a tight smile. "Don't worry. We'll only use you if you're any good. I'll schedule the screen test."

Jarvis picked up a folder he'd left on the table. "Star power opens a lot of doors, maybe even to directing. Look at Dennis Hopper."

Kate tried to say no again, but she couldn't quite form the word. He had a point. She'd be a fool not to grab the chance.

"Good. Just think about it." Jarvis left, with Beatrice dutifully trailing him.

"Oh, how the mighty have fallen." Dylan grabbed another cracker and smeared it with brie.

Lillian threw down her napkin. "Hush. Leave her alone. This is an immense opportunity. Kate, dear, don't be foolish now."

Coming back to her senses, she said, "No. I won't

do it." Fool or not, she wouldn't audition. It was as simple as that. She turned and trudged up the manicured terraced path toward the main house.

"Kate, wait up. I didn't mean to tease you."

She turned to face him.

"Okay, I did." He shot her a sheepish grin. "But this is a great opportunity. You should do it."

She crossed her arms. "I have no interest in Hollywood movies with its promotion of myths: men stoic, women goddesses. It's harmful."

"Is this about Gloria?"

She released her arms and let them fall to her side. "Maybe."

Dylan's gaze moved from her face to the glittery pin on her jacket. "You can't live your life for her." His hand grazed up her arm. "Or even against her."

His expression conveyed a gentle understanding, so unlike his normal bravado. Looking into his dark eyes, she felt safe, and that was a scary thought. She stepped away from him. "I simply don't want to do the screen test because I'm not interested in narrative cinema. That's all."

She turned to leave.

"Wait." He grabbed her hand.

She swung back. He smiled, and she couldn't help it; she smiled back.

"I'm just saying there's also value in a good old-fashioned *narrative* story," he said. "And I have the perfect film to prove my point, Preston Sturges' *Sullivan's Travels*, which happens to be playing tonight at the Regency Cinema. Will you go?"

"With you?" Her voice cracked, and she felt her old inexplicable panic well up inside her when she was around a guy she liked.

Dylan laughed. "Don't look so appalled. It's not a date. It's a challenge. You'll be safe. I'm meeting some friends there."

She shrugged. "I might make it."

Chapter Six

When Kate and Natalie arrived at the Regency Cinema, the theater was packed. At the top of the aisle, Kate scanned the audience. The buzz of chatter from the mostly college-age art house crowd was punctuated by an occasional call across the room, followed by the waving of arms as someone motioned a friend to an empty seat.

Kate spied Dylan down the aisle, leaning against a seat talking to two women. One wore a floppy, wide-brimmed sun hat—ridiculous for an eight o'clock movie—and a puffy jacket adorned with what looked like white dove feathers, as if she had just come from a David Bowie concert.

Natalie followed Kate's gaze. "Oh, that's why."

Kate clutched her friend's arm and turned to leave. "Forget it. I've changed my mind."

Natalie wouldn't budge. "Coward."

"Never," Kate said, much more loudly than she meant to do.

Dylan looked up, waved and headed toward her.

Her legs wobbled. Not because he was so good-looking. He was just so… Well, she didn't know what it was.

"Hey, I knew you'd come," Dylan said.

Oh, right. It was because he was an arrogant jerk!

"Why not?" She shrugged. "I've an open mind."

Natalie giggled, then quickly covered her mouth.

Dylan gave Kate a wry smile. "Right, you're completely nonjudgmental. Everyone knows that."

Natalie laughed again.

Kate glared at her traitorous friend.

"Ah, an ally, I see." Dylan took Natalie's arm. "Come, we've saved a couple of seats." He peered back at Kate. "Just in case."

"Nothing's wrong with having opinions," she mumbled and trailed after them.

A guy about Dylan's age with jet-black hair down to his shoulders was asleep in the aisle seat. Dylan introduced her to Peter Mallick, if one can be introduced to someone who was asleep.

"Just call him Mallick, everyone does," Dylan said.

"Sure." Kate nodded to the slumped individual.

Next to Mallick were three empty seats holding two sweatshirts and a jacket, and at the end was one of her teachers.

"Uh, hi Professor Phillips." It was strange to see her instructor wearing a tight black T-shirt instead of the tan corduroy jacket he wore in class.

He nodded at Kate. "We're out of the classroom. Please call me Steve."

Steve?

Natalie jumped ahead of Kate, bumping into the sleeping Mallick as she squeezed by him and sat next to *Steve*. Mallick didn't react.

Dylan slipped past Kate, leaving her no place to sit except in between him and the slumped Mallick, who reeked of pot.

The lights went down, and the previews began. As if the dinner bell had just rung, Mallick jumped out of his chair. Before the opening credits rolled, he returned and passed down several sodas, a box of licorice, chocolate-covered vanilla ice cream, and best of all, a giant tub of popcorn that had been liberally enhanced with morsels of chocolate. Mallick offered her some popcorn, whispering, "So you're Kate. No wonder you've got Dylan scared."

"Him? Right," Kate said, her mouth full of buttered popcorn.

Mallick slumped in his seat and said in a tone of dead seriousness, "Right."

What was he talking about?

Thoughts of Dylan were soon replaced with the mishaps of Joel McRae and Veronica Lake in *Sullivan's Travels*. In the final scene, the film's fictional director, Joel McRae sits in a movie theater watching his own comedy delight people whose daily lives were a struggle during the Depression and realizing his silly film had value. It gave her the chills.

The lights came up, and she tried not to look at Dylan's smug expression as he caught her brushing away tears. As they left their seats, she noticed Professor Phillips's cheek was smeared with Natalie's coral lipstick. When they got to the lobby, Natalie grabbed her arm.

"Hey, guess what?" Not waiting for an answer, her friend barreled on, "Turns out Steve lives in Los Feliz, practically next door to Silver Lake, so I told him I'd give him a ride home. He's asking if Dylan would take you back to Bel Air. You don't mind, do you?"

"I, ah—"

"Great. You're the best." Natalie jogged over to Steve, and they left.

Kate looked around and saw Mallick walking toward her, but no Dylan.

"I guess you're with us," the black haired stoner said with a big, lopsided grin.

"I guess so."

"Dylan went to get his car. Parking's shit around here."

Outside, the rumbling sound of a stampeding buffalo herd accompanied a shiny black Mustang convertible that skidded to the curb within inches of where they stood. Mallick opened the door, swung up the front seat, and dived into the back.

Dylan sat behind the steering wheel, his lips curved into a sexy smile, his dark eyes soulful.

Get a grip. The guy was about as soulful as an accountant completing an audit. She climbed in. "Just doing your part to increase air pollution, I see."

"Vee eight." Dylan revved the engine.

"Why am I not surprised?"

The car's interior was all black leather and shiny chrome, with an eight-track tape deck and speakers everywhere. "Nice setup. I didn't know Skyline paid so well."

"It doesn't," Mallick said from the backseat. "Dylan's family is loaded."

"Gee," she said. "You should have said so. I would have been nicer to you sooner."

Dylan looked sideways at her.

"Kidding." She examined him. "Is that why you treat women as objects? You figure we're all just after your money?"

Mallick popped his head in between them. "She's got your number. Two points to Kate." He fell back against the back seat.

She turned to Dylan. "You puzzle me. You profess to love old Hollywood movies, happy endings, and all that sentimental stuff. But you may be the most cynical person I've ever met."

He shot her a smarmy grin. "Then let me take you to my place, and I'll tell you where to fit the pieces."

"Gross. Why do you say things like that?"

"Two points to Dylan," Mallick declared.

"No way." Kate turned to him. "That was a complete turn-off."

"Nevertheless." Mallick smiled, but there was a brush of concern on his face as he looked over at his friend.

Dylan hit the gas pedal, and Kate's head snapped back as they sped up Crescent Heights Boulevard toward Sunset. Once on the Strip, there was no choice but to slow down.

Kate rolled down her window and was met with the aroma of marijuana, gasoline, and skunk that wafted down from the hills. But who cared, the street pulsed with the energy of youth. Pounding from everywhere—clubs, car stereos and transistor radios—folk, funk, and heavy metal mixed and mingled into a new L.A. sound.

Yet, even here, there was no mistaking the ghosts of the past. The Rainbow Bar and Grill looked like a small Tudor cottage on acid. Ben Frank's Coffee Shop was all geometric angles, an echo of the 1950s. And even the music clubs, with their psychedelic paint jobs and lines of kids waiting to get inside, Kate couldn't deny these places stood on the shoulders of the likes of Judy Garland or Frank Sinatra, just some of the few who'd performed at spots on the Strip just a generation earlier.

In the backseat of the car, Mallick's waving arms caught her attention. She looked back and saw he lay supine in the narrow backseat with his legs up in the air. He drew lines in the air, as if conducting a song only he could hear or painting on an imagined canvas.

She turned to Dylan and whispered, "Is he okay?"

Dylan glanced into the rearview mirror. "Yeah, he's just working on his new film project."

"Hey, man, I'm stoned, not deaf."

"Why do I think it's from more than smoking weed?"

"Nah, it's from life." Mallick sat up, swaying slightly.

Kate grinned. She liked this mismatched duo.

"What's your film?" she asked.

"It's a horror movie. Real creepy," Mallick said, clawing the air.

"It's *my* film," Dylan snapped.

She was surprised by the sudden flash of anger in his words.

"Hey, man, I thought you were over that jealousy shit."

The warm air in the car had turned frosty.

Hoping to lighten the mood, she looked back at Mallick. "Is this also a Skyline Studio production?"

"Yep," he nodded. "Working at Skyline is just a short-term deal, to get experience and then make movies I want to make."

"It will be temporary for him, too," Dylan said. His anger seemingly gone as quickly as it had arrived. "Mallick doesn't shoot film. He constructs images so beautiful they hurt. Like a Homer Winslow painting. He paints pictures with the camera."

Dylan glanced over to Kate. "So what did you think of *Sullivan's Travels*? No better way to make a point than with a story, don't you agree?"

No way was he getting the best of her, not when debate involved the power of film. "Exactly, that was my point."

"Was it? Funny, I thought entertainment having value was my point."

"I can't fight both you and Sturges. Don't say it, Mallick. I know, two points to Dylan."

Dylan turned the Mustang into Jarvis's driveway. When he stopped near the mansion, she looked at him. So he was a cad. Egotistical and aggravating, too. But she liked him. Like didn't have to imply romance. In fact, it was better if it didn't, particularly since she had to work with him. She held out her hand. "Friends?"

Mallick hooted. "That's a new one for him."

Dylan ignored him. He took her hand. His grip sure and strong and it felt wonderful.

"Friends," he said.

Chapter Seven

The day the first reel of film came back from the developer, Jarvis demanded the restored footage be shown in his home theater after dinner. That night no one seemed to do more than pick at Jimena's scrumptious food.

Except for Beatrice, who sawed her rare steak with zeal, and her plate pooled with blood.

Finally, Jarvis waved off dessert.

Dylan jumped to his feet and hurried to the projection booth. Kate followed him until Jarvis snatched her arm and escorted her to the screening room.

The room wasn't large, but it sure had style.

The seating was raised like in a real theater, with four rows of seats and each with six well-padded leather chairs. In the center of each row was a small table with switches and an intercom built into the side.

Beatrice sat in the back row and lit a cigarette.

In a very un-Lillian-like manner, her aunt wrung her hands in her lap.

Kate patted her arm.

"Tish-tosh, I'm all right," Lillian said. "I just haven't seen Gloria in so long. I stay away from her films normally. Too sad. You see, to me, she wasn't a screen goddess, just my kid sister."

"Ready, Mr. Benjamin?" Dylan said over the PA

system.

Jarvis sat down a few seats away from Kate and Lillian and clicked a switch. "We're ready, Dylan."

"Okay. This is reel one."

The lights dimmed. A grainy picture flickered on the screen, and a film slate appeared with chalk marks indicating Scene 18, Take 1.

While restoring the film, Kate had viewed snippets of it, frame-by-frame, but to see it run together on a large screen and with sound was mesmerizing.

The slate reappeared, indicating Take 2. The scene began again.

"Cut, damn it!" A voice bellowed off-camera.

The film panned to the left, revealing the background, including a young Beatrice in deep conversation with a large, pockmarked man. He looked like a crew member.

Snobby Beatrice wasting time chatting with a crew member didn't make much sense.

Winston Nash stumbled into the foreground of the shot, clearly inebriated. "Good God! Why is this lit like a Carmen Miranda musical? I said I wanted Gloria in shadow! Dave, put a flag on the light. Shadow, damn it!"

Gloria shot him a sardonic look. "We're on take two, and you're just now noticing the lights are wrong? Climb out of your bottle, Winston, and start directing."

"I will as soon as you start acting," he slurred. "Silly starlets."

Gloria flipped her perfectly crimped hair behind her shoulder as she strode to him. "Actress."

Winston rolled his eyes.

She lifted a hand and with the grace of a major

league pitcher, slapped him on the cheek.

He didn't even flinch. His lips curled up in what Kate guessed was a smile except the expression was held tight, and his glassy eyes glistened with pain.

"Did that make you feel better?" Winston said. "Can we do some work now?"

A shadow fell over the set. "Ready, Chief," a voice cried from somewhere off-camera. Kate assumed it was Dave.

"I've been ready all day," Gloria announced, seemingly more for the crew's benefit than Winston's. "You, on the other hand, couldn't tell the difference between a performance by Sarah Bernhardt or her stage-door Johnny. You're sloshed."

"Whose fault is that?"

Gloria balled her fists and took a step toward him. "I told you those were lies. There is no one else—"

Winston stopped her with a look. "Well, maybe you *can* act. I almost believe you. Now let's see if you can perform for the camera." He moved menacingly close to Gloria and gently stroked her hair. "Come, my love. Try to imagine the man you adore capable of doing unspeakable things. Show me how that feels."

Gloria's lips quivered.

Kate trembled.

Winston backed away from Gloria, studying her. "Good. That's it." He yelled off-screen, "Take Three. Action!"

Gloria's lips parted, and she gulped, as if stifling a scream.

The scene began again. This time her performance escaped the narrow confines of the screen and sailed across the decades, allowing Kate to witness the character Crystal Smythe's fear of her husband. Or, was it really Gloria's fear of Winston?

The camera followed Gloria in and out of shadows as she overheard Smythe conspire with other industrialists and his congressman son to appoint Nazi sympathizers to key positions in the U.S. government.

Mercilessly, the scene peeled back Emperor Smythe's benevolent façade to reveal something dark and evil.

Kate was awestruck. Winston's brilliance was in the way he conveyed the malevolence of the man, not by focusing on Smythe, but by seeing through the eyes of Crystal, his innocent wife.

No wonder J.B. Sutton hadn't wanted this scene shown. Rumors were one thing, but millions of people seeing, who everyone knew was supposed to be you and your son, portrayed as Nazi infiltrators on a fifty-foot screen was another. That depiction would be seared into the public imagination forever.

The magic of Gloria's performance stopped again, when mid-scene, she turned and yelled, "Winston, for God's sake stop gawking at the script girl and watch the damn scene!"

The camera kept rolling as it pulled back.

This time Kate caught no glimpse of Beatrice on the set as she had before, but Kate did see something else. The white oblong box. She was sure of it. The one the police thought the killer had used to carry the unknown murder weapon into the dressing room. The box was right there on the set, leaning against the prop table.

Kate glanced at Lillian, wondering if she'd recognized the box, too. But she couldn't tell.

Winston's voice boomed from off camera. "What the hell are you doing ruining my shot!"

"I'm not ruining anything; I'm making it," Gloria said. "No help from you."

"Huh!" Winston's sarcastic bellow echoed from off shot.

Gloria ran her hands slowly down the curves of her voluptuous body. "The crew seems to like my performance. Right, boys?"

As if from nowhere, the director's large frame leapt into the shot as he grabbed hold of Gloria. "Can't you turn off your *femme fatale* bit for a second? Just one second," Winston yelled as he shook her so hard she became limp. She appeared nothing more than a rag doll dominated by his brutal touch.

Kate gasped. She thought Winston would shake the life out of Gloria, right then and there.

From the movie screen, there was a high-pitched scream, and out ran little Audrey.

Kate jumped when her aunt's hands clutched her arm. But she couldn't turn away from the screen and watched in horror, while Audrey, only ten years old, pummeled Winston's stomach with her fists while crying, "Don't hurt my mommy! Don't hurt my mommy!"

Winston backed away.

Sobbing, Audrey then latched on to Gloria who stumbled until she gained her balance.

"I'm sorry," Winston said quietly. He turned away and lumbered out of sight.

Gloria's hand rested lightly on her daughter's head, but her eyes were still on Winston.

"Oh, God." Lillian moaned.

Jarvis clicked the intercom switch. "Stop the film."

The screen went black, and the lights came up.

Jarvis rose and put one arm across Lillian's shoulders.

Lillian gulped the air as if she could barely breathe. She turned to Kate. "Oh, your poor mother. Poor Audrey, I didn't believe her. I didn't want to believe Winston could hurt Gloria. I should've been there. I should've been with Audrey."

"Why weren't you?" Kate asked. "Weren't you supposed to be?"

"No. I didn't arrive until later." Lillian's voice trembled. "Not until Gloria's assistant called me to come to the studio to pick up Audrey. I knew about the argument, of course. The whole crew confirmed it. In fact, that's why I was called to get Audrey." Lillian's arthritic hands lifted to her over-painted face. "But seeing the fight is different. I'd never witnessed Winston treating Gloria like that. So horrible."

Jarvis helped distraught Lillian to her feet and led her out of the screening room.

Dylan came in and sat in the chair in front of Kate's. "Are you okay?"

She shook her head. "Winston killed my grandmother. Did you see how he threatened her?"

"I'm not sure that's—"

"Didn't you see how he bullied her?"

"Yeah, he was awful, but we don't know he killed her. Not for sure."

"Don't we? The only reason Winston got off was a technicality."

Kate turned at the sound of Beatrice's footsteps behind her and sprang to her feet. Feeling so angry and helpless by what she'd just seen, Kate didn't care who she lashed out at. "Why didn't you help Gloria? What were you even doing there on the set that day?"

"My job."

"Meaning?" Kate stood in front of Beatrice blocking her exit.

"Because you're justifiably upset, I'm going to ignore your tone." Beatrice puffed on her cigarette. "I was there because Gloria called Jarvis in New York the day before, complaining about Winston bullying her. Jarvis asked me to check on her. So I stopped by the set before the first of a series of meetings I had that day at the studio. Now if you don't mind." Beatrice swerved around Kate and continued to walk toward the door.

"Why didn't you do something? Why didn't you speak up for Gloria?"

"I would've." Beatrice turned back to Kate. And for a moment the older woman's normally controlled expression faltered, and Kate thought she saw real sympathy in her eyes. But then she wasn't sure as Beatrice's gaze lifted into space and became vague. "Yes, I believe I would have. I didn't see that second outburst. I'd left the set by then." Beatrice patted Kate's arm, and her touch felt oddly cold.

As the older woman walked out of the screening room, Kate rubbed the goose bumps on her arms.

Jarvis stood at the doorway. "That's all true," he said. "Gloria called me the day before, upset. I told Beatrice to look in on her, and then I got the next flight back to L.A."

Jarvis ran his thick fingers through his silver-gray hair. "But, if I'd realized how scared Gloria really was, I would've gone to her first thing, I swear it." He shook his head. "Instead, I joined Beatrice in prepping for a meeting. I don't even remember what my meeting was about that day. Maybe if I'd gone to Gloria instead, maybe, I could've saved her." What looked like real pain darkened his expression.

Kate shook her head. "It's not your fault."

Looking weary and sad, he said, "I've had enough of this for one night, haven't you?"

No! The word shouted inside her before it shot out her lips.

Jarvis cocked his head. "No?"

Watch! The command, the need, reverberated inside Kate.

"I mean, I'd like to see the rest." She touched Jarvis's arm. "Please, there must be a way to prove Winston was the killer, once and for all."

Jarvis didn't look happy about that idea. Still, he turned warily to Dylan. "How much more of the restored footage is there?"

"About twelve more minutes, but there's nothing more of Gloria. After this take, she leaves the set. The next take is a shot over her stand-in's shoulder."

Jarvis nodded and left. Dylan returned to the projection booth.

Each time the scene ended, Dylan rewound the film and ran it again.

After the first couple of times it ran, Kate could see how much she had missed the first time, when she was too busy reacting to the anger in Winston's voice.

She wanted to see every detail. Winston's use of deep focus allowed her to do so. The camera has the ability to photograph a scene in a way the human eye can't see. Human vision is selective. When our eyes focus on something in the foreground, the background becomes blurry, and vice versa.

She struggled to absorb all the visual input. The flickering light from the screen pounded against her skull and gave her a throbbing headache. She couldn't shake the feeling something wasn't quite right in the footage.

She concentrated on the minutiae, cataloging every detail, particularly what occurred when the camera continued to run after a take was done.

There was part of a child's polka dot skirt slipped into the frame after a take.

That must have been her mother.

Burly techs walked at the outer edge of the frame, over thick cables winding across the floor like snakes.

Details, details. All were there, in perfect focus, with deep focus.

"Oh, my God." Kate clamped her hands over her mouth.

It's not what's there, she realized. *It's what's not there.*

She fumbled for the intercom button. "Dylan, stop the film!"

Not waiting for a reply, Kate ran to the projection booth. Despite a fan buzzing in one corner, the booth was a good ten degrees hotter than the rest of the house. Dylan barely reacted to her presence as he remained slumped in a chair, his dark eyes bloodshot.

"Rewind the footage slowly," Kate told him.

"Why?" He shrugged, then did what she wanted, with the projector still on so she could see each frame clearly.

"Stop the film there." She hopped up and down,

unable to contain her excitement. "So, I'm still inclined to think Winston killed Gloria."

"You've made that clear."

"But I saw something. Or, I didn't see it, and that could mean something."

Dylan took off his glasses and rubbed the bridge of his nose. "You're not making sense. Slow down."

"Have you ever seen *Blow Up*?"

"Sure. That's a great film. A photographer catches a murder on film." Dylan chuckled as he placed his glasses back on his aquiline nose. "What? Did Vanessa Redgrave kill your grandmother?"

"Not funny."

"Okay, so what did you see in the footage? Excuse me, not see?"

Kate leaned past him and turned the projector back on. Then she stopped it during the fight, and in the background was the white box with a big bow sitting next to the prop table. "*The* box." She gestured toward it on the screen as if she were Carol Merrill on TV's *Let's Make a Deal* revealing the winning prize behind door number three.

"Huh?" Dylan stared at her as if she was mad.

"Oh, right. It wasn't in news reports, just the police report."

"You've seen the police report?"

"Duh. Of course. The police provided a version of its investigative findings to the family of the deceased."

"Cool. A ton of stuff wasn't made public, can I see the report?"

"You're not listening to me. Forget the report. I'm talking about the box."

"I'd really like—"

"Dylan!"

"Right, the box. Go ahead."

"Well, even the newspapers reported that all that was left of the weapon were bits of marble, a trail of which led straight to Winston's office at Golden State Pictures."

"That, I know."

"The police surmised the murderer must have taken the marble object, the murder weapon, and disposed of it. They knew the weapon was marble and that it had been a violent attack because marble is so difficult to damage and slivers of it were embedded in Gloria's skull. More small pieces were strewn around the dressing room cottage, particularly against pieces of furniture, which must have been where the object had originally chipped. What most people don't know is that an empty white, oblong box, like those used to deliver flowers, was also found in the room."

"So? The newspapers reported that there were flowers in her dressing room. That was another reason they thought Winston had been there."

"The thing is, there was no residue of flowers in that box, only a trace of marble. One theory was the box was not used to transport the flowers but the murder weapon."

Dylan pointed to the screen. "Wait. Are you saying that's the box?"

"Yes."

"How can you be sure?"

"I should know what it looks like. It's in my garage."

Dylan goggled at her. "You have—"

"It was returned to us with the rest of her effects."

"I want to see in your garage."

"Gee, and I thought you liked me for my wit and beauty."

He held her gaze. "That, too."

She gulped.

He pointed at the screen. "So what's the significance?"

"Watch." She turned on the projector, speeding past the argument where Gloria had stomped off the set, then stopped it. "See?" She pointed to the prop table on the screen. "The box is still there. Gloria didn't take it when she left." Kate slowly advanced the film, then stopped it again. "Okay, we're at the first shot, at a different angle."

"So? Gloria's gone now. What's important here?"

"Look at the side of the frame, before they begin the shoot. There's the prop table, but this time the box is gone."

"And?"

"Don't you get it? Gloria's left the set, and if the box did contain the murder weapon, it is also gone. But Winston is still on the set, and he'll be there for at least another hour."

Dylan jumped up. "He didn't kill her. This is big. No, this is astronomical."

"We don't know that. The fact the box wasn't there doesn't mean Winston wasn't the one who ultimately used whatever was inside the package to kill Gloria. I'd still bet Winston is the murderer. It just raises—"

"Sure, it's still possible it was him but not as likely. God damn! Look at the chronology. Gloria leaves the set, nothing in her hands. Yet, by the next shot, the present to her is gone, and I'd posit that it was delivered by the murderer. Who you've just admitted can't be Winston. He's on the set filming."

"Maybe." Kate sighed.

"Maybe? What are you thinking?"

Kate shook her head. "I don't know. None of this gets Winston off the hook. In fact, the missing box could give him a clearer motive. What if the box contained a present from a lover, and that's what threw Winston into a jealous rage? My money is still on him as the killer."

"Hell no!" He looked away and rubbed his chin. "Okay, hell maybe. But we know some things no one knew before. Somebody was in that dressing room with Gloria *after* she left the set and well *before* Winston could have possibly been there. So who was it?"

Kate nodded. "Yeah. And what was in that box?"

Chapter Eight

Next morning, at nine on the dot, Kate called the Kovals, the tenants at her mom's house, to arrange a time to go to the garage. Aggravated that Mrs. Koval didn't want her to come out right this minute and had suggested a more convenient time, Kate hung up the phone harder than she should have.

The back of her neck tingled, as if someone stood behind her. She wheeled around, but the only thing she saw were the painted eyes of Jarvis's elaborate collection of Indonesian shadow puppets staring back at her.

She needed to get a hold of her imagination. The feeling of being watched all the time was just nuts.

Hoping for reassurance from her best friend, she called Natalie. Before she could get a word out, Natalie had excitedly told her that she was leaving town at the end of the week.

"Leaving?" Kate practically screamed.

"Yeah, a friend told me that Johana Gottleib, *the* Johana Gottleib for God's sake, is looking for assistants to help with her art installation in the Mojave Desert. And I was chosen!"

"Oh."

"I thought you'd be happy for me. She's my idol." Natalie sounded hurt.

And she had a right to be. Her friend had always

supported Kate, ever since grade school. Natalie even accepted not being told why Kate was spending her summer vacation not working at Mario's Pizzeria but living in a Bel Air mansion, working on some secret project. Now it was Natalie's turn to have something exciting happen to her.

"Of course, I'm happy for you," she said. "To apprentice with Gottleib is an amazing opportunity, and you totally deserve it."

Still, when she hung up the phone, Kate felt off balance and alone.

When she finally reported to the guest house for work, Dylan appeared to be more exhausted than she felt. His hair was tousled, and she could've sworn he was wearing the same clothes from last night. The small couch looked more disheveled than he did.

"Can we go out to your garage?" Dylan asked.

"No. The tenants have a party today, but we can go tomorrow."

"That'll work." He turned back to scanning some of the footage.

"What? Is that it? We're just going to act like everything's normal?"

"Nothing's normal," Dylan said in a low voice.

"No, it's not. We should go to the police."

He shook his head. "I don't think that's a good idea."

Her gaze narrowed in on him. For a moment his wide, bespectacled face looked sinister.

"Hey, don't look at me like that. Do you know how many contacts the press, not to mention the studios, have at the police department? How else do you think big studio types like Jarvis get tips when their stars are in trouble? If we go to the police, the fact we have the footage will be in the trades by morning and out of our control by nightfall."

"But this is murder."

"It's a murder that's more than thirty years old. And the crime has been written and speculated about *ad nauseam*. Don't worry, if we really had something incriminating, I'd be the first to go to the police. But what do we have now? A box that was there and then gone. That's not enough reason to risk losing the film."

"I guess." Kate sat next to him. "Then should we do some detecting or something?"

He laughed. "Detecting? What do you know about detecting?"

"Well…"

Dylan shook his head. "Don't you dare argue you know how from watching movies. You're the one that says that's all BS."

She shrugged.

"Listen, I'm not saying we don't look into it. I want to figure this out as much as you."

"Really?"

"Yeah, and this is where we start." He pointed to the footage that remained to be cleaned. "More clues may be there. Look what you've found already on the first reel." Dylan got up and retrieved some of the film from the temperature-controlled safe. He placed the strips carefully on the flatbed. "Besides, Jarvis will kill us if we don't stay on schedule."

"You're right," she said. Be methodical. Step-by-step, frame-by-frame. No living on the edge like Gloria, propelled by feelings, drama, illusion, the *grande* play. Stick to the facts. That's what she was good at.

Except everything that was happening *was* dramatic. She looked around the small, almost rustic, guest house, which was perched on one of the most expensive cliffs in the world, where she worked with a cute, hunky guy.

Forcing discipline on her erratic thoughts, she concentrated on the task of cleaning the footage. And for a while, she was able to focus. But by midafternoon the intrusive questions flooded her mind. So many choices—her mother's, Lillian's, even her own—had been made based on what they'd thought had led to Gloria's death.

What if they were all wrong?

She stared at the black-and-white celluloid frame of her grandmother. Gloria's head was tipped back, and a warm light illuminated her porcelain skin and her bright, wide eyes. Even though her grandmother was confined to this single image, Kate was struck by the mesmerizing allure of her face. It wasn't simply that her features were beautiful; it was more than that. Gloria had an intensity of feeling that radiated from her, even in a picture more than thirty years old.

What would it be like to feel things so fully?

Kate peered at Dylan. His large hands meticulously laid out the fragile piece of film as if he were a surgeon in the middle of a life-threatening operation. Watching his attention to detail, his delicacy of touch, Kate's breath deepened. He looked up, and as their gazes met, she felt her body flush.

She turned away and tried to concentrate on the footage. She reached for her cotton swab and magnifying glass on the table. At the touch of them, she jerked her hand away. The magnifying glass was blistering hot. The searing sensation shot up her arm, and flooded her body with an odd but reassuring warmth.

In her mind's eye the celluloid image of her grandmother began to grow. No longer in black and white, Kate saw a medley of rich reds and dark velvet greens that duplicated the faux grandeur of the *Emperor Smythe*'s set. She heard the faint rustling sounds of large cables brushing the floor and the quiet voices of crew members milling around in the background, as she watched the day on the set through Gloria's eyes.

Kate squinted at the bright lights aimed at her, bathing her in their glare while obscuring many of the faces of the people who stared back.

Whose faces?

She struggled to make out the features of the people moving in the darkness. Some she recognized. Winston walking in and out of shadows while talking to some man with a bushy black mustache, wearing coveralls. There were other discernible features of crew members busy setting up the next shot, but no one else she recognized until she spotted her mother as a child.

A weight pressed on Kate's chest at the sight of Audrey, her expression dull, sitting alone upon a large metal case, her small legs extended from her white-and-navy polka dot skirt.

Kate had only tantalizing glimpses of the forms drifting far behind the lights, including that of a woman wearing an enormous hat who moved in and out of the eerie green light of the Exit sign. Lillian? No, it couldn't be her. She did not arrive until after Gloria's body was discovered.

Kate's attention turned to a pool of darkness

behind a discarded set. No form or silhouette was visible. Yet, she couldn't look away. An emotion emanating from that spot drew her. As she walked toward the whirl of dark hunger, a wink of light, perhaps reflected from a watch or jewelry, sparked in the darkness.

She halted. Her heart raced as if she were a rabbit caught in the sights of a falcon. She shut her eyes and told herself what she was seeing was only a dream.

When she opened them, she was again sitting in the guest house. She swayed in her chair like she'd just gotten off an amusement park ride. Grabbing the table, she braced herself until the dizzy sensation subsided.

Dylan stared at her, concern in his eyes. "Are you all right?"

She turned away from his steady gaze. "Yeah, I'm fine."

Insane, but fine.

Kate didn't want to think about what she had seen or imagined. Because then she'd have to choose between being obsessed or crazy. She supposed there was a third option. That these strange memories and sensations of Gloria being part of her, guiding her, were real?

No. That was the crazy option.

"You sure?" Dylan asked. "You're white as a sheet."

She held up a hand to stop him from coming closer, afraid his touch would shatter her sanity, such as it was. "I'm okay. Really."

She returned to her workstation and rewound the strip. The images flickered past her in reverse order.

Poor Gloria.

She probably didn't suspect that she'd never see another sunrise, or kiss her daughter's cheek again, or even have another fiery fight with her lover after that day. Because within hours her skull would be crushed, her body limp and lifeless, and soon most of the world would remember nothing of her vibrant soul except for the photos of the police tape outline where she had fallen.

Kate put the reel back into its canister and shut it. She wished the simple act of concealing the film would finally put the tragedy to rest. But it wouldn't. Gloria's death was only the beginning of the murderer's act of destruction. Kate picked up the film canister. She walked to the safe and locked up the footage.

Her own mother was another victim of the murderer. Audrey had been only ten years old when she entered Gloria's dressing room and found her, not just dead but, if the police report was only half right, with her skull smashed so violently that pieces of her brain were splattered across the room. Despite what medical science might say, Kate was certain the cancer that ultimately killed her mom was as much from the fear and pain that festered inside her from that day on as it was from the alcohol, pills, and cigarettes she later consumed.

Kate hadn't realized that Dylan had moved closer until she felt his gentle hands turn her around.

As if her body had a will of its own, she leaned against him seeking his strength.

"What's going on?" he asked.

Moving into the comfort of his arms, she gazed up into his dark eyes, and her body trembled with excitement. She wasn't sure when this unnerving desire for him had begun. Sometime during the weeks of camaraderie as they'd restored the film, she'd stopped thinking of him as a blowhard and began…

She began to be damned silly. She stepped out of his arms. "Nothing."

He looked unconvinced.

But then again it was better not to look at him.

"You know, you're right." Kate tried to smile, hoping her expression didn't appear as forced as it felt. "I'm not feeling that great. I think I'll call it a day."

She glanced at the clock. She had time to get in a couple of hours of research at the Beverly Hills library before it closed. The library was a place to start detecting.

Dylan was about to say something, but before he could, she dashed out of the guest house.

Once in the main house, she ran up to her aunt's bedroom, hoping to retrieve the police report. She knocked. No answer. She cracked the door open and saw the report on the desk. She grabbed it and headed downstairs.

When she passed by the library, she heard the clink of ice in a glass. Peering in, she saw Lillian ensconced in a Queen Anne chair reading a Harold Robbins' novel and what looked like a stiff drink at her side. Scotch, by the look of it.

Lillian was living history.

Her aunt looked up from her novel, met Kate's gaze, and said, "Yes?"

"Can I ask you something?"

"Certainly." Her aunt placed her book on the mahogany side table.

After rolling up the police report like a spyglass to

keep the pages out of sight, Kate walked to a chair that faced her aunt and sat down. "The topic might be painful."

"Darling, at my age everything is." Lillian sighed dramatically, then smiled.

"Why did you take Winston's side instead of Mom's?"

The words hung in the air. Even Lillian wasn't a good enough actress to hide the glistening pain in her eyes or the stiffening of her posture.

"You put that just like your mother would. It wasn't a choice between the two of them."

"But it was. Mom never forgave you for supporting Winston."

"I wish she…I wish *you'd* understand that my defending Winston wasn't a betrayal of Gloria. I simply knew he didn't kill her."

"Why?"

"He loved her."

Kate scoffed. "That sounds like a motive, not exoneration."

"Try to give me just a little credit. After all, I was there." Lillian stood and posed in front of the large fireplace as if she were about to recite *The Highwayman*. "I'll admit Winston could be a bastard, particularly when drinking. You don't understand, the way they'd argue…" Lillian laughed, which Kate could not help but think was odd, considering the topic.

"They were both so good at verbal sparring, like you are," Lillian said.

Kate was about to retort but bit her tongue just in time to not prove her aunt's point.

"I'm also sure their fighting was never physical,"

Lillian quickly added.

"Mom believed he hit her. She'd seen bruises on Gloria's arms a couple of times. And in the footage, Winston grabbed her and used his brute strength against her."

Lillian shook her head.

"Come on, Winston sounds like a batterer— needing control, an egocentric persona hiding low self-esteem, possessiveness—he fits the mold."

"Thank you for that Psychology 101 treatise. However, those attributes don't describe Winston. He had his demons, mostly when he drank, but those weren't them."

"Tell me about him."

"Why, so you can find another reason to condemn him?"

"No."

Lillian gave her a severe look.

Kate squirmed. "Okay, maybe that's a part of it. It's just that I also think I might have been wrong."

Lillian snorted. "That's a first."

"Please, tell me about Winston."

Lillian's index finger touched her lips, her cheeks lifted, and for a moment Kate thought she could see what Lillian looked like as a girl. "He was my friend, my best friend. I knew him before Gloria did. Did you know that?"

Kate leaned forward in her chair. She hadn't known that.

"Gloria was still a kid when I hightailed it out of our minuscule hometown and landed a job with the Tacoma Repertory Company. It was Winston's first year there, too." Lillian smiled. "We were beside ourselves with joy and ambition, determined to revolutionize the theater. He did. Only a couple of years later, the company was known as the Winston Nash Players." She lifted her arms above her head as if the arthritis Kate knew she had was gone. "He was a magical man. I wish you could know him."

"Know him? He's dead," Kate said gently.

Lillian clapped her hands. "Darling, you know what would be great fun? Let's move our chat to C.C. Brown's, and I'll buy you a butterscotch sundae like we did when you were a child and your mother went on vacation, for a time."

"*Vacation*?" Kate hurled the words at her aunt. "You mean the time mom overdosed on pills?"

Lillian's smile faded. "I didn't know you knew."

"I was young, not stupid."

Old feelings of abandonment welled up in Kate. "The day Gloria died, why did you leave my mom alone for so long after you were called to take care of her on the soundstage that day?"

Lillian looked away.

Kate grabbed the police report she'd hidden behind her and stood. "Funny thing is, it says here the studio's gate attendant logged you in as arriving before one p.m., a good thirty minutes before my mom found Gloria dead. What were you doing for that half an hour?"

Lillian's gaze wandered around the room as if she were searching for something she'd lost. "I did arrive earlier, saw people I knew, said some quick hellos. It's always good to be seen. But thirty minutes? That can't be right. I wouldn't have left Audrey alone that long."

Kate held up the pages. "Then why does the police

report say that you did?"

The sight of the police report seemed to sharpen Lillian's focus. She took in a deep breath that made her appear to grow. "You went through my things?"

"Just to retrieve what was mine," Kate said weakly.

"It's *all* yours, everything."

"I'm sorry, I should've asked. After seeing the footage last night, I had so many questions."

"No. You just wanted to hurt me by accusing me of lying to the police." Lillian paced in front of the fireplace. "I didn't, by the way. I told them I arrived early. I don't know why my explanation is not in the police report. For God's sake, it was no secret. Your mother loved to tell everyone about being abandoned."

"You're right." Kate felt terrible. "I guess spending every day looking at Gloria through a magnifying glass has made what happened to her very real and very, very awful. I hate that there are too many unanswered questions and things not fitting exactly the way the report describes. I just want to know what happened."

Lillian approached her. "Not a healthy activity."

Kate fell back a step. "What do you mean by that?"

"Obsessing over all this. At your age, you should be thinking about your career, about love, not about your grandmother's gruesome murder."

"Have you read this?"

"I wouldn't look for the truth there." Lillian made a dismissive gesture. "I'm not surprised the police report got things wrong. It's a list of cold supposed facts. Human beings can't be measured by that alone."

"The report is a place to start," Kate said.

"No. It's the past. Leave it alone." Lillian shook her head and swept out of the room.

Kate trailed her with the same rush of anxiety and need to make everything better she'd felt when she'd upset her mother.

She halted. No. Not this time.

Lifting her chin, she spun on her heels and headed to her car and the library.

Chapter Nine

Only in Beverly Hills could a warehouse for old books and papers smell of orange blossoms with the astringent tang of ammonia, and not of must and mildew. Kate explored the stacks of the library wondering what it cost to pump the fragrance through the air ducts. It didn't matter. This was one of her favorite places. A true secular cathedral, with its stucco walls and colored Spanish tiles, combined with angular art nouveau trim sweeping the eye up while the inhabitants bowed over large communal tables or in individual carrels seeking enlightenment.

Task one: Find out who Charles Needham was and how he ended up with the missing footage.

In the periodical section, several others wandered the stacks. A girl about twelve with a long, chunky braid down her back paged through a stack of old newspapers as if they were contaminated.

Kate guessed she had been forced to come here for a school project.

At the other end of the spectrum was an old man hunched over a large communal table with a yellowing paper spread out in front of him. She looked at him more closely. Had she seen him before? His face was skeletal, but his expression wistful as he pored over the paper, looking like someone riding on a magic carpet taking him to a different world. No. She didn't know him.

She stopped at the stack that held old *LA Times* issues and thumbed through them until she found the ones dated just before she had received the footage from Charles Needham. She looked for his obit or something else that would tell her who he was. She found his obituary, only a few lines providing his dates, saying he left behind a beloved wife, and giving information about his memorial service in Santa Monica. That city's local paper, *Santa Monica Evening Outlook*, was much more helpful. There she discovered more details, a couple of paragraphs on him, and most importantly, a picture. She recognized that face. In fact, she'd seen it a couple of dozen times the night before. Although the photo in the paper was of an older man, he had the same insignificant mouth and pockmarked face of the young man in the film who had been intently speaking with Beatrice.

This obit said Charles Needham had owned a popular local bar on Fourth Street for the last fifteen years. In his youth, he'd worked as an assistant cameraman on several films in the forties and fifties.

Assistant cameraman. Isn't that handy?

It also said he'd worked for a time for J.B. Sutton, aka Emperor Smythe, in a "security" role.

Bingo!

A connection to Sutton and a connection to Beatrice—very interesting.

Spurred on by her discovery, Kate turned her attention to the time of the murder. The library's pile of newspapers didn't go back more than a year, but the first-floor librarian had told her the older papers were preserved on microfiches located in the archive department on the second floor.

Except for a couple of people working in isolated cubicles, the second floor was deserted. She opened the glass door that led to the archive room.

Behind the counter was a petite woman with long, straight black hair staring at a microfiche monitor. She wore a crochet skull cap and matching cardigan with the sleeves rolled up. Her eyes were dark and serious. When she glanced up at Kate, she gave a slight roll of her eyes, then turned back to her task without a word.

Kate realized she'd forgotten her baseball cap and her oversized jean jacket when she rushed out to go to the library. Always a mistake. Without them, she invariably felt sized-up as either an airhead or a sex-pot.

"Excuse me. I'd like to review the *LA Times* from October 1941 through November." Jeez, she sounded like a supplicant. She couldn't believe how intimidated she still felt by the "smart girls."

The young librarian tapped the eraser end of her pencil against her cheek. "I'm afraid those are currently being used by someone else"

"Are you sure?"

The woman gave Kate a patronizing smile. "Yes."

"How about the *LA Examiner* during the same time?" Kate willed her hands to stop fidgeting.

"Checked out."

Kate got an uneasy feeling. "Really, by whom?"

"We're not Big Brother here." The librarian shot Kate a condescending smile.

"*1984*, I know that."

"Then you'll understand; here people still have privacy rights."

"Sure, of course."

Kate rubbed her cheeks and wondered if her own endless pontification about the need to make film as art was just as obnoxious.

Yes, she realized with shame, it was.

"Is there anything else I can help you with?"

Trying another tack, Kate asked, "Can you tell me what, around that time period, has not been checked out?"

The librarian turned to a large cabinet drawer, where she retrieved three rectangular envelopes opened at the top and handed them to Kate.

"Here's some from the period before your request, from April through August 1941. Will that work?"

"Yes. Thank you."

The librarian escorted her down a hallway lined with little rooms. All the doors were open except for one at the end. Kate had a sneaking suspicion that behind that door would be the person with *her* microfiche. She was tempted to walk down there and find out who it was, but the librarian didn't give her the chance to look. Instead, she directed Kate into the first small room and left.

Kate placed the square microfiche sheet from April 1941 on the clear glass below the monitor and scrolled through a variety of news stories and advertisements. She slowed down at the gossip columns.

By the time she was on the last microfiche sheet from August 1941, her speed at the task had improved. But that didn't curb her frustration. Each time she'd get excited about finding some tidbit about Gloria, the article ended up being no more than a formulaic puff piece with stock quotes about an upcoming film project.

Kate continued further back in time, through issue

after issue until a photo stopped her cold. The other faces in the photo blurred as her focus locked on a child's face. It was her mother, smiling. More than smiling, her eyes were alight with joy. An expression Kate had never seen her mom wear until now.

The caption below the picture read: *Luckiest Little Girl in the World: Gloria Reardon buys out Santa Anita Race Track to stage a colossal tenth birthday celebration for her daughter Audrey.*

Kate studied the entire picture. There were lots of people in the background—children astride ponies, beautiful men and women in their pristine, casual white attire smiling into the camera while waiters all in black served refreshments. In the foreground Gloria stood, her head thrown back in a glamour pose. Next to her was an uncomfortable-looking youth: short, with wide-set eyes, doughy cheeks, and a large face that appeared almost cartoonish on top of his squat, muscular body, like a boxer's.

Kate sucked air through her teeth, astonished when she realized who he was. It was a young Jarvis Benjamin.

Her mind struggled to reconcile this image of Jarvis with the powerhouse he now was. In the photo he looked oh, so out of place in his baggy black suit standing amongst the fashionably dressed golden beauties of Hollywood A-listers. Today, he was the antithesis of awkward or plebian. True, he'd never be Hollywood handsome. But the Jarvis Kate knew had something more. Silver-haired, with the test of experience chiseled into his face, his inelegant features transformed into something magnetic, a look more akin to that of Edward G. Robinson or even Napoleon.

Kate smiled.

Yeah, Napoleon! She thought Jarvis would like that comparison.

She felt a rush of gratitude toward this soon-to-be Napoleon as she gazed at the photo. He was the only one in the big crowd who was paying attention to the laughing Audrey.

Seeing her mom so happy filled Kate with a simultaneous sense of loss and discovery. Her mother gazed at Jarvis with such an easy expression of trust. How horrible that this happy little girl grew up to be the woman Kate knew, one with a bitter expression and an array of prescription drugs at her bedside. Kate slipped the microfiche back into its paper sleeve and flung open the door of the small viewing room, wishing only to get out this place, away from the past, when she abruptly halted, as if she'd slammed into a wall.

There, leaning toward Miss Superior Librarian, was Dylan.

"Are you following me?" she demanded.

He turned and gave her a big smile. "Yes."

"Don't."

The librarian grazed her hand along Dylan's arm and actually batted her eyes at him.

Kate fumed as Miss Intellectual whispered something into his ear as she handed some papers to him.

Why was she getting all worked up? After all, she and Dylan were only friends. That's how she wanted it, right?

She saw the papers the Librarian had handed to him were printouts from the *LA Times*.

Kate clenched her teeth. The librarian knew that

those pages were checked out because she was the one using them. In fact, she was probably doing Dylan's work for him.

Dylan thanked the librarian and sauntered over to Kate. He took her arm and led her out of the archive department.

"Hey, don't be mad," he said. "You were acting really weird before bolting out of the guest house. I just wanted to make sure you were all right."

"Oh…okay." Kate's throat tightened. "I mean, thank you."

"You want to know what I found?" He shot her his jester grin.

****

Thirty minutes later, they were sitting at a small curbside café table, chomping on French fries. Kate told Dylan about her discoveries.

Dylan then handed her a photocopy of a newspaper article he'd found.

She glanced at the caption and pushed the paper back to him in disgust. The article was a gossip columnist's description of Gloria's and Winston's infamous fight at a restaurant a week before the murder. A night Winston was heard threatening to kill Gloria. "That's not detecting. Everyone knows about this. It was one of the big components of the D.A.'s case against Winston."

He handed the page back to her. "Read the article."

Kate shook her head. "No. I already know more than I want to about their torrid affair. The tales of the searing highs of their passions coupled with alcoholic binges and fierce fights. No, thank you. The clever repartee of a Rosalind Russell or a Katharine Hepburn may be fun in the movies, but bantering like that is not—"

"I'm impressed." Dylan grabbed three fries, dipped them into the ketchup, and popped them into his mouth.

"Why?"

"That you even knew who Kate and Roz were. Although admittedly proto-feminist, they still were *merely* studio players."

She glared at him.

He laughed. "Come on, read the article."

The story described how Gloria dumped her chocolate soufflé onto Winston's head and sashayed out of the restaurant. The article said that Winston, with clumps of the sticky whipped concoction sliding down his cheek, shouted after her in his most thunderous Shakespearean voice, "*Passion, hell itself!*" According to witnesses, only then did he notice his audience. Winking at a nearby patron, he waved his arms with a dramatic flourish and bellowed, "*Let come what comes; only I'll be revenged!*" Then he swiped some soufflé off his cheek and ate it. At this, the patrons of the restaurant were reported to have laughed and applauded as he exited.

Kate was astonished by how lighthearted this version of events was, particularly when compared with how she'd always heard the story. That Winston, beside himself with rage, threatened Gloria. That's how the argument was presented at his trial. Kate scanned the article again. There wasn't a hint of that type of malice in the story.

"So what do you think?" Dylan asked when she looked up.

She shrugged. "Maybe what they had wasn't as

destructive as I'd thought. Still, what's wrong with peacefulness in a relationship? That kind of constant one-upmanship has got to be tiring."

"You should know. You argue nonstop."

"I hope that's not true. I don't want to be like her."

His expression darkened. "I'm not sure we have a choice."

"What made you so cynical?"

"Nothing," he said way too quickly. "Let's just say, like most people, I don't want to grow up to be my parents."

He had such a sharp look of pain in his eyes.

She took his hand.

What had happened to him? Who had hurt him so much?

"Defy them. I do," she said.

Feeling his rough skin under her fingertips, she was astonished by the wave of contentment that ran through her just from holding his hand. She wondered why unlike anyone else she'd ever met, she had the urge to do anything, be anyone, to make him happy.

Just like her mother had tried with her father before he left them.

Kate removed her hand, but Dylan grabbed hold of it. "Do you really?" His tone was rough, filled with pain. "Can we really defy them?" He leaned in toward her, his breath warm on her cheek. Her lips inched toward his. God, she wanted to kiss him.

But he backed away, and she reeled with confusion.

The passion in his eyes gone, his gaze fixed upon something down the street. Kate turned but didn't see anything but the usual bustle of shoppers. He stood, his normally animated speech monotone. "Don't you know fighting the past doesn't change it, it only makes the past present." He flipped open his wallet and threw some money onto the table. "I forgot. There's something I've got to do." He pantomimed a buddy-like punch to her arm. "Mind if I head off?"

Before she could say anything, he was gone. Kate leaned back in her chair. Maybe Dylan was more afraid of being close to her than she was of him. She toyed with the glass salt shaker. Or more likely, he was wise enough to know a romance would never work. It was too charged between them to be anything but destructive. Best to remain just friends.

So why did she feel so disappointed?

Her disappointment evaporated when she got back to her car and saw what was waiting for her on the driver's seat—a single yellow rose. She picked up the flower and inhaled its sweet, lovely fragrance. Her heart did a backflip, and she couldn't have stopped the smile on her face even if she'd tried.

The rose had to be from Dylan. Of course it did.

Chapter Ten

In the morning, to hide her "bathing costume," Kate held a plush gray towel around her as if it was a Victorian cloak. Not that anyone else was awake yet to see her.

On the terraced path that led to the pool, her foot slid on the incline. She glared at the half-inch slipper with the powder-puff adornment. Silly things! Although she had to admit something about them made her legs look better. And wearing them beat walking barefoot on the gravel path and less trouble than putting on her boots for a simple stroll to the pool.

She gazed past Jarvis's terraced garden to the other estates perched regally on the hill across the ravine. She lifted her face into the warm breeze. It felt delicious. Strange, for a girl who didn't believe in fairy tales, to have become Cinderella at the castle.

She laughed at the thought. So much for being a rebel. If she stayed here much longer, she'd be genuflecting to Master Jarvis Benjamin like the rest of Hollywood.

When she reached the pool, she flicked off the slippers and dove into the water.

She'd swum in the pool enough to know the water was heated to an absurd ninety-two degrees, unlike the invigorating water of the ocean and the public pools she swam in as a girl. The warm water sliding across her body as she swam soothed her.

Yeah, like a frog in a slowly boiling pot of water.

Or maybe it was her bourgeois attitude that made her think indulgence was a sign of weakness.

She thought about the photo she'd seen of Jarvis at the library. If the rumors were true, he'd grown up poor in a rough neighborhood. He had the right to enjoy his luxurious lifestyle. He'd earned it. In the photo, Jarvis still had those rough edges. In fact, he looked ridiculous, like a gargoyle among the luminous assembly of stars. Yet, with his freakish gift for numbers and the tenacity of a pit bull, he'd risen to become the master of them all.

Jarvis was also the man who'd found time to be kind to her mother when she was a child and now to her, too. Kate switched from doing her regimented laps to playfully twisting her body like a mermaid.

Vanquished was the image of a doomed frog.

When Kate emerged from the water, her body still echoed with the weightless feel of her swim. After drying off with the towel, she stretched out on a chaise lounge.

Her eyes stung from the chlorine and from lack of sleep. Between the nightmares she'd been having since she discovered the film and the anticipation of returning to her garage to examine the box, she was lucky if she'd gotten four full hours of sleep the night before.

But the sun was glorious, seemingly melting her into the chair. The leafy branches swayed, and the only sound was the music of the birds chirping above her. She felt suspended in midair instead of lying on a chaise lounge next to a manufactured oasis made of cement and chlorine.

Her mind drifted to thoughts of Dylan, the warm feeling when he took her hand and his intense expression that at times took her breath away.

Her body tingled as she caressed the curve of her torso, and she felt drowned in the sweet fragrance of that perfect yellow rose, she was sure he'd left for her.

Stretching like a cat, she sighed and drifted off to sleep. In her dream, at first, all she saw were a dozen newly plucked yellow roses standing tall in a blue cobalt vase. Her vision widened, and she could see the flowers sat on a coffee table in a small bungalow. A slightly worn love seat and two dark wood chairs filled out a cozy seating area. Four more vases with different kinds of bouquets were placed throughout the perimeter of the room, each of these with little white cards nestled next to them, with the name Gloria scripted on the front of the tiny envelopes. The two built-in vanities and the mirrors everywhere left no doubt at the place's purpose. It was a dressing room.

Kate couldn't tell why she knew the light that shone through the wood framed windows to be the morning light, but she did. The same way she knew this was Gloria's dressing room, and it was the day of her murder.

Kate scanned the room trying to take in each detail in hopes of finding a clue. The white oblong box with a crimson bow was not in the room. Not that it should be, yet. Her scan of the room halted at the sight of her grandmother.

There Gloria stood in the doorway wearing a lovely pale pink mid-calf pencil skirt paired with a matching silky jacket that scooped in at the waist and broadened at the shoulders. A matching hat, pinned to the side, framed her face like a halo around a face that at any time was beautiful, but now it exuded pure radiance as she stared at the yellow roses, and only at them. She skipped toward the roses.

A woman with sensible shoes and graying hair cut short and curled in loops at the temple walked into the room after Gloria. She held a powder blue make-up case, two purses, one that matched Gloria's ensemble, a movie script, and a newspaper.

"Oh, miss." The woman gazed around the place. "Look at all the flowers."

"Millie," Gloria said to her assistant without shifting her gaze from the yellow roses. "Do you think he's forgiven me?"

She dipped her head closer to the bouquet and breathed in the fragrance. Kate's own senses swam with the rose's complex brew of woodsy musk layered with bursts of fruit. But it was even more than that, it felt like breathing in love.

Awash in the sunlight of Gloria's joy, Kate refused to allow the dark shadows she knew would inevitably overtake this day. For once, she didn't want the shared experience to end.

When Kate awoke from her dream, the dizzy memory of being Gloria was replaced by the startling sight of Beatrice standing by Jarvis's pool and hovering over her.

Kate flinched and sat up in chaise lounge.

Beatrice turned and scribbled something in the notebook she had in her other hand. "Jarvis is waiting for you."

Kate sighed. "Good. Where is he?"

Beatrice tucked the pen behind her ear, and her

notebook she secured inside her black purse. "On the upper patio. He asked me to fetch you." She snatched up the gray towel and dropped it onto Kate's stomach. "Try not to be so obvious. At least pretend to look decent."

"Decent? I'm wearing a bathing suit at a pool." Now fully awake, Kate sat up. That's when she realized the straps had slipped off her shoulders and the bodice was sliding perilously close to her nipples.

"Oh." Red-faced, she tugged the straps back up.

"Save it," Beatrice said. "The coy act doesn't work on me. You like to pretend otherwise, but you're the same as all the other starlet wannabes, using sex to get what you want, particularly when Jarvis is around."

"That isn't true."

"No? Look at yourself. You're just like her, aren't you?"

After so many years, Kate didn't even bother to ask who the *her* was. She'd been compared to Gloria her whole life. But it never had been flung at her with such animosity.

"You hated my grandmother, didn't you?"

In clipped movements, Beatrice turned and walked away.

Kate took her measure of the woman and found her to be no different from the back as she was from the front: all angles and sharp edges.

"How much did you hate her?" Kate called out. "Enough to hurt her?"

That stopped Beatrice. "Never." She marched back until she was so close that Kate could smell stale cigarettes and see the wide-eyed look of fear, before Beatrice adjusted back to her in charge demeanor.

Was Kate acting paranoid? Seeing potential murderers everywhere? Even if Beatrice was a colossal pain, she also had a certain amount of dignity, having clawed her way to the top of this male-dominated industry.

The older woman shot her a condescending smirk.

That was it. Who cared if Beatrice had broken barriers? Kate was sick of being the butt of the woman's snide remarks. Hot with anger, Kate leapt to her feet, ready to fight. Then a laugh altogether strange escaped her own lips.

It wasn't her laugh. Too mocking. Too melodious.

"Maybe, you didn't hate her," Kate's voice cooed, the words tumbling out of her mouth with a volition that didn't seem like her own. Then with a feline sensuality she rolled back her shoulders, and said, "Did you *long* for Gloria late at night? You did, didn't you?"

A fire alarm sounded inside Kate as her body trembled. Those weren't her own words. That wasn't her laugh.

God, what was happening to her?

"Ha!" Beatrice spat. "Gloria disgusted me. And if you care about women's equality, you'd despise her, too."

"I do care." To Kate's great relief, her voice sounded like her own again. She rubbed her temples, trying to make the world stop spinning; just like it had done the other day in the guest house when she'd imagined seeing the day Gloria died through her eyes.

"Your grandmother got what she wanted by spreading her legs. And now you're trying to be just like her."

"I'm not—"

"Save it. Or will you have the temerity to claim you picked *that* bathing suit by chance, out of all the ones in Jarvis's pool house? The one Gloria wore in *Forever Twilight*!"

"What?" Kate looked at what she was wearing as if she was seeing it for the first time. My God, yes. It was the bathing suit from *Forever Twilight*. How had she not realized it was her grandmother's suit?

Kate knew the film, of course. It was Gloria's first featured part. She'd played the young wayward wife of a diplomat who spilled government secrets while she spilled out of her infamous low-cut bathing suit. The scandalous scene had rocketed Gloria and the bathing costume to stardom.

Now the thin, flesh-toned suit Kate wore squeezed her like a fist, no longer the fun, sensuous prop she had enjoyed before.

"For the record, I didn't *desire* Gloria," Beatrice said. "Jumping in and out of bed with men, or women for that matter, was her mode of operation, never mine. I worked for everything I've gotten."

Kate's jaw dropped. "My…my grandmother slept with women?"

"Oh, grow up. Your generation thinks it's the first to do everything. The truth is there is nothing new."

"I don't believe that."

"No?" With a thin smile and a flash of command in her eyes, Beatrice said, "Then let me educate you. If you want to have a sordid life of drugs, sex, and illusion, Gloria and Winston are your perfect models. And if you want to learn about real oppression instead of just whining about it, look up the Hollywood Ten. Have you heard of them? They didn't just demonstrate against wars overseas like your generation. The Hollywood Ten, and many more like them, sacrificed their livelihood to fight oppression here. And women's liberation? Your favorite topic." She pointed to herself. "Look no further, I'm your best example of that."

She was right. Kate knew it. But why did Beatrice have to be so awful? It seemed as if from day one Beatrice had done whatever she could to get rid of her. Why?

Hands on her hips, Beatrice looked like the King of Siam. "I didn't just talk about it, either. I did it." She circled Kate. "I'm the highest-ranking female studio executive in Hollywood. I made it by being several steps ahead of every man I ever competed with and not by using sex or nepotism. Talk emancipation all you want, but are you capable of living it, of competing with the big boys?" The woman stared hard at Kate. "I don't think you are. And if you're not, get out of the way, or believe me, they'll run you over."

"I *am* up to it," Kate said in an annoyingly weak voice. "I want to be a filmmaker, and I'll do it by earning it."

"I doubt it." Beatrice opened her purse and pulled out her pack of cigarettes. "Now run up to the house. Jarvis is waiting for you."

Kate stomped past Beatrice and climbed the terraced path toward the main residence, stumbling in her silly powder-puff slippers. Why hadn't she'd come up with a retort for what Beatrice said? Instead, she'd just retreated. And, in doing so, hadn't she proved the older woman's point?

She couldn't leave things that way. She looked back at the pool patio. Beatrice sat there, puffing on a cigarette.

Kate searched her brain to find the perfect words.

Nothing.

Damn!

She continued to trudge up the slope, mulling it over. When she got to the upper patio, she looked down the hill and shouted, "You're wrong!"

Beatrice looked up at her.

Not exactly pithy, but it got to the point. Then she found more to say. She threw open her arms and cried, "If you believe that the only options for a woman is to be sexless and angry like you or objectified and dead like Gloria well...well..." Kate dropped her arms and said softly, "That can't be true."

"I agree," said a voice behind her.

She turned and saw Jarvis leaning against the doorway between the solarium and the patio. His eyes twinkled with amusement. It made him look much younger than his fifty-something years.

Kate wrapped the towel around herself.

Jarvis shook his head. "But I don't think you do, considering the way you're always covering yourself up?"

"I do believe it." *Intellectually*.

He walked toward her. "Good. Let's talk about the screen test."

"What? Have you and Beatrice been playing good cop, bad cop with me? Was this all a setup?"

He chuckled. "No. But I'd be a chump not to take advantage of the opening."

Kate didn't think this man had ever been made a chump, and she didn't want to be near the person who tried. No matter how polished he now was, she always sensed the hoodlum from the mean streets bristling just below his surface. Oddly, she found this quality both fearsome and attractive.

"Why not take the opportunity to use both sides of yourself?" he proposed. "The screen test is a good place to begin to embrace your sensuality, which is an undeniable part of who you are, and it's also doing what you love, which is film." He winked. "Nice, eh?"

She laughed. "You're good."

He didn't crack a smile, and his blue eyes looked hard now. "That wasn't an answer."

"That's because I've already given you my answer. No. Thank you." Kate walked by him and sat on a wide-cushioned patio chair. Her towel slipped off her freckled shoulders. She saw Jarvis sweep an admiring gaze over her body.

Part of her wanted to wrap the towel around herself again for protection. Then she thought of her recent declaration. Hadn't she in fact made the decision not to be sexless and angry, like Beatrice? Maybe it was time to see if she could be taken seriously without hiding under baggy clothes.

It still terrified her. But she could pretend to be otherwise. Couldn't she?

Kate leaned back and crossed her legs, forming a perfect V.

Like a cat that couldn't resist a dangling string, the great Jarvis Benjamin appeared to be enraptured by her every movement.

She felt giddy for a moment. Is this how power feels?

Meeting Jarvis's stare, she smiled. "Tell me, what's the likelihood we'll win the rights to the footage?"

"Not good. Don't worry. I haven't given up, despite what the lawyers tell me. They're re-researching the matter. At least they better be."

"But I thought Nash had the rights to it, and his family has signed over ownership to us?"

"Not quite. What Winston had wasn't ownership. It was more like an interest. He had rights to the script, right to final edit, and a say about how it would be distributed while he was alive. But from what my lawyers tell me, he had no power to bequeath that interest to someone else."

"And my possessory rights?"

"Only valuable in the movies, I'm afraid. Your possession came from someone who stole it, which legally gets you nothing."

Kate thought about that. "Not quite, because I have it, at least for now. I get to see it before it's buried again. That's something."

"Not a lot. I plan to get more than that out of it, if I have my way, which I usually do."

Jarvis sat on the chair facing hers.

She wanted to shift her angle but fought the need. After all, this was a negotiation. She couldn't show any sign of weakness and be trampled the way Beatrice had predicted.

"Still, if we do lose," she said, "and Sutton gets possession of the film, can we somehow ensure it becomes public? That's what I really want."

"Me too. That's why I want it completely restored before making it public. Then when we do go public, we'll need to make sure everyone knows about it so Sutton can't bury it."

Jarvis leaned back and rested his arms on the top of the patio couch. "Just give me some time. The roll out will be important. I think a party may be in order."

Kate frowned. She wasn't much for parties.

"To screen the footage," Jarvis continued.

"Oh, yes!"

"Good. A party, one that people will be talking about for decades. Lillian can help arrange it. She'd like that."

"Are you kidding? She'd love that." Kate beamed at him, and for a moment his tough guy demeanor softened. It was nice.

He nodded. "A couple of hints here and there, anonymously of course, and we'll get the whole town buzzing with rumors of what we've got. Everyone who's anyone will be at my party for the unveiling, I promise you that."

"Wonderful. You're like Santa Claus."

His gaze clasped onto hers. "I'm nothing like Santa Claus."

Kate gulped.

He continued, "It's great publicity for my studio's remake of *Emperor Smythe*. And my willingness to make it public is not without cost."

She shifted in her chair.

He smiled. "In return, no hiking boots and you'll be decked out in clothes I choose, which trust me, will reveal to the world your uncanny resemblance to your grandmother. The press will love it."

Kate opened her mouth to object.

He shot her a look that told her loud and clear arguing was not an option. "You will wear what I say. Like it or not, *Emperor Smythe* is forever linked in the public's imagination with Gloria. We may not have the best legal argument in terms of ownership, but creating the illusion that we do can help. Trust me. I've won with worse cards." He got up and strode toward the house's back sliding door.

She twisted her hands together. "The press will be there?"

He turned to face her. "Everyone comes when I ask."

"Everyone?" An idea formed. "Is that true?"

"Of course." His gaze focused on her lips.

Kate stuffed down her anxiety and instead cocked her head like the coquettes she'd thought she despised. "Fine. I'll wear Gloria's silly gold-lamé dress. We'll give the press a feeding frenzy."

"Good."

"Hold on." Kate waved her finger. "Nothing's free, remember."

Jarvis lips slanted up ever so slightly. He nodded for her to continue.

"I'll do that if you promise to get J.B. Sutton to the party."

"Huh! My publicity department would be in heaven if I could. But even I can't do that, not for *this* film."

Kate shrugged. "Then I'll be wearing hiking boots."

"No, you won't." Jarvis then appeared to reconsider his tone, for when he spoke again, his voice was solicitous as a salesman. "I can't get him to the party. But if we come to a deal, I think I can set up a meeting for you with that flatulent octopus."

"That would be fantastic."

"Why do you want to see him?" Jarvis's words sliced out swift and solid as an ax.

Kate's toes curled in her powder puff slippers, as she was reminded again that she was negotiating with someone way out of her league. She played with the idea of telling him about the box but felt almost superstitious about letting anyone else know about it. Still, she needed a reason and one to satisfy Jarvis if she wanted to question Sutton.

She looked up. "What if Gloria stumbled upon the conspiracy to steal the film, and there was a struggle? Or Sutton got rid of Gloria to make sure the film never got completed. That's possible, isn't it?"

Jarvis eyes narrowed in on her. "I thought you believed Winston did it?"

"I did, I mean, I do. It's just that explanation is not adding up the way it used to in my mind."

"You're keeping something from me?" he said with a warning tone.

"What do you mean? No one keeps secrets from the great Jarvis Benjamin?" She shone a bright smile, yet her fingers twitched at her side.

"Not for long."

She laughed then got the hell out of there and back into the house before she lost her nerve and told him everything.

Chapter Eleven

Two hours later, she sat in Dylan's rumbling Mustang, heading toward her childhood home. The companionable silence of the drive was made all the more soothing by the summer sun dappling through the shade of the elm trees lining blocks of Claremont Village. That was, until he parked in front of her house.

She felt the now familiar lap of moist heat brushing her skin.

She gritted her teeth. Weren't ghosts supposed to be cold! This feeling was too warm, too seductive to be ethereal.

Ghosts? No. That's crazy talk.

Yet, maybe gothic castles and windswept moors weren't the only places where spirits lingered. Here, at her celery green home with its single car attached garage, small lawn, and one lonely palm tree, she sensed her mother's anger at a world that had taken so much from her. And she felt Gloria as if she sat right beside her.

With a sense of panic, Kate double checked what she was wearing. No swan pin, no revealing bathing attire, only her wonderfully large T-shirt, scuffed jeans, and boots. Yeah! She was herself!

"You grew up here?" Dylan asked.

"So?" She cringed at the defensiveness in her voice.

"Nothing." He shrugged. "It's nice." He leaped out of the car and circled to the passenger door, but she opened it before he could get to it.

"So where did you grow up?" she asked. "In the stately halls of Pemberley? Or perhaps you were raised by apes in the jungle? No mere house for you, huh?"

"Hell, no." Dylan brandished an imaginary sword. "Moats, parapets, a fire-breathing dragon, and a damsel in distress. That's where I live, at least in my imagination. I recommend it."

"And reality?"

"Not as interesting."

"Mother? Father?" she asked.

"More like nannies and boarding schools."

"I'm sorry."

"Don't be. There are perks to a life of luxury. The façades are wonderful. But looking behind them?" His expression tightened as a look of pain brushed across his face. "Not recommended."

"I see why you prefer fantasy."

Was that what she was doing? With her thoughts of ghosts, the wish for a protective presence? Much easier to believe in the fanciful, than the stark alternative, she was having a breakdown.

Dylan's fingers brushed up her arm until resting on her shoulder. The feel of his very real hands on her soothed her worrying mind.

He nodded toward the tree-lined street and at all the neat small houses with manicured lawns. "Tell me. What was it like to grow up on a street with white picket fences and happily-ever-after?"

"Yeah, right." She stepped away from his touch. "Inside all these Norman Rockwell homes is pain, isolation, and broken promises. That's reality."

He moved toward her. "Seeing only darkness, isn't reality either."

She looked at him and noticed the almost pleading tone of her voice as she gazed in his eyes. "Do you really believe that? Or is that too just pretend?"

"Does it matter?" He took her in his arms and kissed her.

His lips were soft, and her head swam with the feel of him as his kiss grew more urgent. She felt flooded by him, by sensation, by need so intense she was lost in it. *She* was lost.

With that thought the beat of her heart turned into a jackhammer, and she could barely breathe. She wrenched herself out of his embrace.

Dylan stared at her, his eyes wide with confusion and a glint of hurt there, too. "I'm sorry, Kate."

She turned away from him, wanting to cry, wanting to scream.

"Are you okay?"

Clearly not.

She hugged herself. Why was she so afraid? Particularly with someone like Dylan, someone she liked, someone she suddenly wanted, she didn't care what it cost her.

And that was it, wasn't it? The same foolish impulse, like her mother who died inside when her father left them, and like her grandmother, who well…died.

Kate marched toward the garage, and away from Dylan.

Fumbling for the key to the padlock, she heard him come up behind her.

But for the first time in her life, she wished she could be foolish, just a little bit. She wished she could be like her grandmother, willing to risk, so she could lie in Dylan's arms.

"Kate?" His rich voice was soft, almost a caress. "Damn. You told me you just wanted to be friends. I'm not used to that with a girl."

"I'm so sorry. I wish…"

"I really like being your friend," he said. "I really like you. It won't happen again, okay?"

Her eyes welled with tears. Funny how an hour earlier, with Jarvis, she thought she'd figured out how to push back her fear of men and begin to embrace her sensuality. But had she really? Or had she done that only by disconnecting from herself and pretending to be someone else?

She couldn't do that with Dylan. But why it was so important to not pretend with him, she wasn't quite sure.

She knelt in front of the garage to unlock the padlock and pulled up the door.

She gasped and stared disbelieving into the garage.

It was empty.

She stood too quickly. Her body waved like an unhinged window in a storm.

Dylan steadied her.

Regaining her balance, she stared at a gouge in the garage floor. It was filled with powdery cement, and long cracks radiated from it.

Had that been here before?

She didn't know. How could she, when as long as she could remember the garage had been filled with supplies, discarded toys, and storage boxes. But not now. It was as if some impossibly large vacuum cleaner had sucked it all away.

Dylan said something, but his voice sounded far away even though he stood right next to her. She shut her eyes tightly like a child making a wish. But when she opened them again, the garage was still empty.

He still had a hand on her shoulder. "We need to call the police. Now." He guided her toward the house. "We need to tell them everything."

When Dylan told Mrs. Koval the garage had been burglarized, she ran back inside, calling her children's names. When she returned to the front door, her children accounted for, she had a crying baby in her arms and a preschooler clinging to her leg.

"Did you hear anything?" Dylan asked Mrs. Koval. "Is anything missing from the house?"

"No. Not that I'm aware of," she said.

Dylan walked in. "I'm calling the police."

Thirty minutes later, an Officer Jansen, who looked not much older than Dylan, swaggered into the living room and took statements. Kate perched on her mother's plastic-wrapped couch, with Dylan and Mrs. Koval standing nearby. Her little boy ran through the house, yelling, "Bang, bang! I'm a robber, I'm a robber."

"I heard nothing." Mrs. Koval said to Officer Jansen. "I had no idea anything was wrong." She collared the boy and dragged him into another room. Kate felt relieved when the child's screams faded.

Officer Jansen turned his attention to Kate and said in a patronizing tone, "You sure you'd locked the garage."

"Yes, positive."

The officer looked skeptical.

"Sir," Dylan said. "I saw the padlock. It was locked when we arrived. Kate used her key to open it."

"Well, okay then." Officer Jansen scribbled something on his pad.

That irritated her. The officer believed Dylan but not her.

"So you have the only key, is that right?" Officer Jansen asked Kate.

"Yes, just me."

"Was there anything of value stored there?"

"I don't think so." Kate shifted in her seat, and the plastic covering on the couch squeaked. "Even my grandmother's belongings, I don't think had any value."

"You inherited the house and contents when your mother died. Is that right?"

"Yes." The plastic squeaked again.

"Is there a list of belongings? Did the trustee do an inventory of your mother's estate?"

"No." Kate shifted.

Squeak.

"I mean yes."

Squeak.

He grinned.

The cop looked as if he thought each squeak told him she was lying. She stood up from the cursed couch. "Yes, there was a trustee, but it was a small estate. Nothing more than the house, my mom's stuff, a checking and savings account. It was all going to me and not worth much; so, no, we thought an inventory wasn't necessary."

He jotted something in his book. "Your grandmother is famous, and you said her belongings were in the garage, but still you claim they had no value?"

"Not intrinsically. Mostly old dresses, knick-knacks, costume jewelry, stuff like that. I suppose to collectors of Hollywood memorabilia they would have value."

"Was it insured?"

"I don't think so. Or, maybe, as part of the homeowner's policy?"

"What's the name of your insurer?"

Dylan stepped forward. "Wait a minute. Why are you grilling her like this? She didn't take the stuff. Kate, tell him what's going on. There's probably a good explanation—"

"Going on?" Officer Jansen said.

"'Going on' is a bit dramatic." Kate shot Dylan a warning glance. She turned back to the officer and said with a smile, "It's nothing. I'm a film student, and I may have mentioned to some people at school I had my grandmother's stuff in this garage. I'm sure my friends had nothing to do with this. But it's possible they told others."

Officer Jansen looked disappointed. "Any other reason you think someone might want to steal these things?"

She shook her head, making sure she did not catch Dylan's eye. "No. I can't think of one."

****

Any guilt Kate felt about not telling the police everything was wiped out after listening to Dylan lecture her nonstop on their drive back to Bel Air. By the time he pulled into Jarvis's driveway, she'd had enough. She slammed the car door and stomped up the pathway toward the house. "You're the one who warned me not to tell the police," she said. "If we did, it would be all over the trades by the next day. That's what you said."

Dylan's bulky form trudged after her. "Yeah, but that was before you were robbed. That's real. And very weird that it happens right after we discovered something about that box. Besides, I was mainly worried about L.A. officers. I don't think Claremont has that type of network with Hollywood insiders. Shit!" He yelled at her. "Don't you get it? Someone broke into your house, and if it wasn't with your key—"

Kate wheeled around too mad to be intimated by his bluster. "What are you implying? That I took it?"

"Of course not."

"That cop sure thought I did. I can't believe you were about to tell him about the footage. He was just itching to make a name for himself."

Dylan grabbed her arms. "Damn it. This is real."

Kate broke from his arm. "You're damned right it is, and I'm sick to death of being gaslighted."

Dylan took a step back with a look of confusion on his face. "Gaslight? What do you mean? Like in the Ingrid Bergman movie? Is someone making you feel like you're going psycho?"

"Maybe. I don't know." Kate for a moment wondered if it could be him. She shook the ridiculous thought away. After all, why would he? She took a breath. "What I do know is the stuff in my garage has been stolen, and I need to know why."

"You need the police to handle this. Don't you get it? The fact that there was no sign of a break-in implies a professional job."

"Interesting." She halted. "I wonder if it also indicates the thief was hoping to delay discovery. I mean, I don't check the garage very often, actually almost never, and the tenants don't have access to it. This could've gone undiscovered for months. Maybe it happened a while ago."

"We need to back off," Dylan said. "This is out of our league. We're not detectives."

"I don't disagree we need assistance. But I can't shut my mind off. I've got too many questions that need answers. I'm not stopping now."

"Get in here. Both of you," Jarvis snapped.

He stood in his front doorway with an expression that could have chilled a volcano.

Jarvis herded her and Dylan into his study. He walked behind his large mahogany desk, which gave a weighted masculine air to the garden view room. "Tell me about the burglary at your mother's house."

Kate gasped. "How do you—"

"I have my sources," he said.

Dylan laughed. "I guess it's true even in Claremont. Jarvis, at least, has *spies* everywhere."

The older man's gaze did not move from Kate's face. "What did you tell the police?"

Figuring it was useless to lie since the guy seemed to already know everything, she ran through the day's events.

When she was done he nodded. "Good. You said nothing about *Emperor Smythe*. You did okay." His demeanor softened. "Don't worry. I'll get someone to take care of this. We'll catch 'em and get your things back. No reason to blow everything up over this,

127

right?"

"I don't care about the stuff. It's just we'd hoped to find a clue to Gloria's murder."

That got Jarvis's attention.

Dylan crossed his arms. "Yeah, that's why we need to go to the police. This could be more than a simple burglary."

Lillian entered the room. "What's going on?"

Kate paced. "Clues, new information. We saw something in the footage."

Both Jarvis and Lillian gave her a skeptical look.

"No, really," Kate continued. "The more we look into the past, the more anomalies we find. Now a burglary. Somehow it all fits together."

Jarvis tapped a gold pen against his chin. "Tell me everything."

She told him. How could she not? The powerbroker with the junkyard fighter simmering below the surface was a man not to be denied.

So she told him about the box. She explained it was supposed to have contained the murder weapon but had been removed from the set after Gloria departed, more than an hour before Winston could've met her in her dressing room. Beatrice was seen talking to Charles Needham on the set, and Charles also had a connection to J.B. Sutton. "That's why we went out there." Kate told him. "To get a look at that box, examine Gloria's stuff, to see if there was something, anything to find some hint of what the murder weapon was. The box, along with everything else, is gone, and we have nothing."

Lillian clasped her hands. "I knew Winston couldn't have done it. He loved her so."

"I wouldn't go that far," Kate said. "What we saw in the footage doesn't clear him completely. It just raises questions."

"Of course it does," Lillian said.

"Fantastic," Jarvis said, stretching out the word. "That's the best pitch for a story I've heard all week."

Kate protested, "It's not a story."

"Maybe." Jarvis smirked. "I'm just saying, look at the bright side. If you don't solve a murder, at least you've got a great premise for a picture." He sat. "The truth is probably more boring than that, what you told the police is probably right, one of your film friends took the stuff. The motive for the break-in was to steal the treasure trove of film memorabilia you had in there. You admitted to telling your school friends that you had a garage full of it. The timing fits. Your school friends or someone they told are the likely explanation."

"Oh, hell! Somber logic, deflating one of my adventures yet again." Dylan shrugged, then turned to Kate. "I agree with Jarvis. As tempting as it is to make a connection between your garage break-in and your grandmother's murder, it doesn't fly. We're the only ones to stumble upon the new information about the box."

He's right. After all, how many times did she have to run the film to see such a small thing in the background? Silly to think someone beside her and Dylan had seen it.

Except, wouldn't the murderer's attention be focused on the box appearing and disappearing in the footage? She looked at Jarvis and Lillian to see if their faces betrayed any knowledge of the information about the box.

Nothing.

Jarvis walked over to Kate. "I tell you what. I'll have my people discreetly check this out." He put a knuckle under her chin and lifted it until she met his gaze. "If they find anything, I promise you, we'll make a report to the police. For now, enough about police and acting like junior sleuths." His gaze darted between her and Dylan. "I've got too much invested in my plan to control the original *Emperor Smythe* film and cash in on the remake. When I took on this project, everyone here agreed to keep it secret until I say otherwise. I expect all of you to live up to that bargain."

Chapter Twelve

Next morning, Kate grabbed her copy of the police report on Gloria's murder and headed straight to the Hollywood police station. She asked if Detective Terrence Sweeney still worked there. She was told he'd left the force over ten years ago. That wasn't good. From the report it was evident he was one of the few people to raise questions about the case. Maybe too many, because he was taken off it.

Kate thumbed through the report and saw the name of a Detective Joseph Robak, who had taken several statements from crew members on the soundstage that day. But the desk sergeant at the Hollywood station had never heard of him. But he gave her a list of all the police precincts in town and told her Detective Robak might work at one of them.

Kate drove to her Silver Lake apartment, thinking it would offer some privacy. She had to admit she'd really come to love living at Jarvis's mansion. Yet, there was something eerie about the place, too. She couldn't get over the feeling of being watched.

To be fair, Jarvis, Lillian, and Dylan didn't seem like the sneaky type. If they wanted to know something, they'd just ask.

God knows, the same was true of Beatrice, although she usually told, not asked. Jimena and Kioshi were the opposite. They had perfected the art of going about their work while blending into the background, so she'd forgotten they were even there. Then there was Gloria. Real or imagined, her presence was everywhere, calling to her, warning her that danger was near.

Now that she thought of it, the moist heat and that warm overtaking sensation she identified as Gloria was qualitatively different than the times she felt she'd seen someone out of the corner of her eye surveilling her. Were they caused by different things? She was beginning to think so.

She unlocked the door of the apartment and was dismayed to find several film students asleep in her living room.

So much for privacy.

Natalie had told her that she'd invited some friends from school to stay there while they were both away. But Kate hadn't expected the entire film graduate program crashing here. Empty beer cans and overflowing ashtrays everywhere. There must have been some party here last night. What a mess.

She tiptoed over to the makeshift bookcase, grabbed the phone directory, and snuck into her bedroom. Some stranger was asleep in her bed. She headed down the hallway to Natalie's room. Kate wasn't surprised, but was sorry, to find it empty. Wasn't she due back soon?

She'd tried several times to leave her a message at the artist's studio Natalie was interning with, but only got the artist's answering machine. They must be out in the desert putting up the installation.

Kate sat cross-legged on the floor mattress and thumbed through the telephone book's government pages. She methodically called each listed police station and asked if a Joseph Robak worked there. On her fourth try, she lucked out and was told he worked out of the West L.A. Station. She asked to speak to him.

She was placed on hold and subjected to an easy listening rendition of *I Wanna Hold Your Hand*. The desk sergeant returned to the phone and told her that Detective Robak was too busy to speak to her today but said she could make an appointment to see him next week.

Kate wasn't in the mood to wait. Besides, she detected something in the sergeant's tone, a hint of a laugh maybe. Whatever it was, she didn't quite trust him. She thanked the officer, hung up, and tip-toed back through the apartment.

Still no movement from the sleeping students. For a moment she felt like a ghost haunting her own past.

She shut the front door and, with a touch of sadness, understood her previous life no longer fit her.

****

The reception area at the West L.A. Police station was a small, rectangular area with linoleum floors, fluorescent lights, and plastic benches against two of its walls. She walked up to a thick plastic window that began midway up the wall and ended at the ceiling. It had a small opening at the bottom and something that looked like a little speaker to talk to the officer on the other side. Next to the window was a door.

A black officer turned and looked at her through the hazy window. He was at least six-two and with the posture of a marine. His uniform looked starched, and his buttons gleamed.

"I'd like to speak to Detective Robak, please."

The officer's eyes narrowed. "Didn't we speak on

the phone?"

"We did."

"And didn't I tell you he wasn't available?"

"You did."

"Yet here you are."

"I am." She suddenly had an irrational fear that she was going to be arrested on the charge of being annoying.

He stared at her as if he was waiting for her to blink first. She held his gaze. The officer shook his head and smiled. "Would you like to tell me what this is about?"

"No, I need to speak to him, only him."

"We're a team here. Let's begin with your name."

"Kate Bloom. It's about an old case, a case Detective Robak worked on. That's why I need to speak to him."

The desk sergeant scribbled something in a large ledger. "What's the case?"

"I'd rather not say."

He gave her a withering look, but she kept her mouth shut. He lifted one hand as if surrendering. "Okay, I don't think it'll do any good, but I'll try again and ask if he'll speak to you."

She sat on the hard bench, her hands fidgeting, until the desk sergeant came back. When he did, he shook his head. "Sorry. Detective Robak's not available. He's got his retirement party this week, and doesn't need—"

Kate leapt to her feet. "Wait a minute. He's retiring this week? On the phone you tried to set my appointment with him for next week."

The desk sergeant wouldn't meet her gaze. "His

joke, not mine."

She sat back down on the bench. "I'm waiting right here."

He shrugged. "Suit yourself."

Two hours passed. Occasionally, she'd see an officer walk by her and wondered if it could be Robak. She imagined what he'd look like. She figured he'd be a grizzled, tired-looking man, with nicotine-stained fingers, a rumpled shirt, and sad, droopy Robert Mitchum eyes. So she was surprised when the desk sergeant surreptitiously pointed to a man with a relaxed, tan face who had just walked out of the building.

Detective Robak had slightly long salt-and-pepper hair and a thin nose with a pointed tip. He wore a blue button-down work shirt, open at the collar and corduroy jacket with suede patches at the elbows. He looked more like one of her professors than how she had imagined a cop.

She thanked the sergeant and ran after the detective. Outside, she looked around quickly. He was heading toward a parking lot.

She caught up with him just when he had swung open the door of a Ford Torino.

"Detective Robak? May I speak to you?"

He turned and looked at her. Or, at least, she assumed he did. He'd glanced over her right shoulder, yet his glassy eyes were unfocused on anything in particular. He didn't appear outright sad but as if he'd forgotten how to smile.

Kate saw that one of her stereotypes had been correct. He did have Robert Mitchum eyes, with that I-don't-give-a-damn-about-the-world expression.

"Listen, I'm on my way home." He said that with a

gentle but firm voice, as if she were a misbehaving child. "If this is an emergency, you'll get more help inside. And if it's not, I don't want to know about it." He turned back to his car, pulled out part of a newspaper he had folded in his back pocket, and threw it into the passenger seat.

Kate saw it was the Sunday crossword puzzle, *The New York Times*, no less, and done in ink. Now she felt even more sure he was the right guy to talk to.

"Please, I've tried to talk to you all day."

He had one hand on the top of his car door. "Oh, you're the mystery girl. Who won't tell anyone what you want to talk about. Go away."

"I have reasons—"

"Doesn't everybody. That's not the way the force works, kiddo. You can't just demand to see anybody you want when you want."

"Except it's your case. That's why I want to speak to you."

"None of them are *my* cases anymore." He looked at her for the first time. "You see this?" He lifted up his lapel. Attached to it was a pin with the round seal of the City of Los Angeles. "My retirement present. Not much for thirty-five years. But I guess it's better than a watch." She thought she detected a note of pride in his voice. But then it was gone when he said, "By the end of this week I'm off duty. So, miss, why don't you march back into the station and explain your problem to a real police officer."

"I'm scared!" Kate blurted.

Why had she said that? It wasn't true, was it? Looking at everything logically, none of this was about her. It was about the past, and that was all it was. She was beginning to sound as overdramatic as Lillian.

"I'm sorry," she said. "I shouldn't have said that. I have no reason to think I'm in danger, not really. And I have a lot of good reasons to keep what's going on secret. In fact, everybody wants me to."

He must have sensed real fear in her voice for the more she babbled the more his eyes darkened and his focus on her became acute.

"Except, what if they're not?" she continued, unable to slow down. "Please, Detective Robak, I need to talk to you."

"Okay, kiddo. You win." He placed a reassuring hand on her arm. "We can go over to Bette's Coffee Shop. You've got until I finish a cinnamon roll to tell me what this is all about."

****

The coffee shop was within walking distance of the police station. It was the type of joint that had a box of cigars in the display case, crayons for kids to draw on the paper placemats, and a large assortment of pies and pastries. Not fancy pastries, but big, sticky ones. It was late afternoon. Most of the people there appeared to be in their sixties or older. Kate guessed they were taking advantage of the early-bird meatloaf special.

Detective Robak and Kate sat in a booth by the grease smudged window. After they each placed their order of coffee and a cinnamon roll, Detective Robak propped his chin in one hand. "So, what's the old case?"

"Gloria Reardon's murder."

Robak rubbed his forehead. "Oh, no. You're one of them."

"What?"

"A nut who thinks she sees conspiracies everywhere. No, it couldn't just be a lovers' quarrel gone bad, not for the illustrious Winston Nash and Gloria Reardon. It had to be that she was really a spy or having a damn affair with Ike or something. Listen, Nash may have gotten off on a technicality, thanks to his high-priced lawyer, but he killed her. It's as simple as that."

The detective rose as if to leave. Luckily, the waitress brought the cinnamon rolls at that moment and refreshed their coffee. From the way Robak gazed at the warm, gooey roll, she didn't think he was going anywhere right away.

After eating his first bite, which he took a ridiculously long time to do, Robak said, "Not to mention the man didn't even deny it. Nash just sobbed and said he couldn't remember a thing. Damn drunk. He had motive, opportunity, and a trail of shards from the murder weapon leading right to his office at the studio. Case closed."

Kate tore off a small piece of her sticky bun. "Your partner, Detective Sweeney, didn't believe Nash did it."

"He thought there were some unanswered questions. That's all."

"Do you know where Sweeney is? Maybe I can talk to him."

Robak's gaze drifted off. "I wish you could. He died a couple years back." He looked at her. "Tell me, what does any of this have to do with you? You a reporter or, I know, look at you, a die-hard fan, a Gloria wannabe. Why anyone wants to be a corpse, I don't know."

"She was my grandmother."

He frowned. "I'm sorry."

"I have questions." Kate hesitated, imagining the angry faces of Dylan and Jarvis if they knew what she was about to tell the detective. "And, I have some new evidence."

Robak's face lit with interest, but then his expression changed as he shook his head. "Listen, I'm retiring this week, I'm not your guy. There's a detective, a good one, assigned to cold cases. That's who you should be talking to."

"Please, they—I mean, where the new evidence is, well, if it gets out, it'll take off like media wildfire, and I can't let that happen, not yet."

"Why?"

"Will you give me your word you won't tell anyone?"

"No." Robak popped another bite of roll into his mouth. "I'll tell you what," he said, chewing slowly. "I'm retired, at least almost. If what you say doesn't require me to report it to the brass, I won't."

"Thank you," Kate practically shouted.

Robak held up a hand. "Hold on, there, kiddo. Let's be clear. I'm not going to keep quiet if I think someone's in danger or it shields a criminal. Got it?"

"Sure." Kate told him about finding the missing footage, about how the head of Infinity Studios was financing the restoration, and that while working on it, she'd seen the box that was supposed to have the murder weapon in it had been moved hours before Winston could've taken it. She also told Robak why she thought some of the statements in the police report didn't add up and about the burglary at her garage.

All the while, he sat listening, his sad eyes looking

at her.

She babbled on, telling the detective, this stranger, things she'd originally had no intention of telling anyone—about the feeling she was being watched, of the strange bumps in the night. She felt so relieved to finally be telling someone of all her fears, someone with no stake in the history, someone she could trust.

When she'd finished, the detective looked as if he was figuring out an algebra problem in his head. "What were you hoping to find in the garage?"

Kate shrugged. "I don't know, exactly. Suddenly, it seemed like the box was the key. Or, more precisely, what had been in the box. I guess I thought if I could examine it, see if any of the tiny shards were still inside, maybe I could figure out what the weapon was."

He smirked. "You don't think we cleaned out the box before returning it to the family, or that we hadn't tried to figure out the same thing a hundred times before?"

"I knew it was a long shot. But maybe, I don't know, because of time, perspective, I'd figure something out. I guess it comes down to questions. Detective Sweeney had them, and so do I. I went to the garage because I wanted to see the box again. Now that I know her stuff was stolen, it makes me even more certain that there was a clue there. And now it's gone."

"It's not all gone. We bagged every speck of evidence found in or near that box before returning it." Robak tapped the table with his sticky fingers. "We still have evidence from the crime scene, including shards from the statue."

"Statue? You know for certain the weapon was a statue?" she said with a rush of excitement.

"Sure," he said. "Give us some credit. We figured that out by analyzing the white shards scattered all over the room. It was made of high-quality marble."

"I knew the shards had been made of marble; it was in the report. But not that the weapon was a statue. Why was that fact not in the police report?"

A hint of a smile played on his lips. "It's not in *your* police report. It doesn't mean it's not in the file."

"Wow." She pushed her cinnamon roll aside. "Do you think the weapon…the statue was an antique?"

"No. An analysis of the marble showed it was new, no more than a year old, but still expensive high-quality."

"If it was new and expensive, couldn't you track down the artist and find out who bought it?"

He shook his head. "We tried, but the little we had of it wasn't enough to go on. What we do know is the crime was very violent. Marble doesn't break easily. The fact it chipped at all shows the killer must have been lashing out and hitting anything in his way. Gloria was the killer's target, but the weapon hit tables and chairs and—"

A whirl of images flashed in Kate's mind's eye as Robak spoke. Images of the dressing room she'd recently seen in her dream, but now that same room was the site of blood and destruction.

Her voice sounded empty, far away, as she heard herself say, "And the statue smashed the vase with the yellow roses from Winston and his beautiful flowers lay crumpled on the floor next to—"

"How'd you know that?" Robak grabbed her hand from across the table.

The dizzying vision stilled, and Kate was once

again staring into the detective's skeptical face.

"From the police report...I guess." She tried pulling her hand out of his grip but he didn't let go.

He shook his head. "Try again."

"Or maybe from an old newspaper. I don't know." She pulled away, and this time he let go of her hands. "I mean, it was everywhere that flowers were found at the scene."

"It was reported flowers were found but not the type that littered the ground next to Gloria. We held that fact back to ferret out the charlatans who get their kicks out of confessing to famous murders."

"You did?"

"Yeah." Robak's eyes narrowed in on her. "So tell me, *who* told you about the type of flowers found?"

Kate looked away from detective's penetrating stare.

Gloria told me. But who'd believe that?

She shrugged. "I just assumed. I mean, how could someone like Gloria not be given roses? And red ones would have been much too commonplace for her."

"You do raise questions." Robak rubbed his chin. "Okay, kiddo, tell you what. I'll pull some strings and review the file."

She wanted to cheer. Instead she tried to remain calm. Hard to do, between sugar, caffeine, and now a cop to help her—who knew relief could be so elating.

"Hey," she said. "Maybe it's better you're retiring. Could I hire you as a private detective or something? That way this can just stay between us."

"Sorry. My wife's already got our bags packed, ready to go live the easy life in Arizona on my pension. The last thing she wants is for me to be a private detective."

Interesting how he had emphasized the word *she* in the last sentence. Kate remembered how his eyes lit up when she mentioned she'd found new information about Gloria's murder. She leaned toward him with a conspiratorial smile. "Your wife doesn't want you to be a detective. What about you?"

"Don't get smart." He gave her a grudging nod. "Maybe I can take a look-see. Mind, I think this is all hooey. The burglary at your garage is probably not connected to Gloria's death. And don't take this the wrong way, but the bump in the night crap you talked about is probably just your imagination. So I wouldn't worry about it. The box being removed at least an hour before Winston left the set… That's interesting. Listen, this is stuff I can't sit on. It'll probably go nowhere, but I've got to let people know."

"We're so close to finishing the restoration of the film. We're just worried that if this gets out before we're done, it'll be taken away from us."

"You mean by J. B. Sutton, aka Smythe?"

"Yes. If he gets the film before we can restore and show it, I'm afraid it will conveniently get lost or be destroyed."

"That doesn't seem very important when you're talking about murder, but then I'm not a film buff."

"Please, can you wait just a little while? Let me talk to Jarvis."

Robak leaned back. "You said he's bankrolling this restoration, right?"

Kate nodded.

"If he doesn't want this out, I guess I can hold onto the information for a little while, but not too long."

"Just short-term. Jarvis agrees with me the film needs to be seen. That's the whole point. Give me a chance to convince him to make it public soon. Once we do, I don't care who knows about my suspicions, real or imagined."

Detective Robak pulled out a pen and wrote a phone number on a napkin. "My home number. Anything else happens you give me a call, okay?"

She felt like launching herself across the table and hugging him. "Thank you."

Chapter Thirteen

Dylan and Kate had agreed it was important they put in six solid hours on the restoration before doing any sleuthing. After a couple of days of this routine, their ideas on how to investigate this old murder staled. Then Kate lit on an idea. "Why not do a list of suspects like they do in books?"

Dylan looked up from the jars of nasty chemicals they used in the restoration and gave her a wry smile. "Novels, you mean."

"Sure. Doesn't mean it's not a good idea. Even fiction can be instructive."

"*I* always thought so." He walked to the sink in the cottage's pocket kitchen and washed his hands.

An hour later they sat huddled over the center table with the police report and four legal-sized pages taped together, on which they had created a chart with columns for name, motive, evidence, and whereabouts at the time of the murder.

Winston Nash was easy. Everyone knew his motive from all the old newspaper articles. Kate wrote: *He believed Gloria was having an affair.*

"And he was known for alcoholic rage, volatile mood swings," Kate said. In the evidence column, she wrote *Winston seen threatening Gloria* and *Found in a drunken stupor with no memory of what had occurred and shards of the murder weapon leading to his office door*.

She looked up at Dylan. "That's pretty strong. He's still the prime suspect, in my book."

"Maybe. But we now know there was at least an hour between the murder weapon being moved and when Winston could have possibly gone to Gloria's dressing room."

Dylan tapped a fingertip on the chart. "J.B. Sutton is my guess. Hell, if half the rumors are true about how he uses his power, this wouldn't be his first murder, or ordered murder, so for my money alibi is irrelevant. He'd hire someone."

Kate shook her head. "I just don't buy it. Sutton orchestrating the theft of the footage is one thing, but killing Gloria, why?"

"What if she saw something, like the person who stole the film?"

She nodded. "Okay, we'll look into that. This leads to the person who had the footage—Charles Needham. What do you think? Did he steal the footage for himself? Like, was he just some obsessed fan? Or did Sutton or someone else hire him?"

"I say Sutton hired him. Gloria catches him stealing the film. Chuck goes all psycho and kills her."

"And that's based on what?"

"Nothing," he admitted. "But it's plausible, isn't it?"

Next on the suspect list was Beatrice Talbot.

"No good," Kate said. "As much as I'd like to pin this on her, her alibi is ironclad."

"What do you mean? We saw that she was on the set that day."

Kate flipped through the police report to the

section on Beatrice and handed it to Dylan. "Our enterprising Detective Sweeney did a thorough examination of her. Look here. The problem is she had witnesses for almost the entire day. The studio gate logged her in twenty minutes before her first meeting. That would have given her just enough time to do a quick stop on the set, which coincides perfectly with when we glimpsed her in the footage. At that point Gloria was still very much alive. After that, Beatrice's whereabouts are accounted for by plenty of witnesses. First, she had a meeting in Bungalow 4B with some studio bigwigs. She's then seen in the very public commissary dining with Jarvis. According to the police report, an eyewitness corroborates the time. They go together to another meeting at the studio, also verified. The police report shows Jarvis and Beatrice remained in that meeting until it was interrupted with the news of Gloria's death. It can't be Beatrice."

"What about Jarvis?"

"Based on what? You don't like him." Kate shook her head. "His alibi's tighter than Beatrice's. He was on the flight from New York in the morning. Lots of people verified that. Logistically, there's really only enough time for him to get from the airport to Sutton's studio in Culver City, where he's seen in the commissary with Beatrice. The studio gate log confirms his arrival was only minutes before he was seen in the commissary. Even more important, if he had a motive back then it was to keep her alive. Remember, Jarvis was just starting out, and Gloria was his cash-cow client."

Dylan tilted back his chair. "Okay, that takes care of that." He thumped his chair back down. "I agree. It's impossible it was Jarvis. The man only values money and power. His motive was to keep her alive."

"That's not fair."

Dylan's dark brown eyes twinkled with amusement. "Why? Are you offended I'm saying that all he cares about is money and power, or that I'm saying that poor misunderstood Jarvis isn't Gloria's killer?"

"Both." She slapped the table to emphasize her point. "I don't buy your premise, and I *do* think he's misunderstood. I mean, even with all his power, doesn't he strike you as lonely?"

"Okay. You win. Jarvis did it." Dylan smiled mischievously.

"You're impossible."

He leaned in closer. He had a musky scent mixed with the sharp odor of the acetone they used in the restoration. Still, she didn't move away. She liked being near him and feeling the soft rhythm of his breath against her check.

In the past, she'd been taken aback by his sometimes broad emotional swings. That didn't matter now. She felt him: his strength, his humor, and even his own feelings of anxiety about being close to her. Yet, despite everything, they were somehow doing it. They were getting closer.

She leaned toward him knowing deep inside that there was no need to be afraid that he'd magically metamorphose into that awful photographer and hurt her.

Besides it was past time that one bad incident kept ruling her life. Dylan wasn't like that. He wasn't a monster.

She'd also not allow herself to be dominated by her feelings for him. They'd stay buddies, and also have sex—after all everyone was doing it.

That was it! She could make that work!

She grabbed his arms, ready to kiss him, except she didn't get further than the grab, which admittedly may have been very rough, for Dylan jerked back.

Rubbing his arm he said, "Hey, why'd you hit me?"

From behind, she heard her aunt laugh.

"I was going to apologize for interrupting, but I see there's no need." Her aunt sashayed from the doorway into the center of the room. "Pathetic."

"Lil," Dylan said, "you didn't interrupt anything."

"No." Her aunt shook her head. "That's painfully clear."

Lillian whispered in Kate's ear, "It's hard to believe we're related. Lessons in seduction are in order." Then the chart of suspects caught her aunt's eye.

Kate cursed herself for not hiding it when she came in.

Lillian leaned over the table to take a closer look. "Oh, dear. You really have become obsessed. I know what you're trying to do, and it's imbecilic."

"We're just trying to figure out—"

"Still, if you're going to list suspects, you should make it complete." Lillian snatched up a pen from the table and scribbled something on the chart.

Kate looked at the chart. Lillian had written her own name there. "I'd never suspect—"

"Well, you should. If you insist upon playing this dangerous game, then no one is above suspicion.

Anyway, I know you already suspect me, whether you admit it or not. That's why you accused me of lying to the police about leaving your mother alone on the set that day." She wrote under the alibi column for her, *None*.

"I'm sorry," Kate said. "That was just my old adolescent anger talking. I know you loved your sister. I'd never think it was you. You had no motive."

Lillian lifted Kate's chin with cold fingers and looked her in the eyes. "Jealousy, my dear. Jealousy."

Her aunt looked at the chart again. "In fact, you could add that to practically everyone's motive column." She tapped a scarlet fingernail on a blank space. "Especially Beatrice."

"Why?"

"Gloria was Jarvis's number-one client. He treated her like a goddess, while Beatrice did all the work and was treated like a grunt."

Lillian pointed to Jarvis's column. "Him, too." She wrote his name down. "Don't let your feelings about people get in your way. That was Gloria's mistake."

Dylan glanced at the chart then looked up at Lillian. Their gazes locked, and although they did not say a word, Kate had the feeling an entire conversation passed between them.

Lillian was the first to break the connection. "I almost forgot, Kate. Jarvis is in his study, and he wants to speak to you immediately.

Turning with a dramatic flourish, the way only her aunt could, Lillian sailed out of the guest house, leaving the aroma of Shalimar perfume in her wake.

****

Kate approached Jarvis's study as if it were the

principal's office, except she didn't know what she had done wrong. When Jarvis opened the door, the answer appeared. Detective Robak stood in front of her.

He looked anywhere but in her eyes as he walked past her. "I'm sorry, Kate. I thought letting him know was for the best."

She watched Robak leave, then looked back into the study. A place with red hues, comforting books, and rich mahogany furniture nonetheless felt as frigid as an ice box because of Jarvis's cold expression.

He waited for her to explain.

She took a deep breath. No words formed. Instead, her mind reeled as she tried to take in the fact that Robak had informed Jarvis about what she'd told him. Robak was probably in Jarvis's pay like everyone else seemed to be. She'd hoped the detective would be someone who'd help her make sense of things, tell her when it was time to back off, and when her fears were justified. She felt alone.

Jarvis tapped his gold pen on his desk.

And in trouble.

"So you lack the honor to come clean," Jarvis said.

Not a hint of anger in his words. That would have required too much feeling. The tapping of his pen showed irritation, disappointment. Yet, his expression was as dismissive and uninterested as if he were dealing with the valet that brought his car back with a scratch on it.

"I'm sorry. I was both trying not to be stupid and not let the secret out. I guess I failed."

"You did. Luckily, Detective Robak is a good man. He came to me and not Sutton. From what I hear, if Sutton picks up one more little hint, he's going to put this whole thing together. But that's my fault."

Hoping this admission signaled a softening, Kate inched toward his desk.

"I shouldn't have given in to your request," he said in a way that made clear he had no intention of doing that again.

She'd grown used to seeing the twinkle in Jarvis's eyes when he looked at her. There was no hint of that now. The rejection punched inside her, the same way it had when she was a little girl of five and had crawled into her father's closet and discovered all his clothes were gone.

Strange, how she'd think of that moment of supreme abandonment. She wasn't sure when it had happened exactly, but while living here with Jarvis and Lillian and working with Dylan, a feeling of belonging had wrapped around her like a comfortable blanket.

Jarvis still tapped his pen. "When I contacted Sutton's people to say Gloria's granddaughter wished to have an interview with him, it sparked the gluttonous bastard to begin digging into what we're doing. But I keep my promises. Sutton's agreed to see you. I'll let you know the details when I learn them."

"Wonderful. Thank you!" She smiled at him, but he wouldn't look at her.

Jarvis's tight expression should have told her to let it go, but she felt a gnawing desire to find a way to restore her fantasy family.

He waved his hand at a garment bag slung over the chair nearest the fireplace. "There's your dress for the party, unless you plan to go back on that promise, too."

"No, of course not."

"Fine. The clock's ticking, which means no more

playing detective. Focus only on your job here. Get that film restored so I can show it before Sutton's lawyers start hounding my ass."

"You *do* want to show it. I *knew* it." She felt a rush of gratitude.

He glared at her. "What do you think this has all been about?"

"Even if it's inevitable Golden State Pictures will take it away from us," she asked.

"Nothing's inevitable. But just in case we don't get it, I'm going to wring every drop of publicity I can get out of this operation for our remake. The party to reveal the footage is critical to that end." He turned his attention back to the papers on his desk, as if she didn't even exist.

"Jarvis?"

Without looking up, he said, "You should have trusted me. I told you I'd handle it. Now we don't have much time before the lid blows off this thing. Get to work."

She picked up the garment bag and unzipped it. The gown had the shape of a 1940's frock, something that could have been worn by Gloria, but is was no replica. In fact, as Kate inspected it more closely, she saw the colors and the design had a contemporary 1970's edge. It was made of silk and had large swirls of understated browns and dark greens. They were colors that fit her unlike the glitter of Gloria's costumes. This dress was luxurious and sexy. She closed her eyes and wished, for once, the old fear of being looked at would go away and she could wear that dress, and be all of those things, and still be herself.

She looked at Jarvis, who was gazing at her now,

his expression soft.

A tingle like a mild electrical current ran through her.

"Oh!" Kate said softly as she pulled the frock free and placed it against her body. It molded against her silhouette perfectly.

Only a minute ago she'd felt cast out, but now she experienced acceptance, approval, and even admiration.

"It's lovely," she told him, hugging the dress to herself. She laughed. "I was afraid you were going to dress me up to look like Gloria for the party."

"Would you have done it?"

Kate suspected her obvious disgust at the prospect was written all over her face. Still she said, "I promised to, didn't I? Yes, I would have worn it."

Jarvis got up and walked toward her. "Don't worry. I'm not that morbid. But that doesn't mean I'm not above taking advantage of your resemblance to Gloria at the party, or in my remake of *Emperor Smythe*." He circled her slowly. "You know, it's not just that you're her granddaughter. Whether you like it or not, there is an indefinable spark you share with her. It pops out when you walk into a room, and I'll wager it will on the screen too, just like her."

Excitement fluttered through Kate. Which was altogether bizarre, considering she stood upon the precipice of the thing she swore she'd never become.

"I'll play that angle for all its worth." Jarvis's tone so matter of fact, so honest. "The press and the public love those connections to the past, stories, rebirths—all that sentimental crap. What makes a blockbuster is finding what's new in an old story. That's you, Kate. I have every intention of exploiting it."

She laughed. "We'll see." A feeling of power swelled inside her. Or was that just an illusion?

"Jarvis? I'm sorry about Robak. I know we agreed to tell no one. I won't do it again."

"You better not." He pointed to the silk dress in her hands. "I want you to wear that to the screen test."

"Yes." She nodded, determined not to be an outcast any longer. "I will."

He looked over her shoulder out to the hallway beyond his study. "Don't you agree, Dylan?" He twirled her around.

She felt her cheeks burn as she faced Dylan, who looked so angry he could have had steam boiling out of his ears.

"Won't she look exquisite at her *screen test*?"

"What?" Kate spun on her heel and faced Jarvis. "We were talking about the party, weren't we? I don't want to do the screen test. I didn't agree—"

"You just did." Dylan snapped his jaw down tight.

Jarvis smiled. "Yes, you did. It pays, to pay attention, Kate. Now you two get back to work. I need this restoration completed. We have a schedule to keep." He closed the door to his study. The discussion was over.

Chapter Fourteen

"You got off on that, on him, didn't you?" Dylan said.

"What?"

"You're so full of shit." He turned and stomped away.

Kate hurried after him. "I don't know what you're talking about." She'd be damned if she'd let his blustering temper intimidate her.

He stopped and looked at her. "Or maybe you don't. Isn't that ironic? You claim to be on a crusade to reveal the truth hidden beneath the surface, but at the same time you're oblivious to your own motivations."

"That's not true," she said.

"Really? Why is it you only want me if it's some bullshit platonic deal, while with Jarvis you don't think twice about acting like a prized trinket? The thing you claim to hate, by the way."

"I don't act—"

"Oh, yes, you do," he shouted, then paused as if regretting his outburst.

She watched his anger dissipate as he took a deep breath and raked his fingers through his wavy hair.

"The funny thing is, I get it," he said. "I've spent my life shielding myself from having any real feelings toward a woman. So afraid I'd lose control."

Had she done the same thing with her own fears?

Was she the biggest fraud of all?

"But the only thing I've gained from running away from passion is a passionless life."

The pain she saw in his eyes was real. With this honesty, he was more courageous than she could ever hope to be.

"For me, that's too big of a price." He took her hand. "What do *you* want, Kate?"

She glanced away.

He dropped her hand, and the world turned cold.

"Fine," he said roughly. "Have that life. You've already figured how to do it, too—playing Jarvis's sex symbol."

"That isn't fair." Or was it?

"No?" Dylan challenged. His wide set face, strong chin, and generous lips now appeared brutish, just like all guys when they don't get what they want, and in that moment Kate hated him.

"Whoa!" A familiar voice, with the drawl of a cowboy calming a spirited horse, said behind her. "What's with the murderous atmosphere?"

It was Mallick. He stood in the doorway between the solarium and the foyer.

Jimena stood near him like a prison guard. "This person was wandering around the gardens. He said he knows you." She looked at Mallick with distaste. "Mr. Benjamin doesn't like unannounced guests."

"I'm sorry," Dylan said. "I'll make sure you're warned next time. Right, buddy?" he said to Mallick.

"Absolutely."

Jimena wiped her hands on her brown polyester pants and marched out.

Mallick pointed after her with what looked like a

rolled-up script. "That's one scary lady. When she caught me outside, she actually dragged me by the ear a couple of steps."

Kate didn't comment. She was too busy willing her heart rate back to a semblance of normalcy.

The lanky Mallick loped around the foyer, peering into all the connecting rooms.

"Come with me." Dylan ushered them into the solarium and closed the door.

Staring through the glass patio door to the backyard, Mallick said, "Wow, this is one big place. Tell me, is the evil Jarvis Benjamin around?"

"Evil?" Kate crossed her arms. "Are the two of you in cahoots?"

Mallick grinned. "Come on, everyone knows he's scary. You must have heard the stories about Jarvis B. With the stable of talent he controlled in the Fifties, he almost singlehandedly brought down the old movie studio titans." Mallick made a rectangle with his thumbs and index fingers and panned it around the room like a movie director setting up a shot. "But instead of destroying the fascist studio structures that made artists into cogs in a wheel, he made a stronger, more imperious conglomerate for himself to rule."

Kate sniffed. "I don't hear anything evil in that. Just smart."

"Tell that to all the artists and producers who quake when he walks into a room. He makes and breaks careers in the blink of an eye."

"Only big Hollywood careers, and I'm not interested in that," Kate said.

"Yeah, right," said Dylan. "Why don't you tell Mallick about your screen test?"

Mallick looked at her, wide-eyed. "Screen test? For Ms. Hollywood is a sellout and I only want to direct art films?"

Dylan looked annoyingly smug. "Guess who enticed her?"

"Jarvis B, of course." Mallick laughed. "See, I told you—evil."

Dylan smiled at his friend. "So what brings you here?"

"I need your help on my horror film," Mallick said.

"I think you mean *my* horror film." Dylan bristled. "Skyline promised me that I'd direct *Satan's Academy*. I wrote it for that damned factory, and I had done some pre-production, and then they give it to you."

"You're huffing and puffing over something called *Satan's Academy*?" Kate said.

"Hey, it's a job."

"Not art," she said.

Dylan rolled his eyes. "Oh, come on."

"She has a point," Mallick said.

Dylan crossed his arms. "Fine, not art. But it's still creative work. At least the way I was going to set up some of the shots."

"Are you going to keep being pissed off," Mallick said, "or are you going to give a guy some help?"

"Sorry, man. Let's just say I've had a frustrating day." Dylan shot a pointed look at Kate before turning his attention back to Mallick. "Tell me what I can do."

"Come out to Skyline today. I'd like to get your input on a couple of things."

"Sure."

"Can I go?" Kate asked.

"I thought you were above B movies," Mallick

said.

"Actually, *Satan's Academy* is more like a C movie," Dylan admitted. Then, he shot Kate a sexy smile that made her toes curl with delight.

How did he do that?

"Anyways Jarvis might get angry," Dylan taunted. "Remember we have his schedule to keep."

"I don't care what Jarvis thinks," Kate said, and those simple words released something in her.

Dylan appeared skeptical.

"I don't. I'd rather be with you guys."

That wasn't so hard to say. She smiled at both of them. "I'm not as snobby as you two seem to think I am."

Both of them stared at her.

"I'm not!"

"Great." Mallick unrolled his script on a table. "I'll take help any way I can get it. The biggest problem is the monster."

Kate made a face. "Monster? No one is doing that anymore. Couldn't it be a psychotic janitor or something more realistic?"

"Monsters lead to metaphor," Dylan said. "Psychotics just to problems with their mother."

Mallick grinned. "You should know. You've got the scariest mom I've ever met."

Intrigued, Kate said, "Really? What's she like?"

Dylan gave Mallick a warning look.

His friend shrugged. "Oh, you know, just your normal everyday housewife. Isn't that right, Dylan?" `

"She's…colorful. Let's leave it at that."

Kate itched to know more, but she remembered what he'd said about his own fears of intimacy and thought better of it. So instead she turned to Mallick. "I believe you had a question about monsters."

"Monster, singular," Mallick said.

"I like metaphors." Dylan shot Kate a wicked grin. "It's very arty."

"She could be right," Mallick said. "Today's audience might not buy it. Even when our monster is created by an old pro like Ted Orlov, who was taught stop-motion animation by the great Ray Harryhausen himself."

"Who?" Kate asked.

"You know, the guy who did the special effects for all the greats, everything from *Mysterious Island* to *Jason and the Argonauts*."

"Never saw them," Kate said.

Mallick looked dumbfounded. "You're kidding me."

"Neorealism they're not," Dylan said. "But if you're looking for fantastic creatures and sword-brandishing skeletons, no one beats Harryhausen, although Ted comes close. You'll like this about him, Kate. He was studying to get his Ph.D. in art history until Hollywood called to him like the Pied Piper, and he never turned back. The guy knows everything about sculpture. Shit! Why didn't I think about him before? Let's go talk to Ted about your monster," he said to Mallick. Then Dylan leaned close to her and whispered, "Bring the police report. He may be able to tell us something about *our* monster, too."

"What?"

"Didn't you hear me? Ted's an expert in sculpture. He knows everything and almost everyone who makes a living at this. Maybe even someone who worked thirty years ago."

****

Skyline Studios didn't look like a studio, or what Kate imagined a production company should look like. It was nondescript in the extreme. A long, rectangular, two-story stucco building that resembled the warehouses and discount furniture stores that lined Washington Boulevard just south of midtown Los Angeles.

She got out of Dylan's Mustang and gazed down the wide street, which stretched for miles. This part of the city seemed like a conveyor belt for people going from one part of the city to another, with no restaurants or movie theaters or anything else to encourage people to stop.

Kate was disappointed to discover the interior of Skyline Studio was just as unattractive as the exterior, with its stained linoleum floors and greenish florescent lighting.

Mallick said he'd meet them later at the special-effects lab. He darted up the stairs to meet with an executive producer on the movie.

Kate and Dylan walked down a long hallway filled with framed posters from every type of pulp movie imaginable and entered the crowded room that was the special-effects department. She delighted in all the exquisite tiny figurines that filled rows of shelves. On the tables and the walls were drawings and watercolors of fantastical scenes. Here movie magic was born.

But, of course, she'd never admit that to Dylan.

The room also reminded her a bit of her mother's collection, which oddly always seemed the opposite of magic to her.

Here, the shelves filled with models, even if some were grotesque, portrayed a sense of whimsy and fun, like a child's collection of beloved toys. Her mother's figurines, each meticulously cleaned and placed, were sealed tight in her china cabinet, like imprisoned dreams.

"Hi, Ted," Dylan said to a man in his forties. He had a rotund stomach and long hair the color of amusement park lemonade, tied in a ponytail. He looked up from a model of a dinosaur that was no more than eight inches high and waved them in.

Dylan took a close look at the model. "Cool. What's this for?"

"New project called *The Realm of the Dinosaur*," Ted said. "Which, of course, has humans and dinosaurs and saber-toothed tigers all living at the same time."

"That's ridiculous," Kate said.

"Yes, but it's fun."

Ted stood and placed his plaster-encrusted hand on Dylan's shoulder. "Hey, I was sorry to hear they took *Satan's Academy* away from you. You wrote a great script, much better than the usual fare that comes out of here."

"Yeah, the bastards promised me I'd get to make it, then they gave my script to Mallick. But, better him than anyone else, I guess. He'll be down in a minute, and before he gets here, I have a favor to ask."

"Ask away, amigo."

"Are you still plugged in with the art scene? I mean people working as sculptors?"

Ted folded his arms over his bulging stomach. "Are you implying I'm no longer a sculptor?"

"Never. You're one of the best, but I don't mean

163

for film. I'm talking about people who sculpt in marble and sell it privately, that kind of thing."

Ted made a face. "That's mostly machine-manufactured crap. You know, every *nouveau riche* jerk wants a copy of Michelangelo's *David* or Bacchus holding grapes for the center of their garden. Usually, they're made with molds, using cement or second-rate marble. In that situation, unless something was stamped with the manufacturer's mark, it would be impossible to tell who made it."

"The one we're trying to ID we know is marble." Kate thumbed through the police report, then read: "It is Bianco Carrara, pure white with no visible marbling."

Ted nodded, appearing impressed. "Expensive. Possibly even ancient."

"I don't think so," Kate said. "The analysis said it had no sign of corrosion and concluded it was new."

"That's probably right, although not definite," Ted said. "I'd need to see it. The good news is if it was recently acquired from the quarry in Massa-Carrara, they'd have logged in who bought it. Why do you want to know?"

"Can you keep a secret?" Dylan asked.

"I would've been out of job a long time ago if I couldn't. Are you going to get to your point?"

Kate handed the police report to Ted.

He flipped through the pages. "You're looking into Gloria Reardon's murder? Don't tell me you're a conspiracy theorist? Everyone knows Winston did it."

"Gloria was my grandmother." Kate watched Ted study her features, then he leaned back in his chair and let out a long whistle.

"We've come up with some anomalies," she

continued.

"Yeah," Dylan said. "The police concluded Gloria was killed by being smashed in the head with a marble statue. But they never figured out what the statue was of or who gave it to her."

"Okay, let me take a look." Ted scanned the report. On page three, he slapped the report shut and handed it to Kate. "Shards? You want me to identify the artist from shards? I'm good, but not that good."

"Please. Anything you can come up with might help."

Ted took the report back. "Okay, let me think."

She smiled at Ted. From afar, the big guy could be mistaken for a tough biker. Up close he had a pudgy face with fine wrinkles and an expression full of kindness.

He pointed to a page in the report. "It says here the box was shiny white, about two-and-half-feet long by eight-inches wide, like a box for long stem roses. So the statue would be smaller than what's usual for a garden unless it was part of a set, which it could have been."

"Anything else?" Kate said.

"Not much more I can tell you unless I can see some part of the workmanship. From what's reported here, I can't even tell if it was handmade or machine-manufactured, much less who made it."

Kate knew she shouldn't feel disappointed. After all, Ted wasn't a wizard that could look at the paltry facts that tons of other people had reviewed before and make discoveries out of thin air. Yet, she did feel let down. Seeing all the wondrous things in this room that he made come to life, some part of her had hoped he was able to conjure up answers.

Ted tapped a finger against his cheek. "Strange to have something like that in a cardboard box. A statue like that would normally be in a wooden crate, not a flimsy box typically used for flowers."

She stepped toward him. "Forensics said nothing about plant residue in the box but a lot about finding specs of marble."

"That's not my point," he said. "It's packaged like it's a gift from a lover."

"Doesn't that suggest Winston then?" she said. "Wait a minute. What if I can get you an actual piece of the marble to examine?"

"How?" Dylan's eyes widened. "Everything you had was stolen."

"Detective Robak said the police have some in evidence. What if we can convince him to let you see it?"

Dylan frowned. "Detective Robak? You talked to him, the rookie in the report, and you didn't tell me?"

She huffed. "I wasn't aware I was supposed to be reporting to you."

"Not *supposed* to, no. I thought we were in this together."

Kate didn't know what to say. Luckily, she didn't have to, because Mallick swung open the door. "Hey, what's happening? How's my Satan coming along?"

Ted handed the police report back to Kate. She tucked it into her army-bag purse.

The SFX guy walked over to his wall of figurines and carefully picked up an eight-inch doll that looked half human, half reptile. "Here he is."

"Ah, good." Mallick moved the hands or claws or whatever they were back and forth, testing the model's full range of motion.

"Was this how you saw him?" Ted asked.

Peering over Mallick's shoulder, Dylan said, "No, this is better."

Kate examined the humanoid figurine, which had green scales and a long, pointed face with razor-sharp teeth. "That doesn't look like Satan. It looks more like a...I don't know what."

"It's not literary Satan," Dylan explained. "Although in the film the school administrators feed and worship it like it was, but in the end it's found to be nothing more than the ever present hunger for more flesh."

Kate shook her head. "Let me guess. The flesh of pretty young girls."

"Naturally," Dylan said.

"Metaphor, my eye," Kate said. "It's just an excuse to show scantily clad women fighting the savage beast."

Dylan grinned. "That sounds like a metaphor to me."

Mallick stepped toward her and laughed. "You know, women fighting off the rapacious hunger of men."

Kate took a step back and wrapped her arms protectively in front of her waist. "That's not a metaphor, that's a sexist stereotype."

"Sure, but an apt one." Mallick shrugged and turned back to Ted.

Dylan remained staring at her in a way that sent a chill through her.

She looked down.

When she peered back up, she saw there had been nothing cruel in Dylan's gaze, in fact, what she now saw was kindness, an expression of understanding.

She smiled at him. Their gazes locked. And for a moment, she felt a sense of knowing, of connection. It was lovely.

"Hey," Ted said. "You're here to talk about your monster, right? So what do you think?"

Mallick turned the figurine in his hands. "It's phenomenal. Although Kate's got me thinking about whether people will buy this kind of creature in the realistic setting of a girl's private school. You know, that suddenly there's this big green monster waving its arms in the middle of a classroom. I'm not sure if an audience will scream or laugh at the sight."

"I've made a suit," Ted said. "You could do some of the sequences with a man in a costume and other shots with the model. That's how *King Kong* was done, and it still works."

Dylan touched the model. "Good idea. I love how you have these very human eyes and then razor-sharp teeth. Pretty cool. That unexpected juxtaposition that will make an audience jump."

"That's it, isn't it?" Kate said. "The shock of the teeth that shouldn't be there or scales on a man's hand. Startling and scary. An image, even from a nightmare, once fully seen, no longer offers surprise. It's the unknown that's terrifying."

Mallick scrunched his rubbery face. "Duh. That's Film 101, but this is Skyline. They want monsters."

Dylan nodded. "Yeah, but I like the idea. We only reveal him at the end, conquered and weak, something to be pitied. But in his predatory power, he is only glimpsed, eyes staring through keyholes, claws scratching on bedroom walls. Maybe the occasional shot of the beast but so fast audiences won't be sure what they saw."

Kate snapped her fingers. "I love that. I saw that in a movie once. It scared me silly and made me crazy. Did I see what I thought I saw? I was left trembling and craving a glimpse of it again."

Dylan grabbed the script and penciled in directions.

"Hold on," Mallick said. "I don't know if the producer will sign off on this. I don't want to blow it."

"Then do it right," Dylan yelled. He hurriedly paged through the script. "Shit!" He exploded again. His booming voice bellowed and he pointed at Mallick in barely contained rage. "You fucking changed my ending."

"No, Skyline did and they own the script."

"I wrote it!"

From behind him, Kate put her hand on Dylan's arm, hoping to calm him.

Instead, he jumped at her touch and swung around, and when he did, he knocked her—hard.

Stumbling from the force of his hit, Kate's head jumbled with images.

Crack! She watched Gloria fall dead.

Slam! The man knocked thirteen-year-old Kate to the bed.

Then an all-consuming picture seared in her consciousness. She was in Gloria's dressing room, furniture and objects tossed and broken. A corpse, with red hair just like hers, lay on the floor drenched in blood. It was more than seeing it. Kate felt the sticky blood against her own cheek, heard the thumps of the assailant's footsteps walk away, and saw the twilight flicker of consciousness as it dimmed. Her view of the scene panned in to the dead body. Kate watched with horror as the corpse's features changed from Gloria's to her own.

"No!"

Kate shook, the room spun, and when her eyes refocused, she saw row upon row of tiny malevolent creatures perched on the shelves in Ted's workshop.

Insane or not, she now felt certain the presence, Gloria, was here to protect her, to warn her to find the killer before Kate becomes his or her next victim.

Dizzy and shaky from the vision, she struggled to lift herself from the floor.

Dylan ran to her. "I'm sorry. I didn't mean...I would never..."

He must have seen the anger in her eyes because he backed away.

Ted knelt by her and helped her up. "You okay?"

Physically unhurt, she still trembled so hard she couldn't form an answer.

Dylan returned, his eyes lowered. "I'm so sorry. Let me take you back to Jarvis's."

Mallick stepped between them and told his friend. "You need to cool off. I'll take her home."

Dylan looked at Kate, his eyes pleading.

She edged away from him, shaking her head.

"Fine," Dylan said. And then he was gone.

Chapter Fifteen

Kate's trembling hadn't yet subsided when she slid into the front seat of Mallick's old Chevrolet Vega. She knew Dylan hadn't purposefully meant to hurt her. She'd startled him. That's all.

He wasn't violent. Was he?

She did know he got angry easily. She'd seen that before. He'd shout and stomp. But she'd never seen him hit or threaten or throw things. God knows, her mom in her darkest moments was worse. But it was different when it was a guy. They were big. They could overpower her.

She also couldn't expunge the vision of her face superimposed on Gloria's dead body. She rubbed her own arms seeking comfort.

Mallick looked at her with concern. He leaned over and opened the glove compartment and pulled out a cough drop tin and flipped it open.

It held an assortment of previously smoked joints and a bobby pin, Kate assumed was used as a roach clip. All she needed was to be in a car accident on top of everything else. "If you're going to smoke, I'm not driving with you. Besides, I thought you were off drugs for the shoot."

"I am," Mallick said. "This is for you. You need it."

Yeah, she did.

She picked the smallest tail end of a smoked joint and lit up. At first the stuff left her more low than high. But after Mallick stopped by a liquor store and she added a little vodka and orange juice to the smoke, she was feeling just fine.

Parked in Mallick's car on a residential street not far from the liquor store, Kate took another drag of the joint before stubbing it out in the ash tray. Between hacking coughs, she asked, "Why did Dylan get so angry? Where did that come from?"

"He had some intense stuff going on when he was growing up."

"Like what?"

Mallick shifted in the seat. "His mom, for one. Very controlling, made everyone keep up appearances, or else. Which is hard when you have a son like Dylan, who is full of big messy feelings. Don't worry, though. I've known Dylan since prep school. The only person I've ever seen him beat up is himself."

"But why explode at all? It's just a horror film."

"That wasn't the only trigger and you know it. When I walked in on you two earlier, something was going on between you. And something's been going on at that house, but Dylan won't tell me what it is. I was hoping you'd tell me."

Kate wondered if affable Mallick had been plying her with grass and alcohol hoping she'd reveal something about the footage. She clamped her dry lips together, determined not to give anything away.

"Then there's you," Mallick said.

That got her attention.

"He's got it bad. It scares him."

"Dylan? No way. He's so sure of himself with

women."

"That's just an act. Or haven't you noticed?"

Had she noticed? She looked out the window, and everything appeared blurry. She wished she hadn't smoked that joint or drank that vodka. Her thoughts moved like molasses, and yet she wanted to think about Dylan.

Her feelings toward him resembled a stoplight that blinked red and green at the same time. Dylan's quirky smile, his funny and at times maddening sense of humor urged her toward him. Yet, a nagging feeling inside warned her to stay away. He couldn't quite be trusted. He was hiding something.

Or were those thoughts due to fear of being close to any man?

Kate tried to focus on Mallick through her inebriated haze. "You've known Dylan a long time, is he…"

"Safe?" Mallick smiled. "Yes. He's a good guy, Kate."

By the time they got back to Jarvis's circular driveway, it was dark. Kate scowled at the sight of Beatrice's Buick Riviera in the driveway. "Eew."

Mallick laughed. "What a face. I bet the camera's gonna love you."

Kate rolled her eyes. "Not you too." She stumbled getting out of the car. Regaining her balance, she opened her arms to the night sky. "Woo, look at all the stars!" She toppled backward. Mallick caught her in his arms when she fell.

"Man, you're a lightweight," he said.

Kate struggled out of his arms. "Who said you could put your arms around me?"

"Whoa. Don't worry. You're not my type."

"I'm not? That's so cool!" She grabbed his hands, and they spun around the way children do.

Big mistake.

Everything continued to spin even after she stood still. She stepped cautiously toward the front of the house, but on her fifth step, her foot landed in a flower bed.

Mallick offered his hand.

She took it and allowed him to guide her up the walkway. "Wait a minute. Why not?"

"Why not what?"

"Why am I not your type?"

"Don't get me wrong, Kate. You're lovely, but I go more for the petite, spunky type. You know, the Mary Anns of this world. You're pure Ginger, even if you haven't accepted it yet."

Kate made a face. "Spunky." The word felt vile in her mouth.

"Said like a true Ginger."

"I have no idea what you're talking about."

A man leapt from the shadows off the entryway and shouted, "*Gilligan's Island* for Christ's sake!"

Kate and Mallick jumped back in surprise.

"How can you not know that?" Dylan said.

"Where did you come from?" Kate slurred. "Where's your car? I didn't see it."

"Hey, man," Mallick said. "What's with the stalking? Are you following us?"

"No. Yes. Maybe… Shit. I came to apologize for being such an asshole. I shouldn't have gone off like that. I wanted to say I'm sorry to both of you."

"It's okay, man." Mallick stood behind Kate,

helping to steady her.

Dylan stepped to within inches of her. "Kate, are you all right? I swear I didn't mean to hurt you."

"I know." She tried to look him in the eye. The world tilted, and she went with it. Mallick had to catch her again.

"Disgusting!" a shrill voice said.

Even in her inebriated condition, Kate had no trouble recognizing the unmistakable drawl of Beatrice's Vassar accent.

Beatrice clopped down the front steps in her black pumps. "Take your *ménage a trois* off Jarvis's property. We can see you from the living room."

Kate scrunched her face. "*Ménage*…are you nuts?" Then she realized she was sandwiched quite closely between Dylan and Mallick.

Beatrice gestured toward the house. "Jarvis and Lillian may be too polite to say anything, but—"

"Not a problem for you, though," Dylan quipped.

"It's always been my job to clean up Jarvis's trash, whether he asks me to or not. You're his guest, Kate. Act with some decorum. This isn't the place for your hippie orgies."

"Orgy?" Kate said incredulous at even the thought.

The porch light came on, and Jarvis, followed by Lillian, walked out the front door. Lillian looked as if she was about to laugh. Jarvis, on the other hand, didn't appear to be so happy. The overhead light exaggerated his scowl and the lines in his face. Kate shrank from the way he seemed to be judging her.

Beatrice crossed her arms. "Dangling two men on a string is a very dangerous game. You of all people should know that."

No way was she going to let Beatrice get the best of to her, not this time. Even if Kate felt like a wimp, she could pretend otherwise. Hadn't she come from a whole family of pretenders? Besides, doing anything was better than behaving the way she actually felt, which was overwhelmed, stoned, and most disturbing of all, a bit turned on by the way both Dylan and Jarvis were staring at her.

She took a deep breath and imagined herself to be witty and confident, with a dash of élan, like Lillian always seemed to be. No, even better, she'd be like…

Her insides caught fire. Kate's shoulder rolled back and she laughed.

She was Gloria.

And that was all it took for the burning presence that Kate had felt hovering nearby ever since she found that footage ignite inside her. This time she let it in, wanted it in, and it filled her completely.

She tossed her red mane of hair and in a throaty voice deeper than her normal register she said, "Yes, why deny it?" She kissed a confused-looking Mallick, then broke for air, and an otherworldly laugh sprang from her lips. "It's true. If Beatrice hadn't interrupted us, we would have done it, right here on the front steps."

Kate flung her arms wide and felt the adrenaline rush of being on stage, which she basically was, because God knows she wasn't behaving like herself.

She leaned into Dylan, threw her hands around his neck, and pressed her breasts against his chest.

Some small part of her felt astonished at her behavior, as if she were watching someone else. Someone who purred, "And then it wouldn't have stopped there." She spun out of Dylan's arms and announced, "Who's for an orgy?"

She turned a sly smile on Jarvis. "Come on, boys, let's take off all our clothes." She tore off her jacket, threw it at Beatrice, and said, "I'll be first."

Beatrice blinked at her. "Gloria?"

At hearing that name, Kate froze with the shock of that implication, but recovered quickly. So what? She was just pretending. Wasn't she?

And if she wasn't, who cares? It was marvelous. Look at them. A moment ago she'd been shaking, afraid. Now she held them all in the palm of her hand.

"Kate?" Her aunt's normally sure voice cracked.

She swung toward Lillian, anticipating applause or for her to one-up her performance. Instead Lillian looked worried. And old, so much older than Kate ever remembered her looking.

Lillian hurried down the steps and clutched Kate's arm with her gnarled fingers. "I think that's quite enough, dear. Let me take you up to your room."

Kate shrugged. "Sure, why not?" Even that felt good, her body loose, pulsed with a feline sensuality, and not her normal boring protective stance.

She turned back to her audience.

There they stood—Beatrice, Dylan, Mallick, and Jarvis, all staring at her. They all looked astonished.

Gratifying.

She winked.

Her aunt herded her into the house. Once in her bedroom, Kate fell onto the bed and was asleep in seconds.

Chapter Sixteen

The next morning Kate stood staring at herself in the bathroom mirror, not sure how it was possible her face showed no sign of the jack hammer that had surely taken up residence behind her right eye. She didn't remember everything that happened last night, although she had a sneaky suspicion it was embarrassing.

So this was a hangover?

At least she hoped the cause was merely a hangover.

Except it didn't hang or droop, as the name implied. No, it seared and throbbed so hard that her entire body weaved as if she was in a boat.

What the hell had gotten into her last night? *Who* the hell had gotten into her? She splashed cold water on her face and tried to shake that thought away. She'd just never drink and smoke pot again. Problem solved. She dried her face and brushed out her hair.

Who was she kidding?

Inebriation or even a dissociative disorder didn't explain all of what she was feeling, of what she'd been experiencing during the past month. She put the brush down.

A dissociative disorder could answer some of the occurrences, but it didn't explain how she knew the yellow roses were found on the floor of the murder scene, when according to Detective Robak that fact had never been released in a report or to the newspapers.

She thought of the other worldly presence—of Gloria—that seemed to bring her strength in times of need or loneliness, as a small child. Now that she thought about it, during that horrible day she was assaulted by the so-called director, she remembered lying there, helpless and passive until she'd been surrounded by the cries of a woman's voice much too old, and much too world weary to have been her own at thirteen.

Was it a ghost?

Perhaps not the kind of ghoul with chains and powdered white skin she'd seen in the movies. But Kate now believed that strong feelings long past haunted the present. They haunted her.

The realization should have scared her. The odd thing was—it didn't.

When Kate returned to her bedroom, her aunt was ensconced on the window seat.

Lillian was dressed in Auntie Mame attire— purple-and-white caftan, strands of chunky beads, and globs of makeup. If she had a long, 1920's cigarette holder, the ensemble would be complete.

"Quite a performance last night," her aunt said.

If Lillian thought she was about to have a nice chat about last night, she was dead wrong. Deciding that the best defense was a good offense, Kate said, "Since when are you up before ten?"

"I wanted to see you. I thought you might need to talk."

"Why should I?"

Lillian's demanding left eyebrow rose.

She ignored it. "I need to get to work. Jarvis will

kill me if the restoration isn't done on time."

Lillian stood and held out some papers Kate didn't recognize. "Yes, work, but not that grueling restoration project. Something more fun. Last night, before your tempestuous scene, Beatrice told me you finally agreed to the screen test and suggested I prep you for it. These are your sides." Lillian handed her the papers.

Kate took the pages. "My sides?"

"Darling, the scene you will be doing for the screen test."

"It can't be today. I just agreed to it."

"Of course not. It's in two weeks. However, after your performance last night, Jarvis and Beatrice couldn't stop talking about how perfect you'd be in your grandmother's role. That's when Jarvis suggested rehearsals for the test to begin as soon as possible, today even, and said that *I* should help you."

Kate thumbed through the pages. "I've got like only one line in this entire scene."

"True. It's a ten-minute close-up while you react to others. That's much more difficult to do well than read lines. But you will be marvelous *if* you're prepared. Which I assure you, you will be. First you must get comfortable with the setting." Her aunt swung open Kate's bedroom door. "And the magic man that Jarvis is—or I suspect Beatrice is, since she does all the grunt work—arranged for us to have access to the soundstage this morning."

Kate stared at her aunt. It wasn't that she didn't know what fun was when she heard about it. Spending the day with Lillian working on a scene at a big studio, was much more interesting than staring at a film strip and picking pieces of dust off it. Still, something didn't feel right with the setup.

"What about the restoration?"

"Tish-tosh, that's for Dylan to finish up. You, my dear, are being groomed to be a star, not a chemist."

****

As Lillian drove them away from the studio and back toward Jarvis's house, Kate had to admit she'd had a great time rehearsing the scene.

It was like being a kid again and playing pretend. Even better than that, because Lillian was the ideal playmate. She had gesticulated, pleaded, and shouted, anything to pull a better performance out of Kate.

Her aunt's love of performing was infectious.

Too bad Lillian wasn't forty years younger. She'd be perfect for the part.

Except the Hollywood system would never choose her to star in any film, even though Lillian Baker was by far the better actress than her sister, Gloria. She didn't have the knockout beauty her kid sister had, so Lillian never played anything better than the sidekick or the shrew.

Just another thing about old Hollywood Kate wanted to change. In fact, wasn't it already changing? Actors no longer needed to look like gods. They could be short with thinning hair like Jack Nicholson or vulnerable and real like Jill Claiborne. True, the big studio pictures, like the ones Jarvis made, continued to demand glamour over talent. But that was just another reason the power of big studios should be changed.

Lillian parked her white Lincoln in Jarvis's circular driveway, and Kate hopped out.

"I'd better get to the guest house," she said. "I'm sure Dylan will be fuming that I wasn't there this morning."

"Be off with you then," Lillian told her, and Kate trotted down the terraced path toward the pool patio.

When she passed the pool house and looked down the stone stairway that led to the guest house, her stomach lurched. Part of the rickety wooden railing was missing. All that remained in that spot were jagged pieces of wood jutting out of the ground like broken teeth. And on one rotted post a torn piece of black fabric fluttering like a small pirate flag.

Kate stepped carefully down the uneven stone stairs to take a closer look. A hot wind whipped up from the ravine and at her, as if it were pushing her back from the edge.

She inched toward the precipice, ignoring her trembling legs, and peered down into the ravine. On a narrow ledge at least fifteen feet below her was a man in a torn black shirt, lying face down.

"Dylan!" she screamed.

The prostrate man didn't move. He was too far down for her to reach. It was a miracle he had landed on the ledge. If he hadn't, he would have fallen hundreds of feet.

"Help!" Kate screamed.

"Miss? What's wrong?" Kioyoshi stood at the top of the steps.

Aunt Lillian hurried up behind the gardener, her caftan flapping.

"Get an ambulance, firemen, quick!" Kate shouted. "Dylan's down there!"

Kioyoshi ran toward the main house. Lillian remained at the top of the staircase, making various sounds of dismay.

Kate looked at the lifeless figure, tears streaming down her face. "Oh God, Dylan."

The creak of the cottage door hinges made her turn and look to the guest house below.

Dylan stood at the entrance, squinting in the bright sunshine.

"What the hell's going on?" he yelled up at her.

She shouted his name and ran down the stairs toward him.

"*Stop!*" he screamed.

Kate put on the brakes and looked down. The next stone step and the one below it had slipped from its place, no longer wedged securely in the ground. It also had a sheen, as if wet. But it was too late in the day for dew to remain on them.

Her knees buckled as she realized one more step and she would have slipped and gone over the edge the same as that poor man had done.

Who was he?

Kate looked down at the unconscious man again. He had the long limbs of a swimmer, black, tangled hair, mismatched socks, and… "Mallick!"

Oh, sweet Mallick.

Dylan scuttled back and forth along the ledge by the guest house landing.

Lillian commanded Kate to come back up the stairs to her.

With the stairs iffy and part of the railing gone, there wasn't anything else she could do. When she was in her aunt's tight embrace, she looked down the stairway and saw Dylan clutching onto a bush, as he backed over the edge.

"*Nooooooooo!*" Kate and Lillian screamed in

unison.

"Don't do this, Dylan!" Lillian cried. "Help is on the way."

He ignored her and kept going. The bush didn't look strong enough to hold his considerable weight. Soon his head disappeared below the edge. Loosened rocks clattered on the canyon below.

Then that sound stopped, and they heard nothing more until Dylan shouted, "He's alive!" Silence again. Then, "His pulse is slow. Where's help, damn it!"

Sirens howled, coming closer. The fire department arrived first, followed by an ambulance, then the police.

Using ropes and harnesses, two firemen descended to the ledge and soon got both men out of there, with Mallick buckled into a stretcher. They slid Mallick into the ambulance with the EMTs and roared away, heading for nearby UCLA Medical Center. He had never opened his eyes.

After the ambulance sped off, Dylan ran from the pool patio up the terraced path to the main house.

Kate followed, yelling, "Wait up!"

"Stay here," he called back to her. "Better if I go to the hospital alone. I need to call Mallick's family, and I don't want them overwhelmed with strangers."

Kate stopped. That was probably right. Yet, she wanted to go to the hospital. Over the past month she'd gotten to know Mallick, and she also wanted to be there for Dylan. She could be of some help. Maybe she could catch up to him before he took off in his car.

His car? That stopped her. Where was Dylan's car? She could've sworn she hadn't seen it in Jarvis's driveway or on the street where he usually parked. Also how did Dylan not notice the loose stones if he'd walked down the stairs first?

Beatrice barreled down the pathway to her, barking orders. "Go get your aunt. Then both of you get up to the house and stay there."

"Who are you to—" Kate began to argue.

"Jarvis is stuck in a meeting, and he told me to handle everything." Her burgundy leather notebook clutched in her hand, she continued to march down the path. Trailing her, Kate saw that Beatrice was a woman of her word, for handle everything she did.

Beatrice began by speaking to the firemen, who were getting ready to leave, and to the police, who with their yellow tape and notebooks appeared to be ready to stay for a while. They all listened to her wordlessly.

Next, she marched up to Lillian. She gently clasped the older woman's wrist and appeared to be taking her pulse.

Kate felt like a heel when she saw how pale Lillian was. Why hadn't she noticed that earlier? She rushed to her aunt's side.

"Stay with her," Beatrice said. "Take her to the house and get her some water."

Kate took her aunt's arm, and they started up the path.

Before taking more than a couple of steps, she heard Beatrice say, "Small world, lieutenant. What a coincidence you were put in charge."

Beatrice spoke to a guy whose dark sunglasses and thick sideburns were not enough to mask his weather-beaten face or petulant lips. He wore an off-the-rack black blazer that had a small polo player logo on it and khaki pants that appeared to be ironed and starched. He tugged at some loose threads on the cuff of his jacket.

His expression seemed to say he knew he was too good for second-rate anything.

The police lieutenant responded to Beatrice with the smarmiest smile Kate had ever seen. "Always ready to help a friend. When I heard the call was at Jarvis's house, I thought you might need a friend."

Kate felt her aunt's grasp of her arm weaken, and she turned back to her and guided her up to the house. An hour later, Kate knocked on Lillian's door and walked in. He aunt was now scrubbed and wearing a fuzzy ice-blue robe. She looked like a little girl. Kate had tea and lemon cake brought up to her aunt's room, and she stayed with her until Lillian fell asleep.

That afternoon Dylan called her twice to provide updates on Mallick. The first call was just to tell her he was at the hospital with Mallick's family and there had been no change. Dylan's second call contained happier news: Mallick was awake.

Remarkably, he had no broken bones. Probably thanks to being one of the most loose-jointed persons Kate had ever met. Dylan told her Mallick had a concussion, but so far none of the tests showed any swelling of the brain. However, because of the severity of the fall, the doctors wanted him to stay in the hospital for observation for a couple of days. All signs indicated he was going to be okay.

Much relieved, Kate hung up the phone. When she turned around, she jumped when she saw Jimena staring at her. Kate hadn't realized she was in the room with her while she was talking to Dylan. Jimena went back to polishing one of Jarvis's antique side tables.

"Do you know when Jarvis will be home tonight?" Kate asked her.

"He won't be. He hates to be here when strangers are around."

"Huh?" He had invited her and Lillian to live in his house for the summer, so this seemed odd. She recalled, though, that he didn't begin to stay here with them until they got to know each other.

"He's at his beach house. He'll stay there until this mess is cleaned up."

"Oh."

"That reminds me," Jimena said. She pulled a sealed envelope from the pocket of her apron and handed it to Kate. "A messenger left this for you."

Kate tore it open and found a letter indicating it was from Jarvis. The note fulfilled a promise. It gave the specifics of her meeting with J.B. Sutton. Noon tomorrow at Sutton's Montecito estate. She should feel grateful for getting an audience with the gazillionaire instead of frustrated. But tomorrow? She wanted to help Mallick if she could.

He was the priority.

Chapter Seventeen

In the morning, Kate arrived at the UCLA Medical Center with magazines and chocolate for Mallick. Dylan, Mallick's parents, and two of his four sisters were already there. All of his family had the same black hair and generous smile.

They told her that Mallick's speech had begun to slur last night, so the doctors had ordered a battery of tests. Kate didn't get to do more than give him a quick smile before an orderly rolled him away. A nurse came in to warn them that after the tests Mallick would need to rest. So she had no reason to stay. She might as well keep her appointment with Sutton.

On the drive to Sutton's estate in Montecito, Kate wasn't sure if she had made a mistake by telling Dylan about the meeting. Gazing at his profile as he drove up Highway 101, she decided she was grateful for the company.

With Mallick in the hospital, whatever squabbles she'd had with Dylan seemed minor in comparison. She shut her eyes and silently prayed for maybe the hundredth time that Mallick would be all right.

After turning off the freeway and heading for several miles up San Ysidro Road, the first thing she saw of Sutton's estate was a thick salmon colored stucco wall that was easily eighteen feet high. It ran along the edge of the road for over a mile, a barricade against all enemies, known and unknown.

Dylan stopped the Mustang at a closed wrought iron gate. He punched the button on an intercom, and after a static-filled conversation in which Dylan identified them, the gate creaked open.

They drove past stables, a string of Spanish roof tiled bungalows, two gazebos, and an amphitheater set into the grassy hillside.

Jarvis had a mansion. Sutton practically owned a town.

Before reaching the top of the drive, they encountered another gate, this one manned by a guy bigger than a Los Angeles Rams lineman. He put down his magazine, which Kate could've sworn was *Better Homes & Gardens*, of all things, and waved them through.

The main house crowned the top of the hill, looking more like a Spanish presidio than a gentleman's hacienda. At each corner of the massive two-story structure, watchmen gazed down upon them from the roof top. It gave Kate an almost uncontrollable urge to run. Instead, she and Dylan marched up to the massive ironclad front door.

Before they could ring the bell, a butler appeared and guided them to the foyer, where two men frisked them before the butler ushered them into an unoccupied room. It was a small, surprisingly normal-looking living room decorated with chunky, mission-style furniture and large paintings of California landscapes on the wall.

Outside a child laughed. Kate looked out a large open window and spied a golden-haired girl of no more than five squatting next to what looked like a gardener.

The child giggled as she dug into the muddy ground with her little pink spade and bucket. Then she ran up to the terraced patio, carrying her bucket in both hands, and hurried toward a long-legged blonde woman, not much older than Kate, who was lying on a lounge chair.

Kate knew who they were. She'd done her research on Sutton, as well as every other suspect on her list. She nudged Dylan and pointed. "That's Sutton's daughter and granddaughter."

The child, giggling, dumped the muddy contents of her bucket right next to the young woman. Looking very proud of herself, the little girl pointed to the pile of dirt and cried, "Look, look!"

The young woman scowled at the mess and without a word to the child got up and walked into the house.

The little girl's face fell. But her smile returned when she sat and started making mud pies.

Kate noticed how Dylan stared at the young woman when she exited the scene.

Typical.

She nudged him. "I bet you'll never guess which one is the daughter and which the granddaughter."

Dylan shrugged. "The older one is his granddaughter, Prudence Sutton. So I'm going to guess the child is the old man's daughter."

"You got it. Sutton must have been like seventy when she was born. How did you know?"

The answer soon became apparent when Prudence slinked in wearing a sleeveless maxi dress with a long slit at the front to showcase her perfectly tanned legs. She then threw her arms around Dylan's neck and kissed him hard on the lips.

"When I asked who was here, I just had to see if it was *my* Dylan Nichols he was referring to, and here you are."

Kate instantly disliked her. And really, it had nothing to do with the fact she used the words *my Dylan*.

As quickly as Prudence had thrown herself at him, she now shoved him away and gave him a coquettish pout. "I'm angry with you. I haven't seen you at any of the Hollywood wrap parties in months. Where have you been?"

"Hey, Pru, some of us have to work for living, you know."

She slowly ran a manicured nail across Dylan's chest. "As I recall, the last party I saw you at, things were just becoming interesting between us." She purred. And for the first time, she glanced at Kate. "But if it was because of *work*, you're forgiven."

Kate cleared her throat. "I don't mean to be rude, but—"

"Don't you?" Prudence said with a venomous smile.

"I…ah…" Kate stuttered.

Dylan put his hand on her shoulder. "What Kate means is we have an appointment with your grandfather, and we don't want to be late."

"That's weird. Granddad hardly sees anyone anymore, and when he does, they are never younger than forty. Unless it's some gold digger trying out to be wife number six or seven. I forget which number he's on." Prudence glanced at Kate. "That could explain *her*. But not you, Dylan. Why are you here?"

"It's confidential," he said.

Prudence stuck out her chiseled little chin. "We'll see about that."

"What's that mean?" he asked.

Prudence waved her hand. "Oh, go have your *confidential* talk. I don't care. Max!" she yelled. The butler appeared almost immediately. "I gather these two have an appointment with Granddad. Is he in his study?"

"No, miss. The library."

"Even better." Prudence smiled. "Take them to him."

Kate and Dylan shuffled behind the butler.

"And Dylan," Prudence called out. "Hope you make the scene again soon, after you're done with your *work*."

When she was gone, Kate glared at him.

"Hey, don't look at me like that. We've just been at some of the same parties. I hardly know her."

"Sure doesn't look that way."

The butler halted before two large closed doors. He gestured for them to wait. They stood in the hallway.

"Pru just likes to run fast, create trouble." Dylan laughed. "Hey, this setup is all very *The Big Sleep*."

"Does everything have to be a movie reference with you?"

Dylan grinned. "I'm just telling you, if we walk into Sutton's library and he's clipping orchids, I'm out of here." He shook his head. "I never understood that damn film. Who was the murderer anyway?"

"I always thought it was obvious. The spoiled *heiress* did it."

"Whoa, Kate. Claws in."

The butler opened the library doors and ushered

them in. Kate was happy to see there wasn't an orchid in sight.

Above a fireplace big enough to stand in was a large painting of a much younger J.B. Sutton, looking even more like the caricature of a bloated industrialist than Nash's Emperor Smythe rendition of him. The painting depicted Sutton with a large barrel chest, a wide Henry the Eighth face, and small, piercing eyes.

Below the painting was a mahogany mantel with photos of Sutton with what looked like every famous luminary of the twentieth century, from presidents to movie stars.

This was a room designed to intimidate. It was the embodiment of the Emperor Smythe persona. Yet the effect was lost when she looked at the man himself. Now old, with a spotted bald head fringed with white hair and sagging pale skin, Sutton sat sandwiched between two large mahogany desks. He was almost unrecognizable as the robust man in the portrait.

Age could explain most of it. Yet Kate sensed the change might be deeper than that. On the credenza behind him were more photos, altogether different from the ones displayed on the mantel. They were ordinary. All in color and almost all of the little golden-haired child they'd seen outside. Kate was able to pick out only one picture of Prudence. She noted there were none of Prudence's father, the former congressman, who was running for the senate when *Emperor Smythe* was due to be released.

"You, I'd know anywhere," Sutton said to Kate in a voice that sounded like a sick car engine. That's when she noticed he had a scar on his throat, which made her wonder if he'd had throat cancer.

He gave Dylan a sour smile. "Jarvis didn't tell me you'd be coming, too."

"Uh, yes. I'm Dylan Nichols." He rubbed his right hand against his jeans and then offered it to Sutton.

Sutton refused Dylan's hand. "Nichols? Right. I understand you're writing a remake of *Emperor Smythe* for Infinity Studios. Don't deny it. I'm well apprised of what happens in my town, Mr. Nichols. You'd be surprised how well apprised."

Kate thought the last sentence was oddly cryptic. She glanced back and forth between the unreadable expressions on both Sutton's and Dylan's face.

"Yes," Dylan said, "I'm writing the remake. And this time *all* the original scenes will be there."

"Not a wise course," Sutton said.

"Is that a threat?"

The old man wheezed as his breathing grew shallow. "Simply good advice. The original stunk, and the public agreed. It bombed, remember?"

"That's because your studio butchered it."

Sutton wobbled to his feet, using the desk for support. "That film is a pack of lies, a travesty, a perversion of the truth. My lawyers will stop your remake. I can assure you of that." His splotchy face and neck flushed red.

Worried the old man was about to have a stroke, Kate tried to calm him. "The film is only a story. We're not here about that. We came to talk about something real, about what happened to my grandmother."

Sutton's gaze softened. "Ah, the incandescent Gloria Reardon. I should know. I'm a connoisseur when it comes to women."

"Collector is more like it," Dylan said.

"Yes, I collect many things—women, companies, information, and *films*."

"Please, I have questions about my grandmother."

"She was exquisite. It wasn't just her looks, either. She had a radiance that ignited men like straw. It was amusing to observe."

"Observe? You were immune?" Kate asked.

"Certainly not." Sutton made a raspy chuckle. "I burned like the rest of them, but I didn't meet her until I took over Golden State Pictures, which was after *Emperor Smythe* began production. Unfortunately, her wildness had subsided by then. She'd plainly fallen in love with Winston. Swore she'd turned over a new leaf and was ready to be a good mother to Audrey and a loyal wife to Winston. But the poor girl lapsed back into her old ways, and the rest, as they say, is history."

Sutton gazed off into space as if he was seeing a scene from long ago. Then he turned to Kate. "Jarvis told me you had questions about Gloria's death. You don't think Winston did it?"

"I used to. I'm not sure anymore."

Sutton's eyes narrowed in on her. "Why?"

"The stolen footage—"

"Stolen?" Sutton dismissively waved his hand. "Don't tell me you're a conspiracy kook."

"Your studio's story that the footage was *mistakenly* thrown away isn't true," Kate replied.

A faint twinkle sparked in his jaundiced eyes. "And how do you know that?"

Hoping she had not given too much away, she gulped down her fears. "What if Gloria stumbled upon the theft? Maybe things got out of hand with the perpetrator. After all, the thief would be staring at an almost certain felony conviction if Gloria Reardon was the star witness against him."

"What are you implying?"

"Only this. If there was a thief on the set that day, that means there was someone else there who had a motive."

Sutton sat down. "That's quite a story. And what do you expect of me? A confession?"

"Not for murder. But perhaps a confession of a different sort."

"You think me the kind of man who would steal a film just to save the reputation of my worthless son?"

"It was more than your son's reputation," Dylan said. "*Emperor Smythe* implicates you as a Nazi collaborator, not just your son, the congressman."

Sutton tilted back in his large leather chair. "That's just one of many things that film got wrong."

"Maybe." Kate smiled. "But it's not wrong about your son, is it? You just said—"

"Watch it, young lady."

Kate stepped closer to his desk. "You're known as the type of person who destroys careers, steals, kills, anything to protect your own. In the public's imagination, you are seen as a villain. I wonder if that's the legacy you wish to have."

He leaned on his desk. "Has it occurred to you that at this point in my life I don't give a damn what people think of me, and I certainly don't care what they think of my son. I haven't spoken to him in years."

Kate stared at the photos of Sutton's little girl so lovingly displayed. "Still, you're her father. I think you've changed. I think she's changed you."

"Do you? Then you're naïve."

"Possibly," she said.

Dylan put a hand on her shoulder. "Forget it. His type doesn't give anything unless he gets something in return. I know what he wants, and there's no way I'm softening the portrait of Emperor Smythe in the new script." He turned to Sutton. "The world still needs to be warned of the power of corporate dictators who operate unseen by the public."

Kate shook her head. "People are more complex than that. Fairy-tale portraiture may be entertainment, but it's not truth. Mr. Sutton's not evil."

Sutton's expression turned cold. "You think not?"

"No." She took a step forward. "In the past ten years, your foundation has been a major contributor to organizations helping with famine relief, medical research, the arts, and many other things."

He shrugged. "Tax deductions."

"And since the falling-out with your son, your bequests have exceeded your income. That's more than tax deductions. That's restitution." Feeling emboldened, Kate placed both hands flat on his desk and leaned toward him. "I'm not here today to ask you for a favor. I'm here to provide you with the opportunity to make reparation to my family."

Sutton smiled. "Nicely done. I like someone who knows how to sell. And I like someone who comes prepared. Ask what you want, and I'll decide if I'm willing to answer."

Kate sat in a black leather chair opposite him and parked her elbows on his enormous desk. "It was you who orchestrated everything. You stole the footage of the scene that implied your son was a member of a fascist origination."

"Not directly."

Dylan shook his head. "Don't waste your time, Kate. He's not going to tell us the truth."

"I think he just did."

"Oh," Dylan said. "You mean it was something like who will *rid me of this turbulent priest*?"

"I didn't say that," Sutton replied. "But I will tell you it was at about that time I learned to be more careful with what I said in front of ambitious people. I'm still careful. I want to talk to Kate, alone. No witnesses. Dylan, you will leave now."

"No way," he replied.

Kate looked up at Dylan. "Please?"

He huffed. "Okay. I'll be right outside the door."

After he left, Kate said to Sutton, "You were going to tell me who the ambitious person was who helped you get the footage."

"Was I?"

"Sorry, I forgot. Nothing direct. Was such an ambitious person Charles Needham?"

Sutton cocked his head, looking genuinely perplexed by the name. "Who's he?"

"The assistant cameraman on the set that day."

Sutton scribbled the name on a notepad. "Never heard of him."

"Later, he worked in security for your studio. You sure you don't remember him?"

"My dear, many people work for me. Thankfully I don't need to meet most of them."

"Okay." Deciding to try another tack, she said, "I know you knew of Jarvis back then, but I don't think you'd choose him. He wasn't controllable, even when he was young."

Sutton nodded.

"Appealing to people's emotions is too risky, so it wasn't my great-aunt Lillian, either. Anyway, I don't think she'd ever be involved with the destruction of art. That's how she saw Winston's work, so it's not her."

"No…hypothetically."

Kate stood. "Beatrice Talbot. She's smart, efficient, and ambitious, and back then she was overlooked because she was a woman." She felt like Perry Mason doing his final revelation. "If I wanted something done right but with, let's say, discretion, I'd think Beatrice would be a very good choice."

Sutton smiled, and it wasn't an attractive sight. "I agree she is very capable. I've always said so."

"Yes, you must have thought so." Kate paced. "The police report indicated she came to your studio early that day to interview for an executive position. Quite a step up for someone who was only an agent's secretary at the time."

Sutton nodded. "You really did do your research."

"The problem is her alibi is airtight. She couldn't have been on the set later that day to take the footage."

"No?"

"You don't agree?"

Sutton shrugged. "If someone is planning to break the law, I'd think they would set up an alibi first." He smiled. "Capable people do."

"Are you saying Beatrice did it?"

"No, I think Winston killed Gloria. However, there were some things that occurred that day that never made sense to me. Not admitting anything, of course."

"Of course."

"You see, I'm in the habit of rewarding people who

do me favors. You understand, it's simply good business to do so. My studio offered Beatrice the job she interviewed for that day."

Kate tried to contain her excitement. Sutton had basically said Beatrice was behind the theft of the footage. Hadn't he?

"It was merely a mid-level position we offered her," he said. "Still, that was a major advancement for someone who at the time was only a secretary. Beatrice is, and was, quite capable, as I said, and—"

"But Beatrice didn't go to work for you. She stayed with Jarvis."

"Yes. That never made sense to me. A week earlier she would have done anything to get that position. Instead she stayed with Jarvis. Knowing how that man operates, I surmised he must have something on her. It's the only explanation that makes sense." Sutton discreetly put a hand under his desk. "Now I have done my good deed for the day."

The butler appeared, as if by magic.

"Thank you for your help," Kate said.

"I'm regretting it already. But you helped me, and as I said, I reward those who do me favors."

"I haven't done anything for you."

"You did. You made it clear you have the missing *Smythe* footage." He smiled, but there was nothing warm in the expression. "If you're smart, you will simply bring it to me before there's an ugly legal battle."

"I don't have it."

"Don't lie to me. You're not good at it."

"I didn't—"

"Of course you have it. I'd suspected it before you

came here, and now you've confirmed it." He held his hand up to halt her impending protest. "You didn't say so directly, but you said enough. Jarvis is a powerful man in this town. He's someone I make sure I'm informed about. My curiosity was more than piqued when I learned Gloria Reardon's granddaughter was living at his house."

"That doesn't mean anything. It could be—"

"Yes, I thought of that." He smiled. "You certainly are very pretty, and Jarvis, like me, is a collector. Or haven't you noticed?"

Kate felt her cheeks grow warm.

"So normally that would be the explanation," Sutton continued. "But that young man, Dylan Nichols, has been coming to his house every day. That type of arrangement is just a bit too liberal for our friend Jarvis. I had my associates investigate Dylan, and among other interesting things I learned about him is that he has a background in film restoration. Very convenient. Add to that your skepticism about your grandmother's murder, and I have every reason to suspect you have recently acquired new information. So what could that be, I wonder?"

Kate felt herself deflate a little more with every word he said. She was a fool. And Sutton was making sure she knew it, too.

"What's more," he said, "several times in this short meeting you've revealed your knowledge of things about the past you shouldn't have, including the fact that the film was stolen."

Kate stared down at her scuffed hiking boots.

Jarvis was going to kill her when he learned that she had let his secret out—again.

"Don't look so forlorn," Sutton said. "You're not dumb. You're just too sincere and easy to read. Heed this warning. You have gotten involved with consummate players, and you're not equipped for this game."

"I don't know what you're talking about." Kate tried to sound convincing but knew she had failed. His estimation of her was so similar to the pronouncements that Beatrice had thrown in her face.

"Yes, you do. That abominable movie and what happened to your grandmother should be left in the past. I'd hate to see what happened to Gloria happen to you. Let it go, all of it."

Game over, Kate thought, and she had lost. But not just lost. Humiliated.

She walked out of Sutton's office feeling much more unsure of herself than she did when she walked in. She evaded, as best she could, Dylan's questions as they drove back to L.A. She had been so stupid. No, worse than that. She was a victim of her own pathetic hubris. That was the right word to use, wasn't it?

Still, she'd be damned if she'd give up.

Chapter Eighteen

It was late afternoon when they got back to Jarvis's house. Only one police car remained in the driveway. They walked around to the backyard to find out what was happening with the investigation.

Jimena stepped out of the solarium door and waved a piece of paper at Dylan. "Someone at Skyline Studios has been calling for you all day. They say it's an emergency."

Dylan took the paper from Jimena and walked inside.

Kate continued down the pathway toward the pool. When she got there, Beatrice was talking to that smarmy police officer she'd heard her speaking to yesterday.

"Well, Lieutenant?" Beatrice said.

The man jotted something on his notepad, then flipped it closed. "It was just an accident. No doubt about it. That is the sorriest-looking stairway I've ever seen. Tell Jarvis not to worry. My men will be out of here today."

"Really? So soon?" Beatrice asked.

"Open and shut," the lieutenant said. "That kid probably went down there early in the morning, when the stairs were slick with dew, fell, and broke the railing. He's lucky to be alive. If he'd missed the ledge, there would've been a hearse here and not an ambulance. Not my business, but Jarvis's lawyer may want to run down to the hospital and offer that young man's family a hefty check before he sues."

"Already taken care of," she said distractedly. Her attention appeared to have shifted and was focused on the pile of rubble made up from the debris railing and the stone steps that had also come loose.

Beatrice's expression darkened.

What had she seen?

Beatrice turned her attention back to the lieutenant. "That's pretty quick for an investigation."

He winked at her. "We aim to please. We'll be gone by nightfall." The lieutenant nodded to Beatrice before turning to talk to a uniformed officer.

With the yellow tape still up, Kate figured she wouldn't get a chance to take a closer look until tomorrow. She climbed back up to the house.

When she walked into the solarium, she found Dylan pacing. "I've got good and bad news."

"Oh, no, Mallick? Is he all right?"

"Yes. In fact, he's doing better. All the tests were negative."

"Wonderful!"

"But he's going to be kept in the hospital for another day or two, just to be safe."

Beatrice walked into the solarium and closed the door behind her.

"The thing is," Dylan said, "even if he's okay and gets out soon, he's supposed to take it easy. Skyline called with fantastic news. They're going to give me a shot. I'm sure Mallick will understand, and Jarvis, too."

Beatrice walked up to them. "Understand what?"

"Skyline wants me to take over directing *Satan's*

Academy—my film. They're such a shoestring operation, they need to stay on schedule or scrap it. It's an incredible opportunity. I've got to—"

"But that's Mallick's job," Kate said. "You're taking it from him?"

"No, not taking. The filming is scheduled to begin in a couple of days. If they can't get a director, there'll be no picture. I have to do it."

Silver pen and notebook at the ready, Beatrice said, "What about your commitment to the restoration?"

Kate gave Dylan a meaningful look. "Yeah, and what about…you know. You're just going to leave?"

"I'm not going far. It's only a week shoot."

"And post production, right?"

He nodded and took Kate's hands in his. "I promise. I'll only be a phone call away. Tell me you understand."

She did, but she didn't like it.

Apparently marginal approval was all Dylan needed, for in the next second he was gone.

"Typical man," Beatrice said. "He has left you to finish the hard work of the restoration." She clapped her notebook shut. "By the way, that project better stay on schedule or Jarvis will blackball him for abandoning it. Or if Jarvis doesn't, I will."

"The restoration has already been delayed, hasn't it?" Kate said. "I mean I'm guessing I won't be able to get back to work on it for a while."

"Jarvis's orders are explicit. He wants that restoration done. He's concerned that Sutton will get wind of it."

Kate looked down and shuffled her feet.

"The police will be gone tonight," Beatrice said.

"So I'll make sure the stairs and the railing are fixed by tomorrow afternoon. You can be certain of that."

Beatrice turned to leave but then spun back. "Do you know what Mallick was doing here? Or how Dylan could be in the guest house without knowing that his friend had fallen? It doesn't make sense to me."

No, it didn't. And it also didn't make sense that she hadn't seen either Dylan's or Mallick's car on the street below or in the driveway.

"And now Dylan has the chance to direct his first full-length film," Beatrice said. "What a lucky boy he is."

Kate hated how her own thoughts jumped to the same ridiculous implication. But Dylan would never hurt Mallick. Not for something as trivial as a film.

No, she corrected herself. Not for any reason. Still, she wondered what Beatrice had seen in the debris pile that had obviously bothered her so much.

****

When Kate peered out her bedroom window the next morning, the backyard was swarming with construction guys. She went down to take a closer look at what they were doing, but they shooed her away.

It was not yet nine when Beatrice told her the men had taken all the old railing down and set new posts in place with quick-drying cement. Obviously, Beatrice had not allowed them to shoo her away. She said that Kate would probably be able to get down to the guest house and back to work that afternoon.

No doubt about it, Beatrice was competent.

Soon Kate would be stuck again, putting in long hours on the restoration, this time without Dylan. Even more important, Sutton had already guessed about the footage. So the time to hide it had passed, she'd need to get it done quickly.

But she couldn't do anything about it this morning, so she decided to visit Mallick.

When she walked into his hospital room, he was staring up at the ceiling. He looked pale.

"Hi," Kate said.

Mallick greeted her cheerfully and hit the button to lift the head of his bed. "I'm sure glad to see you, but I don't think I'm very good company."

"I'm not here to be entertained. How are you feeling?"

"I'm fine except for this killer headache and being bored out of my mind."

"The headache I can do nothing about. But boredom, maybe." Kate fished a deck of cards from her army bag and shuffled them on her knee. "You want to play gin or crazy eights?"

Mallick rubbed his forehead. "Crazy eights is probably more my speed."

Kate dealt out eight cards. They played two rounds of the game, both of which Mallick won. While she arranged her cards by suit for the third hand, she said, "Can I ask what happened the day you fell?"

"Sure." Mallick cut the deck and flipped over a three of clubs. "Everybody else has. Police, insurance representatives, even some ambulance-chaser lawyer."

"So?"

"Yes, I was trespassing. Jarvis's insurance guy was thrilled to learn that." He gave her a hard look. "I knew you and Dylan were up to something, and it must be big since you had Jarvis Benjamin backing it. Plus all those weird cryptic things you've said to each other. It was driving me nuts. From the little that Dylan said, I knew what you were working on was in Jarvis's guest house, so I wanted to take a look-see."

Mallick's pale features made way for a faint blush. "Truth is, I tried to make a surprise visit to the guest house the day before, but that crazy housekeeper nabbed me." He laid down a jack of clubs. "The request for help on *Satan's Academy* was just my excuse to stop by. When I went back the next day to try again, I thought the trick was to get there in the early morning. Some trick, huh? I'm walking down the stairs, and then this one super slippery step comes loose and slides beneath my feet. I grabbed the railing, and it broke." He shuddered. "Man, then pure terror. That's all I remember until I was here."

Kate drew cards until she got an eight and changed the suit to spades.

"You told me Dylan is safe. That I didn't need to worry about him. Do you still feel that way?"

"Whoa," Mallick said. "Of course, what are you thinking?"

She smiled and shook her head. "Nothing. Crazy thoughts."

"You know, I never made it to the guest house, so I didn't find out what you guys are up to. That doesn't seem fair, does it?"

"No, it doesn't."

An hour or so later, Mallick put down the cards and dozed off. Kate tiptoed out of the room and walked down the hallway. A sharp smell of ammonia wrinkled her nose. The roar of a game show's studio audience on the television in one room only emphasized the otherwise strange, sedate atmosphere. Most of the other rooms were dark, and the only other sounds were the rhythmic beeps of monitors.

She rode the elevator down. The doors opened onto the emergency room—a whole different world. This was one filled with noise and activity. A barrage of images: people grimacing with pain, others slumped in faded plastic chairs, and orderlies rushing back and forth through wide swinging doors. A baby wailed, and somewhere down a long corridor a woman screamed.

This wasn't where she came in.

Kate retreated into the elevator. As the doors closed, someone hissed her name. A man's hand appeared between the doors, but he was too late to stop them.

Who the hell was that? With a trembling hand she punched a button at random. All she wanted to do was get away. When the doors slid open, she stepped into a long, eerily deserted corridor. She told herself to calm down. The man who'd called her name could have been Dylan or Jarvis coming to see Mallick. She should go back downstairs and find out who it was. Instead she just stood there, shivering like a wimp. She looked above the elevator door to see what floor she was on. The blinking lights indicated that the elevator had returned to the first floor and was now coming back up.

She ran. She was being ridiculous, but damn it! When she came to a set of double doors with a large square button on the wall beside them, she punched the button, and the doors swung open, then closed behind her.

This corridor was empty, too. As she walked along, the only sound was the squeak of her hiking boots on the vinyl floor and a low-pitched rumble. She wasn't sure if it was the air-handling system or something else. She passed two doors marked "Danger Radiation." Now she felt more paranoid about getting in trouble for being in an unauthorized part of the hospital than about some mysterious man she irrationally thought was after her.

That was until she heard the big doors fly open, admitting a man wearing a doctor's green scrubs, a surgical mask, and gloves. He walked toward her, the rubber soles of his shoes going *screek*, *screek* on the shiny floor.

She leapt to the nearby door, ignoring the radiation warning sign, and desperately rattled the doorknob. It was locked.

The man quickened his pace.

Screek-screek-screek. She spotted a sign labeled "Elevator" with an arrow pointing to the right. She took off. At the end of the corridor, she skidded around the corner. The elevator was near. Just beyond it was a door marked "Stairs."

She stabbed the elevator button beside the door over and over again. The lights showed it coming up. Each second seemed like an hour. *Bong*! The elevator doors slid open. Trying to be clever, she jumped into the elevator just long enough to hit the button for the top floor and then jumped out and bolted for the stairwell.

The heavy clump of her boots echoed as she bounded down the stairs. So much for subterfuge. Her heart thumped in her ears, but she still heard the door above bang open and the sound of hurried footsteps on the stairs behind her. She jumped down two steps at a time until she got to the next landing. She flung open the door and stumbled into a place she recognized—the first-floor reception area, where she'd entered that morning. She stood there for a moment, panting. She spotted a security guard and was about to run toward him until she saw, incredibly, Detective Robak, wearing his familiar corduroy jacket and sleepy expression.

"Detective Robak! Help!"

He rushed to her. "What's wrong?"

She fell against him, gulping for air and pointing to the stairwell. "Hurry, in there, someone's after me!"

The security guard trotted up to them. Robak flashed his badge and waved him off. The detective pulled out his gun and ducked through the stairwell door. Everyone was staring at her.

Where was Robak?

She waited for what felt like hours, but she knew it was only minutes before he returned. His gun now holstered. He shook his head. "Nothing there." He guided her to a row of upholstered chairs. Kate couldn't stop shivering. "Take a deep breath and calm down. Tell me what this is all about."

She explained that a man in a surgical mask had been after her and about someone whispering her name in the emergency room. But she'd seen no one there she'd recognized.

Robak seemed to be trying hard to look as if he was taking her seriously.

"You don't believe me."

"I believe you saw the man you described. I also think you've been under a lot of stress lately. You've been burgled, a friend of yours is in the hospital, and you've been obsessing about a murder. It's not surprising you're, let's say, hyper-vigilant."

When Kate opened her mouth to object, Robak held up his hand. "Don't get me wrong. I actually wish more people were. There are a lot of crazies in this world. My advice, stay hyper-vigilant but not to the point it takes you over, okay?"

Thinking back through the last hour, she realized how she had grown more and more agitated. The screams of pain in the emergency room and then finding herself lost in a land of deserted and antiseptic-smelling corridors. Now sitting next to Detective Robak, it was as if someone had turned the lights on in a carnival's haunted house. She could now see all the elements that had caused fear for what they really were. In this case, merely the harsh realities of a hospital mingled with exhaustion.

Robak stood. "You want me to take you to the station to file a report?"

She shook her head. "No, you're right. What am I going to report? That I saw a man dressed like a doctor at the hospital? Not much there, huh?"

"I said I didn't know. Stay on your toes, and keep me informed."

"Keep you or Jarvis informed?" She peered up at him. "What are you doing here anyway?"

Robak looked at his watch. "I told you I'm sorry about that. I'm not Jarvis's spy."

She looked away.

"I mean it," he said. "I told him before because you didn't want me to go to the brass with your information about Gloria. I thought Jarvis could protect you if on the off chance there was any danger. I'm not on his payroll. Never was." Robak handed her an eight-by-ten manila envelope. "I went to Jarvis's house earlier to give you this peace offering, and Beatrice told me you were here."

Kate began to tear open the envelope.

"Not now. I'm trusting you to be discreet."

She ran her fingers over the envelope. There was something more than papers inside. Was it the shards? No, nothing that sharp.

"Earth calling Kate," Robak said. "What did I just tell you?"

She plopped the envelope into her lap. "Okay, okay."

"If you do figure something out or you get scared again, you go to Jarvis, me, or the police. Promise?"

She nodded. "I promise."

"Good. Now let me walk you to your car."

Robak waited until Kate started her VW bug before he left.

As soon as he was out of sight, she shut off the engine and tore open the envelope. She slipped out a two-page document. The heading identified it as part of Gloria Reardon's murder file. But it wasn't any part that Kate had seen before. This appeared to be the analysis of the shards. Because pieces of marble, which doesn't break easily, had splintered off the weapon and because of the state of the dressing room, the police's working hypothesis assumed the murderer had been out of control, in a frenzy, when he or she struck Gloria. But despite the obvious destruction, the report concluded that most of the murder weapon would have remained intact.

She pulled out a second, smaller envelope and tore it open. In it were twelve photos. They were pictures of three different shards placed next to a ruler, none bigger than one-quarter inch. Each piece of the suspected murder weapon was photographed from four different angles. The corner of each picture was marked with a black felt-tipped pen, designating them A1, A2, A3, and A4, B one through four, and C one through four.

The ones marked *A* were the most promising. They had part of a decorative swirl or part of a snake—definitely a design element. She examined all four photos of *A* closely, but still she didn't know what to make of it.

She wondered if Ted Orlov, the special-effects guy, would know.

The other two pieces were even less promising than the first. At one-quarter inch, *B* was the largest piece. It had a flat smooth surface with the hint of a curve to it. *C* was the thinnest, just a jagged sliver.

She looked at her watch. Time to head back to Jarvis's and work on the restoration. She started her car. When she made a left on to Barrington, she spotted a phone booth. She parked and shut herself inside it. It reeked of urine. Careful to avoid the old chewing gum stuck on the bottom of the telephone box and the filthy, waterlogged phone book hanging on a chain, she dug the folded piece of paper from her jeans pocket that had Ted Orlov's number on it and called him.

He told her he'd be glad to look at the pictures and to come on by and drop them off at his house.

After visiting Ted, Kate finally returned to Jarvis's house and to the work she was supposed to be doing. There, she scarfed down two plums and headed to the guest house.

Most of the construction guys were gone. Only one flatbed truck remained. A grizzled old man stood next to it, not bothering to help a young guy who was unloading stuff from a wheelbarrow.

With a moment of panic, she saw that it was the debris from the staircase. She raced down the terraced path to see if enough of the pile of rubble remained for her to examine. She wanted to take a close look at the stone steps that had loosened—the ones she'd thought glistened unnaturally. She also wondered what Beatrice's uneasy expression meant when she'd stared at the pile of wood that had been the railing.

When Kate got there, she was disheartened to see all of the stone debris was gone. But some of the wood from the railing remained. She knelt and carefully poked through the jagged pieces of wood.

"Hey, I wouldn't do that if I were you. Not without gloves. You'll get hurt."

Kate looked up, and the younger worker with the wheelbarrow walked up to her.

He wore blue jeans and a black—was there any other kind?—Grateful Dead T-shirt and heavy gloves. "You could get some wicked splinters." He gathered up handfuls of wood and turned to dump them into the wheelbarrow.

That's when she saw it. The something that was not right.

It was a piece of wood that looked like it had been part of the base of one of the railing posts. Instead of having a ragged edge, which she thought would be the case if something broke by force, the break on this piece looked smooth. She grabbed it.

The construction guy had filled the barrow and was about to head up the pathway to the truck.

She called to him, "Hey, can I ask you a question?"

215

He turned. "Sure."

Kate held up the piece of wood for him to see. She now noticed it didn't have a perfectly smooth edge, but it had broken at such a precise angle that it just didn't seem natural. "Does this look to you like a natural break?" She pointed to the edge.

He took off a glove and ran a finger over it. "Weird."

"How weird? So weird that you'd say it didn't break? Would you say it was cut?"

"Whoa, Colombo, that's a stretch." He took a closer look. "Well...yes."

"You sure?"

The guy shrugged. "Hey, man, anything's possible. I got to finish cleaning up."

The new railing appeared strong, and the new stone steps had been set into cement that had been poured into a steel frame. The stairs had lost their rustic charm, but who cared. Now they were safe.

Kate took the piece of wood with her on the way down to the guest house. There she wrapped it with a towel and hid it behind the couch.

Why wouldn't the police take a closer look at the railing?

Then she thought of how chummy the lead officer had been with Beatrice. Something definitely wasn't right.

Enough of Nancy Drew for today, and she returned to the task of restoring the remaining footage. She worked well into the night. Her vision blurred. Her head ached from exhaustion, and she was hungry, but she was on the final take in the reel. She couldn't stop now.

She threaded the film carefully into the flatbed so she could examine it a frame at a time. The work required a great deal of focus, but her mind kept wandering to thoughts of marble shards and to the clean break on the railing. She rubbed her tired eyes as the hour grew late and returned to cleaning each tiny scratch frame-by-frame.

Then Kate felt that humid presence infuse all of her senses and Gloria, in that moment in the past, came alive in her mind's eye. This time it wasn't the entire set Kate saw, but only the box. The long gift box with the blood-red bow cried out to her, telling her she knew what lay inside: something familiar about the shape, something itching to be known. She watched her own hand reach across time to untie the bow and lift the lid. She was about to know, to see what the weapon was and—

Someone grabbed her arm.

Startled, Kate opened her eyes. Blinking, she realized her head rested on the table beside the flatbed. She sat up and was confused by a world in color until her focus found Jarvis's reassuring face.

"Time to stop," he said.

"I must have fallen asleep." She rubbed her eyes. "Almost done, I promise. I'll make the deadline."

"Forget what I said. It can wait. You need sleep."

"I'm close, really." She yawned. "I'm at the end of the last take. Or maybe not. I forget. But I'm close to finishing, to knowing—"

"Sweetheart," he said gently. "Tomorrow."

Kate rose to her feet, but her legs weren't quite awake yet, so she stumbled. Jarvis steadied her.

"I suppose you're right," she said. "I had another

Allison Morse

dream."

Jarvis guided her up the dimly lit stairs to the pool patio and up the terraced pathway to the house. It was a warm evening, and there was something reassuring about the gentle but insistent clasp of his hand on her arm. When they reached the kitchen, the great Jarvis Benjamin offered to make her something to eat. Kate shook her head and started toward the stairway to her bedroom. "I want to see if I can get back there. To my dream. I was on the set the day Gloria died. I should know what's in the box, but I don't."

"What?" Jarvis followed her, his arm held her back.

She smiled at him, and felt her cheeks warm with embarrassment. "I know you'll think me foolish or crazy. But I no longer think I am. Gloria is trying to tell me something. Trying to—"

"Stop it. It's consuming you." His hand brushed across her forehead either to offer comfort, or more likely to check if her ravings were induced by fever. But whatever the reason it felt nice. It felt like safety. Compassion in his eyes, he said, "Let it go. You're about to enter a brand-new world. I'm going to make you a star. This is your chance. Gloria's gone. Let her rest."

Jarvis's words made sense, but her body chilled at the thought of trying to block out Gloria's clues and warnings.

He didn't understand. Gloria was helping her.

Chapter Nineteen

In the morning, before eating breakfast, Kate headed to the cottage and finally finished the last of the restoration. No more dreams that night and no more clues had been found in the remaining footage. Still, having the task completed lifted a weight inside her. When she got back to the main house and entered the kitchen, she was met by the wonderful aroma of coffee. The moment she retrieved a mug from the shiny white cabinets, the percolator magically clicked off, indicating the brew was ready to pour.

Jimena really had an almost supernatural sense of timing.

In the refrigerator she found eggs, three different kinds of cheese, bacon, and a large bowl of summer fruit—nectarines, plums, and grapes.

Certainly not like the typical staples at her apartment, where the refrigerator rarely held more than peanut butter and jelly.

She took out a tub of cream cheese—yum!—then went to the pantry in search of bagels. Finding none there, she ambled over to the cellar door and twisted the handle. Locked.

"Good morning, miss," Jimena said behind her.

Kate jumped and turned, feeling as guilty as a teenager caught in the act of stealing liquor. Maybe Jimena was thinking the same thing, since Jarvis had an expensive wine collection down there.

"I…I was just looking for some bagels. Do you have any?"

She shook her head. "But I will put it on my marketing list for you. Anything else you need?"

"No, thank you."

"Fine, sit. I'll make your breakfast."

"Oh, please no. This is fun for me." Kate systematically opened cabinets, looking for a skillet. After opening four doors with no luck, Jimena handed her the pan and left.

As soon as Jimena walked out, there was a knock at the back door. Then it swung open, and in walked Dylan.

"You do know this is private property," Kate said.

"Not yours. Unless there's something you care to tell me about you and Jarvis."

"Very funny. I finished the restoration, in case you're interested."

"Fantastic. I knew you could do it."

Kate opened the refrigerator again. In need of instant gratification, she grabbed a nectarine. She walked over to the sink and washed the fruit. "So what are you doing here? Aren't you busy being the great director?"

His brow furrowed. "I thought you understood."

She took a big bite of the nectarine. Sweet juice ran down her chin. "I do. You're right. I get it."

You abandoned me, she had almost said, but was glad she hadn't. She tried to cover her feelings by getting a paper towel

Man, she needed to get over her daddy issues.

"I'm here to make it up to you." Dylan took her

arm, and despite herself she warmed to his touch. "Let's go, I have a surprise."

"I have work to do."

"Such as? You just said you finished the restoration. Or, is it something to do with the investigation?"

She didn't take the bait. "No, nothing."

"Good, then you can come with me."

"I don't think so. Anyway, aren't you busy in pre-production?"

"I have time for this. I guarantee you'll like it. You need some fun. Come on."

"Oh, okay. But it better be good."

****

By the time Dylan turned onto Third Street, he'd revealed that their destination was Hancock Park.

Not very promising.

Hancock Park was a neighborhood known for stately mansions and for its easy access to downtown for bankers, lawyers, and CEOs. Hollywood types were considered riffraff and not encouraged to buy in the area, although like so many other things, that was slowly changing.

Dylan drove by the mayor's residence and turned a corner, and her heart jumped into overdrive with excitement. Outside one of the large homes was a row of small trucks and vans. A bunch of scruffy-looking guys were hauling equipment such as black cable, floodlights, and film canisters.

It was a film shoot!

Dylan parked his car and turned to her. "Welcome to Skyline Studio's newest production, *Satan's Academy*."

Kate took in the whole scene. The equipment was better than she'd ever used in the student productions she'd worked on, but the size of the crew wasn't much larger. Not a big studio operation by any stretch.

"Your surprise is bringing me to work?" Kate lifted her right eyebrow the way she'd watched her aunt do so many times. "So am I supposed to sit here with bated breath, admiring you while you direct?"

"You could do that. My thought was to employ you."

She was stunned.

"You don't like the idea?"

"Yes!" She leapt out of the car. "This is amazing!"

Dylan climbed out of the car and followed her. "Yeah, we'll see what you say by the end of the day. I'm going to work you, not entertain you."

"I know it can be grueling work and long hours, interspersed with endless periods of waiting and doing nothing, but damn it, this is what it's all about." She threw her arms around Dylan. "It's exactly what I want. Thank you!"

"Even though it's only a shlocky horror film?"

She stepped back. "That's okay. It's a job, right? See, I was listening to your and Mallick's argument."

He laughed.

She rubbed her palms together. "So how long is the commitment?"

"Five-day shoot, that's all. No more than that or else, the money people at Skyline Pictures said."

"The restoration is done so I'm in."

"I take it you like the surprise."

"I love it."

"Good." He gave her one of his most disarming

smiles. Really, it should be classified as a weapon.

She shook the thought away. Back to business. "Where do I report?"

Dylan pointed to the truck that was the farthest one away. Standing next to it was a middle-aged bald guy with a red bushy beard and mustache. "That's George. He's in charge of the lighting. You'll be helping him so he'll also make sure you sign all the paperwork for this gig. And, who knows, if you're really good, I may make you Best Boy."

She said "Ha, ha" and jogged away toward George's truck. On the way she passed the catering truck, the heart and soul of any film shoot, no matter how big or small. Standing underneath a large white tent next to a long table filled with food and drinks were three expertly made-up blondes and one brunette. They must be actresses, judging by their loving gazes at the array of pastries they dared not eat.

Kate, in her loose blue jeans, large T-shirt, and with her red locks hidden under her baseball cap, swiped the biggest, most gooey apple Danish she could find. The actresses glared at her as if eating a sweet was tantamount to declaring war.

Devouring the rest of the Danish, she headed off to find George.

He was easy to spot. He was a large man with a bulbous nose and busy red facial hair. She held out her hand to him. "Hello."

He ignored her and shouted to a young, rail-thin guy who was in the middle of positioning a Fresnel light on top of a tall stand. "Inch to the right. Good. Close the left barn door just a bit."

The young man moved one of the four black panels

that looked like the petals of a daisy.

"Good," George said. "Move on to the next light."

"Excuse me," Kate said.

"Hey, girly, I'm busy." George pointed to the caterer's table, where the actresses huddled. "You're over there. I got work to do."

She took in a deep breath before trying again. "No, I'm here. I'm supposed to assist you. I'm Kate."

George shook his head. "You're Kate? Dylan!" he yelled.

Dylan looked away from a crew member he was talking to. "Yeah?" he yelled back.

"It's bad enough you told me to tutor a girl, but this kid's so scrawny she couldn't pick up a scrim."

"I can too," she said.

Dylan sauntered over. "If she can't, fire her. But I think she's strong enough to do anything you need. Give her a try."

George grumbled some choice curses. "Fine." He pointed to the thin young man. "You'll be working with Chris. What Chris or I says goes, okay? No complaining. This is a tight shoot. We've got over fifteen setups today alone. Don't screw up."

"I won't. I promise."

By noon Kate was covered with sweat. Her muscles burned, and she had a crick in her neck the size of Rhode Island.

No one would confuse her with an actress now.

The only break from lugging heavy equipment and adjusting lights was when the scene was being shot. That's when she had a chance to watch Dylan work. It was a sight to behold. He was amazing at this. Hard to believe it was his first feature film.

As the director, he never had any downtime. Everyone, from the makeup artist to the cinematographer to the actors looked to him for answers.

Was the fabric choice for tomorrow's interior shot right?

Did the blocking make sense?

Did the lighting create the right atmosphere?

How to coax a believable performance from the actresses? Especially from the tall, buxom blonde with the monotone delivery, who also happened to be the producer's girlfriend.

Kate was impressed with how Dylan could take cliché horror scenes like the pretty girls undressing while an eye peers through the keyhole or the frenzied slashing of an ax, and compose almost psychedelic shots of chaotic violence. He elevated the formulaic structure of horror by using surprise and visual richness. All the while, and perhaps most importantly, he got the best from everyone by creating an atmosphere that nurtured instead of demanded.

Watching him work took her breath away. He was a natural. Like the boy who stands out on a little league baseball team because he hits better and throws harder than seems possible, or the math genius who swiftly solves mind-boggling equations as if the solutions were as apparent as the sun.

Then there's the rest of us—her, for instance—who struggle to achieve and sometimes even succeed in mastering certain skills but will never be at the level of the gifted artist.

But she didn't feel jealous as she witnessed such talent in action. Instead she felt awe, a sense of privilege at being able to watch him work.

"Cut!" Dylan's deep voice commanded.

Kate took her cue and moved the lights to the next setup.

It was past eight when she lugged the last Fresnel to George's truck. Chris sat in the passenger side of the truck, his head tilted back, looking exhausted. She could relate. Her legs begged her to sit, but first she needed one more burst of energy to lift the light up to George, who stood in the back of his truck. He grabbed the light and tucked it in with all the other equipment. After climbing out of the truck, he harrumphed before rolling the back door shut and heading for the driver's seat.

Panic ran through her. Had she done something wrong?

She had carried more cables and equipment than Chris. George had yelled at her only once, okay twice, for shifting the light in the wrong direction, but not since the morning. She really thought he'd even been a little impressed when she grabbed a scrim to soften the edge in the shower scene without him asking her to do it.

George stuck his head out the driver's-side window. "Setup is at five-thirty a.m. at Studio B at Skyline. Don't be late." He drove off.

Kate clapped her hands. She'd done it! She made it to day two on her first professional film production.

****

By day four of the shoot, Kate had forgotten what all her excitement had been about. Today all she wanted to do was get out of there, and it wasn't only because she could no longer distinguish one area of pain in her aching body from another. Ted had come by during the lunch break to steal some of the delicious catered food and to tell Dylan and her that he thought he had figured out what the statue depicted. And then he just left!

In any other situation, Dylan would have understood the need to drop everything and track down Ted to get some answers. But not when Dylan was in obsessive director mode.

When the shoot for the day was over, she and Dylan headed to the special-effects lab. Back in the room filled with monstrous models and masks from horror films past, Ted pulled out the twelve photos she'd given to him and placed them on a table in three rows of four—A's at the top, B's next, and C's last.

Ted pointed to row C. "These are useless. It's no more than a sliver." He scooped up the photos as if they were playing cards and slid them back into the envelope.

To Kate, the B's were just as nondescript, but Ted left them on the table while he turned his attention to the four photos marked "A." These were the ones Kate had the most hope for. Although this piece of marble was also very small, it did have a discernible curlicue design on it.

Kate pointed to it. "Is this design part of a border or a costume?"

"Neither. It's part of a beard. I'd stake my reputation on it."

"Are you sure? It looks more like tiny circles."

"Typical for a depiction of the ancients."

"You mean Biblical?" Dylan asked.

"It could be. Or Etruscan or Hassidic, but considering it was bought in the nineteen forties, popular tastes then suggests a Greek or Roman figure. But most Roman males were clean-shaven, although not all." Ted gave them an I-have-a-secret smile.

"So who is it?" Kate asked.

"I wasn't sure at first. I needed more information. After identifying the curlicue design as a beard, I extrapolated the likely size. Interestingly, it comes out to be quite a bit smaller than the two-and-half-foot length of the box." Ted leaned back, looking very pleased with himself. "I'd estimate it at one and a half feet long. Two at the absolute longest."

"Are you sure?" Kate asked. "That would be a pretty small statue for a garden, wouldn't it?"

"Why do you think it has to be for the garden?" Ted said.

"I thought that's what you said before."

"Not impossible, but I think this size makes it more likely an interior piece. Something for the mantel."

"Mantel?" Kate chewed her cheek.

"Now look at the photos marked 'B,'" Ted said. "These are really exciting."

Kate inspected the photo of a small piece of marble. From what she could tell, there was only one distinguishable edge. It was oval.

Dylan pointed to it and asked Ted, "Is it something about this mark? Is it a symbol?"

"No, just a tool of a trade. It's part of an anvil, I'm sure of it which means it can be only one thing. The statue depicts a craftsman. Like me." Ted beamed.

"Since when do they make marble statues of ordinary people?" Kate asked.

"He's not ordinary." Ted opened one of his art books to a bookmarked page. He pointed to the picture of a muscular man with a mangled foot. Held high in his hand was a two-headed hammer, in front of him an anvil. "Hephaestus, also known as Vulcan, blacksmith of the gods."

"You're just guessing," Dylan said.

"A bit, but I think I'm right."

Ted pulled out another art book, titled *The Renaissance*, and opened it to a beautiful painting of a nude woman with long, red, tousled hair standing on a giant seashell. "This is Venus. Also known as Aphrodite. Hephaestus may have been lame and ugly, but he was married to her."

"Oh, my God." Kate stared at the photo of the famous painting of Venus. "*She* was married to the craftsman?" She jumped to her feet. "I've been so dense. You said the statue would be a foot and a half tall?"

"Give or take."

"To fit on a mantel, that's what you said, right?"

"Yes."

"I have it."

"What?" Dylan said.

Ted stared at her in astonishment.

"I don't mean *it*," Kate corrected herself. "Not the murder weapon, but I think I have his mate."

****

Kate, Dylan, and Ted stood at the doorway of Kate's rental house in Claremont. Mrs. Koval, who was dressed for what appeared to be her dinner party, did not look happy to see them. "What are you doing here? As renters we do have some rights, you know. You can't just barge in anytime you feel like it."

"You're absolutely right," Kate replied. "We just

need a minute."

Mrs. Koval stood aside. "Fine."

Kate heard the clank of plates from the adjoining dining room as she walked to the cabinet filled with her mother's mishmash collection. It included two glass mermaids, ivory horses, a Toby Jug, several porcelain dolls, and on the bottom shelf, behind an Indonesian shadow puppet, was a heavy marble statue—a familiar chubby icon with a bow and arrow. Kate knew that was Cupid. Next to that was a statue of a woman. She pulled her out and handed her to Ted. "What do you think?"

He laughed with delight.

Dylan inspected the figurine closely.

The statue was no more than a foot and half high. Braided hair, wound tightly around her head. The face was exquisite. Her head tilted up as if she had just caught the eye of an admiring man. The bodice of her garment loose revealed one of her breasts. Her right hand held a sphere.

"My mother told me she's Aphrodite. Is she?"

"Yes." Ted ran a finger across her shoulders and then pointed to what was in her hand. "This is the golden apple given to her by Paris when he judged her the fairest."

"Why do you have this?" Dylan asked. "I thought all of Gloria's things were stolen."

"I thought so, too. I thought my mom had hidden all of Gloria's stuff in those boxes in the garage. I kept my mother's belongings in the house as part of the furnishings."

Ted looked at the base, then showed it to Dylan and Kate. It had two marks. He pointed at one of them. "That means it's made from blanca Carrera, like the weapon was."

"And the other symbol?" Kate could hardly contain her excitement.

"That's the artist's mark. Give me some time. If he's still alive, I may be able to track him down."

Chapter Twenty

On the last day of the shoot they were back at the Hancock Park mansion. As Kate walked up to the house, she saw that the number of trucks and crew on the set had almost doubled from what had been here before. After four days of long hours with the same crew, she'd felt a sense of comfort in the organized chaos of the set. But not today. The core crew she had come to know, maybe more intimately than she'd wished at times, had been invaded by a whole new layer of people and equipment. Because today was *action* day. All the smash'em, crash'em, blow-up shots were on for today, including the finale where the monster would be revealed.

There was a pyrotechnic crew of about six guys. Each one wore a grim expression, regardless of whether he was assigned to rolling out the detonator wire or setting up the extinguishers or painstakingly measuring the action site.

Also new to the set were a stunt woman, Kala, and a stunt man, Jack. Kala wore a brunette wig and the same outfit as the lead actress. But for Kate's money, Kala, with her muscular arms and no-nonsense manner, seemed to be the superior person. Jack was a different story. He had the manner of someone who thought he was a prime male stud. He gave Kate the creeps when he flexed his biceps and winked at her.

Just before the first shot of the day, a tan Mercedes sedan rolled up. A middle-aged guy, with a thick mustache and sideburns, wearing a shiny purple, open at the collar, shirt and equally shiny black polyester bell-bottomed slacks got out. On anyone the outfit would've looked ridiculous, but this guy took it to a whole new level, with his beer-belly paunch and his insistence that everyone call him Mr. Z, preferably in hushed tones. He was Skyline's action sequence expert.

His job was to swoop down on all of Skyline's productions to make sure each fight sequence, car chase, or explosion hit certain high-octane marks. Unfortunately, they were the same marks for every Skyline picture. Apparently the small studio didn't have the money or the inclination to reinvent the wheel in each film. Instead, Mr. Z and crew became the de facto director of every one of its productions on action day.

Kate felt for Dylan, and she was impressed with how he had to maintain a deferential manner with Mr. Z while persuading him to allow him to do a couple of original reaction shots in the sequences.

She climbed down from a ladder after adjusting a light. Maybe the intensity of the shoot might keep her from obsessing about whether Ted would be able to find the person who had made the statues.

No, probably not.

Once the lights and camera were set for the first of three explosions, Kate went to get some coffee. She had just poured a cup when the first explosion kaboomed and a fireball boiled into the air. Someone must have yelled "Cut!" because a moment later the pyrotechnic guys descended on the blaze and methodically extinguished it.

A long, green, scaly hand reached toward her.

She jumped and turned.

The guy in the monster suit grabbed a bag of sugar and the cream.

He was a big guy wearing what appeared to be a body stocking that covered him from the top of his neck to the bottom of his feet. The skintight nylon had been plastered with what looked like tiny scales painted in army-fatigue-green and the muted red of Southwestern rocks. The makeup on the face was amazing—snakelike eyes, a protruding lower jaw, and razor-sharp teeth like those of a piranha. She swallowed a scream or another laugh, she wasn't sure which. Regaining her composure, she inspected the actor again. The only thing that didn't quite go with what looked like a beast born in hell was the elegant black cape.

"Eck es eee."

"What?" Kate asked.

The man spat his false piranha teeth into his hand. "Oh, sorry, I forgot," the guy said in a thick Brooklyn accent. "Could you hand me the milk?"

"Sure." Kate gave it to him.

"I'm Francis." He held out a scaly hand to her, then clapped it shut when he realized it still held his false teeth.

"Kate," she said between giggles.

Francis tried to balance the teeth and his coffee cup in the same hand, but he spilled some of the coffee, and then he dropped the teeth.

Kate, without thinking, caught the slimy plastic dentures before it reached the ground. Her giggles erupted into a full-fledged laugh. The teeth, the costume, the Brooklyn accent, *and* his name was

Francis. It was too much.

"Nice catch," he said. Francis took the teeth from her, grabbed some napkins from the table, and wiped her hand. "Hey, sorry about that."

"It's okay. Is this your first job as a monster?"

"Nope. I've been a werewolf, a blob of sea kelp, and a Martian, just to name a few. Skyline keeps me busy. But this production only gave me one day of work. I guess the director had some stupid idea that the less you see of me the more frightening it is."

Kate cleared her throat. "Oh?"

"What was he thinking? Look at me. Don't tell me I'm not scary."

"You sure are. But what's with the cape?"

"It's part of this don't-see-too-much-of-the-monster thing." He lifted the cape and wrapped himself with it, as if he were a bat, then extended a long, scaly arm. "See? It conceals my magnificence until the end."

"Cool."

Francis unwrapped himself. "Maybe. Anyway, what's it matter. I sure could use a break from all of this and get back to what I came to L.A. for."

"To be an actor?"

"Nope. The real money is in real estate. That's something I can really sink my teeth into."

Kate lifted up her sticky hand. "Very funny. Listen, I need to wash my hands before I get back to work. Nice meeting you."

"Yeah, same here."

When Kate turned back, something caught her attention across the street. An old man stood there, watching the filming. Nothing unusual about that. Passersby regularly stopped to look on. The man was skeletal and had sunken eyes.

There was something familiar about him. Hard to forget someone who appeared as if life had been sucked from him.

Okay, clearly she'd been on this horror picture too long.

Why did she think she knew him? Then it dawned on her where she'd seen him. He'd been at the library. Maybe other places, too? Had he been following her? Or was it her overactive imagination again?

"You're much nicer than those stuck-up actresses," Francis said.

Kate turned back to him, feeling guilty about how she had forgotten he was there.

He gave her a shy smile, which looked absurd on his red-and-green face. "Maybe we can grab a drink after the shoot?"

"Ah, not tonight, but thanks. Break a leg today."

"Thanks." He smiled and walked away.

She turned and looked back across the street. The old man was gone.

****

The day and evening seemed endless, but finally they were on the last shot. It was the final confrontation, when the monster appears. Then the only brunette amongst the horde of terrorized blonde girls at the make-believe girl's school kills the monster by skewering it with a TV antenna.

"Cut! That's a wrap," Dylan said.

Kate watched him head over to the actress and congratulate her. He placed his arm across her shoulders. Kate bit her lip as the brunette leaned into Dylan.

"Hey, wake up. We're not done," George said. "Help Chris get all this stuff packed and loaded into my truck, okay?"

"Right." She gazed back at Dylan and the brunette. The actress flipped her hair back as if she were auditioning for a shampoo commercial. Then she gave Dylan a come-hither look before she sashayed into the house, probably to change out of her costume, which Kate hoped was not going to be done in front of Dylan. She felt relieved when he didn't follow the actress. Turning back to her task, Kate loosened a light and lowered it on its stand to make it easier to carry. Then she wrapped up the cord.

"You did good." George stood next to her, his meaty hands on his hips.

"Really?" Kate said, feeling excited. "Thank you. I mean wow, I've learned so much. You—"

"Whoa, there. Don't get all gushy," he said with a smile. "Now, get the lights into the truck and find all of my power cords before you leave."

"Will do."

Twenty minutes later, she and Chris had gotten almost all the lights into the truck. Kate looked around and saw that the rest of the equipment was already packed up.

Amazing how fast people can work when it's quitting time. Someone tapped her on the shoulder. It was Dylan.

"Hey." He gave her a goofy smile. The in-charge, somewhat bossy guy she was now used to appeared tentative. He peered down at his shoes, then back up at her. His cheeks reddened. She had never seen him like this, so unsure of himself, so un-Dylan-like.

"Are you okay?" she asked.

"Yeah. It's just, ah…" He cleared his throat. "Now that the shoot's over and the restoration's done, I was thinking, but only if you want to." His baritone voice, which would normally carry to the rafters, softened so much she had to lean in to hear him. "Would you like to get some dinner tonight, you know, with me?"

"What? Like a…"

"A date." He held up his hands. "Don't worry. You don't have to, I mean, we're still friends. We could go on as friends. That's okay. But I don't know, what do you think?"

She giggled, she actually giggled, before managing to say, "Yes."

"Great." His smile was wide and completely disarming, so much so she almost giggled again. Was the overly confident Don Juan she originally pegged him as feeling shy?

"I got to wrap up a couple of things first," he said, his confidence returning. "Let's meet in the staging area of the house in, say, twenty minutes?"

"Sure." After years of schooling, why were monosyllabic responses all she could manage to say? She guessed the bubbly surge of sensation that zipped through her as she gazed at him walk back to the house answered her question.

"Hey, earth to Kate." Chris held a large metal box filled with cables. "We got a couple more boxes."

"Right, I'm on it."

When the last piece of equipment was packed, Chris said, "George and I are going to Canter's Deli to meet up with some of the other crew. Want to come?"

"I would except…I have a date." She smiled and

headed toward the house.

The large, stately mansion seemed empty now, when just hours earlier it had been filled with people and things, serving as the makeup room, costume room, dressing rooms, and offices during the shoot. "Dylan?" Her voice echoed through the empty house.

No answer.

The stillness made the place seem twice as large, or was it that she felt twice as small? She dismissed the feeling of trepidation as being silly, after all not long ago people were streaming all around, they couldn't have all gone. She climbed the stairs to the second floor, looking for Dylan. She wandered around, then headed back downstairs. Halfway down the grand staircase, she saw the unmistakable sight of a man in a scaly green-and-red costume, cape and all, walking toward the front door.

"Francis," she called out. "Have you seen Dylan?" The man-thing halted and pointed to a door off the hallway. It led to the basement, which she knew had been the dressing room for the actors.

She waved to him. When she reached the door, she opened it and clicked on the light switch, a lone bulb at the top of the stairs turned on. She walked down to the basement. The air was cold, which was odd when it was still so warm outside. At the bottom, she flipped the switch for more light, but it didn't work. It wasn't completely dark. A glow came from a room constructed to the side of the large basement's open area. "Dylan," she called out as she walked toward that room.

No answer. Once there, she peered in. There was a lone lamp on a small foldaway table in the corner of the room. Next to the table was a stool. Other than that, nothing and no one was there. She was about to leave when she saw a script that had been left on the stool and thought she'd better retrieve it.

She walked to the stool and picked up the script. She felt a jolt of surprise when she saw what it was. It wasn't a script for *Satan's Academy* but for *Emperor Smythe*. Written in big, red block letters were the words *GIVE IT BACK*.

The lamp light went out.

Kate fiddled with its switch. The door slammed shut behind her, and she heard feet pounding toward her. She darted toward the corner, hoping not to trip on anything in the darkness. She hadn't gotten far when two hands grabbed her arms and twisted them behind her back. He jerked her against his body. A voice, rough and breathy, as if he was trying to disguise it, hissed, "You're only going to be told this once. Destroy the film, or you'll end up like your grandmother."

Kate shifted into fighting mode, twisting her body, trying to break his hold. She pulled free and ran to where she remembered the door to be. But she took no more than a few steps before a heavy fist pounded her head twice. Dizzy, she fell to the ground. The hands of the man were on her again. She screamed for help as he yanked her back to her feet.

He held her from behind. She couldn't see his face. But from the angle he held her, she guessed he was at least six feet tall and very strong. With her eyes now adjusted to the flicker of pale light that poured under the door, she twisted her neck to see the man and glimpsed flashes of red-and-green scales from the monster's mask. She slammed her elbows into him. It did no good. His grip only tightened.

He chuckled. One of his arms wrapped around her waist and pulled her against him, while his hand groped her breast hard. "Come on, wild-cat, fight harder."

Bile rose in her throat as she felt his erection against her back.

She jolted back her leg and struck him.

"Ow!"

She tried to hurt him again, but he threw her to the ground. The man circled her. She protectively clutched her stomach, sure he was going to kick her in the gut. But he didn't. He grabbed her hair again and said in his raspy voice, "Listen, bitch, if that film isn't destroyed, I'm coming back for you. And then we can have some real fun."

He let her go, and in the dimly lit basement she watched him slink away.

Chapter Twenty-One

When Kate could no longer hear any sounds of the monster, she slowly rose. Her head pounded where he'd struck her.

She stumbled to the stairs, held tightly to the banister, and climbed them slowly. When she was in the hallway, she cried, "Help!" The word came out as a whisper. She tried again. "Help!" Her voice was louder, but gravelly. "Dylan? Where are you?"

The house was filled with shadows. She called for Dylan again. Still no answer. She found the telephone, dialed the operator, and asked for the police. Then she called Jarvis's house.

Jimena answered. Kate's voice like sandpaper asked to speak with Lillian.

At the sound of her aunt's voice, Kate sobbed. She broke down so hard she knew Lillian couldn't understand half of what she was saying. But she must have understood enough, because she commanded Kate to get out of the house now and to wait for her and the police there.

When Kate hung up, her connection to anyone was gone, and the cavernous mansion expanded. It felt as if unseen predators peered at her from every dark corner. She ran to the front door. But before she got there it swung open. A pale glow from the streetlights backlit a man's hulking form. She leapt away.

"Hey, there you are," Dylan said easily. "I've been looking for you."

She could see him clearly now. Nothing scary, just Dylan. She exhaled her fear, but anger took its place. "Where were you?" she demanded.

"I—"

"You told me to come into the house. And you weren't here."

"What?"

She shoved him back through the doorway. Outside, she whirled back toward him. "Where were you? Where *were* you?"

He caught her arms and swung her toward him. "Hell, Kate, what's wrong?"

"Get away from me!" She tried to pull away.

He tightened his grip.

"I said get away from me!"

"Never." He took her in his arms. "I'm here now, and I won't let you go. I'll never let you go."

His words were seductive and terrifying. She told herself it was safe. Dylan wasn't the predator. It was another man who had attacked her. She let him hold her until she heard the sound of sirens coming closer, bringing a sense of relief with them. But still she couldn't help wondering. Where had Dylan been?

****

Lillian arrived a few minutes after the police did. Kate ran to her. Her aunt had telephoned Robak, who came and supplied the police with the background. All of it. He told them that things had now gone too far.

The uniformed officers seemed to accept Kate's far-fetched story about being attacked by a masked man in a cape. Between Robak's ties to the force and

Lillian's using every bit of her dangerous Lady Macbeth persona, the officers agreed to keep the event as quiet as they could. The police said they'd file a report and begin an investigation of Kate's attack and of possible new clues regarding Gloria Reardon's murder.

Kate didn't think she needed to see a doctor. What she really wanted was a bath. But Lillian insisted. After getting a clean bill of health at the emergency room, she was grateful to be back at Jarvis's, where Jimena had drawn a bubble bath.

Soaking in the claw-foot tub, she hoped the lavender bath oil would erase the memory of the man's vile hands running over her body.

When the water was long past hot and her skin shriveled, she reluctantly left the sanctuary of the water. Wearing a large T-shirt and cotton shorts, she went to find Lillian.

Her aunt was on the telephone at her bedside table, huffing while she listened to the person on the other end of the line. "I tried, Jarvis. I can't keep an eye on her every second of the day." She gestured for Kate to come in. "Yes, Jarvis," Lillian said.

Another long pause while Lillian tapped her powder-blue slippers. "I will, Jarvis. Yes…Yes. Have a safe flight, see you tomorrow." She hung up the phone. "The man is impossible. But he cares about you and is beside himself that he's three thousand miles away in New York and not here to help."

Kate sat on the bed next to her aunt. "You mean beside himself because the *Emperor Smythe* footage will probably become public before he can announce it at his party and have his lawyers at the ready."

"It's true he's concerned about that, too. In fact, he said we must move the party to this Saturday, if you can imagine. He's going to put the fear of God into the Hollywood elite to make sure the ones he wants there attend." Lillian chuckled. "The man just did the same to me when he insisted all my plans for the party be changed to this Saturday, or else."

"Or else what? Is Jarvis as ruthless as everyone says?"

Lillian put her arm around her. "Nothing you need to worry about. Titans like Jarvis Benjamin are terrifying enemies. You can ask half this town, and they'll tell you so. But like the stellar agent he used to be, he's a pit bull in defense of those he considers part of his family. That's how he felt about Gloria. That's why I was sure he'd help us when you found the footage. And now it seems he feels the same way about you, too."

Kate wondered if Jarvis was Hephaestus. "Were they lovers?"

Lillian laughed. "Gloria had her share of secrets, but I don't think that was one of them. I dare say they had something stronger than romance. He made her a star. And she helped make him very powerful, and not just in terms of the work she generated for his small agency. She recognized his worth behind his rough exterior. The more shallow of us, myself included, thought after she'd gotten her first break she should drop Jarvis and sign with a more high-class agency. But Gloria cared about what was inside him, not about his rough surface. A trait you have in common with her." Lillian brushed a lock of hair back from Kate's face.

Kate had spent a lifetime hating being compared to

her grandmother, but this was something she felt proud to share.

"Gloria was right about Jarvis," her aunt continued. "Being provided with the right entrée into Hollywood, brains and, yes, ruthlessness has made him into a man who makes half this town jump when he walks into a room."

"And Gloria, did he ever scare or intimidate her?"

"No one ever scared my sister. She could take care of herself."

Kate fingered the bump on her head where the man had struck her. The acidic taste of fear burned in her mouth when she thought about being attacked and then the now familiar presence seeking entry. It pulsated hot at her fingertips. She lay back on the bed.

"Darling, are you all right?" Lillian's voice sounded as if it were miles away. Kate closed her eyes, and gone were the sights and smells of the charming guest room at Jarvis's house as she now saw another place. The little bungalow that had been Gloria's dressing room, just big enough for a two-person couch and chair, a small bathroom, and two built-in vanities with a large mirror against the wall. Kate stared into the mirror and shivered when she saw Gloria's face reflected back.

Gloria's face flushed, she laughed either with or at someone in the room with her.

Kate couldn't see who it was but felt his or her lurking presence. The same one she'd sensed in her other dream, hallucination, or whatever this strange time shift was when she peered at the *Smythe* set through Gloria's eyes.

Gloria stood, beaming at her guest. She

nonchalantly lifted one shoulder and was about to turn away, but in that brief moment, her face registered something horrible. Her eyes popped wide, and her mouth contorted into a scream, but before a sound was uttered she fell to the floor, dead.

Kate wept. Slowly she realized she was in Lillian's room, and the cries were coming from her own mouth. Lillian hovered over her. Kate said through her tears, "Gloria was afraid. Oh, God, so afraid."

Her aunt paled. Her eyes glassy as if she too could see the images Kate had just witnessed. "Never afraid was my beautiful sister, never until the end."

Chapter Twenty-Two

During the last two days, Kate had not left Jarvis's house once, not even to walk in the garden or swim in the pool. When she dared to emerge from her room, her pulse raced as she'd scurry to retrieve a book or get a glass of milk, then scamper back to her bedroom and the assurance of its locked door.

She'd been aware of Jarvis's return from New York the night before, but besides having Jimena deliver to her room a startling bouquet of bright daisies and a note from him, he'd left her alone. Dylan, on the other hand, had come by two or three times a day, demanding to see her. Kate had sent word through Jimena and Lillian that she was sick and unavailable.

That wasn't far from the truth. Ever since she'd been attacked, she felt as if her strength, her reason, all the things she thought of as who she was had been replaced by a creature of sensation swinging from frenzied agitation at night to a numbing collapse during the day. The only person from the outside she'd wanted to speak to was her friend Natalie, who had supposedly been back from her internship for over a week now. But what was the point in reaching out to her, since Natalie hadn't bothered to return any of her phone messages since she'd returned. Kate's lower lip trembled and sadness threatened to overtake her. Ever since childhood, Natalie had been the only person she could rely on to be there for her.

Well, things change.

Kate heard a *shhh* sound and saw a neatly folded piece of white paper slide under her door like a hotel bill. It was, in a way. And tonight the bill came due when she had to attend Jarvis's party where the missing footage would be revealed.

No, that wasn't fair. With the daisies, Jarvis had included a kind note telling her she didn't have to go to the party if she wasn't up to it.

But she would attend. She'd struck a deal with him and wouldn't go back on her word. More than that, she felt an even deeper promise to her mother and to Gloria to try to restore at least a part of what had been lost. Somehow she'd needed to find the courage to get through the damned night.

Throwing off the blankets that had enclosed her like a cocoon, she leapt out of bed and retrieved the piece of paper. It read:

Itinerary for Miss Kate Bloom

1:00 p.m. Limousine pick-up

1:30 p.m. Arrival at Beverly Wilshire Hotel

2:00 p.m. Fitting

2:30 p.m. Massage

3:45 p.m. Manicure/Pedicure

4:30 p.m. Facial

5:30 p.m. Hairstylist

6:30 p.m. Make-up

7:30 p.m. Final Fitting

8:30 p.m. Limousine pick-up

The paper read like a young woman's fantasy day.

It filled Kate with dread.

Today she was to be transformed so that tonight

she could step out on to the stage of Hollywood glamour and create a buzz and excitement in the press about the *Emperor Smythe* mystique.

She trudged to her closet and stared at the silk dress Jarvis had bought for her to wear to the party.

It was exquisite. She'd been surprised—no, more than that, touched—by Jarvis's selection of it for her. The gown seemed personal to her, to who she was or, at least, who she wanted to be. Not a costume at all.

How did he know?

She scoffed at her own musings. Who was she kidding? She doubted that Jarvis himself had chosen the dress. He was much too important to bother with that. He must have had some lackey or marketing person purchase the trifle.

Her fingers skimmed the fabric. The dress was more clingy than she would have liked. Still, it had an earthy vibrancy, with its dark jungle green swirling into a rich brown. It evoked sensuality without pretense, a comfort in one's grace. Kate wondered if she could ever allow herself to be like that?

Dylan had been right about one thing. She was scared—no, terrified—to get close to him or any guy she truly liked. Even before the recent bumps in the night and thinking that possible murderers peeked from familiar eyes. Abandoned by her father, left with a bitter mother, and believing her grandmother had died at her lover's hands was beyond a heavy burden to grow up with. If all that had taught her anything, it was that relationships are to be feared, not embraced.

Kate tried to shake off her sense of foreboding. She took the dress and placed it in a full-length garment bag from the closet and laid it on her bed.

The ridiculous thought that it was Dylan who'd attacked her kept circling through her mind. Like a tether ball, no matter how many times she punched the thought away, it came back with equal force. The guy who had assaulted her was big, like Dylan, and strong.

Damn! That awful reminder of her own frailty. Once again she had been defenseless.

She walked to the bay window and peered out at the garden.

Why would Dylan attack her? He wanted the film to be shown as much as she did. Still, she had that nagging suspicion he was hiding something.

A psychologist would undoubtedly say that associating Dylan with her fear of helplessness was her way of shielding herself from falling in love with him. Yet, something lay hidden behind his façade. She felt it.

Or was that simply the truth about everyone?

From her open window, she heard a car come up the driveway. The clock by her bed read twelve forty-five p.m. The limousine had arrived.

Would her attacker be there tonight? Would he follow through on his promise to hurt her if the film was shown? And, what about that strange skeletal man she'd seen on the set and at the library, and maybe other places too, scuffling off into shadows. That couldn't just be her imagination.

Jarvis had explained in his note with the flowers that there'd be no reason for anyone to threaten her if the film was already out. That's why he had moved up the date for showing it.

But Jarvis had not been there in that dark basement and smelled that man's sour breath when he'd promised to hurt her if the film was shown.

Allison Morse

Her toes and fingertips turned cold, as if her blood no longer circulated. She had to get through this night. Clasping her hands like a child praying for protection after waking up in terror from a bad dream, she wished not for her mommy but for Gloria. That's who she needed now. If Kate was to walk out on to the Hollywood stage tonight, with the press, with Dylan, and perhaps with her assailant all gawking at her, she must summon at least a bit of Gloria's legendary aplomb, her joy at commanding attention, her comfort with sensuality—something Kate so obviously lacked. But more than that, she needed Gloria for…

What had Lillian said?

Gloria was never afraid.

A sharp knock at the door. Kate jumped.

So much for aplomb.

Jimena announced that her car was waiting.

Her legs wobbled as she stood. Taking a breath, she pictured how her grandmother would have walked, held herself, felt, while being as pampered and displayed as Kate would be tonight.

She felt feverish. The heat did not just tickle her fingertips as it had done before. It burst inside her, fuel long amassed igniting into flames.

This time she didn't jump at the insistent knock on her door.

A laugh as melodious as a Gershwin tune floated past her lips, and Kate called out that she'd be ready in a minute.

She strode to the closet, ignoring the brown and green frock she's laid so carefully in the garment bag just minutes ago. Because she'd made her choice and there was no turning back. She reached to the farthest end of the closet. Her stomach hopped with nerves as she took hold of her prize—Gloria's gold lamé dress.

No more fear. It was time to shine.

She swung the bag over her shoulder and headed for the limousine. She wondered what Dylan would think when he saw her wearing this dress.

Would he kiss her the way he did before?

Yes. Tonight, she would be Gloria. Maybe this had always been inevitable.

Chapter Twenty-Three

Kate breathed in the cool air of wealth of the Beverly Wilshire Hotel. Built in the Twenties, this hotel had somehow managed to achieve the seamless combination of a European palace, with its ornate façade and faux Roman columns, with Art Deco's long, exaggerated lines in its archways. She had read somewhere that the hotel was built to be a reaction against Art Deco and yet that influence was unmistakable.

Yet another example of the futility of rebellion.

The hotel manager personally escorted her to her room. Waiting for her there was a basket of fruit, a variety of fashion magazines, and a stout woman in her fifties, who shook her head sadly at the sight of Kate. Her name was Mrs. Dolinski. Her job was to make Kate look like a movie star, whether she wanted to be one or not. Four hours later, Mrs. Dolinski clapped her hands, closed the door on the final aesthetician and stylist, and declared Kate *finis*.

Kate had to admit that being massaged, polished, primped, and primed by multiple attendants had been a luxurious experience. Well, not the eyebrow plucking part—that hurt.

Before Mrs. Dolinski left, she instructed Kate to hurry down to the lobby. The car to take her to the party was already waiting.

She stood and stared at herself in the brass-framed, full-length mirror in her suite. A million tiny lights winked off the gold beaded dress. It was like wearing sunlight.

She winked back at Gloria, who was there, in her reflection.

Not bothering to knock, Beatrice swung open the door. "You're late."

Kate shrugged with a catlike air and slowly twirled to show off her dress.

Beatrice cringed as if it were uncomfortable just to look at Kate. Then she said in a voice more world-weary than Noel Coward's, "What? Do you think I'm surprised you're wearing one of Gloria's gowns?" She pulled out her notebook and flipped through its pages of notes. "So…after the announcement's made, I'll make sure the press knows Miss Kate Bloom was dressed for the occasion in her grandmother's famous gold lamé gown. That will add to the titillation, no doubt."

"Can you stop being a jerk for just a minute?"

"What do you mean? I'm thrilled. This is wonderful publicity." Beatrice tapped her silver pen against the book. "It will also be interesting to see Jarvis's reaction. Now, Cinderella, off to the ball."

Kate, chin held high, sauntered past her.

****

Her limousine was one of many inching its way up Jarvis's long driveway. There were also Cadillacs, Jaguars, and Mercedes aplenty.

When her driver stopped in front of the house, a valet handed her out. Because of the three-inch-heel shoes with sharply pointed toes, she should have toppled with her first step, but magically she didn't.

Instead she managed to glide up the front walkway like a blossoming Gigi.

As she approached the arched oak front door, Michael Russo, *the* Michael Russo, the star of last year's gritty police saga, emerged from a group of people who were laughing more loudly than seemed necessary and who all sported variations of the shag haircut.

Michael sidled up to Kate. "I hate these things, don't you?"

Before she could reply, a man she didn't recognize, dressed like a butler in an old Agatha Christie story, opened Jarvis's front door.

Michael Russo swaggered past her, and when he was inside, cameras flashed all around him like firecrackers. He turned back to her and winked, then blasted his hallmark wicked smile at the photographers crowding the foyer.

When Kate stepped inside, several sharp flashes of light popped before the photographers realized she was no one. The press returned to mumbling amongst themselves.

The living room had been transformed. Gone was most of the furniture to accommodate the large number of guests. Additional lights had also been placed everywhere. Kate assumed they were there to assist the photographers. Jarvis's collection of Chinese porcelain was undoubtedly safely packed away from the mob. The place no longer felt like a house but like Grand Central station, with bodies packed close together, banal chatter amplified by the high ceiling of the foyer, and reporters, not normally allowed to mingle with the guests, buzzing around like flies hatching in the summertime.

Kate scanned the room for Dylan, and her stomach did an abrupt backflip when she spotted him in a corner. She took a breath and wove through the horde of glittery people. The only thing she cared about was reaching Dylan. Dressed in a black tuxedo with a white shirt open at the collar gave him the appearance of a rake from some old novel.

She liked that.

But then she saw that he wasn't alone. That brunette actress from *Satan's Academy* was standing with him.

What was her name? Cindy or Sandy, something cute and peppy. Whatever it was, there she stood—no, more like there she leaned close to Dylan, lapping up his every word and batting her eyelashes as if she had a tick.

Kate retreated into the anonymity of the crowd.

What had she expected? Was he supposed to rush to her side, as if she were Cinderella and he her prince?

Well, yes in point of fact, he was.

She knew that was being unfair. Who could blame him if he'd made a move on a cutesy girl? Kate's behavior toward him had been contrary and repressed.

She really didn't want to think about that now. Tonight she may have finally figured out how to break free from her neurotic fears. She was still Kate, but a little melding of Gloria's fire would help.

She glided among the glitterati like an invisible ghost. Everyone was engaged in lively conversation, some in intimate twos or threes, and others in boisterous gaggles of ten or more.

Here she was, dressed to the nines wearing folds of

fabric draped with the sheen of liquid gold that shimmered at her every step and with a bodice that hugged her so tight that it made a mummy's wrapping look like leisure wear, yet no one noticed her, no one cared.

Ironic.

She'd spent her life hiding her looks, and now at her coming-out party, beauty was a dime a dozen. It didn't mean anything by itself.

She spied Jarvis holding court in a corner. She could slip in next to him and remain anonymous. But that wasn't what she was here for. She was here to make a splash, to help market her discovery, and to create excitement for the remake of *Emperor Smythe*. Her throat felt dry at the thought. Yet at the same time her skin burned with excitement, or fear, or maybe both, as she realized she wanted to do it, if only to see if she could. She scanned the room, looking for an opportunity. This wasn't just a party, it was work. And as at any corporate soirée, the name of the game was advancement.

How to attract attention in a room full of exhibitionists?

Kate swiped a glass of champagne from a waiter's passing tray and watched a group of reporters huddled around a bragging Michael Russo.

She was moving toward them before she was even aware of making the decision. Edging up to the outer ring of reporters and like a professional craps player, she hung in the back of them, observing the action, waiting for the right moment to enter the game.

The press asked Michael about the sports car he'd recently totaled and about whether he was having an affair with such-and-such model or such-and-such actress. Finally, a woman wearing a flamboyant purple wide-brimmed hat, whose press credentials identified her as working for the *Hollywood Reporter*, called out, "Michael, tell us, you must know, what's tonight's big secret?"

Michael pantomimed zipping his lips shut while giving a wink, as if he knew.

Kate knew he didn't. But his bullshit had stirred the pot.

Another reporter asked, "Come on, Michael. Jarvis must have indicated something to you. Is it about a new project?"

That was all the opening Kate needed. Like a veritable Mickey Rooney and Judy Garland, she stepped forward, determined to put on a show.

She playfully pointed at Michael. "Of course Jarvis must be thinking of you for the part."

Michal's eyebrows lifted so high they resembled two question marks. "Yeah…of course. The part."

She leaned back and appraised him coolly from head to toe. "Yes, you're an interesting choice."

A grizzled old reporter with yellow teeth asked, "So, girly, I guess you know all about it. What's the deal?"

"Not girly. Kate Bloom. B-L-O-O-M." She looked at Michael again and smiled. "I didn't know Jarvis had told anyone else. It's exciting, isn't it?"

Known as a consummate performer, Michael stammered something unintelligible. She felt a little pang of guilt at using him. But channeling her inner Gloria was working.

The actor regained his equilibrium. "I'm *very*

excited. Who wouldn't be? It's a fantastic part, right?"

Kate waited and let his expectant smile crystallize into a frozen mask. She was fascinated to see how long he could keep that up.

Then she spotted Lillian and got a better idea.

"Right," Kate finally said. She heard a soft pop come from Michael's jaws as he let his face relax. She said to him just loud enough for the reporters to hear. "Of course, the secret is more than about the remake of one of the greatest films of all time."

"Remake? Remake of what?" Someone in the press asked.

Another one grumbled, "Is that all?"

Kate ignored the questions and said to Michael, "Yes, and with one of the best leading roles ever written."

At that point, she'd swear a tiny drop of saliva appeared on the actor's lower lip before he licked it away.

She gave him a nudge as if they were old confederates. "Why don't you give them a hint? Jarvis wouldn't mind."

"Yes, yes!" clamored the press like a pack of barking dogs.

Kate let Michael stew, except this time he gave her his famous wicked grin. "Ladies first."

Believing she was as vivacious as Gloria made her feel as if she was. "Oh, look. My aunt." She waved to Lillian. "Over here, darling."

Darling?

That was over the top. But she couldn't stop the affected words from tumbling from her mouth.

She glided to her aunt with a smile and escorted

her into the circle of reporters and the bewildered Michael Russo. Trying to ignore Lillian's famous admonishing eyebrow, Kate turned back to the reporters. "You all know my great-aunt, the wonderful actress Lillian Baker."

Kate didn't wait for a reply, nor was she bothered by the blank looks on most of the reporters' faces, because she saw a flash of recognition from a couple of them.

Turning to Lillian yet also speaking for the benefit of the reporters, she said, "These nice people want a hint about tonight. Which, of course, made me laugh, for, after all, we are the hint." Kate lifted her long arms gracefully over her head and made a sweeping gesture. "*I'm* the hint. Who I am. What I'm wearing. Everything. It's all to suggest a very important discovery of what was lost in the past and an exciting project for the future."

Some of the younger reporters still looked blank. But not the lady in the hat or the older man with the yellow teeth. Their faces were alight with understanding. The man signaled a photographer in the foyer, who ran over and snapped a couple of shots of Kate with her arm around her aunt.

In the buzz of whispers, she discerned the words *Emperor Smythe* and *Gloria*. Soon a swarm of photographers tightened into a circle around Kate and Lillian, leaving poor Michael excluded from the frenzy.

It all felt so delicious. Like chocolate-covered raspberries melting in her mouth. She smiled with delight as the cameras flashed again and again.

When they had enough photos and saw Kate wasn't going to say any more, the press drifted away.

Michael, on the other hand, stomped away.

"Ta-ta," Kate said as she waved after him. Laughing, she turned to her aunt. "Oh, dear. I guess I stepped on someone's ego." She grabbed her aunt's hands and bounced like a little girl. "I did it, I actually did it. Can you believe it?

Her aunt looked greenish even under her generous application of makeup. "No, I can't."

"You were right about the dress. I didn't think I had it in me."

Lillian tugged her hands free from Kate's. "This isn't you."

"What?"

"*Ta-ta* and *darling*? What on earth? You don't *look*—You don't *act* like yourself."

"A good thing, too. If I was behaving like my normal self, I'd be weeping in some closet right now instead of creating a stir, just the way you always wanted me to."

"Not this way," Lillian said.

"It's too late to change your mind now." Kate scanned the room. More and more guests whispered and pointed at her. "Look, rumors are flying, as planned. I did it. You and Jarvis were right. The boots, my baggy clothes, they were my mask. My protection, and not a very good one. I think I've discovered that gold lamé is a better armor. By wearing this, I can take the offense."

"You sound like Gloria, not Kate."

Kate shook her head and sighed. "Oh, Lillian."

"For God's sake, Gloria wasn't even Gloria. That is, until she started to believe her own press. I loved my kid sister. I did. But Kate, you, who you are in your core, has so much to offer."

"Come on. With everything that's been going on, can't I have a moment to enjoy this?" The heat inside her died down. She took Lillian's hand, and this time her aunt didn't pull it away. "Believe me, I know I'm not her."

Lillian's eyes clouded, and for a moment her sharp gaze was replaced with a look of confusion. "No, of course, you're not. Sometimes the past is too present, that's all." She squeezed Kate's hand. "Do me one favor though?"

"What?"

Lillian smiled. "Promise me, tomorrow you'll wear those ghastly boots of yours."

"Deal. But tonight I'm going to pretend, and if I can get over my self-righteous snobbery about it, have some fun."

Lillian took Kate's arm. "If you can't have fun with your looks, then they are truly wasted on you."

"Now that sounds like my aunt Lillian."

"Dylan is outside on the patio," Lillian said with a mischievous smile. "Are you prepared to make your second entrance of the evening?"

Kate slumped. "I don't think there's much point. Every time I've seen him, that actress is clinging to him. I guess I've blown that."

Her aunt lifted Kate's chin. "I thought you were here to take the offense. That skirmish will be a piece of cake. Trust me."

Kate shrugged. "If he doesn't want me—"

"Enough. I think it's high time both of you told the truth to each other about how you feel."

"And you say *I'm* acting differently tonight? One

more statement like that and I'm going to file a missing person's report. You couldn't possibly be my aunt."

"Oh, please. Everyone around you can plainly see that you're both bonkers about each other."

Her aunt guided Kate into the solarium and perilously closer to the patio, where she'd last seen Dylan. "Now go get him." Her aunt gave her a push and left her to fend for herself.

Now that was pure Lillian.

There were very few people on the patio, perhaps because the night was cooler than expected or because the press was forbidden to be there. However, when Kate saw the heated exchange between Jarvis and Dylan, she suspected it had more to do with no one wanting to be caught in the crossfire, particularly when one of the shooters was someone as powerful as Jarvis Benjamin.

Dylan, taller than Jarvis, hovered over him. Yet of the two, it was the older man's electric blue stare that determined the more menacing presence.

The lead actress from *Satan's Academy* who had clung to Dylan all night had retreated to a safe distance.

Kate took a deep breath and prayed her bravado would guide her as it had done with the reporters.

Unsteady on her high-heeled shoes, she swayed gingerly toward them, repeating to herself Lillian's words *a piece of cake*.

Dylan hollered, "What do you mean the film is going to be moved tomorrow?"

Jarvis, like a snake about to strike, hissed, "Don't question me, boy."

Even Dylan was smart enough to take a step back from him.

Jarvis wore a tuxedo, undoubtedly expensive, but still the baggy way his jacket fell from his broad shoulders gave him the disheveled appearance of a Damon Runyon gangster at a prayer meeting. He just didn't fit in. Not that anyone would dare tell him so. In some strange way, Kate found the great man's inherent awkwardness endearing.

Jarvis swayed back and forth, loose like a boxer, as he circled Dylan. "It's going to be made public. You did notice the press here, didn't you?"

Dylan jutted his chin. "I'll tell you what I noticed. I noticed you have no projectionist and no large rooms set up to show the film tonight, and now I hear you're taking it away."

"I'm doing what needs to be done. When Golden State Pictures and their lawyers knock on my door tomorrow, which, trust me, they will, and demand we turn it over, it will be someplace safe."

"Safe?" Dylan said. "What are you up to?"

"Where are you taking it?" Kate asked Jarvis, forgetting for the moment her goal of making an entrance. But only for a moment, because she was presented with the gratifying jaw-dropping expression from both Jarvis and Dylan.

"Wow!" Dylan exclaimed.

Jarvis's eyes shone as if when he saw her faux gold dress he'd just peered into a treasure trove of the real precious metal. But then he averted his gaze, as if the sight of her hurt and said, "You didn't wear the dress I chose for you," he said curtly.

Kate suddenly felt nervous. "Do you disapprove?"

"No. You look perfect," he said, still not looking at her. "By the way, I've heard you have singlehandedly stirred up the muckrakers' anticipation. Well done."

"But that was only a couple… Is there anything you don't know?"

Dylan cocked his head, making him look like a perplexed hound.

"I predict," Jarvis said, "we'll get front-page coverage tomorrow, thanks to your help and later mine. This evening will build from one tantalizing discovery to the next. The press will eat it up."

Kate turned from Jarvis and saw Dylan gaping at her.

This time she didn't even try to hide the feeling of desire she felt when she looked at him.

Jarvis cleared his throat. "I seem to be one person too many here. Enjoy the evening. It is a party, after all." He gave Dylan an unfathomable smile and added, "But don't go far. There will be a big announcement tonight, as promised." The great man strode into his house.

Kate, allowing her mantra for the evening of *What would Gloria do?* guide her. She gazed right back at Dylan, no longer immobilized by insecurities.

Dylan's normally cool manner faltered at the intensity of her gaze. He peered at the ground, then looked back up at her. "What? Why are you staring at me like that? You seem different."

She took his hand, and she watched his expression change from confusion to longing.

The brunette actress edged closer to Dylan.

Damn. Kate had forgotten the actress had been hovering in the background.

Dylan didn't seem to notice her.

Hooray!

The actress took the hint, stepped back, and faded away.

When she was gone, Kate said to Dylan, "I've wanted to tell you something all evening." She put her lips next to his ear and whispered, "I'm not afraid." And the most amazing thing of all, it was true.

"What?"

"I want you. I want us to be together." She stood on tiptoe and kissed him.

She was surprised when he pulled away.

"Wait. I can't," he said.

She'd felt the longing in his lips. The desire was real, wasn't it? Her mind clouded with self-doubt.

"It's not that I don't want to be with you. Believe me I do. It's just…" He caressed the back of her neck. "My God, Kate, we're in the middle of a party, the press is all over the place, and…" His face tensed. "And, I need to tell you something. You may not want me after—"

"I'll want you." She kissed him again hard, and he kissed her back. It was head-to-toe tingly wonderful.

"Stop that!" a voice commanded behind her. Kate turned and saw Jimena, hands on her hips, shaking her head at them. "Inside. Mr. Benjamin is making his announcement, and he wants you both in there."

"Now?" Kate said. "I thought he was going to do that after he screened the footage?"

Dylan punched the air. "The bastard isn't going to show it. I knew it."

"Of course he's going to. He promised. Right, Jimena?"

Jimena shrugged and turned back into the house.

"Son of a bitch!" Dylan said.

"I hope you're wrong about Jarvis not showing the film. But if you're not, we'll make our own announcement and tell the world about finding it. Together, he can't stop us."

Dylan hugged her. "I love you, you know. Now we'd better get inside." He let go of her and headed toward the house.

"Wait! You can't say *that* and expect me to just go inside to be with all those people, when all I want is to be with you."

He turned and clasped her hand, and led her back to the party. "Let's get this over with so we can get out of here."

"Yes."

"To my place." Dylan's normally self-confident expression turned vulnerable. "Will you?"

She replied by kissing him again.

Ignoring a few disapproving stares, they laughed, and it was if their hands suddenly had a will of their own refusing to behave, compelled to constantly touch and caress each other.

Electronic feedback wailed from a PA system. Arms entwined, they followed the sound to its source in the foyer. The press and most of the guests were already gathered there. The lights had been dimmed a bit so one of the spotlights set up over the banister on the second floor walkway shone brightly on Jarvis, who stood on the staircase, microphone in hand.

Dylan stood behind Kate, his arms wrapped around her. She leaned against him, unable to squelch the feeling of pure joy.

Jarvis glanced at her before he spoke to the crowd. "Thank you for coming to my little gathering. My announcement is…well, I heard the rumors that have been buzzing around here tonight. Many of you have already guessed it."

He paused, and everyone was riveted on him. Kate felt the decidedly unflashy Jarvis was closer to P.T. Barnum than even Lillian was.

At the first sound of restive muttering in the audience, Jarvis continued, "Yes, it's true. I have in my possession the lost footage from Winston Nash's ruined masterpiece, *Emperor Smythe*."

That caused a stir. Jarvis held up his hand to quiet the crowd. "I'm sparing no expense to try to fully restore the footage so the world can see this great piece of film history and its crushing indictment of a corrupt backroom powerbroker."

Dylan whispered into Kate's ear, "What does he mean *try*? We've already done it."

"It's just salesmanship. I think?"

Jarvis continued, "The brilliance of Nash's vision is now clear, so I'm also announcing that my studio will be doing a remake of the film."

"See?" Kate whispered to Dylan.

"The remake will be even bigger, in color, with contemporary resonance," Jarvis said. "After all, look at Watergate. The dangers of corruption resonate even more now than when the original film came out. But I promise the remake will not lose any of the magic of the original. And nothing was more magical than Gloria Reardon in her seminal and final performance. But this time I plan to give the story a happy ending. Here tonight is Gloria Reardon's own granddaughter, the breathtaking Kate Bloom."

A second spotlight swiveled, casting a bright beam

of white light that played over the crowd and then landed on Kate.

She blinked, unable to see through the blinding light, but smiled at the crowd, feeling reassured and happy in Dylan's embrace.

"Kate has assisted in the restoration," Jarvis said. "And I predict that she will fulfill her grandmother's legacy and soon be known as one of the great actresses of the silver screen."

A couple of light bulbs flashed amid the tepid applause.

Jarvis continued, "We are also lucky to have here tonight and fully backing my studio's remake of the film, the son of Marchesa Fiorenza Nicoletti and the great director himself, Winston Nash."

Dylan stiffened.

The beam of light left Kate and swirled about the crowd as if it was looking for the right place to land. Following the light with her gaze, she wondered where was Nash's son?

Jarvis boomed, "I present to you Mr. Ulysses Demoducus Nash."

The spotlight landed on Kate and Dylan again.

"See the lovebirds together, Gloria and Winston's descendants. Who says the past cannot live again?" Jarvis chuckled. "Around town some of you know Ulysses only by his professional name—Dylan Nichols."

Kate jolted out of Dylan's embrace as if she'd been shot.

Cameras erupted into a bombardment of flashes, but she was only half aware of them. She gaped at Dylan—no, Ulysses—or whoever he was, and she thought she'd be ill.

She spun on her heel and fled.

He chased her, shouting her name.

Her escape route was blocked by a wall of reporters and guests shouting questions at her.

Dylan grabbed her arm. "Kate, please, let me explain."

"Get your hands off me!"

He pulled her toward him.

"Stop!"

He didn't let go. "No, not until you let me explain."

She threw a punch at him with her other arm, but the bastard caught her hand.

Fuck that!

She jacked a knee into his groin, and he crumpled onto the floor. "I said don't touch me!"

Flash-bulbs popped like artillery.

Chapter Twenty-Four

The alarm clock read three thirty-five a.m.

Not one wink of sleep. Instead her brain played again and again the shocking news that Dylan wasn't Dylan.

Well, she supposed he was, but he was also Winston Nash's son.

Dylan? She'd actually respected him for what she thought was his ability to display his unvarnished emotions, but all the while he was hiding behind the biggest mask of all.

She rose from the bed, sharp and mechanical like she was a vampire rising from the grave.

God, she was even thinking in horror film metaphors now. Dylan's corrupting influence, no doubt.

After putting on her robe and slippers, she tiptoed down the stairs to the kitchen to find something to ease her stomach.

A glass of water and two crackers later, she still didn't feel any better.

She slipped out the kitchen's back door into the warm night air and wandered on to the patio. She could almost see what was no longer there. She, in Dylan's arms, hours earlier, had been tucked away by themselves. A breeze lifted her red locks. She felt like one of those Victorian heroines standing alone on a cliff overlooking a turbulent sea, pondering the darkness of her life.

Enough!

She'd become more melodramatic than Lillian and Gloria combined.

When she walked on to the smooth pavement of the pool patio, she blinked, surprised to find she'd drifted so far from the house.

A crackle of leaves sounded behind her. She caught only a fleeting glimpse of a raccoon's tail before it disappeared into the shrubbery. Then she saw a light flicker somewhere below. She froze.

Why had she come out here alone?

Taking a deep breath, she assured herself that there were people in the main house who cared about her. One good *Satan's Academy* scream, and they'd come running. She crept closer to the trail that led to the cottage and to what she thought was the source of the light. She also had guessed who was responsible for it—Dylan.

Too many times she'd noticed his disheveled appearance and the equally disheveled couch when she'd reported to work. This had made her long suspect he'd been spending nights at the cottage. But she hadn't figured out how he got in and out unseen by the ever vigilant Jimena.

Kate slowly descended the now secure stone stairs. The glow emanated from the cottage where the curtains did not quite meet.

The light blinked off. She jerked back, and her gaze plunged down the ravine. The darkness of the pit appeared to rush up at her with a suffocating intensity. She clutched the new railing.

She stood only steps away from where Mallick had

fallen. A miracle he hadn't died. She wasn't even sure if Mallick had been the intended victim. Her mind wove different scenarios of the accident. It could have been meant for Dylan or for Mallick or even for her. The only thing she was sure about was that it hadn't been an accident.

Something creaked below, not much louder than the crickets that chirped in the night. A man in shadow slipped out the cottage door, carrying something. He disappeared behind the cottage. Even with only the light of the moon to see by, she knew who it was. Dylan.

No, not Dylan. It was Ulysses, otherwise known as Odysseus. What had her high school teacher said when they studied *The Odyssey*? One interpretation of the name Ulysses meant no one, nobody.

Kind of fitting since she had no idea who he really was.

Interesting. This was another mythological connection to all of this. Had Dylan's mother, the marchesa, whatever the rest of her name was, lived near the marble quarry in Carrara?

Did Winston make trips to Italy to visit the marchesa prior to Gloria's death?

Could it be Winston who'd bought the statue and used it as the murder weapon?

She was jumping to conclusions. Besides, if she remembered the gossip about Winston correctly, he hadn't begun being a professional guest of bored nobility and the nouveau riche until many years after Gloria died. Whatever the truth was, Kate noted that this was another thing she needed to research.

Dylan returned, from who knows where, and

walked into the cottage, leaving the door ajar.

She inched down two more steps to get a better look.

He soon reappeared. He put down what he was carrying before closing the cottage door. Moonlight reflected off a large steel container.

He was taking the *film*!

She had to stop him! Scream? Run back to the main house for help?

But she didn't do any of that. Instead, she just stood there and watched him disappear behind the cottage, carrying away the precious cargo.

The sound of crackling brush receded as Dylan made his escape down some unknown trail behind the cottage.

Kate remained on the steps long after he'd left, willing him to come back.

Birds chirped to announce the first golden hint of sunrise. Wet with dew, she snuck back into Jarvis's house and up to her room.

After another vain attempt to sleep, she emerged from her room with a suitcase in each hand.

The smell of coffee diverted her from her trajectory to the front door.

Ensconced in the kitchen nook, Jarvis read one of what appeared to be several different newspapers spread out on the kitchen table. When he spotted her, his face widened into a satisfied smile that was not dissimilar to the happy and somewhat bizarre expressions of the Toby Jugs that peered down at her from the built-in shelf above the nook.

"You were fantastic last night," he said. "I loved the knee to the groin. Doubled the publicity."

"Bastard!" She dropped her suitcases with an intentional thud.

"I never claimed to be anything but that, both metaphorically and in actual fact," he said.

She was too pissed to be stopped by the biographical tidbit. "You knew who Dylan really was, and you didn't tell me."

"I just found out myself. It seems J.B. Sutton's spies are better than mine. Something I'll square soon."

Curiosity and the need for caffeine trumped her outrage. On the kitchen counter were a carafe of coffee, a bowl of fruit, and easy-to-make meal items such as cereal and bread. Kate figured that Jimena must have arrayed them before she left this morning, since Sunday was the staff's scheduled day off.

Jarvis slathered some jam onto a piece of burnt toast and took a bite. She watched him chew the hapless toast for what seemed like an eternity before he finally said, "Naturally, I had Dylan investigated at the beginning, like I did with all of you. His story checked out. He'd gone to UCLA film school, studied restoration at AFI, and worked in the industry for the past several years, all under the name Dylan Nichols. At the time I didn't see a need to look any further."

Jarvis scraped his butter knife on his plate as if he were sharpening it. "It wasn't until two days ago when J.B. Sutton needled me about Dylan's true identity that I discovered the truth." He scowled, but that look was soon replaced by the expression he normally wore—that of a calculating king. "And by then the party was so tantalizingly close. It was a once-in-a-lifetime promotion opportunity; you've got to see that."

"You could've warned me and still made your

announcement." Sipping her coffee, she sat at the table next to Jarvis.

"I suppose I could've. I suppose a gentleman would've." He shot her a wicked smile.

Her cheeks warmed. In some perverse way, she found him attractive.

"I can't say I regret it," he said. "Your natural reaction, better than I ever could have scripted it."

Kate felt a lot of things about what had happened—pain, anger, shame, but none was the amusement she saw plainly on Jarvis's face. "Yeah, and what if Dylan had been the one who attacked me? Still worth the publicity?"

Jarvis stared into her eyes. "You were never in danger. As soon as I knew who he really was, I made sure you weren't alone with him again. That's why I hired that actress from his film to dog him throughout the party." He reached out to touch her cheek. "I'd never let anyone hurt you."

"Too late." She stood, walked to her suitcases, and picked them up.

He casually looked through the newspapers on the table. "Sure, why stay? Except in the past month your Claremont house was burglarized and you've been attacked. I can protect you, if you're here."

"I don't trust you. Maybe you're the one I need protection from."

He peered up at her. "Could be."

"Stop being so annoyingly honest. It doesn't suit you."

Jarvis laughed. "Now you're seeing me. Admit it, you like me anyway." He got up and walked toward her.

The same height, they stared at each other eye-to-eye. Kate lost the match when she dropped her gaze to hide her smile.

"Stay," he said.

"Thank you. I appreciate it, but I need to go. I'll be okay. Really. I know I shouldn't go back to my apartment. I don't want to put my friends in danger. Besides, they'd never understand all that's happened. I'm not sure even I do. Lillian, though, lives in a secure building, and I have a key. I'll be safe there."

He squinted. "At Lillian's?"

"Yeah… Why?"

Heading back to the kitchen table, he waved his hand. "Nothing."

"When my aunt wakes up, please tell her that's where I've gone."

"She packed up hours ago."

"Without telling me?"

"Before Jimena left this morning, Lillian asked her to tell you—"

"Jimena tells you everything."

"Of course."

"And you wonder why I'm leaving." She kissed him on the cheek. "Thank you for everything. It's been an experience."

"Anytime." He sat back down and returned to the newspapers.

Before leaving the house, Kate stood for a moment at the front door and looked around, taking it all in. She inhaled the aroma of furniture polish and fresh-cut flowers. She wanted to make a clear memory of the fairy-tale mansion she got to live in, at least for a while.

****

No one, it seems, even contemplates getting up before ten on Sunday in West Hollywood. At least that's what Kate surmised from the lack of parking and not a soul in sight. Beyond exhausted, she plodded with her heavy suitcases six blocks from her VW to Lillian's apartment.

At the gate she buzzed her aunt. No answer. After letting herself in the apartment courtyard with her key, she knocked on Lillian's apartment door and got no answer there either. She let herself in to the deserted apartment.

Where was Lillian?

Fine.

She'd get through this alone the way she always had. She promised herself a session of drunkenness later. Right now, all she wanted to do was crawl into bed and shut out the world. She lumbered into Lillian's dusty guestroom and closed the door. With the apricot blackout curtains shut, the room felt like a dark cave. Perfect.

Kate dropped her suitcases, pried off her boots, and crawled under the flowered polyester quilt with the rest of her clothes still on. At last, she fell asleep.

****

She woke to the sound of voices in the living room. Groggy, she peered at the wind-up alarm clock. It was just after three, but in the dark room she had no idea if it was in the afternoon or early morning. She slid out of the bed and cracked open her door. The woman's voice was Lillian's, which was good. The male voice was Dylan's. Not so good.

Kate's first impulse was to barrel into the living room and demand that Lillian throw him out. But something about their low, modulated tones held her back. She tiptoed into the hallway and listened.

"How was your trip?" Dylan asked Lillian. "What did you find out?"

"Nothing, I'm happy to say. But I had to be certain."

What trip? Kate wondered. Lillian had been gone for less than a day.

"And are you?" Dylan sounded like a child who needed assurance after a nightmare.

Lillian was such a gullible fool if she was buying his crap. It was an act, like everything with him.

Her aunt said to Dylan, "The danger is here."

Kate fumed. You bet it's here.

"What are you implying?" he said.

Kate had enough. She charged into the room. "What do you think she's implying? You! Masked son of Winston Nash."

Lillian and Dylan jerked back with surprise.

"Where's our list of suspects?" Kate demanded. "I've got someone new to add to it."

"Come on," Dylan protested. "The murder was more than seven years before I was born."

"So?" She blew a strand of hair off her face. "Okay, you got me there. Still, how do I know you're not responsible for what's been happening now? Huh? Got ya!"

Lillian and Dylan stared at her blankly.

Kate lurched toward him. "Why have you been lying?" Before he could answer she pointed at him. "I'll tell you why. You have some fetish, some need to relive your father's murderous life. That's it, isn't it?"

"You're not making sense."

"Maybe not, but then who really knows why psychotics do what they do."

"Why don't you educate me? You're acting like you could write a treatise on the subject."

"Oh, sure. It's all in my imagination. Did I imagine seeing you steal the footage last night?"

"What?" Lillian asked.

"I—"

"Don't bother lying. I saw you take it."

Lillian paled. "I don't understand."

"Was there another clue in the footage I missed that pointed to your father," Kate said. "Or is it part of your psychosis—only you can have the film, have Gloria, have me."

"That's crazy," he said.

"Did you really take the film?" Lillian looked shaken by the revelation.

Dylan's failure to meet Lillian's gaze spoke volumes.

"Case closed." Kate crossed her arms.

"I can explain about the film."

"Of course you can. Liars have an explanation for everything. I'm still waiting to hear the one you have for luring me into the house that day on the set. I'm sure it's a whopper."

Lillian gave her a stern look. "What are you saying?"

"Dylan told me to meet him in the house, and that's where I was attacked." She turned to face him. "Why weren't you there? Or were you?"

"One of the trucks wouldn't start. I had to help get it towed.

"Which truck?"

"Chris's."

Her breath caught and she backed away from him as far as the walls would allow. "You're lying. Chris came with George that day. I saw them leave together. It was *you* who attacked me."

"I'd never do that. You need to calm down."

"Was it a thrill to terrorize me? I can't believe I actually protected you and didn't tell Jarvis I saw you take the film. I'm like one of those stupid girls in one of your horror movies. Hanging around when everyone knows she's walking into a trap. Not anymore. I'm out of here."

Lillian clutched her hands. "Darling, where will you go?"

Kate wasn't sure. She thought of her apartment in Silver Lake. It seemed like eons since she had belonged there, so much had happened. And Lillian? Kate now saw her to be the woman her mother always said she was. Not to be trusted, because she'd always put a Nash before her own family.

Kate looked around for the army bag she used as a purse. "I'm going back to Jarvis's."

Her bag was by the couch. Dylan saw it too and grabbed it before she could.

"Hell, no!" He held the purse out of her reach. "Talk about acting like one of those B movie ingénues. Jarvis is the one with the fetish, not me."

"He has been nothing but upfront with me. Sure, he's used my relationship to Gloria to his advantage. He stated that was his intention from the beginning. What I want to know is why *you* wanted me to be like Gloria."

"What?" Dylan said.

"Yeah, you were the one who encouraged me to

play the role of Crystal in *Emperor Smythe*. It had to be you that left a yellow rose in my car. I've since learned that was the same type of flower that Winston always gave to Gloria. And last night I saw what I'd suspected. You have a secret way to come and go from Jarvis's house, somewhere near the cottage, down the hillside. It has been you all this time, the person I've felt watching me when no one was supposed to be around. Don't you dare say it's all been in my head."

He reached for her.

"Don't touch me!"

"I love you."

Lillian stepped between them. She was small and old, but she was a formidable barrier. Her presence exuded command. "Dylan, you need to leave."

"Kate," Dylan pleaded.

"Now!" Lillian cried.

He hung his head. "Okay, Lil. Okay."

With Dylan gone, the magnificence of strength that Lillian had displayed dissolved. The elderly woman labored for breath as she retreated to her couch. "Oh, dear," she said with a hollow voice. "I never thought… Do you really think it was Dylan who attacked you?"

"No." Kate hugged herself. "And that's what scares me the most. Even though I know he's a liar, I still want him. I hate myself for that." She knelt and placed her head on her aunt's lap. "Was that what it was like for Gloria? The police report concluded that she invited her murderer into her dressing room. It must have been someone she knew, someone she trusted."

Lillian smoothed Kate's hair. "What do people really know about each other?"

Kate shivered.

"Darling, if I'd thought for one second it could have been Dylan who attacked you, I would have—"

Kate jumped to her feet. "Of course. I'm so stupid. All those cryptic and meaningful looks between you and Dylan. You knew all along who he really was."

"Yes." Lillian looked as fragile as one of her mother's figurines. "You must understand that Dylan was...*is* Dylan Nichols, not Ulysses." Lillian's smile was pained. "In fact, I don't think he ever went by that ridiculous name. When he first arrived in Los Angeles to study film, he wanted to make it on his own, with no baggage, good or bad, from being Winston Nash's son. I saw no harm."

"You never do."

"You're right. I should've told you. I was afraid you'd act unreasonably. We needed the Nash estate's claim to join ours in order to have any chance to control the footage, which meant we needed Dylan, and his price was to be a part of everything. You'd already made it clear that you, like your mother, hated and blamed Winston. I thought if you knew who Dylan was you wouldn't have accepted his help."

"That's bullshit." Kate sighed, trying to dispel her anger. "Fine. Maybe not complete bullshit at the beginning. But there was no reason for keeping the secret for so long."

Lillian looked as if she wanted to say something more, but Kate had enough. She retrieved her suitcases from the guest room. She saw the hurt in Lillian's eyes, her arthritic hands reaching toward her, as if begging for forgiveness.

Kate yanked the front door open and left.

Chapter Twenty-Five

Kate rang Jarvis's door-bell and was surprised when Beatrice answered.

"Jarvis's prediction was off for once. He said you'd be back even sooner."

Kate felt she should be incensed by that callous prediction, except that would take too much energy. "Where is he?"

"In New York. Don't worry. Everything is ready for you."

The house was bustling with activity. Big guys carried boxed-up lights and rolled out racks of folding chairs from the party. She spotted Jimena in the solarium giving rapid-fire orders to a regiment of maids, who were cleaning and putting the house back in order.

Yet everything seemed far away, as if she saw the world from inside a glass bottle—refracted and dulled.

Comforting, really.

Kate followed Beatrice up the stairs. The older woman's voice swirled above her, incomprehensible noise as she walked to her bedroom. That is, until Beatrice swung open the closet door. It was filled with newly bought dresses. The clothes appeared to be conservative, understated. Nothing like the green silk dress Kate had loved or her grandmother's glamorous apparel.

"Your work clothes," Beatrice replied to Kate's unasked question. "The press ate up your performance last night. It would be foolish not to follow up. They all want an interview with Gloria's granddaughter, to learn more about how you discovered the *Smythe* footage. But mostly about your relationship with Nash's son." Beatrice crossed her arms. "It's your choice whether to do it or not."

Kate stared at the curtains by the window seat. They danced like ghosts just as they had in her nightmares. She was unsure if the warmth that kissed her skin was caused by the dry Santa Ana wind or something more sinister.

Shutting her eyes, she no longer cared if Gloria was real or not. No more using a phantom as a crutch. Doing so was eating away at her own identity. And if the last twenty-four-hours had taught her anything, it was that she couldn't trust anyone or anything.

She took a deep breath and opened her eyes.

Beatrice stared at her as if she were crazy.

Kate squared her shoulders, forced a smile. and pretended to be sane. "When are the interviews?"

"As predicted," Beatrice said. "Jarvis said you'd agree."

"What do you mean by that?" A desire to fight back pierced Kate's haze. Again she felt heat tingle her fingertips and spread through her, as if she was being filled by another intelligence.

She fought against it. Not this time.

"Jarvis is very good at what he does," Beatrice said. "Orchestrating people so they do what he wants."

She wanted to lash out at Beatrice, at Jarvis, and at everything. But she wasn't sure if they'd be her own words or Gloria's that would leap from her mouth. So instead she crossed the room toward the window seat. Each step felt as if she fought against a strong wind. Once there, she reached past the billowing curtains and shut the window.

Sitting on the pillowed seat, she was tired but feeling oddly triumphant.

If she didn't know better, she'd think the expression on Beatrice's face almost resembled concern when she said, "Don't take it so hard. There is no reason you should be any different than the rest of us."

"If you have so much contempt for Jarvis, why do you work for him?"

"Ambition." Beatrice said the word as if it were contaminated.

Kate rubbed her eyes, trying to dispel the remains of the fog that had weighed her down. "Is that the only reason?"

Beatrice ignored the question and pointed at a folder on the table in the small nook. "You have two interviews tomorrow and one on Tuesday. In the folder are the answers to the agreed-upon questions. Memorize them and don't stray from the script. Friday is your screen test. You're to be at the studio by eight."

"Oh, I had forgotten about that."

"It can be cancelled. Just say the word." Beatrice's expression brightened in a way that Kate found more disturbing than her normal scowl.

"You'd like that, wouldn't you?"

"Of course not. It's my job to get you there."

Kate stood. "You're lying, from day one you've wanted me gone. Why?"

"You're imagining things."

"I don't think so. Not about you."

"But about other things, right?" Beatrice waved her hand in a dismissive gesture. "I know about your screaming Gloria's name at night in terror and your haunted stares into empty space. You've been the talk of the staff ever since you arrived." Beatrice twisted her hands then let them drop by her side, a more vulnerable gesture than Kate was used to seeing from her. "Take some advice, don't focus too much on shadows when the real world is frightening enough."

Kate looked away, not wanting to show that the words scared her.

"Have you changed your mind about the itinerary? Shall I cancel the interviews?"

She shook her head. "You don't intimidate me. I'll be there."

"Suit yourself." Beatrice opened her bag and pulled out a notebook.

It wasn't the burgundy one Kate had seen her use before, although it was the same handy four-by-six-inch size, with the same expensive soft leather. This book was bright orange, with her name embossed on it in gold. Kate surmised that the burgundy notebook was now retired.

Beatrice made quick notes in it.

Kate imagined that somewhere in Beatrice's home, a rainbow assortment of notebooks lined shelf-after-shelf, looking like a shrine, a place where she could think about tasks accomplished and of tasks yet to do, where she could escape the chaos of the present, which was—What was the word she'd just used? *Frightening.*

Beatrice shut the book and slid her silver pen behind her ear. "If you're sure it's what you want, I'll finalize the details for your screen test."

The woman crossed the room in six efficient steps and shut the door behind her.

****

The next day, Mrs. Dolinski, who had dressed Kate for the party, had arrived early to pick out clothes for her to wear to her first interview at a local news station and something else for her ten-minute segment on the *Merv Griffin Show*.

Although Kate had felt a bit stiff and mechanical, she'd gotten through the day without once summoning her inner Gloria.

She felt good about that but also so alone. No Lillian, no Dylan. Many times during the day she had wanted to call them. But how could she when they'd lied to her?

Beatrice then discovered that the footage had disappeared from the safe in the cottage. By the day Jarvis was due to return from his trip to New York, the police had already been out to his house four times to investigate the theft. A call to Jarvis had ensured that, one, she wouldn't have to answer any more questions until he returned and two, that the police wouldn't leak this news to the press.

Thursday evening, Kate was wearing the same T-shirt and pajama bottoms she had worn to bed the night before. Slumped on the couch in Jarvis's den, she watched reruns. She had never before had the patience to watch the make-believe crap on TV, but the droning of *Let's Make a Deal* and the *Afternoon Schools Special* was just what she needed.

She had to admit she now understood why people got a kick out of the kitsch of *Batman* or the weird mixture of morality plays entwined with aliens that was *Star Trek*.

Yeah, people like Dylan. She stuffed another powdered mini-donut into her mouth.

At the rapid bongo beats followed by a loud, jazzy riff that signaled the beginning of a rerun of *The Avengers*, Kate jumped to her feet. Donut crumbs flew as she slashed her hand through the air in pretend karate chops and kicks at an unseen assailant. The technique was atrocious (both hers and Emma Peel's), but man, it felt good. Kate did a side kick, imagining that her foot slammed into the creep that had attacked her on the set. She threw a hard punch, pretending that her fist hit Dylan's jaw. "Huh!" she yelled.

In mid-kick she saw Jarvis walk in.

"I want to do that," she said, pointing to the TV.

"Play Emma Peel?"

"No, learn karate or something. Self-defense."

He moved in close. "I'll find you the best teachers in the world if you promise to wear a leather cat suit."

"Men! Can't you stop being a sexist pig for at least five minutes?"

"No." He clicked off the television. "Kate, you need to tell me why you won't speak to the police about the film being stolen. Although the fact that you're refusing to answer questions implies the answer. Dylan?"

Kate averted her gaze, but Jarvis's blunt fingers lifted her chin so his blue eyes could look straight into hers.

"I can't stall the police any longer," he said. "You're going to need to tell them what you know, or you'll be in trouble."

Her lips clamped shut.

"Weren't you the one who wanted the film shown, no matter what?" He tapped his finger against his chin. "The motive of the goon who attacked you was to stop the film from being shown. There's likely a connection between your assault and now the footage's disappearance."

She'd be an idiot to not at least consider the question.

It was strange. Even when she had hurled those accusations at Dylan, telling him that he was a liar, a thief, and could not be trusted, the core of her didn't believe it.

Jarvis nodded. "Okay. The police can wait until later. For now, why don't you get dressed and be my date at L'Orange this evening?"

"I don't think I'd be very good company."

"I'll be the judge of that. Besides, it would be good for you to be seen. The publicity has begun to die down."

"You do remember I don't want to be an actress. I'm only doing it so I can—"

"I remember. We leave in an hour."

Kate dutifully chose one of the new dresses that had been bought for her interviews to wear. This one was a simple "little black dress." Gazing at her shoes, she had a momentary urge to accessorize the ensemble with her hiking boots.

That would be the real her. Or would it be a mask? She didn't know anymore. She slipped on sun-kissed color stockings, and slid her feet into black, open-toe pumps.

When she got downstairs, Jarvis was talking on the

hall telephone about some movie deal. He had changed too and was wearing a beautifully tailored light-blue suit. It looked nice. She surmised it was his power suit. Not just because it wasn't boxy from his broad shoulders to his short torso or lose its liquid line and tighten unexpectedly at his muscular forearms, as some of his other clothes did. No, it was because its monochrome color and beautiful workmanship could lull a viewer into thinking the man wearing it was easy and forthcoming. But she knew that was as deceptive as the California sun in a David Hockney painting, where at first the bright, two-dimensional, painting seems to illuminate. But she'd always felt a depiction devoid of shadow only revealed half-truths.

Jarvis had come a long way from the awkward young man she'd heard about. He no longer had to worry about fitting in with the fashionable people. Now he set the trends. If he had been taller and had a marine's ramrod-straight posture, Kate thought it might actually diminish the magnetism of the man. His charisma was not derived from beauty or family name. It was pure force of will.

When he hung up the phone and saw her, he looked altogether pleased. "Tell you the truth, I thought you'd come down in your boots."

"And if I had?"

"Nothing. You'd still be my date at L'Orange." He crooked an arm.

"Right answer." Kate laughed and took his arm. "And don't think I didn't consider it. But you said this was business, so it's not like it's a date date."

"Who said it isn't?" He led her out to the driveway.

Kate felt a knot in her stomach. She was barely

able to mutter an *Oh* before he whisked her into the passenger seat of his Mercedes 450SL.

As merely the trinket on the king's arm, she expected to be bored at dinner. But she was wrong. Sitting at the beautifully set table, with its fine china, glistening silverware, and the glow of candlelight, she watched man after man (and she was sorry to see only men) pop over to their table to pitch some project to Jarvis or ask questions about the final touches to some deal or other. It turned out to be fascinating.

Not the groveling or the rudeness, in that they all spoke as if she wasn't there. But in how Jarvis masterfully orchestrated each conversation. With a smile and a cutting remark, he rebuffed all the second-rate deal makers within thirty seconds flat. He flattered just enough the former sitcom actor who had miraculously landed in the highest-grossing picture of the year.

How he treated his rivals was even more interesting. One of the VPs at Golden State Pictures came over and warned Jarvis that he better get his attorneys lined up since they were about to sue his ass for the *Emperor Smythe* footage.

Jarvis offered the corpulent man a seat and ordered him a drink. Kate was impressed when Jarvis was able to ask after the man's wife and kids by name. The Golden State executive appeared no less surprised, and the way he beamed showed that he was flattered. Jarvis leaned back in his chair and waved a hand. "I always make it a point to know everything about talented persons."

"Really?" The man smiled.

Jarvis needed to ask only one or two leading

questions, and then the guy talked and talked and talked. The spider in a web, Jarvis extracted all the information he could while never betraying anything about his own plans.

When the entrées arrived, people waiting in the wings to approach him retreated, knowing that the royal court was now adjourned.

Kate poured a little béarnaise sauce on her filet mignon. The waiter served them green beans almandine, scalloped potatoes, poured a Chateau Mouton Rothschild Bordeaux, and withdrew silently.

Jarvis slathered some butter on his bread plate and proceeded to salt and pepper it. "Thanks for putting up with that. It's a circus, but part of the job."

"You do it very well." She took a sip of the wine. It tasted luxurious, rich with flavors of oak and spice. Savoring it, she allowed its taste to linger on her tongue before swallowing.

She smiled at him. "Do you always get out of people exactly what you want?"

"Mostly."

"I see." She tried to stifle a giggle. "You did it to us, too. Didn't you?"

"What?"

"At our first meeting, in your office."

His lips curled up into a wicked grin. "What about it?"

"You said just enough to reel us in but no more."

"Of course."

"We were in your office less than half an hour and—"

He lifted his eyebrows. "Much less."

"And by the time we left you had figured us all out.

We thought we were there to persuade the great Jarvis Benjamin, but you played us. We wouldn't have been in your office more than five minutes if you hadn't wanted the film."

"You bet I wanted it. After Lillian dropped that bombshell, there was no way any of you were leaving until I'd gotten it."

"Which meant controlling us. Controlling *me*."

"Control is an unpleasant word. Let's say I needed to know what you each wanted so I could provide it."

"In order to dangle it in front of us?"

"No, to provide it."

"For Lillian?"

"You know as well as I do what she wants. To live again the life of a movie star. I couldn't quite do that."

She smiled at him. "No, but allowing us to live in your Bel Air mansion, giving her the freedom to pretend she was the lady of the manor. Pretty close. Then there was Dylan and me. I suppose we were easy. You handle our type every day. We want to be filmmakers, and you hold the keys."

"That was enough to secure Dylan's allegiance, or so I'd thought. But you revealed a stronger motive. You remember?"

"I wanted the film to be seen. I still do."

"Yes, but it was more than that. You wanted vengeance. There you were, young, an angelic face, and oh, so bloodthirsty."

"Not vengeance," she reminded him. "Justice."

"If that word makes it more palatable."

She looked at her half-eaten steak surrounded by a puddle of its own red juices. She pushed the plate away in disgust. "How did you see that in me when I hadn't realized it yet myself?"

"Recognition." The eyes of the street fighter who'd become a king had for a moment lost his armor and revealed... She wasn't sure what. Sadness? Yes, but more than that. Regret.

She put a hand on his. "What happened?"

At first he looked startled by her touch, and then he relaxed and put his free hand on top of hers.

"Found you!" Dylan rammed into the table like a novice ice skater banging against the rink wall. "And this is the most disgusting display I've ever seen." The reek of whiskey wafted from him. Kate protectively wrapped her arms in front of her waist.

Clamping onto the table and almost toppling it with his weight, he said, "You know Jarvis is maneuvering you into bed," he slurred.

"Go away," she said.

Jarvis gave a discreet signal to the *maître d'*, and three members of the restaurant staff approached, undoubtedly planning to throw Dylan out.

Kate was surprised to see Jarvis lift a hand to stop them.

"Like father, like son," he said. "Bellowing and drunk when you don't get what you want."

"I'm not talking to you." Dylan flailed his arms and almost lost his balance. Gripping the table again, he leaned close to Kate. "You, I need to talk to."

"Go away. You're a thief."

"Thank you for the confirmation, Kate." Jarvis stood.

"I didn't mean—"

"Is it justice for all, or only for some?" Jarvis asked her.

Dylan was too far gone to hear the smirk in Jarvis's voice, but Kate heard it, and she knew what he meant by it.

She lowered her gaze. "For all."

Jarvis smiled, and he offered Dylan his seat. "Then I think you should hear him out, while I make a call."

Dylan dropped into the chair.

Kate watched Jarvis walk to the *maitre d'*, who handed him a phone. Kate knew he would call the police.

At first they just sat in silence. Kate felt like Judas, unable to look at Dylan. And yet he did steal the film. She saw him do it.

Dylan leaned across the table, and his hands clasped hers. "I want to explain."

She pulled her hands away. "I don't want to hear it."

His eyes were glassy from drink but not so much that she couldn't see the vulnerability in them.

"I see it in your face you don't believe those things about me."

Kate turned from his gaze. "Belief is irrelevant next to facts."

"Belief is *everything*. Promise me you'll come with me Monday.

"Why Monday?"

"It won't be ready until then. You'll see, everything will be okay, I promise."

Two uniformed policemen strutted into the restaurant. One stepped forward and said to Dylan, "We don't want to make a scene here, son. Calm down, stand up slowly, and walk out with us, and we won't have to disrupt these nice people's dinner.

"What?" Dylan said.

The other officer, standing behind Dylan, said, "Come with us. You are under arrest for burglary."

"Kate?" Dylan said.

The officer replied, "You stole some film that didn't belong to you, isn't that right, son?"

She couldn't meet Dylan's eyes.

"Fine," she heard him say. When she looked up he was being escorted out by the officers.

He turned and ran back to the table. The cops lunged for him and missed. Someone in the restaurant screamed, and then Dylan was hovering over her. She slid her chair back, beyond his reach, her heart racing.

Then the police were on him. Prying Dylan's hands from the table, the officers yanked his hands behind his back and cuffed him.

Jarvis returned and stood behind Kate.

Dylan shook his head. "You only had to believe until Monday. Just Monday."

The room spun, as if Kate were the one who was drunk. Everything was blurry except for a small piece of paper, about four-by-two inches, that lay in her lap. The edge was perforated, on one side some numbers were printed on it and in blue ink was written the word *Monday*. She clutched the paper to hide it.

Dylan must have left it.

Jarvis placed a hand on her shoulder. "Shall we go, my dear?"

"Yes, of course. Could you get my sweater?"

Jarvis signaled a waiter. While he was looking away, Kate slipped the paper into her handbag.

When Jarvis placed the sweater on her shoulders, she exhaled in relief because he had not seen it.

Although why she felt it needed hiding she wasn't certain.

Chapter Twenty-Six

Several days later, Kate grabbed the crème-colored handbag that matched her wraparound dress and heels and headed for her VW.

After Dylan had been arrested for stealing the film, Jarvis no longer felt any restraint about releasing the fact that the footage had been stolen. This in turn had caused a crescendo of more publicity.

Kate bit her lower lip at the thought. Because that had meant another week she was in demand to do interviews. The only good thing about the new wave of interviews was it postponed the screen test for another week. As before, she'd done her bit and dutifully attended each scripted and vacuous media appearance. She managed to deliver her lines and hit her marks. But she would not allow the spark she'd displayed at the party to reassert itself.

She didn't need Gloria. She didn't need anyone.

She stopped herself from slamming Jarvis's large oak front door in fear of Jimena's scowl. Everything was still conspiring to make it impossible for her to be ready to go back to class when fall semester started in a couple of weeks.

When she reached Jarvis's circular driveway, Detective Robak was there, leaning against his tan Ford Torino, pen and folded newspaper in hand. He appeared to be working on a crossword puzzle.

When he saw her, he threw his newspaper into his backseat, grabbed a file, and went to meet her. "Hey, we got the guy who attacked you on the set of *Satan's Academy*. He's in jail."

"Dylan?"

"No, Jack Wolinski."

"Who?"

"You may have met him. He was a stuntman on *Satan's Academy*."

Kate looked at Robak blankly.

That made no sense.

"Jarvis didn't tell you Wolinski was our prime suspect, did he?"

"No."

"I thought not. Wolinski appeared on our radar almost immediately. He's got a record. Small-time bullshit. The day after your attack we questioned him, and I noticed he was wearing long sleeves on a hot day, maybe to hide some bruises your struggle inflicted. He also was moving like he'd been hurt. So we put a tail on him."

"And?"

"The fool spent the next couple of days getting drunk and spending wads of cash he had no reason to have. We nailed him for lying about his whereabouts during the attack. The idiot didn't even bother to throw away the costume he'd stolen from wardrobe. We found tears in it, like he'd been in a fight. And you'll appreciate this, when I showed his picture to hospital staff, a gal in the pharmacy remembered seeing him the day you were chased."

"But why?" Kate shook her head and wandered toward her car.

Robak followed. "That bugged me. From what the attacker said to you we knew the motive was to stop the release of the film."

She turned back to the detective. "Was he one of Sutton's goons?"

"No. Too sloppy for him. But you're close." Robak opened the file in his hand and took out a photocopy of a page from the *National Enquirer*. The article was from a couple of weeks ago, a salacious report of a wild Hollywood party at Château Marmont. The photo showed a hotel room so wrecked it looked as if a bomb had exploded. Drug paraphernalia and empty liquor bottles were everywhere, and expensively dressed young people were dancing or slouched on wide couches.

"The article lists the names of a bunch of semi-famous people reported as being there, including some B actors, second-rate musicians, and debutantes." Robak pointed to a blonde girl in a glittery tube top and low-riding hip huggers. "Prudence Sutton. And look who has his arms around her. That's Jack Wolinski."

A tall guy stood behind Prudence, grinning as if he'd just won the lottery. He appeared to be drunk. Even in the black-and-white photo, Kate saw spittle running from the corner of his mouth. He seemed to be leaning against Prudence as much to keep his balance as for sexual gratification.

She remembered the guy now. He was that smarmy stunt man on the set the last day of the shoot.

Looking at the picture, Kate shuddered as she remembered his hands all over her and the unmistakable sound of pleasure he took in her fear.

But in actuality it wasn't Jack who tried to terrorize

her. He was just the instrument. Prudence Sutton was the real culprit.

Kate looked more closely at the picture of Prudence. For someone in a wild party scene, she had a surprisingly clear-eyed stare.

Another manipulator.

They were everywhere. And for what? Because Prudence didn't want the film shown and the world to be reminded that she was a traitor's daughter.

Her stupid stunt: to terrorize Kate, to risk Jack going to jail, to risk maybe even herself going there, just so she'd continue to be asked to the right parties?

Examining the photo of the petulant princess, Kate was struck by the injustice of it all. Jack would go to jail, no doubt. But Prudence would be protected by everything money and influence could buy. She'd never take the fall. Sutton would make sure of that.

But this information did not explain everything. She looked up at Robak. "Any word yet about that weird skeletal guy I thought might be following me?"

"No, sorry. Have you seen him again since the film set?"

She shook her head. "No. And the truth is I only saw him, for sure, twice. I guess that could be explained by coincidence?"

"Maybe." Robak shrugged. "But I'm not discounting your feeling that he may have been sneaking behind you more than that. Either Sutton or Jarvis could have hired a gumshoe to trail you—they're both the type to do it. I just haven't been able to pin down which one is responsible."

Kate opened her car door and got in. "At least I'm glad to know it wasn't Dylan who attacked me."

Robak held the car door open. "It's a certainty. Jack confessed to both attacking you on the film set and chasing you at the hospital. After some persuading and fear of serious jail time, he spilled the beans on Prudence. I wanted to tell you in person that your boyfriend was off the hook."

"Dylan's not my boyfriend."

"I also wanted to tell you I'm here if you need me."

"If Jarvis needs you, you mean."

The detective looked away. "I told you I'm sorry. It's just when you first came to me and you talked about all the crazy stuff that was happening, I didn't believe you." He met her gaze. "The thing is—call it a cop's instinct—but the whole picture seems off. Now I'm thinking you could be right."

Kate shook her head. "Great, first you give me the news that you found the guy who attacked me and tell me that he's locked up, and now maybe, just maybe, I don't have to be afraid anymore. Then you lay this cop instinct stuff on me and tell me to stay scared."

"I don't want you to be scared, Kate, just careful. And to know you're not alone."

She whispered, "I am."

"No, you're not. If you need something, if you suspect someone, call me."

"So you can report it to Jarvis?"

Robak rubbed the back of his neck, squinting in the glare of the sun. "I guess I deserve that."

"Yeah, you do." She jammed the car key into the ignition.

"I won't do it again."

"Why should I believe you?"

"No reason, except it's the truth. Be safe." He shut

her door and began to walk back to his car.

She wanted to say something sarcastic to show him she wasn't someone who could be taken in twice. The problem was she did believe him. She rolled down her window and called out, "Hey. What are you going to do about the Prudence connection? Do you have enough evidence to arrest her?"

He turned and walked back to her. "If Prudence was anyone else, I'd say yes. But considering who she is, or more to the point, who her grandfather is, the department doesn't want to go after her. They're probably right. In the end the money and power behind her will mean she'll walk. But I have no career left to ruin, and I figured I owed you. Call it my last hurrah before official retirement."

"I thought you were retired now."

"I stopped working the job, true. But I've accrued so much vacation time and unused sick-leave, I'm still officially on the payroll for another couple of weeks."

Kate considered this new piece of information. "Don't," she said.

"Don't what?"

"Don't go after Prudence, at least not yet."

"Why not?"

"If you go after her and fail, what stops her from hiring some other jerk to do her dirty work and come after me or the film? Instead, we can use the information to our advantage."

"Where are you going with this?"

"The question is where are *we* going. You said you owed me. You and I are going to see J.B. Sutton."

"Yeah?"

"Yeah. Give me a couple of days to think it

through to make sure we get the most out of the information." Kate gave a short laugh. "Sutton said he liked people who were prepared. I hope that's right."

She started her car and headed down Jarvis's long driveway. As she turned on to the street, she caught herself tapping her fingers and smiling. Maybe with Robak's help she could get some real answers.

Then she thought about how she had failed the last time she went up against the Titan. What made her think it would be different this time? Wasn't she being foolish to trust Robak again?

By the time Kate drove into the UCLA parking lot, the late afternoon haze mirrored the lethargy she'd felt ever since the party. It didn't help knowing the reason she was on campus was to request to take a full semester off since Beatrice said the studio would be keeping her way too busy.

Walking past Melnitz Hall, Kate looked around at her old cherished stomping ground. She was struck by how wholly disconnected to it, to her past life, she felt.

Perhaps it was for the best she was not coming back.

People pointed and stared at her. Not because she was their friend or recognized as a fellow student. She was now a celebrity. The worst kind, too—famous for being famous.

When the path led into the sculpture garden, Kate spotted Natalie sitting on the grass, animatedly discussing some point with a group of friends.

For a moment Kate felt happy to see her, there in her familiar broad-brimmed straw hat and bell-bottom jeans, her clothes dappled, as usual, with colorful spots of crusted paint. Kate turned away and kept walking, recalling that her friend hadn't bothered to reply to her message after she'd been attacked. Natalie too had proven to be just another person she couldn't trust.

"Hey, Kate! Wait up!" Natalie jogged over to her. "I can't believe you found the *Smythe* footage and didn't tell me."

"How do you know about that?"

"It's like everywhere, that's how."

Kate flinched when her friend took her by the shoulders.

"Hey, why so jumpy?" Natalie eyes narrowed in on her. "You look terrible."

"Thanks a lot," Kate quipped. She looked down at her own feet and shook her head. Had she actually chosen these dainty, doll-like shoes to wear today?

"Come on, you know what I mean. You're all garbed up and look like a Beverly Hills mistress."

"Am not!"

"Whoa, that hit a nerve. What's going on?"

"Nothing you'd understand."

"I'm sure I wouldn't understand. What I *see* is you with circles under your eyes darker than on a Modigliani painting."

Part of Kate wanted to believe Natalie, to believe she wasn't alone. But she felt too fragile, too afraid to be hurt again. And she dared not allow the specter of Gloria to shore her up. "I've got to go."

She didn't get more than a hundred yards before her attention was caught by two women, about her age. They sat side-by-side on a school bench, practicing an acting scene. The women pantomimed snapping green beans on unseen aprons as they rocked on imaginary chairs. They were completely absorbed in their roles.

Kate could have sworn she could hear the pop of the green beans and she could easily believe that they were sturdy, middle-aged women gossiping on a summertime porch.

That image made Kate smile, even though her muddled mind couldn't tell her why.

These girls weren't possessed. They were *acting*. And sometimes that created a kind of reality, didn't it?

Drip. A part of her began to thaw.

Perhaps she didn't need "Gloria" to fill the hollow part of her own psyche anymore. She could will herself into having the attributes she lacked or was afraid of. To have the necessary bravado when called for, to have courage, or even comfort in her body, with her sensuality and not be swallowed up by them.

She thought back to the supernatural events of the summer and about her grandmother and of herself. Where did the psychological end and the haunting begin?

Whatever the truth was, she wouldn't be taken over again by "Gloria."

She felt a tremble deep inside.

Ignore it. She could do this.

And, if she still wasn't entirely secure yet in facing her fears, then a little acting couldn't hurt. After all, that was her true family legacy.

Taking a deep breath, she believed herself courageous, believed she could open herself one more time and would not disintegrate on the spot, if disappointed again by a friend.

She turned back toward Natalie who had remained planted in the spot Kate had left her. When Kate took the first step toward her, her friend ran to meet her.

Drip, drip.

"Please tell me what's going on," her friend asked. "Except for the rent check you mail every month, I haven't heard from you all summer."

What? That didn't make sense.

Kate had phoned. It was Natalie who hadn't returned her calls.

"I thought we were friends," Natalie continued. "Why haven't you called me back? Did I do something to upset you?"

"You phoned? But…but you didn't return my calls."

Natalie shook her head and her black curls bounced in the wind. "What do you mean? I never got any messages from you. I phoned several times, and each time some stern woman told me you were too busy doing something important to talk."

"Is that true?"

She wasn't alone.

Drip, drip, drip.

Kate shook as the dripping halted, and her senses were flooded with feelings—fear, anger, and relief.

Natalie pulled her into a strong, earth-mother hug.

Kate wept in her friend's arms.

****

An hour later, feeling drained but much happier, no longer like that awful hollow and listless girl she'd been for the last week, Kate munched on tortilla chips and guacamole at Casa Escobar with Natalie.

Kate told her the bare bones of her adventure, too tired to go into much detail. But it was enough to produce the look of horror on Natalie's face when she told her of being attacked on the *Satan's Academy* set.

It was also gratifying to hear her friend's outrage when she heard that both Dylan and her aunt had lied to her.

Guacamole from the tortilla chip Natalie waved in the air as she talked splattered onto the table. "So what are you going to do? You can't hide at Jarvis's forever."

"Hiding?"

"Sounds like."

Kate slammed the table. "I'm sick of this!" People in the restaurant turned and stared at her.

But damn it, she *was* sick of this. She'd been played by everyone—Dylan, Lillian, Jarvis.

"You're right. I've been hiding and whining and being stupid for too long, but no more."

"Good for you," Natalie said. "What are you going to do?"

Kate slumped in her chair. "I don't know."

She thought about Jarvis, the supreme puppet-master, and about Lillian's and Dylan's charade. And God knows what's been going on in Beatrice's mind. The only thing she was certain of is they had all been manipulating her. It was time to turn the tables. No more being a guppy in a pool full of sharks.

She pulled out the piece of paper Dylan had given to her and examined it. It had a serrated edge, like a claim check, on it a list of numbers. "Maybe I start here."

Chapter Twenty-Seven

Mallick hung his head out of Kate's VW bug passenger window like a dog. She felt tempted to do the same if it weren't for it being the second day of a Stage Two smog alert. Still, the weather was well over ninety degrees and just getting hotter, so she gulped in the gunky air as they drove deeper into the San Fernando Valley.

All of the buildings along Van Nuys Boulevard looked the same. Their only distinguishing characteristics were their colorful facades, as changeable as stage sets.

Mallick leaned back in his seat again and downed the last of his soft drink. "Man, this feels good. I was going nuts in that hospital."

"I'm glad you're okay. I was so worried."

"I'm fine."

"Good." She smiled. "Now, will you tell me what this claim check is for?"

"Don't you like surprises?"

"Not anymore. If this is dangerous, maybe we should call Robak."

"Hey, man, no fuzz."

"He's ex-fuzz. I mean cop."

"Man, I've still got such a cotton mouth. Let's stop and get a drink or something."

Kate rolled her eyes. "Not again. So why no

Robak?"

"Let's say the place we're going to doesn't do everything according to the letter of the law." Mallick pointed ahead. "Hey, that's the turn."

She slowed to make a right. "I don't even want to know how Dylan learned about such a place."

"That's easy, through me."

Kate sighed. "Why am I not surprised."

Mallick tilted his car seat all the way back and stared up at her car's faded headliner. "In college I got work as a cameraman on some porn films."

Her body tensed and she cringed.

"Hey, it wasn't that bad," Mallick protested. "Everyone was an adult and there by choice. I got film experience, and it paid for my schoolbooks."

"Sure, who cares if you were perpetuating the objectification of women."

"Come on, all movies do that. Besides, look who's talking. I saw those pictures of you in the tabloids, dressing in the clingy gowns of your dead grandmother. Even you've learned that objectification sells."

They were now so deep in the valley that the rows of small strip malls had been replaced by large warehouses. Mallick pointed to a narrow driveway, and she turned in. It led to a cracked asphalt parking area for a one-story steel building shaped like an L. It was divided into fifteen boxy units.

She parked.

Before Mallick jumped out of the car, she grabbed his arm. "So tell me, what does working on porn in college have to do with where we are?"

"Before you get all angry all over again, let me say again the stuff I worked on was strictly soft-core and legal."

"How noble."

"The thing is, when I worked on the porn films, I heard about some film developers known for their silence. You know, when the footage crossed the line."

Despite the nauseating implication of that statement, she perked up at the realization of why they were here. "Oh, my God, you're taking me to the film, aren't you?"

He smiled.

"Why didn't Dylan tell this to the police? I mean, they have a flimsy case against him as it is, since he's arguably one of the people with a right to the film. You can't steal from yourself."

"He's not the only one with a claim, and the case isn't that flimsy because of *your* testimony." Mallick stepped out of the car and slammed the door, not bothering to hide his anger.

She didn't blame him. She was pissed at herself for the whole thing, too. She followed him. "But if Dylan was just making copies of it and we return it, there's no crime. Why hasn't he told the police?"

"I guess for the same reason he took it." They walked by the first unit. Its roll-up door was open, and she could see what looked like a thousand typewriters piled on tables, with an old guy sitting at a bench tinkering with one. They passed several padlocked doors, then some type of artisan's studio with weird iron statuary. Mallick halted at the end unit. The door was shut, and there was no sign except for one identifying it as Unit 15B.

Mallick rang the bell. A low-pitched buzzing replied, unlatching the door. He opened it, and they stepped into a small, windowless but air-conditioned space and up to a bare counter.

A young man the size of a freight truck appeared from behind a dingy curtain.

Kate handed the claim check to him. He took it without saying a word. He retrieved a box of index cards from under the counter and flipped through them. He pulled out a card and disappeared through the curtain.

The guy reemerged carrying six 35mm film canisters and placed them on the counter. He went into the back again and returned with another six 35mm canisters.

"Your original is on the top of each pile," he said in a gravelly voice.

Kate stared at the canisters.

Mallick nudged her. "Blink."

"So many copies. Brilliant!"

Mallick smiled. "Let's get out of here."

She opened her army bag, not sure how she would pay for this.

The man waved her off. "It's paid in full."

Mallick and Kate took the canisters out to her car. They tried to secure them as best they could, but it was a no go, so Mallick crawled into the backseat with the film to keep them from falling.

Once she was settled in the driver's seat, she peered into her rearview mirror at all the shiny canisters. "I still don't understand why Dylan didn't just tell the police where they were."

"He didn't want the developer to get into trouble. He couldn't say anything until he got the copies into the hands of someone he trusted. I think he wanted the copies because for some reason he thought they might help exonerate his dad from Gloria's murder." Clinging to the silver canisters, Mallick shook his head. "Man, you think you're the only one who has issues about being like your family. Dylan is so like his dad, which scared the shit out of him as a kid. Think about it. All the evidence pointed to his dad murdering the woman he loved, and Dylan's temperament was just like his. That messes with your mind."

Kate thought back to how, particularly in the beginning, Dylan seemed to keep women at an emotional distance, but he'd begun to break free from that and allowed her in. She thought about his smile, the tentative touch of his fingers, to all the things he'd said to her that she only now could make sense of.

"Don't you think we'd better get going?" Mallick said. "We need to get this film out of the heat."

"Right." She started the car.

Mallick clung to the canisters when they got into the stop-and-go traffic on Van Nuys Boulevard.

"You know," he said as she turned on to the freeway, "maybe the biggest reason Dylan didn't tell police about the footage is because of you. He's a romantic. I think the film is an offering. You'd been threatened over it, so he, like some pathetic white knight, is handing it to you like it was the golden fleece."

Kate smiled. That did seem like Dylan.

Mallick continued, "He wants you to decide what should be done with the film. Destroy it and be safe, or hand it back to Jarvis. He's left it up to you."

They drove the rest of the way in silence.

When she pulled up in front of Mallick's West

L.A. apartment to drop him off, she said, "Will you take the film to the police, call Dylan's attorney, and get him out of jail?"

"Why don't you do it? He'd want to see you."

Kate shook her head. She wasn't ready for that. "When you take the film, tell them you're bringing in the two originals and four copies of each."

"Only four?"

She smiled at him. "We don't want them all to go missing, do we? Can you store one of each reel someplace safe?"

Mallick grinned at her. "You bet."

Chapter Twenty-Eight

Later that afternoon, Kate skidded down the dry dirt trail she was sure Dylan had used to sneak off with the film the night of the party. As she trekked the steep incline, dust swirled around her hiking boots, turning them from tan to brown. Ridiculous to think this was the first time she'd worn these boots for real hiking and then to discover they weren't very good at the task. She came to a turn with another steep decline, but here the narrow trail she'd been on joined with a wider one.

A man, thirtyish, jogged past her with an Irish setter at his heels. Kate followed him down the wide path.

At the end of the trail was a low steel gate painted white, with a brown-and-white park sign on it providing hours the trail was open.

Past the gate, Kate stepped on to the smooth pavement of a typical suburban cul de sac. But unlike the cul de sac's in Claremont, that were bordered by modest three-bedroom houses, here wide, gated driveways faced the road. Kate surmised that they each led to a monstrous Bel Air estate.

The jogger now leaned against a green Gremlin stretching his back legs. His panting dog peered through the car's oddly shaped vertical back window. She'd bet the jogger wasn't a local, and his Gremlin didn't cause a second glance from the residents. Neither would've Dylan's Mustang, which he must've parked here anytime he wanted to come and go unseen.

Why he did this, she still didn't know.

Dylan's motive for taking the film was now clear. He was trying to protect it. Even so, she knew he and Lillian were still keeping something from her. She couldn't trust them. But it was time she trusted her own instincts, which told her Dylan wasn't the one who jimmied the staircase. In fact, the more she thought about it, the more she wondered if he'd been the target that day, and not Mallick. She was sure that someone had sabotaged the steps and railing.

After all, no one knew Mallick would be there. He'd told her that his curiosity had spurred him to sneak onto Jarvis's property that morning. And she had been conveniently occupied then, far away from Jarvis's house working on the scene for the screen test with her aunt. Kate also knew Jarvis's staff had been forbidden to come near the guest house during the restoration of the film. Therefore, if the saboteur didn't know about Dylan's secret way to the cottage, then Dylan was the one expected to slip on the loose step that morning and fall through the railing.

The stakes rose tenfold in her mind. She needed to catch the killer. She jogged up the hill. It was time to execute the plan she'd formed after she remembered that before Natalie became an abstract painter, she'd been schooled in Classical fine art techniques. Kate had seen her sketch books filled with precise renderings of masters' works.

Back at Jarvis's guest house, she phoned Natalie, who picked up on the first ring. "What did you think of Chuck Needham's handwriting?"

"Easy as pie," Natalie said. "Don't worry. I wrote it just like you said and put the letters in the mail today, one to each—Beatrice, Jarvis, and your aunt Lillian."

"Good. Then all we've got to do is see how they react."

"You're crazy, you know?"

"I know. But I'm not stupid. Detective Robak knows about this. He's got our backs."

Kate hung up the phone and trekked up to the main house.

When she got there, she heard whistling of what she thought was Rogers and Hammerstein's *Getting to Know You.*

Kate followed the happy sound to the kitchen. An incongruous sight greeted her. Jarvis, his sleeves rolled up and wearing an apron, stood at the counter grating cheese, pieces of which had managed to find their way into his silver hair. It was almost surreal. Jarvis waved at her and went back to his jaunty whistling. She'd never seen him being so free with his emotions before. She liked him this way. "Where's Jimena? I thought her regular day off wasn't until tomorrow."

"I told her she could take off early. I'm going to make us dinner."

Kate walked over to him and looked at what he was doing. There was a small bowl with freshly sliced red onion, two pieces of sourdough bread generously buttered on one side, and cheese everywhere.

He smiled at her, looking abashed. "Grilled cheese. It's the only thing I know how to make."

Kate squeezed his arm. "Wonderful. Let me get cleaned up, and I'll be right back."

She hurried upstairs and shed her clothes. As she

stepped into the shower, she caught herself humming that tune he'd been whistling. Clean and back in the dressing area, she found a nice compromise of styles by pairing one of the recent skirts bought for her interviews with one of her own three quarter sleeve with a scoop collar T-shirt. Barelegged she slid on a pair of sandals. She was about to go downstairs when the phone rang. Thinking it might be Natalie, she picked up the receiver on her bedside table. "Jarvis Benjamin's residence," she said.

"Get out of the house," replied a rough masculine voice.

Kate's pulse jumped into overdrive. "What? Who is this?"

"It's Ted. Kate, get the hell out of there."

"What?"

"I found out who bought the Hephaestus statue. It was Jarvis. In fact, he bought the whole damn pantheon from the same artist."

"Are you sure?"

"Absolutely."

The world contracted around her. The fine furniture, prettily painted walls, and gently billowing curtains suddenly made the room look like a plush prison.

"Kate, are you there?"

The sound of Jarvis's whistling was outside her closed bedroom door, and it was coming closer. She held her breath.

Three brisk taps on her door. "Dinner's ready," he said. The doorknob turned.

Kate called out, "I need another minute. I'll be down soon."

"Don't be too long." The sound of his footsteps faded.

Ted said over the phone, "Do you want me to come get you?"

"No. I'm leaving now."

"Good. Meet me at the studio. If you're not here in thirty minutes, I'm coming after you."

Panic gripped her.

Jarvis. How could it be him? She didn't want it to be him.

She ran to the main closet, grabbed one of her suitcases, and threw some things into it. The rest of her stuff would have to wait.

She cautiously opened the door to the hallway. Nobody there. She dashed through the hallway and down the stairs. When she reached the foyer, she heard the clinking of plates in the nearby dining room and tiptoed the rest of the way to the front door and out of the house.

Chapter Twenty-Nine

Once Kate got safely away from Jarvis's house, Ted took her to his place to hide out. There she called Robak and told him what Ted had discovered about Jarvis. The detective proceeded to grill Ted, but the facts held up. Jarvis had bought the statues. But that alone wasn't enough. There were still too many variables.

The game needed to be played out. The post office should deliver the forged letters to the primary suspects—Lillian, Beatrice, and Jarvis—in a day or two. And Kate was determined to keep the appointment with Sutton.

The next day, in the early evening, Robak drove her up to see Sutton. He warned Kate again that it was too early to drop her guard with anyone.

Robak had arranged the audience with Sutton by threatening to expose his granddaughter, Prudence, as the one responsible for Kate's assault. There was no pretense of welcome as there had been the last time. Instead of a butler opening the door, they were confronted by two big thugs straight out of central casting, who patted them down before saying, "Sutton says he'll only speak to one of you. No witnesses."

"But—" Kate began.

"Who has the power to negotiate here?" the thug continued.

Robak gave Kate an encouraging smile.

"I do," she said.

She had taken only two steps into Sutton's office when he shouted at her from his giant desk, "What kind of proof do you have?"

In no mood to waste time, Kate opened the file folder she carried and handed him a photocopy of the picture of Prudence and Jack, Jack's confession implicating Prudence, and a bank statement the police had dug up showing that Prudence had withdrawn $20,000 from her account, along with another bank statement showing the same amount had miraculously appeared in Jack's account the same day.

"Idiot!" Sutton said.

"Why do I think your disapproval has more to do with how sloppily she did this rather than the fact she did it?"

"Well, you'd be wrong." He looked thoughtful for a moment and then said, "I'm not happy about it on either score, *if* this were true. But I've cleaned up worse."

"You've had to do that a lot for your kids, and now grandkids, haven't you?"

Sutton looked pale, but his eyes were like steel darts when they focused on Kate. "All right. Hypothetically, if what you say is true, then what do you want so the information about my granddaughter disappears? Money? Backing for a film?"

"I want…*hypothetically*, of course, three things, none of which will cost you a dime."

He looked suspicious. "Go on."

Kate sat in the chair opposite him. "First, I hope you can ease my mind about any more attacks on me and about anyone trying to stop the release of the complete restored version of *Emperor Smythe*."

Sutton waved his hand. "That's already a certainty. I'm admitting nothing, but I can assure you that you will not be bothered again about the film. Request number two?"

"You implied an answer before, but now I need to know for certain. Who did you hire to steal the film the day Gloria died?"

"I did no such thing."

She stood and walked toward the door. "Fine. I guess the next thing on my list is having a chat with the police about my attack."

"Hold on," Sutton called to her. "You don't expect me to say otherwise. My man checked you for wires. But I'm not a fool. Devices can be planted or missed."

Kate turned and strode back toward him.

Sutton gave her a crooked smile. "You're not a fool either. In fact, you're much better at this than I anticipated. I'm impressed, Miss Bloom. You've been very careful with your words. You are just making *requests* even though we both know what you're doing is blackmail."

"What an awful word. I'm doing no such thing. Like before, I'm simply seeking information from someone who might know about things that happened the day my grandmother died."

"Ahhh, still looking for murderers."

"Or am I looking at one?"

"You don't expect me to answer that."

"It wouldn't surprise me to find you're capable of murder. However, I'm more inclined to think you're like your granddaughter and would hire people to do your dirty work."

"What else do you think you know about me?"

"Suspect is more accurate."

"And?"

"Let me try again. *If* you were interested in hiring someone back then to remove an item from your film studio, who would it be?"

Sutton still said nothing, but he nodded at her as if encouraging her to continue.

"A smart businessman like you wouldn't be as foolish as Prudence was and hire a loser like Jack or, back to the day Gloria died, like Chuck Needham. You already implied as much last time, that you'd hire someone known to be a hard worker, ambitious, and underappreciated, someone like Beatrice Talbot, perhaps. It was Beatrice, right?"

Sutton nodded. He looked her straight in the eye. "Is the answer clear this time?"

"Yes. Thank you."

Sutton began to smile, but it quickly morphed into a cringe. "You are a lot like Gloria. And I don't mean in looks, but in smarts."

"Gloria was smart?"

"Like a razor. Don't look so surprised, many a breathtaking starlet teetered on genius and some in fact were. Like exquisitely beautiful Hedy Lamarr, with a list of scientific inventions to her name. Kate Hepburn, with her degree in history and philosophy and the ability to master anything she set her mind to. And Gloria matched them all in wit and steely determination."

Kate shook her head at her own idiocy. The revelation was more illuminating about herself than

Gloria, and so ironic she almost laughed.

She'd been the one guilty of objectifying Gloria more than any man or studio ever did, maybe more so. Gloria was not a one-dimensional Hollywood bombshell but so much more than that. In fact, if anyone had been living a flat existence, it was Kate more than her grandmother ever had.

She smiled at Sutton. "Thank you for telling me that." Kate spun on her heel and headed again for the office door.

"Miss Bloom," Sutton called out. "You said there were three things."

She turned back to him. "Oh, don't worry. The third you have already done for me."

He looked puzzled.

"You've sent a threatening letter to Beatrice, Jarvis, and Lillian, anonymously, of course, but everyone will know it's from you."

"But I didn't."

Kate shrugged. "No, but people will think you did. Because you're the kind of person… How did you put it the first day we met? Oh, yes. The kind of person who collects information. You see, in the letters is a copy of part of a confession from Chuck Needham, in his own handwriting—very convincing. In it he says he saw someone, not Winston, leaving Gloria's dressing room just before she was discovered dead." She paused and winked at Sutton. "The blackmailer, that's you, threatens to turn Needham's whole letter over to the police, naming that person unless the killer returns the missing *Smythe* footage and brings it to a drop point." She smiled. "All very clandestine and exciting, isn't it?"

"That's a dangerous game. Why are you dragging me into it?"

"I need it to be believable. Who else but you could possibly have such a confession in his possession?"

"No one, and I don't. Therefore, neither do you."

"True, but they don't know that."

"Are you mad? If you're right and one of them is a murderer, that could make me a target."

Kate swung open the door, then turned back and smiled at Sutton. "I guess you'd better hope we catch who *did* do it. Any additional information you wish to supply on the matter, you are free to contact me or Detective Robak. Good evening, Mr. Sutton."

Chapter Thirty

Kate was surprised at how nervous she felt when she rang the bell to her aunt's apartment. Lillian buzzed her through the courtyard gate. Not until Kate reached the second floor landing and saw her aunt waiting for her, the apartment door open, did her case of nerves begin to dissipate. Lillian, wearing a purple caftan trimmed with gold thread at the collar and with wide V-shaped sleeves, enfolded her in a hug. The aroma of vanilla and spice from her aunt's liberally applied perfume saturated the air.

It was nice.

Lillian pulled back and looked at Kate. "Darling, I've missed you." She clasped her hands and lifted them into the air as if in a prayer of supreme thanksgiving, "Thank you, thank you."

"I've missed you too." Kate edged past her. "But you're overplaying it a bit."

"Nonsense." Lillian entered her modest apartment's living room, her arms gesturing widely and gracefully as if she was wearing a butterfly costume in a big Broadway musical. "Certain monumental events, like rain at the end of a drought, cessation of military action, and *you,* my darling, forgiving me, incite great feeling."

On the coffee table sat Lillian's English tea service. Kate sat on the couch next to the table and eyed the butter cookies. "I'm still angry with you."

"Oh." Deflated, Lillian descended, elegantly, onto the chair across from Kate.

She smiled at her aunt. "I'm not that angry."

"Wonderful!" Lillian rose, fluttered to her desk, and picked up a sheet of paper. "I have a surprise for you." She handed the paper to Kate. "I received this letter this morning. Look. I'm being blackmailed." Lillian acted positively thrilled by the prospect.

Kate took the letter and pretended to read it, because she knew its contents. It was one of the three letters Natalie had mailed. Beatrice and Jarvis should have received their letters by now, too.

Lillian hovered next to Kate and pointed to a paragraph. "It isn't signed, but I bet that octopus J.B. Sutton wrote it. You see, it says that Charles Needham, the man who sent you the footage, wrote a confession of sorts, not for murder but for stealing the film. The blackmailer, Sutton, intimates that later in Needham's confession he reveals seeing someone other than Winston leaving Gloria's dressing room prior to Winston leaving the set."

"What are you going to do with it?" Kate asked, terrified her aunt would say the wrong thing. "I mean, this letter could place the murder at a time when you didn't have an alibi. Aren't you worried the release of Charles's confession could make you a suspect?"

Lillian shook her head. "Tish-tosh, that's ridiculous. I'll tell you what I did. First thing this morning I called that Detective Robak and told him about the letter and asked him to find out for certain who sent it. Don't you see? It's at last proof that someone other than Winston killed my sister."

Lillian didn't do it!

Kate was so relieved she thought she was going to weep. This time, she threw open her arms and hugged her aunt.

"What's this all about?"

"I'm just happy," Kate said. And she was. That feeling had begun when she saw Natalie. And now, again, she realized that turning away from people who loved her was idiotic. "I still have a screen test to do, and don't be shocked, I want to nail my performance. Will you help me?"

Her aunt clasped her hands together. "Marvelous!"

"Realism, Lillian. I want to do a realistic performance," Kate said.

"Right, right you are." She wrinkled her nose as if she smelled something dreadful. "Less is more and all that—such a terrible idea. Unfortunately, it happens to be true." She took Kate's face in her hands. "Of course, I'll help."

Lillian poured herself some tea and made a small plate of Danish butter cookies for Kate as if she were a child. "Now tell me about getting Dylan out of jail. I heard it was you who proved he had taken the film to make copies, not to destroy it. So romantic! Were you waiting for him, stalwart as he was released from the big house, then fell, at long last, into each other's arms?"

"No." Okay, so maybe she wasn't ready to accept everyone who supposedly loved her. Her aunt could be forgiven. Dylan was just too damn confusing. Kate nibbled on a cookie.

"Mallick brought the evidence in, not me," she explained. "It's better I don't see Dylan again. There's just been too many lies."

Lillian's tea cup rattled against its saucer.

Kate put a hand on her aunt's arm. "Don't worry, I won't cut you out. That is, if you don't lie to me again."

"Oh." Lillian's gaze shifted to the ceiling.

"Oh?" Kate stiffened. "There's not something else, is there?"

"Darling, sometimes there are good reasons to tell stories. Lying is such an ugly word."

"Not when it's accurate. Tell me."

"This modern need for truth all the time is so vulgar."

"I mean it, Lillian."

Her aunt dabbed the corners of her pink-lipsticked mouth with her napkin. "Very well. I won't make the same mistake I did with your mother." She folded the napkin and placed it on the tea tray, then stood up. "I'll take you there."

"What?"

"I think it's better I show rather than tell."

****

After it was clear that Lillian wasn't going to answer Kate's questions until they arrived at wherever they were going, they drove in silence. Kate stared out the window of her aunt's Lincoln Continental and watched lettuce fields zip by. She wondered what possible good reason there could have been for her aunt's lies.

Whatever it was, she'd rather have it out in the open. If she was going to stop being merely a pawn that others maneuvered, she needed to know the full extent of the games being played around her.

A couple hundred miles northeast of Los Angeles,

Lillian finally turned off Highway 99. The exit looked like so many of the others they had passed along the way. A coffee shop and a gas station shone brightly in the sun next to the freeway exit, but beyond that nothing but cultivated fields.

Then a couple of miles farther along, Lillian turned on to a two-lane road that climbed a small hill and took them past a large oil field, and then they drove through a bustling small town. The main drag boasted two old brick movie theaters, three banks, many shops and restaurants, and even an old-fashioned train station. They drove past the town's outskirts and wound through neighborhoods where kids rode bikes or played basketball. At the top of a hill, Lillian pulled the Lincoln into a large parking lot.

They were at a kind of park. It had green grass, oak trees, and benches to sit on. There were also two buildings near each other by the parking lot. One, a small cottage with beautifully tended yellow roses in the front of it, the other a larger octagonal structure, in front of which a sign read "Almond Tree Playhouse."

An old man walked slowly out of the door. He looked as brittle as fallen leaves. When he turned toward them, Kate flinched. It was the old man she'd seen on the *Satan's Academy* set the day she was attacked. And if she wasn't mistaken, she'd swear she'd seen him before, there in the corner of her eye, but sneaking away into the shadows when she turned.

Not far behind the old man came Dylan.

Was this what their trip was all about?

Kate disentangled herself from the seat belt and almost toppled out of the car. Was her aunt trying to force a reconciliation between her and Dylan? The last thing she wanted was to see him again. But okay. Let's get this over with. She marched toward him.

When Dylan saw her barreling toward him, instead of smirking or smiling or whatever a co-conspirator might do, he leapt in front of the old man like a lineman protecting the quarterback.

"Get her out of here!" Dylan yelled to Lillian, who was trailing Kate. "Are you nuts? They'll lock him up."

The old man nudged Dylan aside and doddered past Kate to Lillian. "Lil, darling. Are we to read *Merry Wives* today, or are you in a bloodthirsty mood and prefer the Scottish play?"

He looked at Kate with milky eyes. The old man's mouth twitched, and the animated expression that had been there a moment before disappeared. His eyes shifted like a bird's, flitting from one point of focus to the next. His jerky movements stopped when he stared at Lillian.

She turned him gently toward Kate. "This is my great-niece. This is Kate."

"M'dear, you finally brought her. Thank you." The old man's pupils appeared to grow larger as he continued to stare at her. The gaze was all too familiar. It was like Dylan's.

Kate stepped back, but the old man clutched her arm with a gnarled hand and said, "You're in danger. That's why I've been watching after you, to protect you." His head jerked to Dylan and then to Lillian. "But they won't let me."

Dylan unlatched the man's hand from Kate's arm, and when he did the old man's expression became blank.

"Let me take you inside," Dylan said to him.

"No, please." His creaky voice sounded plaintive. "Not inside. I need to watch after her, please."

Dylan relented and escorted the frail man to a bench in front of the theater.

Kate now knew who he was, even if that was impossible. She marveled at the number of lies necessary to protect *that* man.

He no longer bore any resemblance to the last caricatured image the world had known of him—the fallen golden boy who'd become an obese, dissipated clown. But yet, glimmering through the old man's decrepit being was the suggestion of the harlequin's grace that had once been there, the same flair she'd seen in Dylan but had never made the connection.

Why shouldn't they be alike? Like father like son, right? The old man was Winston Nash.

Kate turned to her aunt. "How can he still be alive?"

Lillian averted her gaze.

Kate shook her head. "Mom was right. You choose him every time, even with all that's been going on."

"I can explain," Lillian said.

"Forget it." Kate turned away, ready to walk the two hundred miles back to LA rather than spend one more second in her aunt's, or in Dylan's lying presence.

She didn't make it more than twenty paces before Dylan caught up and stopped her. Before he could say a word, she said, "The yellow rose left in my car wasn't from you, was it? It was from him. Your father has been following me this whole time. You've both been protecting him, letting me believe the feeling of being watched was all in my imagination. How dare you!"

"You've got to understand," Dylan replied. "My

dad's not well."

Kate laughed. "That's a lot better than dead. Anyway, I really don't care. You forget, during the last month I've been burglarized, threatened, and attacked. And Mallick was almost killed."

Lillian trudged toward them, her breathing labored.

Kate continued, "Still, neither of you thought to tell the police that the most likely suspect for all of it was alive and well."

"He didn't do any of those things," Dylan said. "And if it was known my dad was on the set the day you were attacked, he'd have been arrested. The scapegoat, just like before. He couldn't survive that again."

"Him? What about me? What about Gloria?"

"You've got to believe me. He'd never hurt you. I was about to meet you that day on the set when I discovered that my dad was there. Hell, that's why I was late meeting you. I needed to get him in a cab and safely out of there. I hate I wasn't there when someone hurt you. But discovery would have destroyed him. What would you have had me do?"

"To have told the police!" She took a breath and tried to say in a less hysterical tone, "Or at least have told me."

"Yeah, sure, so you could carry on like you are now? Ready to run to the cops, throw him in jail? No way."

"Enough!" Lillian lifted her arms, the loose sleeves of her caftan sailing in the breeze, making her look like Charlton Heston parting the Red Sea. Then, just as dramatically, she dropped her arms in defeat. "You're right. We should've told you. We were wrong. You must understand that never for a moment did I think Winston capable of harming you or Gloria. I still don't. I've known and loved him for over forty-seven years. Dylan is not exaggerating about the damage to Winston if the press found out he was still alive." Lillian's eyes gleamed with tears. "But, my darling, you must know something your mother never did. If I had to choose between you and Winston, I choose you."

Lillian, her marvelous aunt, stood before her, the very picture of loss and regret. And Dylan, his shoulders hunched as if he were encumbered by a crushing weight.

Kate wanted to stay angry. She had every right to be angry. Yet, right or wrong, these were the two people she loved best, and they were both in pain.

"Talk to Winston," Lillian pleaded. "After that, if you think the police must know he's alive, I will report it myself."

Winston sat alone on the bench, staring at the swaying branches of the large oak tree above him, his expression childlike. Here was the undisputed master of film and theater. Also the monster of her childhood. He didn't look like much. Once thought of as a lion of a man, he now looked as frail as cracked glass.

She walked back to the theater and sat beside him. His gaze took a circuitous route but finally landed on Kate's face. His palsied hands quivered, yet there was still a certain amount of elegance in the way he lifted her hand and kissed it. He said, " 'A wither'd hermit, five score winters worn might shake off fifty looking in your eye.' "

She pulled her hand away. "Who are you seeing, me or Gloria?"

"You. 'The prettiest Kate in Christendom.' "

"Will you please stop that and talk to me?"

Winston's smile faded, but Kate would not be deterred. "Please, tell me what happened the day my grandmother died."

He shook his head, his hands fidgeting in his lap. "I don't remember. I don't remember anything. Ask anyone, Doctor Rosen would tell you, the past for me is a jumble."

"You've managed to remember Shakespeare quotes." Kate stood. "I'm not buying this crazy act."

"Quotes, huh! Of course I know the lines of great works. That's not memory, it's my soul speaking." His eyes flashed, and for an instant she could see the fire he was reported to possess on stage. A mastery so compelling, the legend was that when he played Oedipus, at the ridiculously young age of nineteen, and he came onstage in the final act with his eyes blackened to look like vacant sockets, women swooned and men fled the theater swearing that in his hands was a bloody, gelatinous goo that had been his eyes.

The amazing thing about that story was that nothing had been in his hands, not even fake blood, much less fake eyes. His belief in that reality was enough to make it the reality for the audience.

Despite herself, she smiled. She was beginning to like him and the direct approach wasn't working, so she decided to take a different tack. "I need help with a scene. I need to put on a performance, and it has got to be convincing. Any advice?"

His eyes shone. "Ah, that's a question I can answer."

"Any chance I could learn to convey even half of

what Lillian or Gloria could?"

He chuckled. "That's the wrong question. You could try to be Lil or Gloria, you have the bearing and beauty for it. You might even fool some. But why? In the end it would be hollow."

"That's what I was afraid of. I guess even you can't make someone into a great actress with less than a week to prepare."

He looked questioningly at her.

"That's when the screen test is," she explained.

His shaky hand patted her knee. "Don't despair. I said it would be hollow if you tried to be Gloria or Lil. I didn't say you couldn't be a great actress." He winked. "I've been known to be a pretty good judge of that. Fiction comes alive when you find the truth of it in yourself. I believe you can do it as long as the lines you speak are true."

Kate laughed. "That makes no sense. By definition they're not true. You're not Othello or Hamlet or Lear."

"Aren't I?" He had that jester's grin, just like Dylan's. "The task is to find them in yourself, not in your aunt or in Gloria."

"But Gloria was so larger than life."

"We all don't glitter gold. That was true of her. I suspect you are a bit more subtle."

"Boring you mean." Kate thought of the silk dress Jarvis had given to her that had called to her from somewhere deep within. She smiled. "I'm just brown and green. No one would pay to see that?"

"If you are brave and give yourself fully to all of who you are, I, for one, would wish to see it. The world would wish to see that truth." He looked at her with pride, and a hint of loss.

She believed him.

No, she needed to stop that.

He is, or once was, the greatest showman in the world. He could be playing her right now. And she hadn't learned anything about Gloria. "Please, tell me what happened the day my grandmother died."

"Oh, Kate." He turned away from her.

She waited.

He stared at the theater for a while, then said, "Do you know I'm hoping they'll let me direct *Taming of the Shrew* this year?"

Kate shook her head.

He continued, "I see you scowl at the notion of the play. People misinterpret the moral in Katharine's speech at the end. Some people interpret it as saying a woman's place is to kneel to man. But that's wrong. Her speech is about kneeling to love. That, m'dear, is a rare and courageous act." Winston gazed into space. "Once upon a time, I was ready to submit to love, to partnership. Alas, Gloria was not."

"Did you kill her?" Kate held her breath.

"I, I, I, I…" He continued to repeat the word as if his thought was stuck in an endless loop. It stopped, and that was scarier, because he had frozen. He turned ash white, fell to the ground, and writhed with convulsions.

She reached to help him, but then she was afraid she might make it worse. Winston's body jumped and twitched with such intensity.

Dylan ran to them. He turned his father onto his side and cradled the old man's head in his arms while the rest of Winston's body shook.

Lillian stood beside Kate, looking down at Winston, her face lost in pain. Then as quickly as it began, Winston's body stilled, and his breathing slowed. It was over in less than a minute, but it had felt interminable to wait so helplessly while another human being writhed out of control. Looking at Dylan's face, she could only imagine how horrible it was for him to see his father that way. How many other times had Dylan held Winston like this, trying to soothe him the way he did now, waiting for his father's eyes to regain focus?

Dylan assisted Winston to his feet and turned to lead him away.

"No," Winston said. "Kate asked me a question. She deserves an answer." He glanced at Dylan and then at Lillian. "You all deserve one. I just don't have one to give. I was drunk. I blacked out. After leaving the set, the next thing I remember was the police shaking me. I woke to find myself slumped in my chair in my office. Drops of blood and shards of white were under my feet. I suppose I must have killed her."

"No!" Lillian wailed.

Winston caressed Lillian's cheek. "Who else could it have been? I was hurt and angry that day. A week earlier she'd promised to be my wife. We had previously agreed we'd have a normal life together. No more jet-setting, no more lovers. We'd be committed to each other, to Audrey, to being a family." His face and neck flushed red. "It took Gloria less than a week to break that promise and jump into bed with the bloody valet at the Dorfman's party."

"Don't you remember something more about that day?"

"Enough," Dylan said to Kate. "Please."

Winston raised a hand to halt Dylan. "It's all right.

I do remember walking off the set and heading to my office. I saw members of the crew wrapping up."

"Who?" Kate asked. "Did you see anyone out of place? Did you go to Gloria's dressing room?"

"I don't remember." He hung his head, then lifted it. "Except…" His voice grew stronger with excitement. "Yes, there was someone out of place that day, who didn't belong." His face scrunched up as if he were straining to remember. He shook his head. "I can't remember who. I'm sorry. I'm so sorry."

Dylan led his father to the bench. "It's okay, Dad. Rest now."

Kate trudged back toward Lillian's car, trying to grapple with the fact of Winston being alive and still learning no more about Gloria's death. Kate slumped against her aunt's car door and watched as they settled Winston once again onto the bench under the large oak.

Her aunt walked back to Kate. Dylan soon followed. "Do you want me to tell the police about Winston?"

Lillian's and Dylan's expressions were filled with pain. Just beyond them sat Winston, looking so frail, so confused.

Kate sighed deeply. "How is it possible everyone thinks he's been dead for over ten years?" she asked Dylan. "I mean why? I need to know exactly how many lies your family has told. Where does it end?"

"It began with one lie." Dylan shook his head. "No, the truth is my family never claimed he died."

"Oh, come on."

"I know, I know," Dylan said. "We didn't deny it either. When the rumor appeared first in some small paper, it seemed like an answer to everything. Perhaps he'd be left alone and have the space to get well."

"What happened to him?"

Lillian gazed sadly at Winston. "In 1962, he fell into a coma. The press reported it as an overdose."

"But it wasn't," Dylan said. "My dad had been trying to get his life back together. A year earlier he'd begun a diet to lose the weight, and then, like an idiot, he decided to go cold turkey on the alcohol and pills. When I came home from playing field hockey that day, I found a trail of vomit leading to my dad, and him lying in it, his tongue bleeding so much I thought he bit it off." Dylan's expression looked as if he were reliving that frightening experience.

"To the film industry," Lillian said, "Winston had been dead for a long time. The papers reported him being in a coma. No one heard anything about him again. I guess it didn't take much for Hollywood and the media to assume he was dead. They all were sure they'd heard it somewhere, and people took it as confirmation when on the rare occasion the public became curious about Winston Nash, or his legacy, and they'd be directed to his estate to ask their questions. Soon his death was reported as fact."

"But he wasn't dead. He was in a conservatorship," Dylan said bitterly. "My mother had him locked up in a sanatorium under the name *Nichols* to avoid any more unpleasant publicity. The place she'd sent him to in Italy was beyond backward. They gave him electroshock treatments and pumped him full of drugs."

Dylan placed his hand on Lillian's shoulder. "That's where he stayed until Lil saved him. She got him out of that hole and found him a place where they actually wanted to heal his mind—The Center for

Wellness. It's just a couple of miles from here. They made him better mostly by just taking him off the antipsychotics. He was discharged to outpatient status in less than a year, but he's never been the same. No one's sure about the precise cause of his seizures and confusion. Maybe it was the coma and loss of oxygen to the brain, the shock treatments or the drugs or a combination of all three. The doctors say it's probably permanent. But sometimes I think he's close to coming back to the man he once was." Dylan lowered his eyes. "Other times, I'm not so sure."

"I'm sorry, Dylan," Kate said.

"Will you expose him?" he asked her.

She looked up and saw Winston was walking toward them. He appeared to be broken in more places than she'd have thought possible. Yet, he'd been right about one thing. He still had his soul. "No," she said. "I don't think we should tell the police. Like both of you, I don't believe Winston's capable of murder, even if he does." Both Lillian and Dylan looked relieved. "But don't get me wrong. I may believe that he's not a threat, but that doesn't mean I'm not pissed off that you two lied to me."

Dylan and Lillian looked crestfallen.

Kate shrugged and smiled at them. "But I suspect I'll get over it with time."

Winston grabbed his son's arm. "I remember. Someone was out of place." He turned to Kate. "A woman, near Gloria's dressing room. She tried to duck out of sight, when she saw me and then I got called back to the set. It was odd."

"What woman?" Dylan asked.

"I'd met her before, but she didn't belong there."

His head bobbed as if he was on a train instead of standing on solid ground. "My brain, my addle, addle, addle," he repeated like a stuck record.

"It's okay, Dad."

Winston babbled, "There was much to do. No, that's not right…much ado, yes, much ado…"

"What?" Dylan asked him. "Why are you saying that? Does it have to do with who you saw?"

"Yes, but I don't know why."

"Oh, my God," Lillian said.

Dylan and Lillian exchanged knowing glances.

"What?" Kate asked.

Dylan looked so excited he was practically quivering. "The play, *Much Ado About Nothing*."

"So?" Kate said.

"Oh, dear." Lillian lifted her hands and let them fall again, indicating she was exasperated by having such an ignorant niece.

Kate, on the other hand, wanted to kill both of them on the spot if they didn't explain.

"Beatrice is the name of the heroine in the play," Lillian said. "I performed that part myself once. It's a marvelous role—such a strong, smart woman."

"Dad, was the woman you saw in front of the dressing room Beatrice Talbot? She worked for Gloria's agent back then, remember?"

Winston's eyes lit up. "Yes! That was her name." Then his moment of clarity faded, and he mumbled. "Why, why was she there? Gloria didn't like her. She didn't belong outside of Gloria's dressing room."

"It's okay, Dad. I'm going to take you in now. You need some rest."

"Yes, yes, yes," the old man said.

Kate gazed at Dylan as he took care of his father. She realized those two were just as much a prisoner of that awful day in 1941 as her own family had been.

When Dylan returned to them, he walked with his old jaunty gait. He pumped a fist. "That places Beatrice at Gloria's dressing room well after she claimed to have left the soundstage."

"It makes sense." Kate nodded. "Sutton confirmed she was the one he sent to steal the film. She was probably there to take the footage from Needham, and something went wrong. Gloria saw her, and Beatrice killed her. Or, there is always Lillian's theory—jealousy."

"But didn't Beatrice have an alibi for that time?" Dylan said.

"Clearly bullshit. Beatrice has a lot to answer for."

Light danced in Dylan's eyes. "Right. Her alibi was Jarvis. If she doesn't have one, neither does he."

Chapter Thirty-One

After a playful knock, Kate glanced up and saw Mallick open the door and push a bewildered-looking Dylan into Ted's house.

Looking at Dylan, her breath caught, even though it had been less than a week since she'd been unsure if she could ever forgive him for lying to her about his dad. But then again maybe she had known it would not take her long before she wanted to see him again.

He appeared befuddled until he spotted Kate and then he focused in on her as if she were the only one in the room, the only one that mattered.

She tingled and smiled and really didn't know what to do with herself. He may not be Hollywood handsome, but there was something about his slightly unkempt soft, light-brown hair, his dark eyes made bigger by the frameless glasses, and his slightly goofy expression that did it for her.

Gaining her bearings, she rose from Ted's clay-and-plaster-encrusted dining room table. Despite its location near his kitchen, she hoped it was never used for eating. The creation of sculpted fantasy was clearly its higher purpose.

On the table was Kate's statue of Aphrodite. Next to it was a matching in size re-creation of Hephaestus. Natalie and Ted, working on Hephaestus, discussed whether the musculature of the right arm that held the god's hammer should be more humanistic, like a Renaissance depiction, or idealized in the neoclassical tradition. These subtleties being way over Kate's head, she left them to it and walked through the stucco archway to the living room.

"Welcome to our command post," Kate said to Dylan.

"Huh?" He looked at her, eyes big with longing and a just a hint of tentativeness.

Mallick pushed Dylan toward her. "Don't worry, she must have forgiven you or you wouldn't be here."

She shrugged. "Yes, we do need someone to play the lover."

Mallick laughed. "Yeah, she's forgiven you."

Kate turned and walked back to the dining room.

Regaining his voice, Dylan said, "What's going on? Play? Command post? This is just Ted's house."

"Currently mine, too," she said.

Dylan's ears turned red at that news.

"Hey, Dylan," Ted yelled from the table. "Get in here, amigo. We need all the help we can get."

Ted stood, his large beer belly thrust out, and his thick hands on his waist. "Is what I read true? Are you really Winston Nash's son? Man, I can't believe you didn't tell me."

"Or me," Natalie said.

Expecting the final chime-in, all eyes turned to Mallick.

Holding up his hands as if in surrender, he confessed, "Okay, okay, I knew, but that's only because I've been unlucky enough to meet Dylan's mother."

Dylan stormed up to Kate. "What do you mean you're living here? I mean, hell!" His bluster did not bother her. Because she knew with him, it was just bluster.

"Cool down," Ted said. "She's in the guest room, if it's any of your business. Kate needed a place to stay where no one would think to look for her. I'm not entirely sure I should be flattered, because that meant with me."

"Gee, Dylan," Kate teased. "If it bothers you, I could go back to Jarvis's house."

Dylan grumbled until he spotted the two statues on the table. He pointed to Hephaestus. "Wait. Where did you find that? I thought that thing was smashed?"

Ted shook his head. "Smashed? I don't think so. Marble isn't porcelain, you know. It takes a lot to shatter it. Even though we know from the evidence it had struck several pieces of furniture in the attack, my guess is only small slivers fell off. Most of it would've remained intact. Extrapolating from the photos of the larger remaining shards, it broke here, here, and here on the left side of the statue." Ted pointed to the statue's beard, which appeared to have a piece missing, to the top of the head, and to the anvil, which also had a chunk missing. "These are the places where I think the marble broke and crumbled. The shards at the murder scene and in your dad's office at the studio came from these spots."

"But how do you have it?"

Everyone grinned at clueless Dylan.

"It's not the real thing," Ted said with pride. "It's a replica."

"I think we're close," Natalie said. "Ted's amazing. The art professors at school have got nothing on him." She ran a finger down the statue. "The size and the texture of the marble we could recreate because of Kate's statute of Aphrodite. That is assuming it was part of the set, which we do. Yet, how to know the exact configuration from just photos of shards? Impossible. Particularly in this case, where the artist purported to make his statues from his own original designs. But Ted's a researching fiend."

The phone rang.

"Saved by the bell, it was starting to get embarrassing," Ted told them. He walked into the living room and picked up the phone.

Natalie continued, "Ted unearthed allegations from some of the sculptor's rivals that he'd forged his designs, even though they didn't match any known depiction. Ted kept looking. Did you know he has privileges at both the Getty and the Huntington? How cool is that!"

"So," Natalie continued, "he finds in some dusty sketchbook from the late eighteenth century this little-known Danish neoclassical artist's drawings of the entire Greek pantheon. And there it was!"

"What?" Dylan asked.

"A drawing in the exact pose as Kate's Aphrodite statue."

"I get it," Dylan said. "You're hoping the statue of Hephaestus, the murder weapon, was the same design as this Denmark dude's sketch."

"Precisely," Kate said.

Ted walked back in. "Hey, that was Detective Robak on the phone. Guess who's been out sick from work ever since receiving your letter?"

"Beatrice?" Kate asked.

"What letter?" asked Dylan.

Ted ignored him and said to Kate, "Bingo. Robak also found out she went to the Fed building a couple of days ago to renew her passport. He's heading out to her apartment to question her now."

Kate clapped her hands. "And then there were two."

Natalie echoed, "Two remaining suspects."

Dylan paced. "I don't like the sound of any of this. A letter? A replica of the murder weapon? What are you up to, Kate?"

"I'd think it's obvious. After all, I'm taking a page out of your book to see if there is indeed truth in fiction. The statue is for my mousetrap."

"What the hell are you talking about?"

"You know, *Hamlet*. Heard of it?"

"Of course *I've* heard of it," Dylan shouted. "Since when have you?"

"Even little old me knows at least one line from that play."

" 'To be or not to be'?" Natalie swung her arm in a large dramatic gesture.

Kate grinned at her. "Okay, so I know two lines from that play. That one and one Lillian's told me: '*The play's the thing wherein I'll catch the conscience of the king.*' "

"Are you freaking nuts?" Dylan cried. "There's a murderer out there. This isn't a game."

She raised her chin. "I can handle it."

"What's gotten into you? Where did all this insane confidence come from? Who the hell are you?"

She did feel confident, but this time she knew it was her own and not Gloria's, and she liked this newfound part of herself.

Dylan eyed her suspiciously. "You're acting kind of like you did at the party but without the edge. I want my restoration partner back, neurosis and all."

She could have kissed him right there. It was the nicest thing anyone had ever said to her. "Don't worry. I'm still here, neurosis and all," she said grinning at him. "Except, interestingly, now that I know there's something real to be scared about, like a murderer, I'm finding my more prosaic fears silly."

"But that's just it. There *is* a real killer. You can't go around setting someone up as if it were a play." He halted in mid rave. "I mean you do know how *Hamlet* ends, don't you?"

"Sure. I mean...I think—"

"Everybody *dies*, including Hamlet!" Dylan shouted.

Mallick raised his hand like a kid in a classroom. "No, that's not true. The friend lives. In this case me."

"No way," Natalie said. "I'm the friend."

"No one's going to die," Kate declared. "I'm not dumb. My play has backing. We're working with Detective Robak. He'll be there when the trap is set."

"Then he's crazy, too," Dylan said. "Do you know how many things can go wrong?"

Kate glared at him. "Sure, but it seems less crazy than sitting around and letting other people pull the strings. I'm not doing that anymore. This time, I'm the director."

He gripped her arms. "And the bait, right?"

"Well...yeah."

He pulled her to him. "Kate, don't do this."

Natalie smacked her hands on the table and stood up. "Okay, that's it." She stepped up to them like a referee. "You two take your bizarre foreplay outside. Or, even better, get it on already, Jeez!"

Her words hung in the air until the silence was broken by the sound of Mallick trying to stifle a giggle. This was followed by snickers from Natalie until Ted released the tide of merriment with a boisterous belly laugh, and the rest joined in.

Kate thought she might just dissolve into embarrassment on the spot. She glanced at the floor, and when she peered back up into Dylan's dark eyes, she thought, why not? It was about time.

She clasped Dylan's hand and tugged him toward the door. "Good idea."

Her friends laughed and applauded as Dylan and she stumbled out of the house.

Outside, Kate breathed heavily, as if she'd run a marathon and not simply walked the fifteen or so feet from Ted's house to the sidewalk. She looked at Dylan. He gazed straight out toward the street with a dazed look in his eyes and a goofy smile plastered on his face.

She would've laughed if she wasn't afraid of hyperventilating.

He finally looked at her. His expression had changed from stunned to enthralled, his dark eyes no longer unfathomable, no longer full of uncertainty.

On the drive to Dylan's house, belted in and apart in the Mustang's bucket seats, they didn't speak. What was running through Kate's mind was too intimate for words. She gazed at him as if for the first time, drinking in every detail. How his frameless glasses had left small marks on the bridge of his aquiline nose, how the lines too soon etched on his forehead betrayed a childhood filled with worry. He concentrated on the road, not touching her, yet she could feel a part of him reaching for her, as if an invisible tether already connected them.

Dylan's small craftsman house perched on a hill in the shadow of the Hollywood sign. They held hands as they climbed the four steps to the wood-framed porch bookended by thick pillars firmly set into a cobblestone base. Before opening the door, he said, "Are you sure?"

In answer, she kissed him. His lips were warm, and their taste ran through her like the salty zing of a stolen sip of a margarita.

In his bedroom, he pulled her to him. He kissed her. At first, he touched her almost with a shyness, as if he was afraid his desire might damage their hard-won friendship.

This was the last thing she had expected from the guy she had originally pegged as a womanizer.

She unbuttoned his shirt. He lifted her into his arms and kissed her deeply, and then all tentativeness was gone for both of them. A frenzied stripping of clothing ensued until they were naked, and they toppled onto his bed.

The linens had a light fragrance of soap, while Dylan smelled of musk and heated skin. Kate knew that outside these walls her world was infected by murders and manipulators. But it didn't matter. At least for now, she held her funny, sexy, aggravating Dylan in her arms, and all was well. The masks she'd righteously advocated be torn from society, had in this moment, fallen away easily as their hands, lips, and bodies discovered each other.

Chapter Thirty-Two

Today was the screen test. Kate sat in one half of a partitioned bungalow located on Infinity Studio's lot. It was her dressing room for the day. The cozy room had large wood-framed windows on one side and a built-in vanity on the other, along with a bathroom, mirrored closet, and a small living room area. It was almost an exact replica of Gloria's dressing room she'd seen in her visions.

She was lucky to have it. An unknown like her would normally never be assigned to such a nice room, particularly just for a screen test. She'd have normally been lucky to get a closet-size room in a long trailer.

It was good to have friends in high places. Thank you, ever efficient Beatrice.

It was also the perfect place for her scene. She looked at herself in the mirror and thankfully all she saw gazing back at her was her own reflection.

She wore the dress Jarvis had bought for her. She really did love it. It had a pattern of now and a structure of then.

Perfect for the *Emperor Smythe* remake and the other part she was to play today.

She twisted and watched the greens and browns of the silk dress ripple like the leaves held aloft by a strong tree.

Strong was the last thing Kate felt.

Nausea, abject terror, and a certitude that she'd flub every line she had diligently rehearsed was a more accurate description.

She paced the room. What had Winston said about acting?

Something about fiction comes alive if she could find the truth of it in herself.

Good advice, but could she do it?

She looked at the boxes she'd brought with her. One was a white, oblong flower box. She undid the red ribbon around it and removed two dozen long-stemmed yellow roses, which she arranged in a vase on the coffee table. She arranged even more carefully the oblong box so it was propped against the wall opposite the door, ensuring that it would be the first thing seen when someone entered the room. The second package was a generic brown box that Ted had stuffed with newspaper to keep his prize safe in transit. That box she placed in a dark corner of the opposite wall.

Standing straight, she exhaled.

Right. Show time.

She strode toward the door to head to the soundstage.

She could do this; she could do this.

When the dry, hot air of the late summer day smacked her in the face, her stomach clenched. She spun on her heel and tore back inside to the bathroom. She made it just in time to hurl out the piece of toast she'd forced herself to eat that morning.

Ten minutes later, she entered the soundstage a bit ashen and with a bitter taste of bile in her mouth.

Oh, what a glamorous life.

An assistant ushered her to one of many empty

chairs placed around the periphery of about two hundred square feet of perfectly lit space. Beyond the bright light she spotted Lillian and Dylan. She'd gotten them on to the set by saying one was her agent and the other her acting coach.

The assistant introduced Kate to the man who'd be playing her husband in the scene. He wore jeans and a t-shirt, and his hair spiked out haphazardly, as though it had been years since he'd bother to use a comb.

He must be a member of the crew and not an actor. But it didn't matter. This was her screen test. There would be only one camera set to take a medium shot of her.

The assistant cried out "Last look."

The tall girl with thick framed glasses, who'd done Kate's hair and make-up earlier appeared and dabbed face powder on Kate, and re-clipped her hair. The lady smiled and said, "You'll do great, honey," then left her in a pool of light.

She tried to ignore the lights, the people around her, and concentrated on the character she was about to play. It was the same part her grandmother had played—Crystal Smythe, the young wife of Emperor Smythe. In her screen test for the remake, she was to perform the pivotal scene she and Dylan had ironically spent the summer restoring. It was the moment when Crystal discovers her husband had lied to her. Worse than that, she learns he's a traitor.

Kate looked at Dylan.

Yeah, she knew what it felt like to think that about someone you loved. However, instead of pushing out the painful memory, she allowed it to grow inside her. She layered on top of that what she imagined it would be like if something that awful happened to someone as sheltered as the character Crystal must have been. Crystal Smythe was a pampered heiress who'd never been taught how to do anything for herself. So opposite from Kate's own self-parenting childhood.

Could Kate play that, be that?

Take one.

"Roll!" said the director.

The word reverberated as if God had spoken it, and time evaporated.

"Action!"

The guy in jeans threw out the dialogue Crystal was supposed to overhear. Without thinking about the part she was playing history or her own, Kate responded. All the details she'd diligently sketched out about the character entwined with her own life story. There, in the give and take of the scene, Crystal Smythe flickered into being. But not completely. Another part of Kate was cognizant of the marks on the floor she needed to hit, how to modulate the rhythm of the scene, and remembering each line. Even as she gave herself over to feelings outside her comfort zone, she remained in control. That alone was an electrifying discovery.

"Cut!" the director said.

Before Kate could take another breath, her aunt rushed to her with open arms. "You did it, darling!"

Kate felt foggy as the heightened state of creating fell away. "Was I really okay?"

Lillian beamed at her. "Brilliant!"

"Like Gloria?"

Her aunt smoothed Kate's hair. "No, like *you*."

The voice of the director jarred Kate out of her moment of bliss. "I'd like to do another take, if you don't mind," he said.

Lillian frowned at him. "Why? It was perfection."

Kate saw Jarvis standing beside the director. She gulped.

The director called to her, "I'd like to see another one."

Take two.

Take three.

Take four.

Not a good sign for a screen test.

She tried not to think about that or about her emotional fatigue or about Jarvis standing next to the director, impassive but an undeniable presence. Instead, she took it all as a challenge and focused on nailing the scene again and again.

Take five.

Take six.

After take twelve, Kate saw Jarvis place his hand on the director's shoulder. The director yelled, "That's a wrap!"

Jarvis did an about-face and headed for the exit.

Kate ran after him. "Please don't go."

He turned to her, his face blank. Still, she sensed a simmering rage that made her mouth go dry. "I want to apologize," she said.

"You ran out of my house without bothering to tell me."

She heard a hint of a hurt boy in the tone of this older powerful man. "I'm so sorry. You've been nothing but good—no, more than that, extraordinary to me. You didn't deserve that. It's just that things have been so confusing, I don't know if I can trust anybody."

He exhaled, and the fierceness in his eyes dimmed.

He glanced at Dylan and Lillian. "You seem to have forgiven them."

"I don't know if it's forgiveness. Lillian's my family, and Dylan... Well, I realized I love him and don't want to be without him." Kate sighed. "I guess I should tell you the news. Dylan asked me to marry him. Isn't that amazing? I've never been so happy."

"Amazing," Jarvis said without expression.

"Crazy, I know. It happened so fast. Or maybe not. Even though I fought it, I think I fell in love with him the second I saw him."

He gave her hand an awkward pat. "I'm happy for you." He turned to leave.

"Oh, wait, I have a present for you, to thank you." She leaned in closer and whispered. "Lillian and Dylan don't know about it. It's a secret. They've been a little overprotective. I have it in my dressing room. Will you meet me there?"

Lillian and Dylan walked up to them. Dylan gathered her into his arms and gave her a deep, luxurious kiss. "The scene was wonderful! Congratulations."

Jarvis took a stiff step back. "I should be going."

Kate placed a hand on Jarvis's arm. "Oh, not yet. I have that thing, you know, what we need to discuss."

"What thing?" Dylan asked her.

"Oh, nothing." Kate shrugged. "I need to return Jarvis's house key. Stuff like that."

"Keep it," Jarvis said. "You have an open invitation to stay there anytime you want." He gave Dylan a pointed look. "For whatever reason." A hint of a smile played on his lips before he turned to leave.

He strode across the soundstage, but he didn't get

far before one person after another stopped him and petitioned him for who knows what, but all no doubt wanting something from him. To Kate, somehow that seemed more lonely than being alone.

She suppressed an impulse to run up to him, take his hand, and walk out beside him.

As if Jarvis could sense what she was thinking, he glanced back at her.

With a ridiculously possessive gesture, Dylan turned her around and kissed her again. She felt annoyed for a moment, but then was lost in the taste of him. When Dylan released her, she looked back, and Jarvis was gone.

****

Kate sat by herself on the couch in her dressing room and waited.

There was a rap on the door.

She smiled. He had come sooner than she'd predicted.

The door swung open, and Jarvis walked in.

She was almost ashamed of feeling gratified that the first thing he looked at was not the oblong box but her. She felt sexy, strong, and like no one's pawn anymore.

Then Jarvis saw the box. And as she knew he would, he let his gaze linger on it longer than he should have if it meant nothing to him.

Jarvis looked back at her, his expression neutral.

Damn! The man was such a consummate gamesman. She couldn't read him.

He walked by her to the vase of yellow roses on the coffee table. He sneered. "You'd think Dylan would try to be a little more original. Same flowers Winston always gave Gloria. Kind of perverse, if you ask me."

"You knew those were the flowers Winston normally gave her? I didn't think that was common knowledge. In fact, before Winston, the magazine articles on Gloria said she preferred mixtures of flowers and found roses mundane."

"Of course I knew. I knew everything about Gloria. She trusted me."

"I don't."

"I've noticed. That's a mistake," Jarvis said. "Marrying Dylan is another."

"I love him." Kate turned her back to him and walked to the corner where she'd placed the other, nondescript box. Her imagination danced with images more absurd than the ones used in *Satan's Academy*. The rustle of steps behind her were not Jarvis's but those of some metamorphosed monster.

She tried not to let her imagination get the best of her as she prattled on. "I guess everyone saw how I felt about Dylan even before I did. You knew, you saw it in my eyes, I know you did." Her back still turned to Jarvis, she bent over to pick up her gift for him, trying her best to stifle the desire to scream. This was absurd. She was safe. She knew it.

Kate grasped the statue of Ted's replica of Hephaestus. She heard the shuffle of Jarvis's feet as he moved closer. When she stood and turned around, he was so near she felt his hot breath on her neck.

"Dylan's wrong for you. I can protect you. You need protection."

"Yes, I do." She held up the statue of Hephaestus. "From *you*."

Jarvis stumbled back, gaping at the statue as if it

were an apparition.

Kate took a step toward him, running her finger along the left side of the statue, where the top of the head and part of the beard and anvil were missing. "You're the one who bludgeoned Gloria to death."

"That's not true."

Jarvis's expression appeared placid. But Kate sensed the monster would soon appear. Couldn't she see it quivering just beneath the surface of his carefully constructed veneer?

She couldn't stop now. She thrust the statue in front of his face. "It's you, isn't it? The tough kid from the streets, so crude and awkward among all the beautiful people of Hollywood. When you couldn't have your Aphrodite, you killed her."

"You're crazy." Jarvis snatched the heavy statue from her and held it like a baseball bat ready to be swung.

Time slowed. Kate shrank away from him and braced herself for the blow. From the corner of her eye she saw the closet door crack open and Dylan peek out. Could he get there in time to stop Jarvis's assault?

But that didn't happen.

Instead, Jarvis threw his head back and laughed.

She saw Dylan slip back into his hiding place.

Jarvis chanted, "Come out, come out, wherever you are." He sneered at Kate, his eyes dancing with a wicked mirth. "You're fantastic. Completely wrongheaded, Nemesis. Still fantastic."

Kate stood there, struck dumb.

"I was supposed to confess there, wasn't I? Which means we're not alone, right? You'd want witnesses for that." He clapped his hands like a schoolmarm and yelled, "Okay, children, amateur hour is over."

Silence.

Jarvis gave her a stern, patronizing look. "Kate."

She sighed and called out, "Okay, he's right. No point now. Come on out, everyone."

Dylan appeared first at the closet door. Unplugged earphones dangled from his neck. In the closet was a small soundboard hooked to a reel-to-reel tape deck, which was recording everything from the radio transmitter microphone Kate was wearing.

Ted and Natalie shuffled out of the bathroom, looking guilty. Mallick was the last to join the party, because he'd been stationed outside, where he'd been filming the scene with a super-eight camera through a slit in the window curtains.

"Nemesis, the Greek goddess of retribution, you called me that the first day I met you," Kate said. "That's your thing, right? Assigning the qualities of metaphorical gods to people. *You* gave my grandmother the Aphrodite statue. And you bought Aphrodite's mate, Hephaestus. Don't deny it."

"I don't. Why should I?" He gazed about the room, looking as if another thought had come to him, and his expression darkened. "Oh, no." He looked at the statue, running his finger over the jagged edges. "Of course. You said that something made of marble cracked her skull."

He now looked ashen. "Are you telling me this is what struck Gloria?"

"The original one did, yes," Ted replied.

"I had no idea." Jarvis sank into a chair. "Then I *am* responsible, at least partly. I did buy it. But not for me." He laughed bitterly. "I'd never see myself as

Hephaestus—the tradesman, the worker, the deformed servant to the gods. I'm too much of an egotist for that, or haven't you noticed? I picked Zeus for myself. Hephaestus I bought for someone else, as a joke. Maybe it was too cruel of a one?"

"Who did you give it to?" Dylan demanded.

"Isn't it obvious? Beatrice."

"What? Why?" Kate asked.

"What's more, I supplied her alibi." Jarvis stared into space, appearing almost disoriented until his gaze landed on Dylan. His focus returned, he said to him, "I'm sorry. All these years I thought it was your father who killed her. And all the time it was Beatrice, my supposed loyal worker." Jarvis punched his right fist into his left hand. "How could I've been so stupid?"

Kate placed a hand on his shoulder. "It's not your fault."

"Damn, I forgot." Jarvis leapt to his feet. "She's going out of town. We've got to call the police right away."

"Of course," Kate said. "Call Detective Robak, he'll know what to do."

"Let me," Dylan said. "I saw a phone outside the soundstage." He ran out.

"Hey, man, not without me." Mallick followed, slamming the door behind him.

Jarvis stared at the statue. "It really is remarkable. How did you reconstruct it? How did you know what it looked like?"

Kate nodded toward Natalie and Ted. "Thank them. They're geniuses."

Natalie beamed at Ted. "It was mostly him."

"Impressive," Jarvis said.

Ted looked positively embarrassed by the compliments from both Natalie and Jarvis.

They all stood there in an awkward silence until Dylan returned. "Hey, Robak said the police will try to track down Beatrice before she gets away. But he needs Jarvis to come down to the station pronto to make a statement. Can you?"

Jarvis nodded. "Of course. I still can't believe it was Beatrice that killed Gloria."

"Yeah, and not my dad," Dylan said.

"That may take me even longer to get used to. I've hated Winston for so long. I took it out on you, son. I'm sorry." Jarvis held out his hand to Dylan.

Dylan took it. "Well, that's something." He turned to the others. "Mallick and I are going down to the station, too. I'll call you when we're done."

Kate slung her purse onto her shoulder. Ted and Natalie carefully wrapped up the statue and placed it back in the brown box.

Jarvis turned to Kate. "I guess I'm getting slow in my old age. You're not really engaged to Dylan, are you? That was part of your set-up too, wasn't it?"

Natalie giggled.

"Of course it was," Kate said. "Jeez, I'm *only* twenty-two. I'm not getting married for a long time, if ever."

"Amen," Natalie said with a wink.

Jarvis strode toward the door.

"Wait." Kate rummaged through her purse and dug out the key to Jarvis's house. She held it out to him. "You'll want this back."

"No, I told you before, it's yours. You have an open invitation, always."

"I can't believe you don't hate me."

He looked puzzled.

"You know, for thinking you killed Gloria, for trying to set you up."

"Not a bit," he said, not hiding the irony in his tone. "I recognized your need for the truth the first time I met you. It's who you are, nothing to apologize for."

Ted picked up the box with the statue and stood by Kate. Ted asked Jarvis, "Then, uh…can I take that to mean no repercussions for any of us? I mean, you're known in this town as a pretty scary dude."

Jarvis chuckled as he headed for the door. "No repercussions, at least not for this performance." He opened the door and turned back.

"Kate, I don't mean to frighten you, but based on everything that's happened, you're still a likely target. I never realized the depth of Beatrice's jealousy. As long as she's out there, you should be careful. Call or come by if you need anything. I mean it."

Chapter Thirty-Three

A short article buried in Friday's newspaper, reported Beatrice Talbot, long time executive of Infinity Pictures, had been detained as a "person of interest" in an unsolved murder case while trying to board a flight to Argentina.

Kate waited until Sunday, the day the staff was away, to go to Jarvis's house. She could have packed her belongings, been gone before noon, but she remained for a while looking out the window of what had been her bedroom and taking in the view of the terraced backyard, knowing it would be her last time to do so.

She opened the window and a familiar humid breeze wrapped around her like a hug.

Gloria.

The curtains flapped in a flurry.

"It'll be okay," Kate assured the wind. "It's okay."

In the house the slam of the front door echoed. A couple of minutes later, Jarvis strolled out to the patio. She shut the window and headed downstairs to join him.

Once by his side, she turned to him. "I'm sure you already know that Beatrice was caught at LAX."

"I heard."

"She denied everything, of course. But Robak says the evidence is mounting. Your testimony about her

Allison Morse

alibi being a fake, the murder weapon belonging to her, and Beatrice's known animosity toward Gloria creates a compelling narrative."

He tapped his chin. "There's more. One of my connections on the police force told me they got a warrant to search her place, and they found bank records showing she'd been writing checks to Chuck Needham all this time. Needham must have been blackmailing her. And with the evidence of the recent blackmail letter, Sutton must have been trying to continue the practice."

The hillside's licorice air tasted acrid in Kate's mouth. "I guess there's no doubt anymore who killed my grandmother."

Jarvis rested his hand on her arm. "You don't need to leave. I'd like to have a caretaker around the place, someone I trust."

"You have Jimena and Kioshi."

He let go of her. "I'm hardly around, if that's what worries you."

Melancholy weighed on her as they slowly meandered back to the house. "I don't think so. I don't belong in this grandeur."

"You do." Jarvis opened the solarium door for her. "Your screen test was great, and it's not only me saying it. Several of my producers can't wait to sign you for the remake. I'm going to make you a star, so you'd better get used to it."

He raised a hand to halt her inevitable protest. They both laughed. For a moment they were just two people who liked each other. But then Kate felt awkward again.

The great Jarvis Benjamin looked down at his

368

shoes. "Do you think we can get back to where we were before?"

She shook her head. "I don't think that's a good idea. I may not be engaged to Dylan, but I am in love with him. I want to make it work and…well, you confuse things."

"All I was talking about was finally making you my culinary specialty, grilled cheese sandwich *a la Benjamin*. The meal you skipped out on the last time you were here."

Kate grinned. "That I would love."

"Good." Jarvis headed toward the kitchen. "Two grilled cheese sandwiches coming up."

"Wait."

He turned to her.

"I brought you something. It's in my car. Except it could be a really bad idea." She looked at Jarvis, then at the ground, then at Jarvis again. "I'm not sure. I wanted to give you something special, to thank you and apologize—"

Jarvis made a dismissive gesture. "You don't need to give me anything."

"But I *do*. You've been phenomenal. You've given me so many opportunities. And you're not easy to shop for, I might add, being a man who has everything. If you don't like it, just tell me."

Jarvis chuckled. "Okay, okay. So what is it?"

"My mom's statue of Aphrodite."

Jarvis stopped as he was taking a large skillet from a cabinet and looked at her. His smile had vanished.

"I mean, I guess it was Gloria's statue, the one you gave to her. I thought you might like to have it back. At least, I'd like to give it to you, if you want it." Kate sucked in her lower lip. "Dumb, huh? Particularly on the heels of my fiasco with the replica of Hephaestus. A statue of Aphrodite is probably the last thing you'd want. All the bad memories."

"No, good memories," Jarvis said haltingly. "Thank you. I'd like her back."

"Cool! I'll go get it." She ran out to her car.

When she returned to the kitchen holding beautiful Aphrodite, Jarvis was standing at the counter, grating cheese. He was whistling as he held up a red onion and said, "This is what makes the sandwich special." Jarvis unsheathed a butcher knife and thinly sliced the onion.

Kate placed the statue on the kitchen table and sat down. While he worked, she peered up at the familiar sight of his Toby Jugs collection on the built-in shelf above the breakfast nook. Smiling, she pointed to the squat, round body of one that looked like an inebriated Ben Franklin. "My mom had a Toby Jug similar to that one. I think I still have it in her mishmash of a collection."

"I know. I gave it to her."

"Really?"

"Sure, it was our thing. I'd take Audrey treasure hunting, that's what we'd call it."

"Oh, how nice. Come to think of it, it makes sense she got that from you." Kate swept her gaze around the kitchen. "I've noticed you like to collect things."

He kept slicing the onion. "When you start with almost nothing, *things* become like prizes." He glanced back at her and grinned. "Particularly pretty ones."

"Yeah, right, like those grotesque Toby Jugs. They're so attractive."

Kate thought about the antique matchboxes and

pipes she'd seen in his office the first time they met and the Indonesian shadow puppet collection in his living room and many other things. "But you're a purist, a real collector. My mom's stuff was a hodgepodge of items, but when you choose something, you take it seriously. Ted told me when he traced your purchase of Hephaestus, you didn't buy just one or two. You commissioned the entire pantheon." Her gaze fell on the always locked door to the cellar. She stood up, went to it, and jiggled the doorknob. Locked. "I bet that collection's in the cellar. Except why hide it? Unless… Oh, God, Hephaestus is there."

She turned, not daring to look him in the eyes. But she felt his gaze on her, pictured him standing there, staring at her, the butcher knife clutched in his right hand, looking like one of his Toby Jugs, squat and dissipated in a way that made him look fiendish.

"What did you say?" His words sharp, staccato.

With only a quick glance at him, she inched toward the kitchen doorway. "Nothing, ah, except, you know, I left something else in my car. Let me go get it."

He crossed the room in three swift strides and seized her arm, still grasping the knife in his other hand. "Say it! Say what you're thinking!"

"Nothing. I'm thinking nothing." She struggled but couldn't pull her arm free out of his iron grip.

All her alarm bells went off, commanding her to run. She twisted her body in a frenzy. His grip tightened. She couldn't break free. Still, she had to know, had to play out this scene. She willed herself to calm down and control her breathing.

"Where is it?" she demanded. Her body trembled, but her voice was strong. "Where is your Classical collection?"

He smiled as though he had waited decades for someone to ask.

"You're too much of a collector to have gotten rid of it. Particularly that one. Greek gods are the metaphors you speak in. I'm right, aren't I? You still have it."

"You don't care about my statues," he snapped, his outburst so incongruous with the supremely in-control persona of the Jarvis she'd thought she knew. He jerked her close to him, the point of the knife only inches from her now. "You're only interested in seeing if I kept a particular one. You *need* to know, don't you? Yes, he's there, even more battered and deformed than before. And here you are, my little Nemesis."

Jarvis put his face close to hers, and for an awful moment she thought he was going to kiss her. She jerked and turned her head.

His grip stiffened and he shoved her to the ground as if she were contaminated. "Not again."

She trembled and looked up at him. "Not again what?"

His expression grew icy, and his blue eyes turned black.

She looked up at him. "Losing control? Is that what happened with Gloria?"

He grabbed Kate and pulled her to her feet. Securing her in a headlock, he placed the tip of the blade under her chin. Together they walked to the kitchen table. He pointed the knife at the statue of Aphrodite. "Pick her up. It's time to put her where she belongs."

Kate grabbed the statue and hugged it tightly.

Jarvis dragged her to the cellar door and pinned her against the wall with a beefy shoulder while he keyed the lock. He pushed her through the doorway onto the landing, holding the blade against her back. Luckily, he didn't notice the scrapes near the latch.

Jarvis switched on a light. It barely lit the steep stairs. Unable to hold the railing because she carried the statue of Aphrodite, Kate had to depend on Jarvis for support. They clumped in unison down the wooden stairs. Her legs wobbled. The darkness below was terrifying, her need to scream out almost overwhelming.

Her mind whirled with fear and doubt. She'd been so foolish. What if he threw her down these steps, in this dark place? What an easy solution to the problem of her.

But no, he wouldn't do that. After all, the last thing he'd want was a reason for the police to search his precious cellar. It was too risky, much more than the way he had planned to kill Dylan on the steps to the guest house.

Yes, he was the one who did that, it must have been him. All the pieces were falling into place.

"You tried to kill Dylan, didn't you?"

He didn't answer. They took another step down the cellar stairs.

Her mind raced. It must have been Jarvis who'd tampered with the stone steps and railing. He'd arranged for her to be away that morning, so the only person expected to go down those stairs was Dylan, his perceived rival, but his plan had failed. He wouldn't be fool enough to try such an unsure method of disposal again.

She trembled with relief when they finally arrived on the cement floor.

Jarvis relaxed his grip. With an odd gentleness, he put a stocky arm around her waist and guided her to a stool far from the staircase. Before leaving her there, he nodded like a Victorian gentleman escorting his lady back to her seat after a dance, instead of to this windowless prison.

He clicked a switch. Fluorescent lights flickered on, filling the room with greenish glow until it had the over-lit quality of an all-night drugstore. The ceiling was low. The room, however, was vast. It appeared to be more than half the length of the house. Along the west wall, wooden racks held a modest number of wine bottles. On the opposite wall, and less dusty, was Jarvis's true prized collection. Two shelves high and at least thirty feet long, a glass display cabinet held marble figurines, all in the same style as the Aphrodite statue that Kate held in her hands.

Lesser known classical figures populated the bottom shelf. Some she recognized, such as Sisyphus rolling his rock and the Minotaur, with the head of a fierce bull and the body of a man. Jarvis clicked another switch, and twelve separate spaces on the top shelf lit up. A marble statue stood in all of them but one. From her research, Kate knew that each one was a member of the Greek pantheon.

Jarvis took the statue of Aphrodite from her and placed it in the empty spot.

"*She* was who you were looking for when you arranged to have my garage cleared out, right?" Kate protectively wrapped her arms across her waist. "You thought she might lead us to the person who bought her mate. You."

The knife in his left hand, he continued to adjust the statue so the light would hit her just so. "I saw that you'd become gung-ho about playing detective after we viewed the footage."

"Aphrodite did too. She's what led us to you, to your weapon."

And there it was. Next to the newly installed Aphrodite was the statue of Hephaestus. The real one, with all of its telltale signs of damage. Kate had felt sure it would be here. Jarvis was too obsessed, too much of a collector, and too tied to this past to have gotten rid of it. Of all his collections, this one had to be the most important to him. The one he'd want to gaze at. The one he'd want close.

Finally, there would be recompense for all the harm he'd caused her family. Kate stood. No longer submissive, she recited her indictment. "Motive: jealousy. Opportunity: no alibi. When Beatrice's alibi was blown, so was yours. Evidence: You bought and still have the murder weapon. What's more, you recently planted those bank records in Beatrice's files to direct suspicion to her."

He cocked his head, looking confused, but his body was tense, as if he was ready to spring into action.

She took a deep breath and held her ground. "Chuck Needham never made a confession. My friend Natalie forged that." Kate pulled up her shirt half-way and tore off the small transmitter that had been taped to her stomach.

Jarvis blanched at the sight.

"Everything you've said and done today has been recorded. True, it's not the full confession we'd hoped for, but I think we've got enough to make it stick." She went over to the stairs and called out, "What do you think, Detective?"

"Open and shut, if you ask me," Detective Robak said as he came down the steps. Two uniformed officers followed him. All three had their guns drawn. When Robak reached the floor, he said, "Drop the knife, Jarvis. It's over."

The two officers walked up and flanked him.

"You are under arrest for the murder of Gloria Reardon," Robak said.

Jarvis quickly recovered from the surprise. "I don't think so. I know a little bit about the criminal justice system. None of this production is admissible."

"We'll see about that," Robak said.

Jarvis gave Kate an admiring look. "I knew you could act. Do I know my business or what? You fooled me. Still, it won't work. You have no warrant. Any supposed evidence will be thrown out." Smiling, he said to Robak, "My lawyers will eat you for breakfast."

The detective's droopy eyes hardened. "Warrants aren't the only legal way for the police to enter a house." One of the officers grabbed Jarvis's arms and pulled them behind his back while the other officer cuffed him.

"Hey!" Jarvis said.

The handcuffs clicked into place and something snapped in Jarvis. He shouted at the officers, "I'll sue your ass for entrapment. Ruin your careers, take away your pensions. Don't think I can't. I've got a lot of influence in this town."

"We know," Kate said. "Your influence and spy network was why the warrant route was problematic."

Jarvis stuck out his square chin. "That's right. What you've done here is illegal."

"You said you knew about criminal law." She walked up to him. "Then you must know that a guest residing in a house has the authority to *invite* the police in. No warrant necessary."

He smirked. "I'll deny you were a guest here. Jimena and Kioshi will testify you moved out more than a week ago."

"Yes, that posed a problem. Fortunately, the day of my screen test you invited me to live here not once but twice and in front of witnesses. So today I moved back in. I spent the morning carrying my stuff in, not out."

Jarvis glared at her. "Are you telling me the setup at your screen test was not to force a confession of murder but to get invited back here?"

Kate shrugged. "Don't get me wrong. We wouldn't have minded if you had confessed. But, yeah, that's all we thought we'd get."

Jarvis made a wheezing sound. Clutching his stomach, he doubled over.

She lurched toward him thinking he was having a heart attack, but then Jarvis's wheezing segued into high-pitched, laughter.

She gasped at the sight of him.

It was so out of character for Jarvis, the man who had held himself in such suffocating control all the time.

Well, not all the time.

"Brilliant, Nemesis. Brilliant." He laughed.

Robak said to the uniformed officers, "Let's get him out of here." Each officer grabbed one of Jarvis's arms.

"Wait, please." He stood straight, and she watched him fight to gain back his composure. "Tell me Kate, why didn't you believe it was Beatrice? There was so much evidence. You should have believed it."

Her eyes narrowed. "Too much evidence. Some of which you planted. Robak had searched her files previously and found no such records. And then, after you visited Beatrice, miraculously they appeared. Also, she gave no hint of recognition when she saw the replica of the Hephaestus statue, unlike you did at my screen test. You were Hephaestus."

Pain glistened in his blue-flamed eyes.

The officers shepherded Jarvis up the stairs. She followed. When they reached the grand circular driveway, Robak walked over to a squad car and called in to dispatch.

Jarvis stood silently in the officers' grip, hanging his head. He looked lost.

She moved close to him. "I wish it hadn't been you." She took a step back. "But facts are facts. After interviewing Beatrice, Robak was convinced she had been acting scared and suspicious because she was afraid of being accused of stealing the footage and withholding evidence in a murder investigation. It was very clever of you to use her need for an alibi to create one for yourself. I'm guessing you saw her steal the footage."

He didn't answer.

"Yeah, I think that's it. Master manipulator that you are, I bet you made her feel indebted to you for providing an alibi. But I think as time went on she began to wonder, began to suspect, in moments when she'd allow herself to reflect, that all along it was you who killed Gloria. I think that's why Beatrice wanted me out of your house. She wanted me away from you."

Kate shook her head. "I misjudged her, and when we knew for certain it wasn't Beatrice, I thought about your collections, all meticulously displayed. The possibility you still had the statue got me wondering about your always locked cellar door. I confess to trying to jimmy it on my own, but that didn't work. The police, even when legitimately invited into a house, aren't allowed to unlock doors without a warrant. We needed you to do that, and you did."

Jarvis lifted his head and gave her a malevolent look. "You are just like Gloria. Calculating, vindictive…" Then a strange smile contorted his features. "And glorious."

Kate turned away from him. She felt a familiar damp heat, like breath, touch her skin. A roar of sound, and she looked up to see the green canopies of Eucalyptus trees shaking the way they did the first day she'd come to stay at Jarvis's place, without any wind.

Detective Robak motioned to one of the officers, who nodded and recited to Jarvis as he escorted him to the squad car, "Jarvis Benjamin, you are under arrest for assault with a deadly weapon on Kate Bloom and for the murder of Gloria Reardon. You have the right to remain silent, anything you say can and will be used against you in a court of law. You have the right…"

The officer pushed Jarvis into the backseat of the squad car.

As the car pulled away, the branches above her stilled, their restless thrashing replaced by the sounds of birds chirping.

She walked slowly to her car and wondered if she

had just felt Gloria for the last time.

Kate had once asked herself, where did the psychological end and the haunting begin?

But that was it, wasn't it? There had been two distinct aspects to her perception of Gloria's presence.

First were the times she felt "possessed" by her. This aspect had way too conveniently manifested at times when part of Kate yearned to be less afraid, to face a situation with bravado and sensuality. The psychological implications of that were too obvious to ignore.

But the second aspect Kate had experienced, the dreams and visions filled with warnings, these had held undeniable clues to things she would not otherwise know.

Whether it made her crazy or not, she chose to believe it had been her grandmother's sprit trying to help.

Kate got into her VW and turned on the ignition.

Because Gloria, her Gloria, had not been some one-dimensional object of mere fantasy. She was so much more than that. A spirit so bold, she transcended the barrier of time and physical form to warn and protect her granddaughter from a murderer.

As Kate drove away from Jarvis's manor, she was now positive Gothic castles and windswept moors weren't the only places where tormented spirits lingered.

But today, in Bel Air, peace came to Gloria.

Epilogue

Ten years later

Perfection is Malibu beach. At least Kate thought so. She gazed at the view from her porch. The expanse of yellow twinkling sand, topped by dark blue sea, and above that a band of azure sky reminded her of the layers of color found in a Rothko painting.

Winston Nash, much better now after years of love and care, hobbled across her imagined artwork, with her three-year-old daughter, Lily, trailing after him.

Kate shook her head. Winston, like his son, was once again forcing narrative on her. In his lush baritone, with only a hint of his old tremors, Winston recited to Lily something about the sky. It sounded like Shakespeare. Dylan would know.

Undaunted by her blustering grandfather, Lily giggled as she attempted to climb up his leg, only to fall to the soft sand. Facedown, she waved her arms about. Then she got onto all fours and proceeded to dig like a dog.

Winston barked and joined in the fun.

Dylan yelled to Kate from the kitchen, "Hey, Natalie just arrived, and Mallick's going to be here soon. You need to get ready, or you'll miss your own opening."

"Right." Kate jogged into the house, showered, and

slipped on an Armani pantsuit. Her red hair fell loosely below her shoulders in soft waves. She did her own makeup, an advantage of being the director this time and not the actress.

When she was ready, she walked out of her bedroom. Dylan, Mallick, and Natalie were in the family room sipping coffee and chatting as if it hadn't been almost a year since they'd all seen one another. It had ultimately been Mallick, and not she, who had eschewed Hollywood for "art." He was now a professor at Reed College in Oregon. His short films played the festival circuit, and last year several of them were shown at the Portland Art Museum.

Before she had the chance to sit, Mallick looked at her with a grin. "So your sellout is complete, huh? First an actress, and then for your directorial debut, a traditional Hollywood picture, filled with gothic elements." He shook his head. "*Tsk, tsk.*"

"Well, it's not like it's *Satan's Academy IV*." Kate sat on a wide-cushioned couch next to Natalie. Her friend defiantly still wore peasant blouses even though it was now the 1980s and the yuppies had taken over.

"Hey," Dylan said. "That franchise has been a blockbuster, and it paid for this house, I might add."

"And, I'm grateful." Kate smiled at Dylan, who was ensconced in his favorite plush chair before turning back to Mallick. "My film may be Hollywood, but it's based on the truth."

"I heard you've been visiting Jarvis in prison." Mallick's brow furrowed.

"But she has no reason to visit him anymore, right?" Dylan said to Kate. "Now that your film about him is done."

"Leave her alone," Natalie said. "Her meetings with Jarvis and making this movie about Gloria's death are cathartic. It's an important part of her emotional processing."

Yay, Natalie!

Her friend had recently completed her Master's in Marriage and Family Counseling, because making feminist collages didn't pay the bills, and besides the work really suited her.

"Although…" Natalie made a face. "It really creeped me out when we discovered he was the reason I got that internship that summer, all to isolate you."

Mallick shuddered. "I don't know how you can stand talking to him after everything he did."

Kate shifted her gaze to the open window and listened to the rhythmic beat of the waves crashing on the beach. The powerful sound usually offered comfort, but now the distant rumble seemed lonely. She thought about Jarvis, alone, growing old in his cell and about the story he had told her. She shivered.

"I just wanted the truth for my film." She looked back to her friends and forced a smile.

****

After the last frame of her film finished, the lights came up at the Director's Guild theater. The audience of her peers applauded, but not before Dylan leaned over and gave her a playful nibble on her ear.

Kate laughed.

"Your film was great," he said.

Mallick sat on the other side of Kate and had fallen asleep—some things never changed.

After the post-screening party, Kate, Dylan, Mallick, and Natalie went to Canter's Deli, where they talked about film, children, and just life in general for hours.

Later, back home, Kate sat propped up in bed reading, unable to sleep. She tiptoed out of the bedroom so she wouldn't wake Dylan.

Wandering toward the kitchen to get something to eat, she saw the TV flickering in the den. Winston had reclaimed some of his *joie de vivre* since moving in with them, but he still had trouble sleeping. Before returning to bed, Kate felt a chill run through her. Something was wrong.

Times like this she wished for Lillian. The longing for her aunt in that moment weighed in on her as much as the night she was told her great-aunt had passed away in her sleep. Kate thought about how, if Lillian was here she'd have quipped something fun and sarcastic, and just thinking that made Kate feel better.

She peered into her daughter's room and saw Lily sound asleep.

All was right with the world, except...

Kate checked the house again, and in the living room the curtains were whipping in the strong ocean breeze. She hurried over to slide them shut. Then she noticed something on the floor, against the wall. It was a white, oblong flower box with a thick red bow. Stuck to it was a note. It said:

Congratulations.

Kate undid the ribbon, lifted the top off the box, and pulled out a marble Greek statue. She'd never seen this statue before, but Kate knew who it was supposed to be. Typical of the classical depiction of women, the statue was naked and beautiful, although her face was a bit more pointy than most. A determined mouth, a hint of pity in her eyes but not enough to stop the sword she wielded from striking, if she had to.

Kate placed the statue in the center of the coffee table and smiled.

No, she wasn't Gloria.

She was Nemesis.

A word about the author...

Allison Morse is the author of two novels: *The Sweetheart Deal* and *Fallen Star*. She lives with her family in a house in the hills that's filled with books.

For book club resources and to learn more about Allison and her upcoming works, please visit her website at allisonmorseauthor.com